Praise for *The Chemical Cocktail*

**A *FINANCIAL TIMES*
BEST SUMMER BOOK OF 2022**

'What sets *The Chemical Cocktail* apart…is that Erskine has applied the intellectual and scientific rigour of her writing to a high-speed, gripping and fun story.'

E&T

'A terrific read.'

Literary Review

'The plot is tight and after a luringly steady start the final hundred pages explode with twists and turns…an action-packed adventure perfect for any thriller-lover ready for a modern heroine to blow their socks off.'

Swansea Bay Magazine

'Fast-paced, roller-coaster ride.'

Financial Times

'Revenge is an act of passion, vengeance of justice.
Injuries are revenged; crimes are avenged.'

Samuel Johnson

Praise for *The Chemical Detective*

SHORTLISTED FOR THE SPECSAVERS DEBUT CRIME NOVEL AWARD, 2020

'Action, intrigue and a stonkingly modern heroine. It's a blast.'
Sunday Times Crime Club

'Intricate, seductive and thrilling. Erskine's writing glows with wit and danger. And can't help reminding you, with every page turned, of how close we all are to detonation.'
Ross Armstrong, author of *The Watcher*

'A very readable debut thriller with a feisty and likeable heroine.'
Irish Independent

'Just the right blend of suspense and tension… I recommend this original and compelling debut novel for fans of mysteries and thrillers, as well as for those looking for a credible female protagonist in a genre dominated by male superheroes. Already, I am looking forward to reading the next instalment in this series.'
Forbes, Editors' Pick

'Explosive science, strong women and snowy landscapes, all within a gripping, smart, fast-paced read.'
Helen Sedgwick, author of *When the Dead Come Calling*

'Imagine the love child of Jack Reacher and Nancy Drew…a delicious cocktail of dating and detonations. Call it Mills and Boom.'
Evening Standard

'A stunning, cinematic debut that's going to land on the 2019 thriller scene like a half-kilo of silver fulminate.*
*stuff that goes bang.'
Andrew Reid, author of *The Hunter*

THE CHEMICAL CODE

79
Au
Gold
196.967

Fiona Erskine

POINT
BLANK

A Point Blank Book

First published in Great Britain, Australia and the Republic of Ireland by Point Blank,
an imprint of Oneworld Publications, 2023

ISBN 978-0-86154-203-1 (paperback)
ISBN 978-0-86154-036-5 (ebook)

Typeset by Geethik Technologies
Printed and bound in Great Britain by Clays Ltd, Elcograf S.p.A.

Oneworld Publications
10 Bloomsbury Street
London WC1B 3SR
England

MIX
Paper from
responsible sources
FSC® C018072

To my beloved Aunt Alison – you were ahead of your time.
The Death of Uncle Joe (1997)
The Portingale (1976)
The Trusted Servant (1972)
The Jesuit (1972)
The Muscovite (1971)
No Need of the Sun (1969)
The Heretics (1965)
Thank you for the stories, the inspiration and all your kindness.

Alison Selford née Macleod
(1920 – 2022)

Mensagem

Valeu a pena? Tudo vale a pena
Se a alma não é pequena.
Confie primeiro no espírito santo
Com anel, nome e número do canto
Desmonte a caixa com gaveta falsa
A chave para o oriente, esconde na alça
As mapas poente, cobre entre aço e couro
Mas tenha cuidado, nem tudo que brilha é ouro
Deus ao mar o perigo e o abysmo deu,
Mas nelle é que espelhou o céu.

Fernando Pessoa and Isabella Ribeiro
da Silva (with sincere apologies to the poet)

The Message

Was it worth it? Everything is worthwhile
If the spirit is versatile.
Trust first in the holy spirit
With ring, name and verse implicit.
Take the box with fake drawer, dismantle
The key to the cast hides in the handle.
Between leather and steel, western maps unfold
But be careful; all that glitters is not gold.
God gave the sea danger and the abyss, why?
For it is a mirror to the heavens above the sky.

Translation Jaq Silver

Cast of Characters

Main characters

Jaq – Dr Jaqueline Silver (née Maria Jaqueline Ribeiro da Silva). Born in Angola to an Anglo-Portuguese mother and Russian father. UK-trained chemical engineer with expertise in explosive safety
Graça – Graça Neves. Trainee Federal Police Agent attached to the Financial Crimes Division based in Curitiba, Brazil

Friends

Marina – Marina Queiros (née Paulo Santos). Aeronautical engineer, pilot and inventor. Chief Technical Officer Áerex, Chief Concept Officer Transform
Carmo – Maria de Carmo Centeno. Portuguese lawyer based in Lisbon
Xavier – Portuguese kite-surfing champion and environmental activist with ECPOTO

Enemies

Frank – Frank Good. Director of the Clean Energy Division of Zagrovyl
Crazy Gloves – Raimundo Elias. Head of Ecobrium
Colonel Cub – Head of RIMPO
Beefcake – Oskar Guerra. RIMPO assassin

Family

Isabella – Isabella Couto Roubado Ferreira Ribeira da Silva. Jaq's grandmother (Angie's mother), now deceased
Angie – Maria dos Anjos Couto Roubado Ferreira Ribeira da Silva. Jaq's mother, now deceased
Sam – Manolo Samuel Ribeira da Silva. Jaq's brother, now deceased
Anton – Anton Oleich Sakoshansky. Jaq's father, now deceased

Other

Yuko Nakamura – Owner of a bio-ethanol factory in Ituverava, São Paulo, Brazil. She reached an out-of-court settlement with Hélio TV after claiming that an actor impersonated her missing father in the reality TV show *The Missing*
Éder – Security guard at Florianópolis airport car park
Zélia – Zélia Neto. Boss of Agent Graça Neves at Financial Crimes, Curitiba, Brazil
Carlos Raposa – Lawyer for Pelupent, Brazil
Clara – Clara Sousa. General manager of Zagrovyl, Brazil
Salty Walter – Walter Salgado. Director of Exploration Africa, Cuperoil
Major Moura Gomes – Head of army base, Florianópolis
GG – Grandmother of Graça Neves
Roberto Covelli – Chief prosecutor with Federal Police Financial Crimes, Curitiba, Brazil
Hugo Gao – University researcher
Kléber – Police officer, Florianópolis
Marcia – Cleaner, Florianópolis
Alfredo – Gardener, Florianópolis
Nick McLean – Anti-corruption lawyer working for Pelupent
Graham – Graham Dekker. President of Global Operations, Zagrovyl

César – Reality TV show host of *The Missing*

Gilda – Maria Beatrice. Assistant presenter on *The Missing*

Karina, Lucas and Noah – Reality TV participants on *The Missing*

Chico – Security Guard at São Paulo apartment complex

Bruno – CEO of Tecnoproject, consulting engineers based in São Paulo

Marco – Salesman at Tecnoproject

Deborah Ives – Director of Corporate Integrity, Zagrovyl

Pedro Carmargo – Head of private banking at the Bank of the Holy Ghost, Rio de Janeiro and 'guest' of Colonel Cub

Maria, Luis, Chica – Family of Pedro Camargo

Busco – Private investigator, São Paulo, Brazil

Aline – Aline Aldo. Maid, musician and undercover federal police agent

Fergus – Fergus Podger. Australian geologist consulting in Brazil

Cândido – Driver for Fergus

Luis – Mining engineer, Iron mine

Tiro – Blasting technician, Iron mine

Amado – Assistant blasting technician, Iron mine

Lars – RIMPO assassin, Europe

Advogado Castanho – Elderly lawyer in Salvador, Brazil

Advogado Nogueira – Junior lawyer in Salvador, Brazil

Rafael Barata – Clerk in Banco Espirito Santo, Rio de Janeiro

Dr Rao – Head of Emergency Medicine at Blessed Martyrs Hospital, Rio de Janeiro

Professor Jean Parker – Toxicologist

Mercúrio – Code name given to an actor hired to impersonate Jaq's son

Organisations

ÁEREX – An aeronautical engineering innovation and test centre in São José do Campos, Brazil

CASTANHO E NOGUERIA E ADVOGADOS ASSOCIADOS – Salvador Law firm

CUPEROIL – A state-owned oil and gas company and one of Tecnoproject's main clients

ECOBRIUM – Ecology Brazil. A direct-action environmental protection pressure group known to employ violence and take illegal action

ECOPTO – Ecology Portugal. An environmental protection pressure group that remains within the law

HÉLIO TV – Brazilian TV company, producers of *The Missing, Surf Rescue, Love on the Beach*

JALI – *Jardinagem e Limpeza*. Florianópolis Cleaning and Gardening Company

OPCW – Organisation for the Prohibition of Chemical Weapons

PELUPENT – International anti-corruption NGO with headquarters in Cambridge, England

RIMPO – A paramilitary organisation set up to support the artisanal miners, the *garimpeiros*

SUCOBRAS – Agrochemical complex, sugar and ethanol

TECNOPROJECT – A firm of consulting engineers based in São Paulo who employ Jaq in Brazil

TRANSFORM – A high-technology shoe company

ZAGROVYL – A multinational chemical company. Jaq's previous employer

47
Ag
Silver
107.868

Brazil imports more silver than it exports. In 2012, 200 tonnes of silver were produced with an estimated value of US$ 150 million.

Most silver is produced as a by-product of copper, gold, lead and zinc refining.

The precious metal is used in solar panels, water filtration, electrical contacts and conductors, as a catalyst for chemical reactions, in photographic and X-ray film, as disinfectants and microbicides, and in currency, investments and jewellery.

2,000km from the gold mine, Ituverava, São Paulo State, Brazil, February

The attack comes at the end of the day when I am least expecting it.

Steam billows from the top of the factory chimney, casting a living shadow onto the footpath. Swirls of black and grey, constantly moving, create a negative map of the white plumes rising behind me. The smell of sugarcane, a foetid mix of sweetness and rot, lingers in my nostrils. The machinery noises: mills rumbling; conveyors clattering; molasses slurping in huge metal vats fade to the thrum of traffic as I walk from the main office block towards the exit.

The factory owner leaves first. Yuko drives an open-topped sports car towards the main gate as I approach the security office. She raises a hand in farewell.

'Good luck!' she calls as she passes.

I don't believe in luck. It's the choices we make that matter. After what Yuko told me, I may have to rethink some of mine.

The barrier opens and Yuko speeds off down a dusty road. Only directors get to park inside the perimeter fence. My car is on the other side of the factory gates, in the visitors' car park.

Inside the gatehouse, I unclip my pass and push it over the counter to the sleepy security guard. He opens the SucoBras logbook at today's date and runs a finger down the page searching for the right entry.

Nom/Name: Dr Jaqueline Silver
Empresa/Company: Tecnoproject
Função/Occupation: Chemical Engineer

Officially, I came to conduct an energy efficiency audit of the sugar-to-ethanol factory. In truth, that was just a ruse, an excuse to speak to the owner, Yuko Nakamura. To find out how far I'd been duped, to winnow the chaff of lies from the grains of truth.

It's hot; I am distracted by Yuko's disclosure, the conspiracy she claimed to have uncovered. Little black flies buzz around my ears, but it is the swarm of contradictions inside my head, the dissonance clamouring for attention that dulls my senses.

'*Doutora?*'

The security guard hands me a pen.

I sign out, return the pen and pass through the turnstile. The staff car park is almost empty; the day shift must have left while Yuko and I were talking. A skeleton staff keep things running overnight.

Fields of sugarcane surround the ethanol factory, a patchwork of green stretching as far as the eye can see. The plants yet to be cut tremble in the slanting sunlight, a light breeze caressing the fronds. The cane stumps of the recently decapitated bleed and shrivel in the summer heat. A combine harvester trundles into the aural landscape, and a freight train hoots in the distance.

Time to get away from here, to find somewhere quiet to reflect on what I've learned.

I pass the employee bike shed. It's empty of push bikes, but a few motorbikes have muscled in. A pang of longing grabs me by the throat. I borrowed a Harley Davidson from my absentee landlord not that long ago, enjoyed a glorious spell of freedom as I meandered down the coastline from São Paulo to Florianópolis, following the surf. That motorbike caused a great deal of trouble in the end, attracting far too much attention from the police, but I miss it now.

I'm almost at the visitor's section of the car park when I hear boots on gravel and turn to see that men are following me. One is tall and bald, wearing jeans and a floral shirt, another is short and wide and dressed like a soldier, the third has red hair and wears loose grey overalls. The three men break into a run. Call me suspicious, but I don't think they're rushing to make friends.

I've made a few enemies since I came to Brazil, that's the trouble with inheriting a gold mine you don't want. Others do. Some will stop at nothing to gain control. Some for political reasons, some for greed.

Whoever these gentlemen represent, I don't like the look of any of them.

I have a choice.

I can go it alone, make a run for my car, lock the door, press the gas pedal to the floor and unleash the power of fermented sugar.

Or I can seek safety in numbers, return to the factory, duck under the security barrier, rattle the turnstile of the gatehouse, pummel the safety glass window and hope that the dozing security guard lets me back in.

And what then? Is this ambush a coincidence? Or has someone at SucoBras tipped them off, told them where to find me?

Who?

When I think of all the people who've betrayed me, it has often been those I've liked, loved even. Yuko? Was that why she opened up to me? Because she knew I wouldn't live to tell the tale?

I stopped trusting other people a long time ago. The only person I can rely upon is myself.

I make a dash for my car, fumbling in my bag for the key, almost at the driver's door, when the taller man grabs me, pinning my arms to my sides while another presses a damp cloth to my mouth and nose. I smell the sickly sweet anaesthetic and try to hold my breath, kicking at the shins of the man behind me then raising a knee to attack the one in front. The red-head steps to the side, releasing the pressure on the anaesthetic pad long enough for me to take a breath. My ears start buzzing. My head is swimming.

I close my eyes and force myself to go limp.

It works. Carrot-top drops the pad and takes my feet.

My heart races, my thoughts chaotic and movements clumsy. Think. Make your brain work. Keep the grey cells awake. Was it chloroform, oldest of anaesthetics? Surely nobody used trichloromethane any more? Not that these thugs cared about side effects. Ether then. Yes. Diethyl ether is faster-acting than alcohol, but the effects don't last as long. My head is becoming clearer. The longer I breathe fresh air, the sooner I'll get my coordination back.

The men are carrying me away from my car. I don't dare open my eyes for fear that they'll apply more ether and knock me out properly, but I can tell where we're going by the sounds and scents of the factory. The hot treacly smell of burning bagasse suggests we are near the utilities section where the waste from the sugarcane is used to generate electricity. The whoosh of steam and *psst-psst* of condensate traps confirm my hunch. We must be skirting the perimeter fence, outside the factory, heading to the back gate and the goods yard, the place where lorries and vans make deliveries to the stores.

Or take away waste.

I need to escape from these goons before they bundle me into a van and drive me far away.

I am not as strong as any of these three men. I don't stand a chance in a fair fight, but I understand the principles of physics. Energy is force times distance. My legs are the longest levers I have. Power is the rate of energy transfer. I can't rely on a single kick; I need to deliver frequent blows. Momentum is mass times velocity. I am lighter, so I have to move faster.

I wait until I hear Shorty rattling a set of keys. I open my eyes in time to see him unlock a white van. Baldy still has a tight hold on me, but his red-haired accomplice drops my feet. I remain limp, all my weight carried by a single captor as Carrot-top opens the rear doors and bends to lift my feet. I kick him in the nose with all my might. *Crunch.* He recoils, hands flying to his face and my next kick lands where it hurts the most. Thank heavens for safety boots.

Shorty runs at me, raising a fist for a punch, but I duck. His momentum drives him forward and he hits Baldy in the gut. I twist my leg round their tangled limbs, causing them to fall and smash head-first into the van doors, slamming them onto the legs of Carrot-top who was perching on the rear hatch platform and howling.

I only have a few seconds before they gather what wits they have left.

They are fighting for gold. I'm fighting for something much more precious.

I didn't come to Brazil because of a gold mine. I came to this country to find my son. I thought he was dead. Yuko's revelation gives me a reason to fight on.

If I perish here, now, in the goods yard of a sugar-to-ethanol factory in the farmlands of Brazil, I will never understand what happened to him, I will never uncover the truth.

I can't give up now.

The wail of a police siren gives me a rush of hope. Did the security guard spot the assault, call for help?

The men are moving again. I can't wait here to be rescued. I need to defend myself, and I know exactly where to find the most effective weapons.

I run towards the factory.

The back gates from the goods yard to the sugar factory are chained closed, but a pedestrian gate has been left slightly open. I make a dash for it.

I run past the stores and enter the power plant, sticking my fingers in my ears against the din, the rumble of mills grinding the solid biofuel, the roar of the burners, the whoosh of steam, and the turbines spinning copper coils in magnets at 3,000 revolutions per minute. Like most modern power plants, it appears unmanned, everything regulated by intelligent sensors driving automatic valves, supervised by a small number of human technicians in a central control room.

That's where I'm heading, but I only get as far as the evaporators before I see the reflection of Shorty in the shiny aluminium cladding. He's moving fast, gaining on me. Quick, I need a weapon, something to slow him down. Think!

I feint a right, weaving between the vacuum ejectors before making a left, towards the feed tanks.

The raw cane juice, *garapa*, is treated with sulphur dioxide. Sulphur removes impurities, including the chromophores that colour the sugar crystals and spoil the bright white we associate with purity. Sulphur destroys the bacteria, putting a stop to their competing fermentation routes that would reduce the yield of ethanol.

Sulphur, administered in the form of sulphur dioxide gas, is also highly toxic to humans. It smells vile, causing your eyes to stream, your chest to tighten until it's hard to breathe. I may not be as strong as my assailants, but I'm smarter. I can deliver a chemical punch to the solar plexus without raising a fist. With the added advantage that a release of SO_2 will set off the toxic gas alarm and alert the night-shift technicians, forcing them out of their comfortable control room and onto the factory floor.

Of course, there is a risk. A risk of death. High concentrations of SO_2 cause pulmonary oedema, death by drowning in your own fluids. The factory workers should be OK, they're trained and have emergency breathing apparatus to protect them while they find and fix the leak. I intend to remain upwind. But there is a risk of death to the men trying to kill me.

Seems fair to me.

I grab a spanner and screwdriver from the shadow board. In three anticlockwise twists, I detach the hose manifold from the SO_2 cylinder and with one jab, I ram the point of the screwdriver into the flow-limiting safety device.

The screech of high-pressure gas almost drowns Shorty's screams as he runs into a face-high jet of freezing poison. Almost, but not quite. The toxic gas alarm blares into action, yellow light flashing and 100 decibels of warble drowns his last gasp as he collapses to the floor. My eyes begin to water as the foul gas flows over him and creeps along the basement.

I'm already on the stairs, racing up above the catastrophe. I burst into the control room, the one section of the factory guaranteed to be manned overnight. Alarms shriek, lights flash and three emergency breathing sets are missing.

The control room is empty.

The night shift has either run away or are out tackling the crisis I created. I grab the emergency phone and scream at the gatehouse to call an ambulance. Then I vault over the control desk and grab a spare breathing set. Struggling with the fittings designed for male facial geometry, my ears ringing from the alarms, I don't hear the men creep up behind me. Baldy slaps the mask from my face and catches my arms, pinning them to my side. Carrot-top wrenches the air cylinder from my back and throws a hessian sack over my head and shoulders, winding a rope round and round, tighter and tighter, trapping my arms inside.

I shout for help, but my pleas are muffled by the thick fabric of the bag.

When we start to move, it's away from the emergency. I let them drag me along until I detect the distinctive smells of the fermentation hall. On the open grating, I stumble and feign a fall, freeing myself from their grip. I'm on my feet in an instant, running for my life.

I have a bag over my head, my hands are trapped under the rope that coils around my waist. There's no time to free myself.

For a few seconds I think I might make it as far as the laboratory, might manage to barricade myself in before my assailants catch me. Might concoct a new chemical weapon until help arrives.

But the men are too fast for me. One of them grabs me and together they drag me away.

Fresh air tells me we're outside. My legs are struggling to keep pace with my captors. I need to conserve energy. I can tell where we are going by the changing tone of machinery. We pass the rumbling mills at a gallop, the swish-swish of the cutting knives is getting louder and louder. I have a sinking premonition where they're taking me.

The threshing machine.

Was this always part of the plan? Were the factory staff in on this?

Would Yuko really want my flesh and bones to mix with her sugar? How would the carefully selected strain of yeast, *Saccharomyces cerevisiae,* optimised to turn sugar molasses to ethanol, react to my blood and bile? How would it cope with the competing microbiota from my body? *Actinomyces viscosus, lactobacillus iners, candida albicans.* Would there be enough sulphur to counteract human contamination? No one at SucoBras would willingly take such a risk, deliberately introduce sixty kilograms of concentrated biohazard into the fragile fermentation process.

These men are improvising. They just want me dead.

But I'm not leaving this life until I know the truth.

Is my son still alive?

As we reach the steps of the threshing machine, the sweet smell of macerating sugarcane is almost overpowering. My feet stop moving. I refuse to climb to my death.

I hook my feet around the handrail. Mistake. A pair of strong arms lifts me bodily, slinging me over a broad shoulder, carrying me towards the platform, to the hopper above the machine with rotating blades. High-speed threshing knives that can slice through sugarcane will mince flesh and shatter bones.

It's two against one now. The tall, bald one carrying me, slung over his shoulder like a sack of potatoes and the red-haired one in front. I can hear his footsteps running up the metal stairs to the platform, breathing hard.

'*Mexa-se,*' he shouts '*Pressa!*'

Hurry up! Easy to say when you're not the one carrying a struggling captive.

The squeal of metal on metal as the safety gate is raised sends my heart in the opposite direction. This is it. I'm out of time. Do something. Anything. I go limp, wait until we stop climbing and get my sense of direction from the sound of the accomplice's low chuckles. *Monstro.* I lift my knees, fold them up into my stomach and then kick out and back. I make contact, hear the scream as the man swings on the safety gate, suspended over the threshing machine. I scissor my legs, wrapping myself around the face of my abductor. He curses and falls backward. I roll over him, down the metal stairs. A corner of the sugar sack catches and tears and I can breathe again, see again.

I hear a cry.

The safety gate wasn't designed as a swing, it is bending under the weight of the man, and the chuckling Carrot-top is chuckling no more. He's dragged in shoes first. The worst way to die. First the feet, then the ankles, the shins, the knees, the thighs. Bones are tougher than sugarcane – the machine groans and the man screams as he descends into the rotating knives, the smell of a burning rubber belt mingling with the metallic scent of blood. The motor races and the belts slip, but the drive train has been sized to handle anything. The victim shrieks as the knives reach his groin, his hips, his torso. A final gurgle and then he's silent.

The machine chomps on. I turn away before the crunch of his skull.

There were three men. Now there is only one. The bald survivor stands open-mouthed in a state of shock.

I run.

Terrible noises follow me as the threshing machine crunches through the remnants of the man who tried to kill me. His grisly end was exactly what he intended for me. I feel no remorse, for this death at least.

My hands are still bound; the rope around my waist secures a sugar sack over my head. I gulp for air through the tear in the hessian, extend it with my teeth so I can see where I'm going. I can't look back; I don't dare look back.

I run to the nearest row of sugarcane and dive in head-first, momentarily glad of the rough fabric that protects my face and arms from the worst lacerations. I wriggle like a worm, twisting through the dense stalks, using my knees and toes to push forward, loosening the rope as I go.

I pause to listen. Where's the other man? Is he coming after me? Will he wait until heat and thirst drive me out? Are there others coming to back him up? I can't risk going back to my car.

The mournful hoot of a locomotive gives me an idea.

My progress through the dense crop of sugarcane is slow and painful, but it's easier once I've wriggled free of the rope and removed the sack. I can't cut straight through the field; I keep to the edges where the planting is thinner. If these canes were fully grown, ready for harvest, I wouldn't stand a chance. As it is, I can just about squeeze between them. There are other creatures here that move more easily. Lizards and snakes, rats and mice. And flies, so many flies.

I hear the hum of resonating steel rails, then the click-clack of advancing wheels. Nearly there. By the time I emerge into the culvert, the diesel engine has already passed. The wagons follow. I start to run. *Clank, clatter, clank clatter.* It's too fast. Usain Bolt managed a top speed of 27.78 miles an hour in the 2009 World Championships in Athletics. Florence Griffith-Joyner ran 100m in 10.49 seconds, that's what … 21.3 miles an hour? I'm fit, but no Olympian. If I sprint, maybe I can reach fifteen miles an hour for a short burst, but this locomotive is travelling at more than twice that.

I look for something to catch, something to grab on to, but the chains between the wagons are fastened tight, and even if I did manage to reach one, chances are it would wrench my arm out of its socket or drag me under the wheels.

The immensely long train trundles past; I watch the last wagon with a sinking heart.

I'm ready to give up when I hear the interplay of horns. A call and response. Toot and an answering toot. There's another train coming in the opposite direction. But this is a single-track railway. Where's the passing place? At the screech of metal on metal, the squeal of brakes, I break into a run. The smell of hot iron gets stronger as I race round the bend. My train is continuing but there's a second train in a siding, on the other side of the tracks. I cross the empty track and duck down as I pass the engine. The driver doesn't notice me, he's watching the long train go past. I grab hold of a chain, pull myself up onto the bogie between wagons and, with one last effort, hurl myself up and over into the first truck.

It doesn't matter where this train is going. I just need a safe place to think about what Yuko told me.

If it's true, it changes everything.

Until I understand how I got here, I will never be able to move forward.

I need to go back to when it all went wrong.

Back to Christmas Eve.

24
Cr
Chromium
51.996

Brazil's production of chromium, 336,000 tonnes in 2012, was worth about US$ 120 million.

Chromium is mainly used in electroplating and to make stainless steel.

Graça loathed multistorey car parks, hated the low ceilings, dim
lighting, tight curves, narrow ramps and sudden slopes. Concrete
pillars jumped out at her from unexpected angles, dark shapes
slithered in the shadows as the walls closed in. Taking a deep
breath, she gripped the wheel. Federal Police Agents – *Agentes de
Polícia Federal* – were meant to be able to go anywhere, do anything.
As she rounded the final corner, her headlights caught a flash of
chrome.

Gotcha!

The motorbike was partly hidden, tucked behind a concrete
pillar, hard up against a breeze-block wall. Graça got out of the
car and ran a flashlight over it. The registration checked out –
SAL·1064 – as did the description: wasp-shaped with the teardrop
end of the petrol tank pointing to an oval leather seat. The chrome
gleamed in the torchlight. The bike might be old, but someone
had lavished it with care and attention. Not the most recent rider
though.

Graça crouched down to inspect it more closely. Sand between
the spokes and wheel rims, mud under the seat. A helmet dangled
from the handlebars, the fingers of a pair of gloves creating a
leather fringe. She extended a hand and then pulled back.

Don't touch the bike.

Stay with the bike.

Those had been her instructions, and she wasn't about to
disobey.

Graça exited the multistorey and parked up outside the security
office. The door was locked, but, peering through the grimy
window, she could see the back of a man with his feet up on a

desk, a heavy-set middle-aged man in a security uniform. On the TV monitor in front of him, a sallow-faced military man emerged from the jungle to a split screen with the studio titles of the hit reality-TV show *The Missing*.

She'd planned to watch the Christmas Eve special at Grandma's, curled up on the sofa with a tray of hot, sweet *rabanadas*. But the best laid plans were no match for the demands of police work.

Graça jiggled the door handle. Locked. She banged on the window.

The man inside the office glanced over his shoulder and pointed to a sign in the window. *Fechado*. Closed.

She banged harder until he got to his feet and lumbered to the door.

'Can't you read?' he shouted through the glass. 'The office is closed for Christmas.'

'Do you have CCTV on the entrance to the car park?' she shouted back.

'Who's asking?'

Graça flashed her badge at the window. 'Police.'

The key turned in the lock, and the door opened a few centimetres, restrained by a heavy chain.

'Show me your warrant card.'

Graça removed the plastic card from her wallet and passed it through the gap.

'Curitiba?' he handed the card back. 'A Paraná cop has no authority in the state of Santa Catarina.' He tried to close the door, but Graça had anticipated his next move, thrusting her foot in the doorway.

'Federal police,' she said. 'Brazil-wide jurisdiction.'

He pushed the door hard against her foot.

Standard police-issue boots were robust, but a misguided revolt by a group of fashion-conscious female police agents had led to the introduction of a raised-heel court shoe, a lighter option which had neither style nor substance. The pressure against the pad of her big toe was beginning to hurt.

'Let me in,' she said.

'Not without a warrant.'

He opened the door a little and then slammed it against her foot. She yelped at the sudden pain in her little toe and stepped back.

The door closed, the lock turned, and a blind rattled down over the window. Footsteps plodded over ceramic tiles followed by the whoof of a heavy body lowering itself onto a padded seat. The TV volume rose in time for the dramatic music that signalled another success for *The Missing*.

And another failure for trainee investigator Agent Neves.

Graça limped back to her car. She took off her shoe and rubbed her toes. Nothing broken. She started the engine and reversed the car to the barrier, swinging it round so that it was blocking both entrance and exit to the car park. She locked the doors, turned up the music and opened the glove box to extract a box of treats picked up from the *pastelaria*.

When the car horns started blaring, the door of the security office flew open. The security guard, dressed in a shabby uniform that didn't fit him, waddled towards the car blocking the access.

'Move,' he yelled. 'Now!'

Graça ignored him.

'Oi!' A good-looking young man, about the age and build of her youngest brother, leaned out of the passenger side of a ramshackle car with a yellow surfboard on the roof. He tapped his watch, miming the words *I've got a plane to catch*.

The security guard reached Graça's car and banged on the windshield.

'I'm calling the police.'

She rolled her window down a few centimetres. Her music blared out. A bossa nova from Sérgio Mendes' album *Timeless*.

'Go right ahead.' The Curitiba office had already been in touch with the military police at the Floripa station and they had shown zero interest in her mission. She raised the paper box of uneaten pastries. 'Fancy sharing? These would go down much better with some CCTV footage.'

'You're causing a disturbance.'

'No, you are.' Graça smiled. 'All you have to do is let me in to your office and I'll move out of these good people's way. It would be a shame to ruin their Christmas.'

'Causing an obstruction at an airport is a serious offence ...' he began.

'You a lawyer?' she asked.

No reply.

'An ex-cop?' she tried.

No reply.

'Strikes me you know a little too much about the criminal justice system for a night-shift security guard in this little backwater. So maybe it's best not to attract more interest from the police than necessary.'

His flush told her she'd struck gold. She turned down the music.

'Look, mate, it's Christmas Eve. Neither of us wants to be here. I just need to look at a few CCTV tapes and then I'll get out of your hair. Give me a break?'

He sighed. 'You'd better come in.'

Graça followed the security guard in her car, driving it onto the pavement directly outside the office, continuing after he opened the door and stepped inside, leaving a narrow corridor between metal and breeze block, just enough room for her, but not quite enough for him to escape.

Inside the office, the TV was still blaring. She could hear the presenter, César, through the open door.

Christmas is a time to be with family ...

Well, it might be for some, for those who don't get landed with the shitty jobs.

She wound up the window and squeezed through the gap between car and building.

César was in full flow now.

Hold them close, for you never know what is around the corner.

Grandma would be upset if she didn't make it back in time for church tomorrow. Every year GG claimed it would be her last Christmas; every year she was proved wrong.

Graça slipped through the office door.

And to all of you out there with a loved one who is missing ...

Grandma would be missing her, the only one who would even notice her absence. The rest of the family disapproved of her career choice. Her older brother objected so violently that family reunions usually descended into bitter argument.

The guard motioned for her join him at the single CCTV monitor.

... have faith, get in touch. This year alone we reunited hundreds of families who had given up ...

She placed the box of pastries on the desk. The guard reached forward but she drew it back.

'What's your name?'

For a moment she thought he was going to refuse to answer. She kept her face impassive as he wrestled with his animosity. What had the police done to make him hate them so? The scent of nutmeg and caramel broke through his reserve.

'Éder,' he growled.

'Turn off the TV, Éder.'

He pressed the remote and the dramatic theme music of *The Missing* was silenced.

'And now, load up the CCTV,' she ordered.

'What date?'

She checked her notes. 'Let's start with December 22nd and work back.'

Once the tape was loaded, she opened the box of pastries, and he grabbed a pastel de nata.

'Take a seat.' He nodded at a battered metal chair. 'What are we looking for?'

The CCTV was grainy, poor quality. Car after car pulled up to the barrier and took a ticket. Graça was beginning to give up hope when she spotted the bike.

'There!' she shouted.

Leaning forward, she jabbed a finger at the screen.

'There – see?'

Éder grabbed the keyboard and pressed pause, then edged back, frame by frame.

There was no mistaking the distinctive wasp shape of the Harley Davidson Knucklehead. Graça noted the time stamp. 06:08 December 19th. Five and a half days ago.

'Can you get a better shot of the rider?'

A woman – no doubt about it. Underneath the leather motor-cycle jacket, she wore a summer dress and sandals.

He inched the tape further back and then forward.

'There!'

In jerky frames, the rider glanced up at the camera. She wore an open-face helmet, her dark hair caught in the chin strap framing a honey-coloured, heart-shaped face with full lips, large eyes and a small, straight nose.

A face that was curiously familiar.

Where had Graça seen her before?

Where am I?

Splish.

My hand is wet. Why is my hand wet?

Not just my hand, my arms, my shoulders, my neck, my hair.

Splash.

I can hear it now. The water. Moving all around. And I'm moving with it. Bobbing up and down. Up and down. Up and down.

Why is it so dark? Is it night already? Or are my eyes closed?

Splosh.

I wave my head from side to side to clear my thoughts. My thoughts don't clear. My head is full of mercury. Why mercury? Because mercury is liquid like my surroundings? Because it is heavy like my limbs? Because it's silver like me?

Silver. Jaq Silver. At least I remember who I am if not where I am. Or why.

I raise my head and force my eyes open, lashes tearing, eyes stinging.

Everything is blurry, as if I'm in the middle of a monochrome set, floating in a blue-grey mist. Am I underwater? I raise a hand and open my fingers, bringing the palm down with force. *Splash.* There is definitely an interface. I take a long breath. Air above, water below. Sea and sky all around.

How long was I asleep? What day is it?

We wish you a Merry Christmas. The song arrives unbidden from my memory, the music of a light breeze, the rising wind clearing a space in the mist. *We wish you a Merry Christmas.*

Christmas Day?

Not yet.

Christmas Eve perhaps?

That's not quite as daft as it sounds. Christmas is a time to avoid other people. Every year I find a place to hole up and hibernate for a couple of nights. This particular location seems a bit extreme, but there's a familiar twisted logic here.

But where?

The water is cool, but not freezing cold. Too mild for Europe in December. If this were the north-east coast of England, or even the Western coast of Portugal, I'd be dead by now. Could it be Africa? My childhood was spent splashing in vast, temperate seas. But I am no longer a child. So, Asia then? No, there's a faint moon and it's upside down. Southern Hemisphere. South America? Yes, of course. Brazil.

I'm in the middle of the South Atlantic Ocean on Christmas Eve. Alone.

Alone? Not quite.

Porra!

Something is floating beside me.

Splash. Splash.

As I move away, it follows. Ghostly shapes flutter all around me. Are attached to me.

Hahahaha!

It's a dress. A summer dress. I'm wearing a summer dress with a wide skirt. In the middle of the ocean. I laugh out loud with relief as my flowery skirt billows around me. Flowery? When do I ever do flowery? What's got into me?

At least I have a lifejacket on. That's sensible. I pat the collar until I find the whistle. I bring it to my lips and blow.

Fweee.

Pathetic. The noise is lost amidst the waves and wind. Try again.

Phweeeeeet.

Better.

Longer and harder this time.

Phfffwheeeeeeet!

Silence.

24

Just the swell of the ocean, the swirl of breeze and splish-splash where they connect.

There's no one to hear.

No one is coming.

Silence.

The shivering starts and builds momentum.

I don't want to spend Christmas alone again.

I want to spend it with you.

Mercúrio.

As the full horror comes flooding back, grief overwhelms me and the salt from my eyes spills over to join the salt in the sea.

Florianópolis, Brazil, December 24th – Christmas Eve

Graça left the security office, got back in her car and followed the road to the back of the airport car park. She found a spot where she could remain partially hidden while maintaining a clear view of the multistorey exit.

Stay with the bike.

The bonus was a view of the airport runway through a chain-link fence and three bars of phone signal.

Graça called Zélia.

'Hi boss. You still in the office?'

'Where else would I be? It's my shift.'

Tell that to her colleagues who'd all knocked off early on Christmas Eve.

'I'm sending a photo from the CCTV.'

'Motorbike man?'

'Woman.' Graça clicked send. 'Tall, dark-haired, Caucasian female.'

Ping.

'Hmmm, let me see.' Zélia's nails clattered on the keyboard. 'Not sure it's clear enough for an ID.'

'Cross check with passengers on flights out of Florianópolis after 7 a.m. on December 19th,' Graça suggested. 'If you've got access to security footage, she's wearing a summer dress, sandals and a leather motorbike jacket.'

'I'm on the case. Anything else?'

Graça sucked air through her teeth. 'What's all this about?'

'Way above your pay grade.'

'So is being sent to Floripa unsupported. C'mon Zélia – how am I supposed to do my job if I don't know what my job is?'

'I can't share the file without permission.'

'Who can give permission?'

'Only the chief investigator.'

'And where is he?'

'On holiday.'

'And his deputy?'

'On duty, but conspicuous by his absence.'

'You're the only one in the office on Christmas Eve?'

'More fool me.'

'Then you're in charge.'

'I wish!'

'Please.'

A pause and then the click of a file being sent.

Ping.

It was a lawyer for Pelupent Brazil, an anti-corruption organisation, who'd called it in.

Carlos Raposa had been trying to return a hire car after a surfing weekend when he noticed something in the basement of the airport car park. A keen biker himself, he recognised the Harley Davidson as one of only a few civilian bikes made in the early 1940s before US manufacture was diverted to military requirements. The fully restored twin-engine Knucklehead was worth a fortune, so he was astonished that there was no immobiliser, not even a U-bolt or a chain lock in sight. Even the helmet was unsecured, dangling from the handlebars with a pair of gloves stuffed inside. Something tugged at his memory; he took a couple of photos on his phone – position, numberplate and chassis – before checking the time and hurrying away.

Back in Brasília, the bike preyed on the lawyer's mind. Or, rather, a connection to the bike that floated in his memory, just out of sight, just out of reach. He zoomed in to the photo of the chassis and looked up the frame number. The last time that particular Knucklehead had changed hands was at auction in a rare lot of three bikes, including a 1952 Vincent Black Lightning. They sold for an undeclared sum to a mystery buyer in Brazil. The same secretive buyer who'd come to the attention of those investigating international money laundering when he imported millions of dollars' worth of European art.

Carlos called his friend in Blumenau, 150km from Florianópolis, a man who had no interest in motorbikes, but had access to the full database of all vehicles registered in Brazil. The registration document for the motorbike with licence plate *SAL·1064* was not for an antique Harley Davidson Knucklehead, but for a six-year-old Honda 120, one of the cheapest and therefore most popular bikes in Brazil. Interesting. When the name of the registered owner appeared on the screen, alarm bells started ringing all the way to Curitiba, 250km further north.

By the time the right department – the financial crimes division of the federal police – received the message that a valuable asset belonging to a person of interest had been spotted, apparently abandoned, in a Floripa airport car park, it was Christmas Eve, and all the senior staff were heading home to their families.

The first responders filed the report in pending. Interesting but not urgent. Any investigation could wait until after the Christmas break.

Zélia, who had pulled the short straw and was working over Christmas, disagreed with their assessment. She thought it unlikely that the bike would remain unclaimed. What if the owner had intended it as a gift for someone else? And when did people normally exchange gifts?

At Christmas.

Her bosses prevaricated. There was no honour among thieves, they said. The bike had probably been stolen.

If the bike had been stolen, Zélia countered, why would the thief leave it to rot in the basement of an underground car park at a small regional airport? More likely it was payment for something. Someone was waiting for a quiet day to go and recover the asset. A day when there were no flights in or out of the airport.

Christmas Day.

The bike was unlocked. How likely was it that it would still be there when the financial crime investigators came back from their holidays? This was a job that couldn't wait.

They told her that if she felt so strongly about it, she should organise the investigation herself. Organise, that is, without leaving Curitiba where she was on duty, and good luck getting an officer to cancel their Christmas plans and go on a wild goose chase to Florianópolis.

So, Zélia handed the job down to a junior police agent, a trainee still on probation whose prearranged leave could be cancelled without explanation.

Graça Neves.

And here she was.

High in the sky a plane began its descent into Florianópolis airport. It looked like something from another planet; an alien spacecraft, a twin-bodied, silver-skinned glider.

Graça peered up from her phone, shading her eyes against the sun as the plane landed and taxied across the shimmering apron towards her, coming to rest on the other side of the fence from where she sat in her car.

A domed hatch, like the top of an egg, opened and the pilot clambered out of the futuristic plane, shaking out her long hair.

Was it a her? The mysterious motorbike rider from the CCTV footage? A spark of excitement fizzled out into disappointment as the pilot on the other side of the fence strode past the floodlights. Her hair was much longer, fairer and curlier, her skin colour was lighter, between porcelain and vanilla, her face broader and squarer and her cheekbones sharper than those of the suspect.

Graça finished reading the file from Curitiba before calling Zélia.

'Any luck on the ID, boss?'

'Patience, my child, patience. Visual searches take longer.'

'I read the file.'

'What file?'

Graça laughed. 'The file I'm not allowed to see.'

'Keep it to yourself, OK?'

'Who owns the motorbike?'

The notes hadn't named anyone, referring to the person of interest being investigated by the Curitiba police only by codename NaCl.

'Who's NaCl?' Graça asked.

'I can't possibly reveal that.'

'The chemical formula for salt, so I'm guessing it's your old friend, Salty.'

'Smart arse. Did you study chemistry or something?'

'Pharmacy,' Graça replied. 'So it's Walter Salgado?'

'I'm not saying anything.'

'But you're not saying no.'

'Interpret that any way you wish.' Graça could hear the smile in Zélia's voice.

Walter Salgado, nicknamed Salty Walter, was a director of the exploration arm of the state oil company, Cuperoil. A Brazilian national working in Angola, with a net worth many, many times what you might expect from his official salary and bonuses. And therefore, a person of interest to the financial crimes unit. And to Zélia in particular.

'So, the motorbike rider is Salty Walter's girlfriend?' Graça asked.

Zélia sighed. 'Whoever she is, why did she leave such a valuable bike unlocked?'

Graça thought back to the CCTV images of the rider.

'In a hurry? Distracted? Forgot?'

'What could be so urgent that you fail to lock a motorbike worth millions of reais?' Zélia sounded positively angry about it. Which was understandable given the value of the toys cast aside by the super-rich in comparison to the size of the federal police budget. The Brazillionaires and their hangers-on had no idea how hard it was to live on a police salary or how rarely it was paid on time.

'It's an old bike.' Graça said. 'Maybe she didn't know how much it was worth.'

'Or maybe it was deliberate, an act of revenge.'

Zélia liked that idea. Graça could tell by the change of tone. Her boss's long-term partner had walked out on her after eighteen years, and Zélia was still hurting.

'Nice move,' Graça said to be supportive, but she was unconvinced. If you wanted to dispose of your boyfriend's prize possession in his absence, Floripa seemed a long drive when you could sell it in São Paulo, city of 20 million people and a good proportion of the nation's crooks.

'We'll find her and bring her in,' Zélia said. 'If she's angry, she might be happy to testify against him. This might be the missing link we need.'

'You want me to leave the bike and go look for her?' That sounded a lot more interesting than being stuck behind a multi-storey car park on Christmas Eve.

'No. Stay with the bike. Don't touch the bike. I'm sending reinforcements.'

The sky darkened before night fell, the clouds gathering. With a flash of lightning and a crack of thunder, the heavens opened.

Graça sat hunched in her car, listening to the rattle of raindrops on the metal roof, her stomach rumbling.

Why had she left the box of pastries with the security guard? Éder had eaten most of them, but there was a *Pāu de Deus* – a yeasty bun with a sweet coconut topping – that she could murder right now.

She was going on a diet after Christmas. Or maybe the new year was a better time to begin, although that was also the start of her summer holidays, so perhaps she'd wait until after Carnival. But it certainly hadn't started yet, and if she was going to be stuck here much longer, she'd need something to keep her energy levels up.

The evening flight was late, perhaps hovering above the storm. It wasn't until the rain eased a little that Graça saw the lights emerging from the dark sky.

She turned her attention to the runway as the plane landed, the wheels bouncing on the tarmac and little puffs of black smoke following on their heels. A whiff of burnt rubber reached her as the plane taxied past the silver glider and turned towards the arrival building. The engines stopped, the wheels were chocked, and mobile stairs wheeled out to the front and back. Graça scrutinised the passengers as they disgorged under floodlights. None looked remotely familiar. Once the plane was empty of passengers and their hold luggage, the fuel tanker trundled up. After refuelling was completed, it was the turn of the cleaners and finally the catering truck.

Fifteen minutes after landing, the car park came to life. A sports car approached the barrier, a hand stretched out to present a ticket, the barrier rose, and the car roared off into the night. Graça turned the key in the ignition and leaned forward, listening out for the throaty growl of a motorbike, ready to set off in pursuit of whoever picked it up. Twenty-seven cars later, silence returned.

Graça checked her watch. There were still a few hours before the night flight came in. The diet book said it was a false move to skip proper meals. If she was going to get dinner, now was the best time.

Don't touch the bike.

Stay with the bike.

She drummed her fingers on the steering wheel. Orders were all very well, but then don't send a lone police agent on a mission that needs back-up.

She grabbed her water bottle and drank until it was empty.

South Atlantic Ocean, December 24th – Christmas Eve

Swim
    right arm
    kick and kick
    left arm
    kick and kick
    breathe
    rest

Swim
    so thirsty
    the water is cool and salty
    salty
    wait
    stop
    STOP
    salty means seawater
    sodium potassium magnesium boron strontium
    carbonates chlorides sulphates bromides fluorides
    too much salt for the kidneys
    fastest way to dehydrate
    water water everywhere but not a drop to drink.

Swim
    right arm
    kick and kick
    left arm
    kick and kick
    breathe
    rest

Pitter-patter, plish-plosh
    rain
    head back
    mouth open
    sweet, sweet raindrops
    gulp
    gulp
    not enough of them
    slow down, let them collect

Swim
    right arm
    kick and kick
    left arm
    kick and kick
    breathe
    rest

Florianópolis, Brazil, December 24th – Christmas Eve

As night fell, the rain hammered down with renewed intensity, and Graça could no longer ignore the need to pee. The closest toilet was in the multistorey. She locked the car and slipped in through a side entrance.

The place felt eerily empty. Her footsteps rang out, echoing between smooth concrete walls. She cursed the stupid police shoes; it would be soft-soled boots next time.

The ground-floor toilet was disgusting. She retched at the filth, fought the urge to vomit, turned round and walked away. Maybe there was another one in the basement?

The ceilings seemed to get lower as she descended. She turned on her flashlight and focussed on the concrete walls. There was no toilet in the basement, but the whole floor stank of urine. If you were a man, every wall was a toilet. Could she go here, in the corner? Even the thought of it made her blush. She walked over to the bike.

They said don't touch the bike, but no one said anything about the helmet. She reached inside. A pair of black gloves nestled under the chin strap, hand in hand. She picked them up for inspection: nice quality leather with a silk lining, female size. As she brought one up to her nose she caught a whiff of petrol, a darker note of machine oil and something else, something lighter, vaguely floral. Under the gloves lay a patterned scarf made of something soft, silk perhaps. The scent of jasmine was stronger here. She brushed the scarf against her upper lip, the section of skin just under her nose, and breathed deeply.

Graça pushed her fingers back into the helmet, probing under the protective padding and fished out a key. An ordinary key, like her grandma's house key. Checking that no one was looking, she slipped it into the ignition. A perfect fit. She moved it a quarter turn and the lights came on. She turned the bike off again, returned the helmet, scarf and gloves to the handlebar and added the key to her keyring.

This bike wasn't going anywhere.

Time to find a clean toilet and something to eat. Graça turned round and walked out into the rain.

She drove to a fast-food take-away on the other side of the airport and ordered a meal deal to get the free soda and hot apple strudel.

The toilets were bright and clean, and she took advantage of the hot water and clean paper towels to freshen up.

'Agent Neves? Supersized cheeseburger meal?'

'That's me.'

'Merry Christmas.'

Graça grabbed the food and drove back to her stakeout, settling down to dinner with a view of both the multistorey exit and the airport. She ate the food while it was hot. Once she'd finished, she walked to the multistorey, removed the key from her keyring and returned it to the helmet of the bike.

The airport floodlights came on ten minutes before the night flight appeared in the sky. Graça scrutinised the passengers as they disembarked. Not one even vaguely resembled the motorbike rider.

The silver spaceship was refuelling now. A long hose snaked out from a covered bay where the tanker driver was sheltering from the rain.

Graça turned her attention back to the car park. The passengers from the night flight, or those who had come to meet them, were retrieving their cars. Over the next thirty minutes a stream of vehicles approached the barrier, inserted a ticket and drove away. Not a single motorbike among them.

She washed her meal down with a can of *Guaraná Antarctica*, a fruit soda and one of her five-a-day, then relaxed in her seat, almost dozing off to the rhythm of raindrops hitting the windscreen and rolling down the glass.

And then it happened.

CRACK!

The first explosion lit up the sky with a pale blue glow.

The blast wave that followed rocked the car and shattered windows.

CRASH!

And then the sound wave.

BOOM!

Frank Good checked for messages on his phone, frowning on discovering his inbox empty. Since when had everyone in China used Christmas as an excuse to do nothing? In a 24/7 global business any lack of productivity had consequences. He'd be kicking some backsides tomorrow.

He clicked onto LinkedIn to check if any of his team were working. His phone purred and he lifted an eyebrow at the caller ID lighting up the screen: Clara Sousa, general manager of Zagrovyl in Brazil.

'Merry Christmas, Frank.'

The way she said it lightened his mood, straightened his spine, uncoiled his reserve. Her husky voice conjured memories of their time together, the night they slipped away from the Zagrovyl international conference to explore more intimate international relations – the very best sort of networking.

'Merry Christmas, Clara,' he said. 'What time is it in Brazil?'

'You're eleven hours ahead of us. It's still Christmas Eve here, but I saw you come online and I wanted to say thank you.'

'For what?'

'The board approved my rare earth metal project.'

'In Brazil?' Frank tried to keep the surprise from his voice. Sourcing metals with rare properties had been key to Frank's own success in the Green Energy division of Zagrovyl.

'Whatever you added to the strategic sourcing report opened the door.'

While delighted by confirmation of his influence within the multibillion-dollar global company, if truth be told, he hadn't added anything. All he'd done was taken out the qualifier. It was a matter of fact that Brazil possessed the third-largest reserves of rare earth metals in the world – but that statement was usually followed by a warning that they were spread out and hard to extract economically.

Well, she definitely owed him a favour now. Payback time.

'Remember I asked you about a former Zagrovyl engineer working in Brazil?'

'Dr Jaqueline Silver? Yes, I read her paper, "Natural Danger",' Clara said. 'Very interesting. I may use it—'

Frank interrupted. 'Did you find out what she's doing in Brazil?'

'She's working for Tecnoproject – but they aren't a serious company, more of a vector.'

'A vector?'

'Come to Brazil, Frank, and I'll explain how things work here.'

As if he cared.

'I invited her to come and talk about jobs with Zagrovyl.'

Frank felt a chill descend. If Silver returned to Zagrovyl, she might be invited to give evidence against him. Something to be avoided at all cost.

'But she refused to even discuss it,' Carla added.

He straightened with relief until an uncomfortable thought caused his shoulders to hunch again.

'You didn't mention my name, did you?' he asked.

'Of course not, Frank. You asked me not to.' Carla's voice dropped an octave, suddenly husky. 'I like a man who knows what he wants.'

A warm surge of memory made him stretch and smile.

'Thanks for trying, Carla,' he said. 'Forget about Jaq Silver.'

He only wished he could do the same.

Florianópolis, Brazil, December 24th – Christmas Eve

BOOM!

Darkness gave way to a halo of blue flame. The car shook, the glass flexed and turned white.

Graça punched out the shattered passenger windows, the side that had faced the blast, and floored the accelerator.

She'd passed her advanced driving exam with flying colours, top of her class in fact. Give her an open road and she was a Formula One winner. Except that she rarely got the chance. Not one of her male colleagues allowed her to put her foot down in anger. They might be slow to share the boredom of surveillance, reluctant to shuffle along in city traffic without lights or siren, but quick to take control if there was any chance of a high-speed chase. Was it adrenaline or glory they sought? And was she always relegated to a passenger seat because of her gender? Or her skin colour? Or her weight? Probably all of the above.

But those men weren't here, and she'd just witnessed a massive explosion in the airport.

Fire engines were already screaming over the concrete, sirens wailing, lights flashing. She screeched up to the barrier and flashed her badge at the airport security.

He shook his head. 'No one's allowed in.'

'What happened?'

'Some sort of fire, I guess.'

She peered into the darkness. Whatever it was, it had taken out the floodlights. 'It looked more like an explosion to me.' A short, sharp burst of energy. 'Anyone hurt?'

'No.'

She felt a rush of relief to see the glider pilot walking towards the airport building. Everything looked eerily normal. No fire. Just the flashing blue lights of the fire tenders.

By the time Graça got back to the car park, the army had arrived.

The soldier clicked his heels. 'Major Moura Gomes.'

Graça resisted the urge to salute. 'Agent Graça Neves.'

'I'm here to take over surveillance.' He twisted his mouth in a simulacrum of a smile that lacked any warmth. 'You'll be wanting to get home to your family for Christmas.'

She felt a surge of irritation. What did he know about her family? Was he suggesting she was somehow less committed to her job than he was? She hadn't asked for bloody reinforcements.

'Where's the bike?' he demanded.

'Basement of the car park.'

'Show me.'

Graça heaved herself out of the car and followed him into the dark maw. She glanced up at the single security camera over the entrance. The glass was shattered. No lights came on.

'Wait.'

Graça returned to her car and fetched a flashlight. She pointed the beam at the entrance.

'There was an explosion at the airport.'

He raised an eyebrow.

'Looks as if it has taken out all the electrics.'

He walked fast, with long, even strides. She had to hurry to keep up with him, her stupid police shoes clack-clacking against the concrete ramp. He reached the basement before her.

'Where is it?'

'Over here—' She stood, frozen to the spot, staring at the empty space where the bike should have been. 'How the hell …'

'Where?' he couldn't hide the irritation from his voice.

'It's gone,' she whispered.

'Gone?'

'The bike is gone.'

'What?' He sounded alarmed. 'When?'

'I'm guessing it was taken during—'

'I don't do guesses.' And neither should you, his frown told her. 'Give me facts. When did you last see the bike?'

'I checked at about 9 p.m.' Returning the keys to the helmet, but no one needed to know about that. 'Then I watched the parking exit from my car.'

'Show me.'

They walked out of the car park in silence. Graça pointed to her surveillance spot by the airport perimeter fence.

'Right there.'

'You didn't see anything leave?'

'Only cars.'

'No motorbike?'

'No.'

'No van or lorry that could be carrying a motorbike?'

She shook her head.

'And you were watching? All the time?'

'Until the explosion at the airport took out two of my windows.'

'Show me.'

They walked round to the passenger side, and she pointed at the missing glass.

'I went to see if they needed help, but the airport fire brigade had everything under control, so I came back here.'

He stared at the fast-food packaging on the passenger seat.

'Via the *Happy Hamburger*?'

She could hear the disgust in his voice as his eyes slowly looked her over, deliberately tracing every curve and bulge, from her thick ankles up to her round face. She couldn't help the tell-tale blush.

'That was earlier. I had to pee.' What was she supposed to do? Men might take a leak against a wall, but a female officer squatting with her trousers around her ankles was not a good look for law enforcement. 'I put in my order, went to the toilet, collected my food in less than five minutes.' It sounded lame even to her. 'And I checked the bike after I got back.'

He raised an eyebrow as if he didn't believe her.

'So sometime before midnight the motorbike that you were supposed to be watching disappeared and you missed it. Is there CCTV footage?'

'You'd have to ask Éder.' Good luck with that.

'Who is Éder?'

'The parking security guard.'

'Been making friends, have we?'

Deus, this man was insufferable.

As they reached the exit, Graça shone her torch up at the security camera. The glass of the lens had shattered, and the recording light was off.

'I think it's safe to assume that there won't be any footage after the blast,' she said.

'We assume nothing.'

Graça blushed again.

'Well, this is a fine mess.' The Major made a dismissive gesture. 'You can go now, Agent Neves.'

Merry Christmas to you too.

Graça stopped to fill up with fuel: ethanol for the car, cake and coffee for the driver.

The cashier wiped sleep from her eyes. '*Feliz Natal.*' She hadn't been thrilled about being woken up but appeared happy enough with the tip.

'*Feliz Natal!*' Graça replied.

Merry Christmas to you too.

At the memory of the Major's contempt, she lowered her eyes and turned away. Her first mission had been simple. Surveillance of a valuable asset to see who collected it. Any corruption investigation had to start with evidence.

She'd let it slip through her fingers.

Back in the car, Graça brushed a few fragments of glass from the passenger seat.

Had someone engineered the explosion, distracting her long enough to remove the bike she was meant to be watching?

Was it the owner, Salty Walter? Did the crook who registered the motorbike at a fraction of its true value collect it himself? Salty didn't look much like a biker. More likely he bought the bike as an investment.

Was it the mysterious woman caught on CCTV riding the bike? Did she return to collect it? The feds in Curitiba would very much like to talk to her – a potential witness against Salty.

Or was it someone else?

She'd never know.

Sent on a simple mission, she'd failed.

As Graça drove through the night, determined to get to church in time for the Christmas Day service, the image of the mysterious woman in the CCTV footage remained with her.

The dark-haired woman didn't look like a criminal, but then white-collar crime followed different rules: never judge a book by its cover.

Why did the face look so familiar?

Who are you?

Where are you now?

South Atlantic Ocean, December 25th – Christmas Day

The sun is high in the sky.

I am a smooth, flat stone, skimming the surface of the ocean. Pale, five-fingered shapes move through the water ahead of me, wrinkled from immersion, grey with cold. Hands. Are these my hands? I test the connection between my thoughts and these hands, willing the left to clench, the right to wave, but they just keep on swimming, and I am none the wiser.

I focus on the smudge of land to the west, allowing my phantom limbs to propel me forwards. I can no longer feel my fingers or toes, my hands or feet, my arms or legs, and the injury to my shoulder is only a distant memory. If I stop moving, I will freeze. If I lower my head, I will drown. I am not ready to die. There is something I need to do first. Afterwards, I don't much care what happens. But I cannot leave this life with unfinished business.

I hear the plane before I see it, the thump-thump-thump beat in the air.

Marina?

With the very last of my energy, I roll onto my back, stretch out my limbs and splash the water with hands and feet to make myself visible from the air.

I put the whistle to my mouth and blow. Will Marina hear me above the noise of air swept by the blades of unsynchronised propellers? Why is my friend, test pilot and inventor, flying an old propeller plane and not her beautiful hydrogen-powered jet?

Perhaps it's not Marina, but I'm beyond caring. I'll take whatever form of rescue comes my way. I raise my hands and wave at the sky.

And that's when the bullets start raining down.

2km from the gold mine, Tocantins, Brazil, Christmas Day

Deep in the jungle, high above the waterfalls and rapids that tumbled towards the giant river Tocantins, smoke rose from a cooking fire. Inside a quarry, a dozen conical huts with wooden floors and thatched roofs were connected by rope walkways to form the headquarters for RIMPO, para-military defenders of Brazil's poor, landless miners, the *garimpeiros*.

Colonel Cub emerged into the light and led a little procession towards the prison hut.

'Merry Christmas!'

The bank clerk from Rio lay shackled on the beaten-earth floor of his cell. He kept his eyes tightly closed in the hope that the Colonel was addressing the guards rather than their prisoner.

'I said, Merry Christmas, Pedro Carmargo,' the Colonel boomed. 'My dear, dear little man.'

Pedro opened his eyes, taking in the black leather boots with neatly tied laces, the camouflage trousers and shirt that hung so loose on the Colonel's bony frame, the white hair and gaunt face. He blinked at the fire in the eyes of his captor.

'I have some good news.' The grin split the Colonel's face in two, yellow teeth filling his skull from ear to ear. 'We found Silver.'

Silver? Not gold?

'And Pedro,' the Colonel said. 'I have a present for you.'

Rough hands seized his arms and Pedro cried out in pain as the guard pulled him upright and nudged him in the ribs. 'What do you say?' he growled.

'Thank you, Colonel Cub,' Pedro said.

'Do you have a present for me?'

Pedro bowed his head. Here it comes. Whatever he said next would be wrong. He said nothing.

The Colonel waggled a trembling finger. 'I suppose it's because you're a communist,' he said.

I'm not a communist. I'm a banker.

'Communists don't believe in God, do they?'

I once believed in God. Now I'm not so sure.

'If you don't believe in God, you don't believe in Jesus.'

Jesus can't save me now.

'And if you don't believe in Jesus, you don't believe in Christmas.'

How can I give anything, imprisoned in the jungle by a madman, far from my church and my family?

'But I am a generous man. A Christian man. I brought a present especially for you.'

'Thank you, Colonel.'

'I've noticed you're looking a bit pasty.'

That's what happens when you chain a man to the floor of a windowless cell and starve him apart from a daily bowl of beans and rice.

'I think you need some fresh air and sunlight.'

Pedro jerked his chin upwards, a rising helix of hope twisting his stomach into a helter-skelter. Was the lunatic finally going to let him go?

'Would you like that?'

47

Pedro threw caution to the winds. 'Very much, Colonel Cub,' he said.

The Colonel nodded to the soldier who placed a cloth bag on the table in front of Pedro.

'Open it.' The Colonel nodded at him.

Inside was a metal dog collar, in two parts with a hinge and pin, attached by a ring to a long leather leash.

'Put it on.'

The soldier fastened the metal ring around Pedro's neck and handed the leash to his boss.

'Walkies?'

The Colonel started to laugh. The braying grew loud and louder, reaching a peak of hysteria as Pedro's sobs turned to barks.

Curitibanos, Brazil, December 25th – Christmas Day

The congregation rose to their feet and spoke with one voice.

Jesus is born!

The pastor led the drumming, establishing a syncopated rhythm by pointing to each section of the congregation in turn. A slow beat using feet for the bass, cascades of off-beat triplets to fill the pause, a finger-clicking jive and a bossa nova cascade of palms hitting thighs. Once he had four sets of human percussion clapping and swaying, he raised his voice to sing. He might lack the rich gravelly bass of his predecessor, but he could certainly hold a tune.

The familiar call and response of the *Church of Jesus Christ our Lord and Saviour* filled the church.

All that is good, comes from Jesus.

Praise be to Jesus Christ our Lord.

Federal Agent Graça Neves had driven through the night, pulling up at the Church just before the Christmas service started. She found her grandmother in her usual pew, right at the front.

'Merry Christmas, GG.'

They embraced.

All that we have, we share with Jesus.

Praise be to Jesus Christ our Lord.

The pastor held up both hands and the congregation fell silent.

'What does Jesus want on his birthday?' He answered his own question. 'To see us succeed.'

'Hallelujah!' echoed the audience.

'Why does he want us to succeed?' He barely paused, declaiming with passion. 'Because he loves us, he trusts us, he knows that we are strong and capable and good. He sees our struggle. He knows how hard life can be. He wants us to take care of ourselves. He wants us to reap the rewards of our labour on earth as well as in heaven.'

He spread his arms wide and cried out.

'Jesus wants you to be happy, he wants you to be hopeful, he wants you to be confident, he wants you to work hard. Jesus wants you to be rich!'

Graça quite liked the pep talks. She could see why her grandmother had switched from the dry, old Catholic church, with all its hectoring on sacrifice and abstinence, restraint and denial, sin and misery to this happy-clappy God loves you and wants you to prosper alternative.

But there was a catch. There's always a catch. The elders were coming round with the collection trays.

'Invest in Jesus. Whatever you give will be returned to you tenfold, a hundredfold, a thousandfold.'

Graça patted her pockets, but the pastor was way ahead of her.

'If we are pinched and mean with Jesus, then we are only hurting ourselves.'

Graça extracted a roll of notes, unpeeled one and placed it in the tray. The elder stared at her, pushing the tray closer.

She blushed and added another.

Her grandmother nudged her, and she dropped a third and then a fourth note into the tray, before turning away.

Deus, what had she done? She still hadn't been paid this month, and there were debts to cover. Instalments on the car loan, and she needed to get the windows fixed. Rent was three months overdue. A police agent's salary was barely enough to cover her outgoings at the best of times, but when it was paid late, things got worse.

The congregation was chanting again.

Trust in Jesus, so Jesus can trust in you.
Invest in Jesus, so Jesus can invest in you.

Give to Jesus, so that Jesus can give back to you.

Graça drove her grandmother home. The little house wasn't much to look at from the outside, more of a shack with unrendered breeze block walls and corrugated tin roof; one of several – all different shapes and sizes and textures and colours – that fringed the unpaved road as it wound up the hill.

The front door opened directly onto the road. Graça parked right outside, then walked round to open the passenger door.

'What happened to the windows?' asked GG.

'Long story.'

Graça went ahead and put her key in the lock. It didn't fit.

'It's open!' GG called from behind her.

Graça turned the handle, and the door sprang open.

'You should lock up,' she remonstrated.

'Pah,' the old woman snorted. 'I've nothing worth stealing.'

'What about the TV?'

Graça nodded at the large screen that graced the main room.

'Everyone's got a TV, mine is probably the oldest in the neighbourhood. Nobody would bother with a heavy old thing like this.' GG shuffled forward, heading for the fridge in the corner. 'Check what's on while I get us something to eat.'

Graça couldn't find the remote, so she switched the TV on at the side. The jangling chords of *The Missing* filled the room and the face of César Correa appeared on the screen.

'Did you catch the episode last night?' GG asked.

'Not really,' Graça said. 'I was working.'

'There's a new series of *Love on the Beach* if you prefer,' GG said over her shoulder.

'I have a present for you,' Graça said, placing a gift on the kitchen table.

The congregation had exchanged presents at the celebration. The pastor insisted that these be low-value gifts, with only one giver and one receiver selected at random, railing against the materialism that encouraged people to spend money on trinkets instead of 'investing' it with Jesus.

'Naughty girl,' GG admonished.' I told you not to.'

Graça smiled as GG tore open the wrapping paper, opened the box beneath and removed the pieces. Five tin plates of decreasing size, painted with birds and flowers, a set of steel rods and hoops inside a large muslin bag.

'Lovely.' GG beamed, then frowned. 'What's it all for?'

Graça laughed and pointed to the picture on the front of the box. 'It's a cake stand. An English one.' She twisted a metal rod into the centre of the largest plate and then added the others one by one, constructing a tower, finally slipping the muslin over the carry ring at the top and draping it over the pyramid.

'I thought it might be useful for your market stall. You make the best sweets in the world. You could charge more for things if they're nicely displayed.'

'But people can't afford ...'

'Remember what your pastor said.' Graça smiled. 'Jesus wants you to be successful.'

GG laughed. 'Then I have a present for you too.'

On the stove top was a tray of freshly made *brigadeiros*, balls of condensed milk and chocolate rolled in chocolate crumb.

'But first,' GG opened the lid on a casserole and ladled out a generous helping of meat and bean stew. 'Feijoada.'

Graça's mouth began to water. The diet would definitely have to wait.

The smooth silk of water is pockmarked with danger. Someone is shooting at me from a plane flying low above the ocean.

At the sound of missiles hitting the surface, my body reacts. The ache in my muscles vanishes. I take rapid shallow breaths. My heart rate increases. A burst of energy banishes exhaustion, like a gale-force wind sweeping through the sea mist, bringing a moment of complete clarity.

This plane has not come to rescue me.

Someone is trying to kill me.

But who?

I've made a few enemies in Brazil. But which of them knows I'm here? Who has access to a plane and a repeating rifle?

A burst of fire strafes the water to my left and then my right.

Whoever it is, they're a good shot. I have a few seconds while the plane turns. The shooter won't miss next time. It doesn't matter who's shooting. What matters is how I survive.

The horror of my stupidity hits me. Not only have I deliberately attracted this assassin with whistles and splashing limbs, fluorescent lifejacket and wide, bright flowery skirt, I've made myself the largest target possible.

The plane turns and makes a new run, even lower this time.

As my conscious wizard brain, the cerebral cortex, tries to calculate how much time I have left, the autonomic lizard brain unleashes a chemical carnival. At a shrieking whistle from the amygdala, the hypothalamic percussion begins, the drumbeat of my nervous system cueing a melody of hormones.

Epinephrine bursts from the alto-sax section of my adrenal gland. It circulates through the body, increasing my heartrate, pushing blood to my muscles. Small airways open in my lungs so I can take in more oxygen with each breath. My senses become sharper. Glucose is released from the bass section, tubas and sousaphones, and floods into my bloodstream, supplying the clarity and energy that I need. Only one way I can go. Underwater.

Dive!

Water is 800 times denser than air, sea water even heavier, and once a bullet hits the water, it decelerates faster. The missile changes trajectory, sinking as it slows down.

My first dive is a disaster, the buoyancy of the life jacket pulls me back to the surface. I rip it off and dive again, turning myself into a sleek torpedo, morphing from a giant, luminous, flowery dartboard to a tiny bull's eye, the soles of my feet presenting the minimum mark for the shooter.

I dive deeper and deeper until my lungs are ready to burst. I count to sixty then turn underwater to swim sideways before coming up for air.

The chemical carnival is developing new melodies. As the initial surge of tenor epinephrine subsides, the secondary theme emerges. The trombones take over as corticotropin-releasing hormones signal to the bass drum of the pituitary gland, prompting a thrum of adrenocorticotropic hormone, triggering a cadenza of cortisol from horns of the adrenal glands.

Diving again. Down.

It's as I come up for the third time that I take the hit. The searing pain in my left arm is accompanied by a flower of red blooming around me as I dive down again.

For the very last time.

Curitibanos, Brazil, December 26th – Boxing Day

GG's house might be Graça's favourite place in the world. Everything familiar. Everything just right. A small, simple house consisting of four rooms: a single main room spanning the whole ground floor and three small bedrooms upstairs. It was hard to imagine GG raising five children here, with an outside toilet and washroom, but perhaps the secret was the huge garden at the back, which GG tended with skill and care.

Graça woke to the crowing of a cockerel. She remained dozing in bed, luxuriating in the familiar noises of country life until the delicious smells from the kitchen could no longer be ignored.

They ate breakfast in the garden, seated on plastic chairs either side of a rickety iron table. GG's *rabanadas* were definitely the best in the world; thick slices of white bread soaked in beaten egg and cream, fried in oil and then coated in cinnamon sugar.

'I have to go back to Curitiba today.'

'Can't you stay a little longer?' GG asked.

Graça shook her head. The summons left little room for doubt.

'Can you come to church with me?'

Again? 'No, but I can give you a lift there when I set off.'

'Let's go out for coffee. I want to make sure the neighbours see you.'

Graça smiled. At least someone in the family was proud of what she did.

As they left the house, Graça turned to lock the door, but the key didn't fit.

'GG, have you changed the lock?' she asked.

'No, dear.'

'Can you try?'

'My granddaughter is a policewoman. No one would dare rob me for fear that you shoot them.'

Graça frowned. 'You should still lock the door.'

GG rummaged in her handbag and took out her own key. It fitted smoothly, and the lock clicked shut.

Graça ordered two coffees at the bar. The café opened straight onto the main road. Through a curtain of beads, she saw her grandmother settle down at a table outside.

Men and women stopped to talk to her, a few pulled up chairs and soon there was a crowd of GG's friends and neighbours with an average age of seventy.

Before long, a traffic jam formed. The blast of horns soon drowned the chatter of conversation. Cars could have taken it in turns to pass the café in single file, one direction at a time, but impatience caused a logjam.

An elderly man took it upon himself to restore order, controlling the access around the obstruction created by GG and her friends, signalling to the northbound, then southbound traffic in turn.

But the self-appointed traffic policeman gave up when a truck carrying building materials rumbled up the potholed highway, the load too wide to pass. The driver sat on his horn until the pensioners got slowly to their feet and moved chairs and tables out of the way.

Graça brought the coffees out to a table for two and helped to rearrange the seating.

'What were you doing in 1970?' she asked.

GG shook a packet of sugar, tore off one corner and poured it into her small black coffee. 'Why do you ask?'

'I watched an old clip from *The Missing* after you went to bed last night, all those students who disappeared in the 1970s, did you know about it at the time?'

GG stirred her coffee. 'I don't feel sorry for communists. If they'd stuck to studying instead of playing at revolution, they'd have been fine.'

Never talk politics with GG.

'Things were better when the army were in charge,' she continued. 'Everyone knew where they stood.'

Best to change the subject.

'Shall I get a new key cut before I leave?' Graça asked.

'Let me see yours.'

Graça separated her copy from the keyring and GG compared it with the original.

'This is the wrong key.'

'Let me see.'

Graça held them both up to the sunlight. They were the same size and basic shape, but one of them had the words Briggs and Stratton engraved across the head.

A motorbike key.

With a sinking heart, Graça realised what she'd done.

Army base, Florianópolis, Brazil, December

A convoy of camouflaged trucks squealed to a halt at the edge of the runway. A sleek fighter plane roared down the smooth strip towards the sea and took off into the summer sky, banking over the ocean before flying back over the island of Santa Catarina towards mainland Brazil. The trucks rumbled across the runway and parked up at a long, low building.

The army had a small base at the military airport; they provided support activities, like security and baggage handling, tasks the Air Force felt beneath them.

A civilian in olive fatigues was waiting outside the officers' mess and saluted as Major Moura Gomes jumped down from the lead vehicle.

The officer clocked the tattoo of a smoking cobra on the man's arm and gestured for him to follow.

It took both men a moment to adjust from the bright sunlight outside to the dim lighting in the long corridor. Major Moura Gomes led the way to his office and closed the door behind them both.

'The Colonel sent you?'

'Yes, sir.'

'Do you have a name?'

'Oskar Guerra,' the man announced. 'RIMPO.'

The paramilitary organisation, RIMPO, was founded to support the *garimpeiros*, landless artisanal miners. Since Colonel Cub had taken over leadership, the line between supporting and exploiting was increasingly blurred.

'And what can I do for the Colonel?'

The Major listened carefully. Not to the words, which were simple enough, but to the spaces between the words, the things left unsaid, the things that might trip him up. He'd worked with RIMPO before and had learned that nothing was ever quite as it appeared. But the Colonel had influential friends; it was wise not to cross him.

'I'm not sure how we can help you.'

'I believe you have a motorbike,' said Oskar.

How did the Colonel know about the motorbike? The same leak in the military police that had alerted the army? Or someone in his own battalion? RIMPO must have eyes and ears everywhere.

Major Moura Gomes frowned. 'Our orders are to return the bike to its owner.'

'Yes, sir. You have it, sir?'

The Major nodded towards the window. A grey army truck was parked directly outside. 'We staged a little diversion to recover it from an airport car park.'

'Diversion, sir?'

'To distract the federal police who had taken an unhealthy interest.'

'Can I see the motorbike, sir?'

'Why?'

'Colonel's request, sir.'

The Major rang a bell and barked at the young lieutenant who entered from a side door.

'Any sign of that federal police agent from the airport?'

'No sir.'

'Keep a lookout. Tell me if she comes snooping around.' The Major gestured at Oskar. 'Take this man and show him the bike.'

Oskar felt a little shiver of anticipation as the soldier unlocked the doors of the lorry. The bike was old, but even Oskar, neither a fan of motorbikes nor of antiques, could appreciate the chrome, the geometry, the beautiful waspish curves of the body.

He climbed into the cargo space and walked round the bike. He ran his fingers over the leather saddle. It was warm to the touch.

Unlike the last rider.

News had just come in. Silver was dead, shot from a plane as she floated on the sea. With her death, any claim on the gold mine became less of a threat. But the Colonel liked things to be neat and tidy. He wanted an old, portable safe that had belonged to Silver's family, a safe that she had recently brought to Brazil.

'Have you removed anything from the bike?' Oskar asked. 'Top box? Panniers?'

'We haven't touched it,' the soldier said. 'Our orders were to pick it up and keep it safe. What are you looking for?'

Oskar didn't answer. He moved to the helmet hanging over the handlebars and extracted a scarf, bringing it to his nose. Soft, so soft. And what a scent. Oh yes. He recognised the scent. Silver's scent. There was nothing else, just a pair of gloves.

'Can I take these?'

The soldier frowned. 'Ask the Major.'

Oskar took one final look and climbed back down.

The Major was sitting at a long table covered in maps.

'Did you find what you needed?'

'Not exactly.' Oskar held up the scarf and gloves. 'But I'll take these.'

The Major nodded.

'What happens next?' Oskar asked.

'We return the bike to its rightful owner.'

'Is Walter Salgado back in Brazil?'

'No, still in Angola. We're waiting for instructions with a firm address.'

'You're taking it back to São Paulo?'

The Major shook his head.

'He has properties all over Brazil.'

Silver had been living in Walter Salgado's flat in São Paulo; if he had a house nearby, Jaq Silver might have stayed there too. The safe might still be there.

'When will you know the delivery point?' Oskar asked. 'Today?'

The Major shrugged. 'It's not a priority. We have other, more pressing matters to attend to.'

Oskar tried and failed to control his impatience.

'Tomorrow?'

The Major barked an order and a soldier entered, carrying a clipboard.

'Sergeant, contact this man once you know the delivery address for Walter Salgado's recovered property.'

'Yes, sir.'

The soldier turned to Oskar. 'How do we contact you?'

Oskar took out a new burner phone and read off the number.

The soldier wrote it down.

The Major waved him away and turned to Oskar. 'Are we done now?'

'Yes, sir. Thank you, sir.'

'Send my regards to the Colonel.'

Curitiba, Brazil, December

The modern office block looked impressive from the outside. A curved glass façade supported by painted concrete pillars created a grand atrium with the words *Justiça Federal* in large gold letters on a semi-circular portico above the main entrance.

Inside it was less inspiring. Graça's workstation was a hot desk on the fifth floor. The natural light and ventilation had been stolen to create private offices for the important people: the judges and chief investigators and senior managers.

Zélia was now on holiday, so Graça had a busy morning. She was preparing to go out for lunch when the summons came from the chief investigator.

Roberto Covelli sat at his desk, lips pursed, brows meeting in a storm-laden V, drumming his fingers on the paper file in the centre of his polished metal desk. He barely glanced up as she entered the room.

'Yes?' he barked. 'What do you want?'

'I'm Agent Neves, sir.' Graça coughed. 'You asked to see me.'

He raised his head and looked at her before letting out a long sigh.

'The agent responsible for the fuck-up on Christmas Eve?'

Better not to argue. 'Yes, sir.'

'Sit.' He gestured at a seat opposite his desk. 'You only had one job. What was it?'

'Stay with the bike.'

'And did you?'

'There was an explosion ...'

'Someone set off Christmas fireworks and you panicked.'

'More than fireworks ...'

'Not according to the army report.' He tapped the file. 'They

62

carried out a full investigation into your ...' his lip curled into a sneer, '... claims and could find no evidence, no trace of any explosion at the airport.'

'How do they explain the shattered CCTV camera, the failed electrics?' She'd been there. Seen it. Felt it.

'If you wanted to steal something, isn't CCTV the first thing you'd sabotage?'

'What about the broken glass on my car windows?'

'Bad driving?'

She ignored the jibe.

'The fire brigade attended. There must be a report of the blast from the airport. Someone must have recorded it. I saw a blue flame, then a fireball. It blew out the glass from my car windows and the parking security cameras.'

'I told you. The army checked, false alarm.'

'But—'

'So, let's drop this explosion nonsense. Why didn't you stay with the bike?'

Graça bit her lip. 'I left my station because of an ...' she corrected herself, 'an incident at the airport. I went to see if I could help, and when I got back the army had arrived, and the bike was gone.'

'Why not just admit it? You left your station to get food.'

This was hopeless. If she told him that she'd gone for food earlier then she'd have to confess to removing the bike key. If she told him about the bike key, she'd have to confess to something else.

She said nothing.

'The Major saw the fast-food wrappers in your car. You abandoned surveillance to get a hamburger and fries. Why not come clean?'

Stay with the bike.

Don't touch the bike.

Graça straightened her spine and took a deep breath.

'It's true I stopped off at the Happy Hamburger to use the toilet.

I was on my own: no partner, no back-up. I didn't know how long before reinforcements arrived. What do you expect me to do?'

'I expect you to find another job.'

Her jaw dropped.

'You're pathetic Agent Neves. All you had to do was to watch the bike until reinforcements arrived.' He sighed. 'But you people just can't control your impulses.'

You people. The bastard.

'Consider yourself suspended pending investigation.'

'But—'

'You're off the case.' He closed his eyes. 'Get out of my sight.'

As she slunk from the office, Graça put a hand into her pocket, wrapping her hands round the metal ring of keys. She'd failed not on one but two counts. She might not have the motorbike, but she had the key.

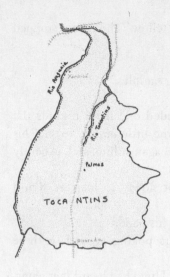

20km from the gold mine, Tocantins, Brazil, December

Hugo Gao cut a handful of scrubby grass and tied it with string. He scooped up a trowel full of crumbly soil and brought it to his nose, deconstructing the earthy smell into its constituent parts, rust and roots, mushrooms and moss. He poured the russet-coloured sample into a zip lock bag. Placing the sheaf and bag in his rucksack, he extracted a plastic bottle, unscrewed the lid and knelt beside the stream.

He had almost filled it with river water when a shout made him look up.

'Stop!'

A man limped towards him waving his hands. He had the pinched features of one of the villagers, hardy farmers who scraped a subsistence existence from this poor soil. Racing ahead of him came a barking dog – a brown-and-white terrier.

Hugo remained still and averted his gaze. He let the small dog approach him, turning away slightly while reassuring the animal in a low, calm voice. 'Hello there little fellow.' The terrier stopped barking as its master approached.

'You can't fish here!'

Hugo held up his hands. 'Just taking samples.'

'Why?'

Hugo dropped his arms and extended one hand towards the dog, keeping the palm flat, allowing the little animal to sniff his knuckles. A damp, velvety nose rubbed against him, and he gently scratched the animal under the chin.

'Checking water quality.' Hugo got slowly to his feet. 'I'm a university researcher.'

The villager backed away, wringing his hands.

'The Colonel doesn't like strangers poking around in these parts.'

The Colonel. It wasn't the first time Hugo had heard that name. Colonel Cub. People whispered it with fear in their eyes.

The dog rolled onto its back, and Hugo bent to rub its tummy.

'Does the Colonel have a mine near here?' Hugo asked.

The man backed away. 'How would I know?'

'Lights at night, machinery noises?'

'Machines?' The man laughed bitterly and shook his head. 'Why use machines when you can cripple men instead?'

Hugo observed the man more closely. His right hand was missing three fingers and his left leg was bent, as if it had been broken and badly set.

'If you know what's good for you, you'll leave now.' The man gestured downriver. A tremor shook his outstretched arm.

Hugo straightened up and the dog jumped to its feet.

'I'm on my way.'

Hugo stoppered the water bottle and added it to the other samples. He hefted the rucksack onto his back and gave the dog a final pat before setting off. The terrier bounded at his side until its master whistled, and it reluctantly turned back.

Hugo felt the man's eyes boring into his back. At a turn in the path he looked sideways to see the man climbing the hill, still watching him. Hugo raised a hand in farewell, but only the dog barked a response.

Hugo entered a thicket of spindly bushes and ducked down, waiting until the man and dog were out of sight. He surveyed the grassy slope and the ridge beyond. If he climbed a little further, he could investigate what was going on up there.

A wingless insect dropped from the bush onto his neck and began to crawl towards his face. Hugo brushed it away, catching it in his fingertips to inspect. A nasty piece of work: *Triatoma infestans,* a blood-sucking bug that probably carried the Chagas disease parasite *Trypanosoma cruzi.* These kissing bugs came out at night to feed from the face and lips of their prey. This one would have to remain hungry. He placed it on the ground and watched it scurry away.

Hugo checked his watch, then shook his head. It would soon be dusk. Best to get the samples back to the laboratory.

Analysis came first. Hunches had no place in science. It was the data that mattered. The numbers, plotted on a hydrogeological map would determine where he should go next.

He was getting closer.

UBERABA

1,900km from the gold mine, a freight train, Uberaba, Minas Gerais State, Brazil, February

Clatter, clank, clatter-clatter, clank.

The train is picking up speed.

I lie back in the empty wagon and stare up at the sky. It's almost dusk, fingers of pink caressing a faint blue sky. The moon emerges, pale and silver and upside down. A reminder that Brazil is in the Southern Hemisphere. February is high summer, and the crescent moon has an overhanging brow instead of a protruding jaw.

Rainwater or condensation has collected in a runnel used to strengthen the steel plates. I sniff it cautiously, dip a finger in and taste it. It's cool and ferrous but I'm thirsty and in no position to be fussy.

I lie on the floor of the wagon. Little hard grits press into my back. I sit up and sweep away the kernels of yellow corn. I'm not hungry now, but they'll make an acceptable meal when I am. I use the hessian sack to make a rough mattress and coil the rope to form a pillow.

It's not the most comfortable bed, but the steel walls of the train wagon mean that no one can see me.

I'm safe here.

I have food and water and no one knows where I am.

I think back to the three men at the sugar factory. The man I attacked with sulphur dioxide looked like a soldier. RIMPO, the military-style protection for freelance miners, have been trying to kill me since I arrived in Brazil. What the Colonel's thugs lack in intelligence, they almost make up for with persistence. The tall bald one in the flowery shirt was dressed like a supporter of Ecobrium. I can understand why the militant eco-warriors might feel they had a score to settle with me, but would they team up with soldiers? Their distrust of the military ran deep. And what about the red-head in mechanics' overalls? Not a SucoBras employee, but perhaps a contractor? A screech of metal brakes on metal rails remind me of his fate. The memory of Carrot-top sinking feet first into the rotating knives of the sugarcane thresher makes me retch. That fate was meant for me.

Suddenly I'm exhausted.

I close my eyes.

It's dark when I wake. The only light comes from the stars, huge and bright. The smell inside the open-topped wagon is musty and nutty – propyl pyrazine from the corn. The warm breeze brings other scents, fresh green vegetation from the plants in Brazil's vast fields. The train moves slowly through the flat agricultural landscape. Too dark to see, but I am content to guess at the chemical codes, those signature chemical cocktails that give every living thing on earth it's unique scent. We move from sugarcane to soy to corn.

Where am I headed? Escaping the sugar factory, direction was unimportant. All that mattered was to get away from the men trying to kill me.

Now that I've put some distance between myself and the assassins it's time to get my bearings.

My limbs are stiff, sharp crystals of lactic acid in muscles unused to sprinting. I try some slow stretches as I stare up at the stars. Which direction am I heading?

The last time I remember moving under a sky this clear, it was on a yacht in the Black Sea, the water lapping against the hull, the wooden planks creaking as they cooled on deck, the sails luffing in the wind. Staring into the dark eyes of the man lying beside me, I wish I'd paid more attention when he started to explain the principles of navigation without instruments, but the closeness of Giovanni's body was always so distracting.

In any case, it's not as if I can steer this train. I am at the mercy of the freight schedules.

Think about it logically. This train carried corn. Brazil is one of the largest exporters of corn in the world. Cargoes sail to Mexico and Germany, Iran and Japan, all from the port of Santos. Now it's empty, so it's on its return journey. The train is travelling inland, back to the farm.

The wrong direction.

How long have I been travelling the wrong way?

I search the sky for any hint of dawn, but it is inky black.

A couple of hours? Four? More?

Many, many more.

I force myself to face the truth.

I have been off course since Christmas Eve. I have burnt so many bridges. I'm not sure I can ever find a way to take me back to where I should be.

But while I still have breath in my body, I have to try.

25
Mn
Manganese
54.938

Brazil produced 1,164,000 tonnes of manganese in 2012, worth roughly US$ 166 million.

Manganese is mainly used in iron and steel production.

Praia de Moçambique, Florianópolis, Brazil, December

The air shimmered above the hot sand, blurring the line between land and sea. Today was warming up to be the hottest day of the summer so far, and the sun worshippers were out in force.

Graça pulled into a car park and found a narrow space between a battered old camper van and a brand-new open-topped Mercedes. A group of surfers approached, beaded dreadlocks swinging and clacking as they walked past.

As the machine dispensed her parking ticket, Graça reflected on the beach as the great leveller. Rich and poor, young and old, black and white, all possible body shapes and sizes mixed on the beach, relaxing side by side in a way they rarely did once they put their clothes back on.

She put the paper ticket in the windscreen of her car and locked it before remembering that anyone could break in via the two plastic sheets serving as passenger windows. Following a narrow path through the dunes, tall grasses brushed her bare legs. She could have driven the last kilometres, but she wasn't sure how her car would handle the sandy, single-track private road, and given that she wasn't on official police business, she preferred to approach unseen.

The list of Salty Walter's properties, or suspected properties given that they were registered in the name of family members or shell companies, was as long as it was depressing. Most were abroad: Key Largo, Florida; Upper West Side, Manhattan, New York; Quinta del Lago, Portugal; Kensington, London. The ones that interested Graça were in Brazil, especially the one closest to Florianópolis airport.

Graça had printed out the file before her interview with

the chief investigator. It was still in her handbag when she was escorted from the building.

She might be officially off the case, but she wasn't going to sit around watching daytime TV until Zélia came back to defend her.

The first glimpse of the isolated beach bungalow filled her with envy. From the path it looked deceptively small and simple until you got up close and saw how far it extended. A gentle breeze brought scents from the lush garden, a riot of succulents and flowering vines. Floor-to-ceiling windows and a teak veranda commanded an uninterrupted view of the coastline. What a location.

You had to be practically at the front door before you could appreciate the view it commanded of the beach, the dunes, the sea, the headland. How did someone get to own a place like this? How did someone have a place like this as one of several holiday homes?

There was no car in the driveway, no Harley Davidson motorbike either, and no sign of life in the bungalow.

On the other side of the garden stood a garage. Graça followed the road and tried the handle, but both the double doors were securely locked. She peered in through a small window. Empty apart from a sink, a deep freeze, a washing machine, a portable gas-powered barbecue with several bottles of butane and a small diesel generator. No sign of the precious motorbike.

She walked back through the garden. It wasn't as productive as GG's, more for show than to reap nature's bounty, but it was well cared for. The absentee owner must employ someone to look after it.

She cut down to the beach and walked past the front of the house and then climbed up the rocky bluff on the far side. From the top of the hill, she spotted a silver glider coming in to land.

She retreated to a spot where she could observe both house and road unseen and pulled out her phone.

'Zélia, hi.'

'Graça.' The tone was cold.

'How was your holiday?'

'Brief.'

'I'm at the beach.'

'Good for you.'

'Looking at Salty's beach house.'

A tsk of irritation. 'I thought you were off the job.'

'There's no sign of the motorbike.'

'Leave it, Graça.'

'You certainly left me to face the music.'

The silence told her that the barb had struck home.

A noise from the beach made her swing round. The silver glider had landed and was taxiing down the beach. She took a picture with her phone.

'Look Zélia, can you do me a favour?'

'No.'

'There's a plane here. On the beach. Pretty sure I saw the same one at Floripa airport before the explosion. Any chance of finding out who flies it?'

'No.'

'I'm sending you a picture.'

'Didn't you hear me? I'm in enough trouble as it is.'

'What sort of trouble?'

'There's no love lost between our boss and Major Moura Gomes.'

'Why did you get the army involved then?'

'I didn't. I asked for help from the military police in Floripa. They were the ones who called in the army.'

'I didn't need help.'

'I couldn't leave you on your own. You needed to rest. To eat.'

Graça steeled herself for what came next.

'But you couldn't wait, could you?'

Even Zélia despised her. Why did thin people feel they had the right to judge?

'I left my post because there was an explosion at the airport.'

'So you say. But why would Major Moura Gomes lie?'

'Maybe he had something to do with the explosion.'

'Now you're getting paranoid.'

Ping.

'Was that the photo arriving?'

'I'm not opening it.'

'Please Zélia, just take a look. It's like some sort of silver spaceship.'

'*Bolas*. Never seen one like that before.'

'Call me when you have something.'

'No. I'm busy.'

'I know it's tricky, but if anyone can do it, you can.'

Graça settled down in the shade of a palm and unpacked her beach picnic. She'd gone for something healthy, no meat today: *pão de queijo* – cheese balls made with cassava flour, crisp then chewy then liquid; *Romeu e Julietta* – a sandwich of white cheese and red-guava jelly encased in pastry and, of course the *brigadeiros* – condensed milk truffles rolled in chocolate.

A woman strode across the beach, instantly recognisable as the pilot of the silver glider. Graça snapped a couple of photos and sent one to Zélia.

Minutes later her phone rang.

'You're completely out of your depth.'

Graça smiled. 'Hi, Zélia.'

'Do not, on any account approach that glider. It's an Áerex prototype. There are only a couple of people who can fly it, and both are ex-military and extremely well connected.'

'Is one the woman whose photo I just sent?'

'Marina Querino. Formerly Paulo Santos.'

Graça blinked and looked again.

'A pilot, engineer and inventor. And a very close friend of Salty Walter.'

Bingo.

Hospital, Florianópolis, Brazil, December

The sea is calmer now. The lapping waves replaced by the regular thrum of a motor. A boat? A plane?

My eyes flash open.

The sea is no longer black. Nor is it blue. Nor red with my blood. It's white. All around me, bright white.

There is more than one sun above me. I look to the side.

I'm no longer swimming. I am lying on my back. There's a pillow behind my head, a bandage on my left arm and crisp white sheets all around me, tucked in tight.

A bed.

A hospital bed.

Where am I? What day is it?

On Christmas Day, I remember the noises above the water changing. No more bullets strafing, the whirring propellers receding to be replaced by the rapid chuff-a-chuffa-chuff-a-chuffa of a helicopter.

As I broke through the waves and gasped for breath, I saw a figure in the water, racing towards me, coming to kill me?

The carnival of chemistry had run out of steam, the timpani slowed, soft sticks on cymbals as my cortisol levels fell, the parasympathetic brake bringing the *Frevo* number to a close.

I remember thinking that I had no energy left to fight.

It wasn't until Marina wrapped her arms around me and brought water to my parched lips that I knew I might be saved.

But when I remember everything that had happened before, I wish she'd left me to die.

I open my eyes, but I see nothing.

People are talking, but I hear nothing.

I run a swollen tongue around the inside of my mouth, but taste nothing.

I'm lying in a hospital bed, hooked up to a drip to ensure I feel nothing: no thirst, no hunger, no pain.

Only longing.

Longing for a connection I didn't know existed and is now broken. Longing for something I didn't know was missing and can never be mine again. Longing for someone I found and lost.

I take refuge in sleep.

The machines whoosh and thrum as I doze in my hospital bed. The oxygen valves and peristaltic pumps, the heartbeat and pulse monitors, the occasional whoosh of the blood-pressure cuff inflating and then deflating, all these noises lay down a percussion, the rhythm for my dreams.

My mother is playing the piano. Schumann I think, but which one? Robert or Clara? She always loved the romantics. Schubert, Brahms, both Schumanns. Perhaps she felt a special connection with those who saw the world as they wished it to be, not as it really was.

Angie is seated at the piano, on the carved rosewood stool that doubles as a music chest. Her hands fly across the ivory keys of the Broadwood that my father bought for her after they eloped. She once told me that it was a poor relative of the Bechstein grand she left at home, but she can coax magic from it. She has her back to me, her thin frame under a flowing dress. The evening sun is shining on her hair, a single, long plait down her back.

I want to say something, but the words won't come. I want to step forward, but my feet won't move.

And then the music stops, and she turns. It is not my mother. It's a skeleton. And the skeleton has no face, just a gleaming white skull. The eye sockets are empty, the nose is just a pair of holes. The jaw opens wide.

'You killed him!' it shrieks.

There is no escape from my guilt.

Praia de Moçambique, Florianópolis, Brazil, December

The picnic spot above the beach had many advantages. The shade of a large tree, a gentle sea breeze and a view of all access points to Salty Walter's beach house. The wrap-around veranda was clearly visible, but the garage was partly obscured by the bungalow and garden.

Graça had barely finished the last of the cheese balls when a convoy rumbled up the sandy path, a car, two lorries and a scooter.

The pilot came out of the house, directing the lorry towards the garage before walking across the garden to meet them.

Graça almost choked at the sight of the uniformed officer stepping out of the lead car.

Major Moura Gomes.

The man who lied about the airport explosion.

The man whose lies had caused her suspension.

She thought back to their last conversation when the army came to take over surveillance of the car park.

'You didn't see anything leave?'

'Only cars.'

'No motorbike?'

'No.'

'No lorry that could be carrying a motorbike?'

What was Major Moura Gomes doing here?

And what was in that lorry?

Federal Agent Graça Neves abandoned her half-eaten picnic, straining to see, to hear. What was going on down there?

Every muscle, every sinew in her body tensed, ready to march down and confront the Major, but he had a battalion with him, and she was alone. Her job was on the line and if there was one thing she had learned at police training school, it was the importance of evidence. Corroborated evidence.

She bit her lip and waited.

Before long, the army convoy trundled back past the house and set off down the sandy track that led back to the main highway.

Minutes later Marina left as well, pulling on a flying jacket, swinging a cap and goggles as she strode across the beach to the plane.

What was Marina's relationship to the mystery woman who had ridden the motorbike? What was her relationship with Salty Walter, the owner of the motorbike?

Graça retreated behind the tree as the strange-looking aircraft gathered speed across the sand and soared into the air.

The hospital smells of bleach and artificial violets.

'Good afternoon.'

I keep my eyes closed.

'Can you hear me?'

The voice is deep, commanding. I do not respond.

'Here's an interesting case.' The consultant is doing the rounds with his team. 'The patient is in good health and has recovered remarkably well. She should be able to go home soon.'

Home? Where is home?

The prospect of moving – getting dressed, walking from the hospital to a car, boarding a plane – is unbearable.

'However, she is completely unresponsive, so we are unable to ascertain her wishes.'

My wishes?

I have only one wish. For none of this to have ever happened. To start all over again. To go back to the beginning. But that can't happen, can it? Once something is known, you can't unknow it.

Leave me alone.

I close my ears.

Let me sleep.

Someone is talking about me again.

'... catatonic trauma.'

I grimace. Is that what they think? That my refusal to engage, my wish to hold myself separate from the terrible reality is some kind of mental illness. Perhaps they know my family history. How my mother reacted to grief.

Is this how Angie spent her last days? Locked in a living hell?

Unable to communicate with the outside world. Or choosing not to.

'She needs specialist help …'

I'm not my mother. I'm stronger than that. And unlike my mother, I have no one else to blame for my predicament. Only myself. I am the cause, and I am the solution.

Time to get a grip. To take control again. To pretend that I'm OK. To act now. before they move me to some psychiatric unit and start on the drugs. Blunt what I feel. Restrict what I do. Change who I am.

If I let them fix me, I'll never be able to complete the task.

I started this and I must finish it.

With a supreme effort, I open my eyes.

'Jaq.' Marina leans across the bed and puts a warm hand on my shoulder.

I wrench my hand from under the sheet and grasp hers, squeezing it with all my might. I make eye contact and force a weak smile.

'At last,' Marina says. 'I was beginning to think we'd lost you.'

I try to sit up but there's a needle in my arm. A clear polyethylene tube snakes up to a drip stand beside the bed. I sink back down.

'Here, drink this.'

A glass appears at my lips. I sip slowly, my lips are swollen, my throat burns. The liquid is salty and sweet at the same time. I gag and force myself to stop.

'Slowly now.'

I open my mouth, but only a croak comes out. Marina hands me a pad and pencil.

Where are we?

'A hospital in Florianópolis.' Marina squeezes my hand.

You came back for me.

'Of course! Did you ever doubt me?'

In truth I gave up hope for a while out there in the ocean, that vast cruel canvas with nowhere to hide. Gave up because I blamed myself for what happened, because I didn't consider myself worthy of saving, because drowning felt like a fitting punishment. And if I doubted myself, is it any surprise that, for a moment, yes, I doubted you. And perhaps you should have stayed away. Perhaps you should have left me there.

Marina strokes my cheek.

'How do you feel?'

I'm OK.

But am I? The light is too bright. The whoosh-whoosh of machines too loud. It hurts to swallow, my muscles throb, my skin stings as if someone has taken sandpaper to every inch of flesh. Everything aches.

Tears well in my eyes.

'You're safe now, Jaq.'

I bring Marina's fingers to my lips. *Thank you.*

If there is one person I feel completely safe with, one person I totally trust, it's Marina.

I fall asleep holding her hand.

Curitiba, Brazil, December

Graça watched Zélia's battered old car pull into the police station car park. Early for night shift, as usual. A few minutes later, the day-shift supervisor roared away on his motorbike, more interested in his evening plans than conducting a rigorous shift handover.

Graça drove round the building – checked that Roberto Covelli's Range Rover was nowhere to be seen – and parked up in a visitor's bay.

Time to confront her boss.

She strode up to the semi-circular portico expecting the large glass doors to open.

They remained obstinately closed. Without her electronic pass, she would have to wait for admission. She pressed the buzzer and waited for the intercom to light up.

Best not to identify herself. 'Delivery for Zélia Neto.'

'Leave it in the lobby, I'll let her know.'

'I need a signature.'

'I'll send someone—'

'I need her signature.'

'She's busy. Who's it from?'

Graça thought fast. 'Knucklehead.'

Zélia's dark eyebrows leapt from a tight frown to arched surprise as she opened the outside door.

'Graça! What are you doing here?'

'There is something I need to show you.'

Zélia looked around to check they were alone, then ushered Graça into an interview room.

'You shouldn't be here. It could prejudice the disciplinary hearing.'

Graça clenched her teeth against the rising anger. 'Our chief investigator was right not to trust Major Moura Gomes.' She handed Zélia her phone.

Zélia clicked through the pictures: the silver glider, the army convoy, the meeting of Marina and the Major, the exodus. The final pictures showed that the valuable motorbike discovered in a Florianópolis airport car park was now back in its owner's garage.

'Shit.' Zélia let the phone fall from her hand onto the metal table. Her sigh continued after the clatter of metal on metal stopped. 'Tell me, what do you think is going on here?'

It was a favourite trick of Zélia's, perhaps it gave her time to think. Graça wasn't in the mood.

'You tell me! You were the one who sent me! You were the one who called in the army! Did you set me up?'

Zélia slammed the table with the palm of her hand. 'Don't go all emotional on me, Agent Neves.' Her voice was hard and brusque. 'I already told you it was the Floripa military police who contacted Major Moura Gomes, not me.' She leant forward, eyes blazing. 'We need to stick together on this one. Go back to the beginning. Knowing what you now know, tell me how you see it.'

Mollified by the return of her title, Graça took a deep breath.

'Someone caused an explosion at the airport to distract me. While I was responding, the army cut the electrics, smashed the CCTV camera, put the bike into a lorry and then blamed me for its disappearance.'

'Sounds about right. The question is why?'

'Salty Walter clearly has friends in high places.'

Zélia picked up the phone again and looked at the final pictures.

'I can't make out the registration.'

'I took the pictures through a window. The garage was locked. I couldn't get a good angle.'

'How do you know it's not a different bike. He owns several.'

'I looked inside the garage before the army convoy arrived. It was unlocked and empty.'

'You have a before picture?'

'No.'

'We need the evidence to be watertight. I need a picture from inside the garage showing the numberplate. With a certified time and date.'

'You want me to go back?'

'Wait here.'

When Zélia returned it was with a police badge and a special evidence camera.

Graça smiled 'Am I reinstated? Suspension overturned?'

Zélia shook her head. 'Better not.'

'But—'

'We don't know who is leaking information from the inside.'

'So you want me to stay suspended?'

'It'll be safer for both of us.'

'What do you need me to do?'

'Go back to Floripa.'

'I need wheels. I can't afford to fix my own car.'

Zélia opened a drawer and took out an official police pad. She scribbled something and then signed it.'

'Take your car to the police garage.'

'And my gun? Can I have it back?'

Zélia ignored the request. 'Get some better pictures. Then wait. I need someone on the outside. Unhampered by rules and protocol. Someone clever and resourceful. Someone I can trust.'

Although trust, Graça reflected as she drove to the garage, is a two-way commitment.

Hospital, Florianópolis, Brazil, December

The hospital ward noises – ringing phones, squealing castors on ceramic tiles, beep-beep of monitors – make it difficult to sleep.

A nurse approaches and picks up the chart at the end of my bed.

'*Bom dia*,' he says

'Hi.'

'How are you feeling?'

How indeed? Bereft.

My stomach rumbles.

'Hungry,' I say.

The nurse smiles. 'That's good. But we need to take it slowly. I'll make up an energy drink for you. We have to introduce solids bit by bit, so your gut has a chance to start working again.'

'Thank you.'

'I'll let your friend know you are awake.'

Marina arrives not long after I finish the liquid meal. It tasted of nothing, but my stomach is no longer growling.

'Jaq, good morning!' She pats the side of the bed and I grab her hand.

'Thank you!' I say.

'For what?' she laughs. 'Seems to me that my delay in refuelling almost killed you.'

'How long was I in the sea?'

'Good question. When you jumped out of my plane on Christmas Eve, you were heading for a ship. What happened?'

'It's all a bit of a blur.' Not a complete lie.

'What did you see?' I ask.

Marina squeezes my hand. 'I saw you land on the *Tartaruga*. Sweet parachute work by the way.'

87

'Great jet pack,' I say.

Another of her inventions that saved me.

'Much improved by your nozzle design.' Marina says.

I acknowledge the compliment with a nod. We work well together. 'And then?'

'Once you were safely on the boat,' Marina continues. 'I flew to Florianópolis airport to refuel, but there were ...' she looks at the ceiling. '... problems with the hydrogen connection. In the end I had to persuade the coastguard to get involved. What happened to the boat, Jaq?'

It was my decision to blow up the Ecobrium research vessel. I chose to weaponise Marina's technology. It's not her fault. I am wholly responsible for that.

'It sank,' I say.

She narrows her eyes, but she doesn't ask why.

'And you were marooned at sea.'

I nod.

After I fell to the sea, I remember fragments. Swimming. A shower of rain. More swimming. Darkness falling. Swimming. Dreams, vivid dreams all night long. Bullets strafing the sea ... No, that must have been a dream. Or a hallucination.

'How did you find me?' I ask.

'When we couldn't raise the *Tartaruga* on the radio, air-sea rescue let me accompany a reconnaissance mission. We started with the boat's last known position, but it wasn't until late on Christmas day that we found you.'

So, I was in the water for twenty-four hours. 'What day is it today?'

'December 30th.'

I sit up at that. 'I've been in hospital for five days?'

'You were asleep until yesterday. How do you feel?'

'Getting better. Getting stronger.'

'You'll be able to leave here soon, convalesce at the beach house.'

The last place I was happy. Really happy. The one place I can never return to.

I grip her hand. 'I don't want to go back there.'

'What happened, Jaq?'

I can't tell her. I don't have the words. All rationality has left me, washed away in the ocean. Now, I have only emotions. Passions that have to be obeyed. If I tell her the truth, reveal my demons, she will guess what I'll do next. And try to stop me.

I close my eyes. 'I'm tired.' So tired. So bone-achingly weary that it is all I can do to keep my head upright and my eyes open.

'A lot of people want to talk to you,' she says. 'Starting with the police.'

I twist my mouth and wrinkle my nose.

'They're waiting until you are well enough to talk.'

Best to get it over and done with.

A single policeman comes to interview me. He is tall and blond and wears his uniform well. He looks more like an athlete than an officer of the law. He is polite and courteous.

'Dr Silver, how are you?'

'Recovering,' I say. 'Thanks for asking.'

'Can you tell us what happened?'

How much did they already know? Marina must have told them that I jumped out of her plane. What else did she see? What else did she reveal? I wish I'd checked my story with her first. The best policy is to be as truthful as possible. Lies are harder to remember.

'I boarded the Ecobrium research ship, the *Tartaruga*.'

'How?'

'I jumped from a plane.' I add. 'With a parachute.' Best not to mention the jet pack.

'Why?' he asks.

'I'm an engineer.'

Nonsensical as an explanation, but then people have many

strange ideas about what professional engineers do. They think engines before ingenuity.

He frowns and writes it down.

'The boat was malfunctioning?'

I choose my words carefully. 'There was an explosion.'

His eyes light up 'Before you arrived?' I see where his logic is taking him – an engineer jumping from a plane to attend to a stricken ship sounds almost plausible. But I have to stick to the truth wherever I can.

'After I arrived.'

He writes this down as well.

'What caused the explosion?' he asks.

I shrug. 'A malfunction.'

I don't add that I engineered the malfunction with the express purpose of blowing up the ship.

His pen scribbles noisily.

'How did you get off the boat?'

'I was thrown clear.' This is partly true. The blast wave of the explosion had certainly assisted the jet pack in getting me away from the disintegrating boat.

'Into the sea?'

Not immediately, I had a few minutes of flight before the jet pack ran out of fuel and I fell into the water. But that's splitting hairs, information he doesn't need.

'I fell into the sea.'

'How many people were on board the ship?'

'I only saw two crew members.' Only two men, because they'd just murdered the third. The kidnap victim I was too late to save. Mercúrio. My son.

I close my eyes and ask for a glass of water.

'Are you OK to continue?'

No, but I also want this over and done with. I nod.

'What happened to the crew?'

'I fear they were killed in the blast.' Served them right, the murdering bastards.

He shakes his head.

'I believe, like you, they survived the explosion.'

My eyes open wide as I struggle to process this information. 'They're alive?'

He shakes his head. 'Unfortunately, they're both dead.'

I try to disguise my relief.

'They were found in a lifeboat,' he adds.

I'm confused. 'They died from injuries sustained in the explosion?'

'No,' he says. 'Both men were shot at close range.'

I'm swimming again, moving towards a smudge of coastline that appears and disappears in the grey sea fog. Nothing is defined; everything is possible.

My son is still alive.

Hospital noises. The border between dreams and reality sharpens. As hard as I try to remain afloat in this misty, liminal world, the arms of Morpheus, god of sleep, are opening. My refuge is fading. I must face up to my guilt.

I failed my son.

The definition hardens and suddenly I'm in a hospital bed with sharp bright lines and everything is black and white again and I can't pretend any longer.

My son is dead.

When I open my eyes, Marina is asleep in the chair at the side of my bed. I study her face. It is both strong and delicate, square and round, fine and firm – all winning combinations. She is a handsome woman. And a true friend.

With my right hand I explore the injury to my left arm. Just a flesh wound, the doctor said, but it still hurts like hell. How did I cut myself so badly, out in the open sea? Was it a bullet that tore through the flesh of my arm?

Waking up in hospital, I'd almost dismissed the memory of being shot at, suspecting a hallucination brought on by exposure and dehydration. Then I heard what happened to the crew of the *Tartaruga*. Did they somehow survive the explosion, scramble into a lifeboat only to be shot by a sniper firing from a propeller plane? Did the same assassin then come for me?

I'd assumed it was a false memory, because the hail of bullets coincided with Marina's arrival. I remember diving to escape the missiles, then surfacing to see her in the water, swimming to my rescue.

Marina opens her eyes and smiles.

'You're awake,' she says.

'And you were asleep.'

'Power nap.' She smiles 'To make up for a lack of beauty sleep.'

I take her hand. 'You're beautiful, Marina.' And I mean it.

She looks away.

'Marina, what were you flying when you came to rescue me?'

'I was a passenger in a helicopter.'

'I thought I heard a propeller plane.'

'There was a light plane in the area, flying low, circling something. That's how we spotted you.'

'Who was in the plane?'

'No idea. It flew away when we arrived. I was more concerned with rescuing you.'

'Did you find the *Tartaruga*?'

'The trawler vanished without a trace.'

'What about the crew?'

'The second chopper found them in their lifeboat.' She grasps my hand. 'I understand they didn't survive. You were so lucky, Jaq.'

If only she knew.

'Is there anyone you need to contact?' she asks. 'Friends, family. To let them know you're OK?'

I unpick that backwards.

Am I OK? No. But best to control that message.

Family? I have none. Not now.

Friends? Yes, there is one person who might be concerned. Someone who knows about my habit of disappearing for a few days at Christmas and always checks up on me before the new year. I should call Johan to let him know I am OK.

'What happened to my phone?' I wonder aloud.

'I have it.' Marina says.

'You do?' I have no memory of giving it to her.

'I charged it this morning.' Marina produces it from her handbag.

I scroll through. Multiple missed calls and texts.

Nothing that can't wait.

Shanghai, China, December

On a Shanghai skyscraper, coloured lights formed patterns on the towering wall of glass.

A cartoon deer leapt over a clear forest stream, disturbing a flock of little birds that flew over the treetops and into a leafy glade where children were playing on a swing. The blue roundel with the letter Z – the corporate symbol for Zagrovyl – appeared, and the film ended with the slogan in Mandarin then English.

净零 – 为了我们的孩子
Net zero – For the children

Inside the roof-top restaurant, the Lazy Susan groaned under the weight of the food as dish after dish was added and spun round to the principal guest: broccoli spears with tiny red chillies; steaming triangular dumplings stuffed with mushrooms; a whole fish, silver skin scored with diagonal cuts to reveal the white flesh underneath.

Frank had hosted so many banquets for government and business contacts that he had literally no idea who this delegation represented. His speech was always the same – he'd learned enough now to be able to rattle off a few platitudes in Mandarin (or occasionally, rebelliously, Cantonese). The advantage of a musical ear was that he could listen and copy. Of course, he had no idea what anyone said to him in return, but that was what his translator was there for – as much a cultural as a linguistic interpreter. Alice also knew to fill his jug of *baijou* with water so he could toast the night away and remain stone cold sober, while all around him his guests became drunker and drunker.

He sat up straight when he saw the caller ID.

'Frank Good,' he answered, rising from his chair and stepping into the antechamber of the private dining room.

'Can you talk?'

'Give me a second.' Frank closed the connecting door.

His boss rarely called direct. It was hard finding a time window that worked for China and east-coast USA with business hours that were 12 hours apart. The monthly one-to-ones with Graham Dekker were arranged by Vanda, his PA, with military precision.

'Fire away.'

'I need you back in England.'

Frank clenched his jaw. For all that he complained about the food, the language, the crowds, Frank adored China. Correction, Frank loved his life in Shanghai. Great flat, private chauffeur, obedient staff, thrilling night life. The prospect of returning to Teesside was far from appealing.

'When?'

'Straight away.'

This was a blow. Things were going well. The Green Energy division was flourishing under his leadership. He had a Chinese team who understood how to make things happen, how to turn ideas to action.

'Why?'

'Trouble.'

'What sort of trouble?'

'Not the sort we can discuss on the phone. I'll meet you in person. Get your PA to tie in with mine.'

As Frank finished the call, he was struck with absolute certainty that whatever this was about, he could already guess who would be found at the epicentre of trouble.

Jaq Silver.

Blumenau, Brazil, January

By the dawn of the new year, the news had travelled right around the world and back to where it started. Many of the military policemen in the state of Santa Caterina were ex-forces or had relatives in the military. Kléber had served with Oskar and would have joined RIMPO when he left had it not been for his wife who was pregnant with twins. Since the divorce he was re-evaluating that decision. He called his friend.

'Someone's been lying to you,' Kléber said. 'She's alive.'

'Who?'

'Silver.'

'That's not possible.' Anyone who survived the explosion on the boat was picked off in the sea. 'No one could have survived.'

'And yet she did.'

'How do you know?'

'My colleague just interviewed her in hospital.'

'Where?'

Oskar took down the details, gathered his tools and set off.

Dangerous places, hospitals.

Hospital, Florianópolis, Brazil, January

I test my legs, swinging them round the side of the bed, placing the soles of my bare feet on the smooth floor, experimenting with my weight. Standing is one thing; walking takes more coordination. I use the bed frame and the walls to steady myself.

'What do you think you're playing at?' Marina enters the room. 'You need to rest.'

'I need to move.'

'You're not going anywhere until you're well.'

I'll never be well until I find the man who murdered my son.

'The sooner I move, the sooner I'll recover.'

Marina comes forward and takes my arm, leading me back to the bed. I sink onto the pillow.

'Do you want to tell me what really happened?'

And then the anger comes, and I can't speak, can't give it voice.

Marina sits down on the bed and puts an arm around me.

'At least Mercúrio is safe?' Marina asks.

I shake my head. I can't bring myself to tell her. Not yet. But I can't hold back the tears.

'We'll never see one another again,' I say.

Marina misunderstands, as I intended.

'Never say never. You both just need time.'

I want to shout at her. You don't understand. We ran out of time. The kidnappers killed him. I failed him and now it's too late.

I want to scream at the world.

My son is dead. Because of me.

Florianópolis, Brazil, January

It was dark by the time Oskar got inside the hospital. Day-shift security was absurdly tight, and he had to wait until night shift to slip inside with a food delivery. By which time it was too late.

The bed until recently occupied by Dr Jaqueline Silver was empty.

He called his contact in São Paulo, but there had been no sighting of her at the Jardim flat for some time.

The following morning, he dragged his police friend to the hospital to demand the patient's forwarding address.

It took some persuasion to drag the information out of the frightened receptionist, but Kléber guessed where her children went to school and the implied threat of an unfortunate accident at the nursery gates proved very effective.

The registered address for Silver was Casa do Sal, a detached property on the seafront of Praia do Moçambique.

A place Oskar knew well.

Both the São Paulo apartment and Floripa beach house belonged to the same man, Walter Salgado.

Oskar had accompanied the army convoy when Major Moura Gomes delivered the old motorbike. He'd stayed behind to search the house and garden for the old safe. At the time, he wasn't looking for Silver. Turned out she'd been in a hospital just twenty kilometres away.

By the time he got back to the beach house, his mood had gone from bad to worse to abominable.

Praia de Moçambique, Florianópolis, Brazil, January

In the garden of the beach bungalow, everything was quiet. The only noise came from the crash of surf onto sand, the chatter of marmosets and squawk of parrots in the wilderness beyond.

Graça's car was still in the Curitiba police garage. She'd taken it to the official repair shop to get the passenger windows fixed. Unfortunately, someone had decided to make further checks and it had failed every test of roadworthiness: tyres, brakes, exhaust, emissions. When she'd remonstrated, they'd given her a courtesy vehicle: a Honda 120 motorbike and a helmet.

It was a long, hot, dusty drive and she was almost tempted by the sea as she roared up the private road to the beach bungalow. She slowed on spotting a van parked outside the main door, JALI – *Jardinagem e Limpeza* – emblazoned across the side.

An elderly man in overalls emerged from the house, carrying a suitcase under each arm. A much younger woman in a maid's uniform followed with a couple of cardboard boxes, and the man loaded everything into the back of the van.

The maid extracted a brush, mop and bucket and returned to the house. The man took out a sack of fertiliser and carried it to the garden hut.

Graça parked behind a tree and debated what to do. The decision was made for her when she saw the woman leave the house with a basket of dirty laundry. Graça waited until the maid had unlocked the garage doors, then followed her in.

'Oi!' Graça stepped forward to greet the maid, who almost dropped the pile of sheets she was carrying.

'This is private property.'

'I was just looking for a tap to fill my water bottle.' Graça offered her a chocolate truffle.

The maid eyed her suspiciously, then wiped the palms of her hands against her apron and took one before gesturing at the sink.

'Thanks. I'm Graça by the way.'

'Marcia.'

When she smiled her whole face lit up. She was very young, probably still at school, just helping out in the holidays.

Graça filled her bottle from the tap. 'Nice bike.' She pointed at the Harley Davidson Knucklehead.

Marcia wrinkled her nose. 'Looks pretty ancient to me.' She began stuffing sheets into the top-loading twin tub. Graça waited until her back was turned before snapping a few pictures of the bike with the police camera, making sure that the numberplate *SAL·1064* was visible this time.

The maid reached up to a shelf and filled the soap drawer from a box of washing powder.

'D'you know the woman who rides it?' Graça asked.

'What?'

'The motorbike.'

'I don't know anyone.' Marcia sniffed, returning the washing powder box to its shelf. 'I'm just the cleaner.'

Graça held out another sweet. Marcia hesitated and then accepted. Difficult to refuse, GG made the finest *brigadeiros.*

'Is she moving out?'

'Who?'

'The woman who rode that motorbike.'

'My grandad says that a foreigner and her Brazilian fancy man were renting the beach house over Christmas.' Marcia wiped her lips. 'Some people can't even be bothered to pack up their own stuff, never mind leave the place half decent.' She sniffed. 'I better get on.'

'Did she leave a forwarding address?' Graça asked, placing the box of treats in the empty laundry basket. 'For her stuff?'

The maid stared at the *brigadeiros* for a moment then picked up the basket up with a smile.

'Ask Alfredo,' she said.' He's in the garden.'

Except he wasn't.

The gardener was standing beside the van, wringing his hands as a man shouted in his face. Something about the interloper gave her pause and she held up a hand to stop Marcia rushing to Alfredo's side.

'Wait,' she whispered.

Although the stranger wasn't in uniform, he was clearly a soldier. Not just the clothes: short-sleeved T-shirt, khaki trousers, black lace-up boots, but the buzz cut, the clean shave, the tattoos and the barely supressed violence.

'I tell you, there's no one here.' Alfredo protested. 'Whoever was renting it over Christmas has moved on.'

'Don't lie to me. She checked out of the hospital. I've just been there.'

'Well, she didn't come here.' Alfredo opened the back of the van. 'Look, we're sending her stuff into storage.'

The soldier began pulling things out and hurling them to the ground

'Where is it?' the soldier shouted.

'Where's what?'

'The old safe?'

'I don't know what you're talking about.'

'A leather-covered metal box.' He held his hands about a foot and half apart. 'This size. A square box with brass handles.'

Alfredo shook his head.

'I haven't seen anything like that.'

The soldier raised his hand to strike the old man, and, with a cry, Marcia ran to her grandfather.

The garage doors flew open, and the soldier thrust Marcia forward. She fell onto the concrete as he turned and locked the door behind them.

He began opening cupboards and pulling things crashing to the floor.

'Where is it?' he shouted.

'I don't know,' she sobbed. 'Please let me go.'

Someone was banging on the door outside, 'LEAVE HER ALONE!'

'Who is that man outside.'

'My grandfather.'

'Would you like me to hurt him?'

'No.'

'Then tell him you're OK.'

She nodded and put her mouth to the keyhole.

'I'm OK, grandad.'

'Then come out, NOW!'

'Tell him not to shout,' the soldier said.

'Don't shout, grandad.'

'LET HER GO!'

'Tell him I have a gun.'

'Don't make him angry, grandad. He has a gun.'

The shouting stopped.

'Good girl. What's your name?' His tone softened.

'Marcia,' she whispered.

'Ask me what my name is?'

'What's your name?'

'My name is Oskar.' He grinned. 'Now, why don't you ask me what I want?'

'I heard you asking about a metal box, but I don't have it, I've never seen—'

'Maybe you don't have the safe, but you might have something else I want, that would make up for it just a little bit.'

'I don't understand.'

'Oh, I think you do. Do you have a boyfriend, Marcia?'

'No.'

'I don't believe it. I bet a pretty little thing like you has lots of boyfriends. I bet you know exactly how to make a man happy.'

'Please …'

'Come closer, Marcia.'

'No.'

Oskar raised his gun.

'Do you love your grandfather, Marcia?'

'Yes.'

'Do you want me to shoot him?'

'No.'

He turned and pointed the gun at her. 'Do you want me to shoot you?'

'No.'

'Then turn round and face the washing machine.'

Oskar advanced towards the trembling woman, slamming her against the pulsating twin-tub.

Placing the gun on a shelf, jammed between a box of washing powder and a bottle of fabric conditioner, he put one hand on the back of her neck as the other loosened his belt buckle.

'Bend over,' he ordered and pushed her down, squashing her face against the lid of the vibrating spinner.

'Don't move.'

He yanked up the skirt of her uniform, wrenched down her panties and began to fiddle with his zipper.

Marcia screamed.

Graça stepped out from behind the fridge freezer. In one smooth movement she retrieved the soldier's gun from the shelf and pointed it at his back.

'Let her go,' she ordered.

Oskar whirled round. 'And who the fuck are you?'

She released the safety catch.

'I'm your worst nightmare, pal.'

Graça's finger found the trigger. Nothing would have given her greater pleasure at that moment than to blow Oskar's head off, but she'd seen what hard, fast bullets did to soft tissue, and she didn't want Marcia to witness it. She lowered the muzzle until it was pointing at his crotch. Perhaps castration by kinetic projectile would be lesson enough.

He ran at her then, a raging bull of thwarted power and libido.

She stepped aside at the last minute, letting him crash into the heavy door, before smashing the barrel of the gun against his temple.

Oskar slumped to the floor.

'Marcia, honey,' Graça said. 'Come and open the door.'

She searched the unconscious soldier as Marcia released the bolts with trembling fingers.

'Shall I call the police?'

Graça flashed her badge. 'I am the police.' She smiled as she bound the soldier's wrists behind his back with a plastic cable tie. 'You OK?'

Marcia nodded.

'You want to report an attempted rape?'

Marcia shook her head. 'I just want to go home.'

'Go then. Get your grandad to take you out of here.'

Graça unlocked the door and Alfredo dropped what he was carrying to embrace his granddaughter.

'Are you hurt?' he asked.

'She saved me.'

He took in the scene at a glance. The unconscious soldier on the floor, his arms and feet tied behind his back. He turned to Graça.

'Thank you.'

Graça smiled.

'I found it.' The old man pointed to the object he'd dropped to embrace his granddaughter. 'The metal box that bastard was looking for.'

Graça bent down to take a closer look. The old safe had seen better days. The leather covering was in tatters and the silk lining looked to have been colonised by the wildlife of the garden. There was even a plant growing in a narrow gap between metal sheets. What was so important about this battered, rusty old thing? Well, if it mattered to the military, it must be worth a closer look.

'Thank you. I'll take things from here.'

'What about him?' Alfredo spat at the soldier.

Graça checked the safety on the gun and slipped it inside her jacket, along with the extra ammunition clips she'd liberated from the man on the floor.

'Help is on its way. I'll be fine.'

Marcia hugged her. 'You sure?'

'Just go.'

Once the van had gone, Graça sat outside. It was cooler now, the sun hiding behind a cloud and a sea breeze rising. What to do now? In the white heat of anger, she could easily have shot or wounded the soldier. It was harder to kill him in cold blood. And wrong. Her police training was too recent to ignore.

If she called Zélia, it would be hours before Chief Investigator Roberto Covelli would even consider whether or not to send the feds. If it meant a tussle with the army, he'd probably just let it go. And once the army came for their soldier and he reported what happened, or at least a version of events that made him look less like an idiot, Major Moura Gomes would put two and two together and figure out that she was the same federal agent they'd tricked before. The army would remove the bike and all evidence of their involvement, and it would be her word against theirs.

The soldier would regain consciousness soon. The man was solid muscle, even cable ties and rope wouldn't restrain him for ever.

Her best hope was to alert the local police. After she'd preserved the evidence.

By the time Graça had finished documenting the scene, the soldier was beginning to stir.

She placed the metal box in a laundry bag and fastened it to the passenger seat. Straddling the 1941 Harley Davidson Knucklehead, Graça put the key in the ignition and roared off into the sunset.

Possession, after all, is nine-tenths of the law.

5km from the gold mine, Tocantins, Brazil, January

A light rain started to fall, a relief after the intense heat of the day. The water droplets hung, shimmering from the seed heads of grasses, rolling off the leaves of herbs, disappearing into the petalled cups of delicate wildflowers, evaporating to release a smorgasbord of scent.

Hugo sniffed the perfumed air and smiled. After long days analysing samples in a cramped laboratory, mapping the results in an even smaller office, it was good to be back.

The beaten earth track stopped where two rivers joined, the turbulence carving out a deep pool before tumbling down a series of waterfalls.

Hugo took an empty bottle and descended towards the river. The rain had turned the soil liquid. He lost his footing and slipped the last few feet, the seat of his shorts and calves, the back of his shirt and forearms gaining a coating of red mud. With a long, hot drive ahead of him, the pool looked inviting.

After taking his sample, Hugo removed his boots and socks, his glasses, shirt, shorts and pants and waded naked into the river.

He dived under the water and swam to the other side of the pool, only to bump up against something soft. He rose to the surface to find himself surrounded by the glassy eyes and smooth shiny scales of dead fish, their swollen bellies uppermost. As he thrashed around to escape, the putrid smell hit him with full force.

Hugo swam back, pulled himself out of the pool and retched onto the riverbank.

Panting as he pulled on his clothes, he grabbed the sample, climbed up the muddy slope and returned to his jeep.

He didn't need toxicology results to tell him that something was wrong.

Very, very wrong.

He looked up the valley. The mountain remained wreathed in mist even though the rain had stopped.

Hugo pulled out a map.

Time to investigate.

Hugo found the perfect spot to camp, in the lee of a sandstone bluff with a view of rolling grasslands stretching out to the west and forests to the east. This was the part of fieldwork he loved best, to forage a meal and then stretch out under the stars.

He continued up the river at first light. The smell of human habitation hit him long before he saw the flies buzzing around a ramshackle collection of buildings crowded into a fold in the valley, hidden until you crossed a low ridge.

The shacks closest to the river were constructed from local materials – timber and stone, twine and straw, but the accommodation at the edges of the encampment consisted of poorly laid brick with black plastic bags over doors and windows. A sheet of corrugated iron provided both shelter and drinking water, the rainwater from the roof draining into a steel drum. An open sewer ran parallel to the main street.

Hugo had seen this kind of town before, but never one quite so dismal. Mines attracted the desperate and deluded, *garimpeiros* drawn by rumours of great riches. They razed the forests and ripped up the grasslands and burrowed into the earth with nothing but their own muscle. A collection of men with little in common and even less to lose had come together to fight over a few nuggets of gold.

Right now the place was deserted, a few stray dogs patrolling the beaten-earth streets. The only human Hugo spotted was a crippled man heating water on a wood fire as he scraped pans outside a *cantina*. Judging by the residue, the eatery served only beans and rice – cheap fuel for the miners.

Hugo passed a locked-up general store. Peering through the steel grating he spotted overpriced picks and shovels, mosquito nets and flip-flops. Further down the main street, a rudimentary medical clinic offered tooth extraction. The only buildings that looked as if they wouldn't fall down in the lightest puff of wind were the liquor stores, which were built and armoured like Fort Knox.

The place gave Hugo the creeps. He shivered, and was turning to leave, when the soldiers arrived. Two clean-shaven white men with buzz cuts and tattoos, dressed identically in lace-up boots, khaki trousers, short-sleeve T-shirts and an alarming amount of semi-automatic weaponry slung across their muscled chests.

Hugo slipped into a narrow alleyway, hoping they hadn't seen him.

A little dog ran up to him and began barking excitedly.

Hugo bent to reassure the terrier, but the damage was done.

'You there!' One of the soldiers blocked the alleyway. 'Come here.'

Hugo returned to the main street, hands away from his body so they could see he posed no threat. The dog came with him.

'Papers?'

He swung his rucksack to the ground and began to unbuckle the waterproof pocket.

'Leave that. Step away.'

One soldier kicked the bag to the other. The dog, thinking it was a game, seized hold of a strap and began to fight it.

'Who are you?'

'A research scientist at the University of Manaus.'

The younger soldier shooed the dog away and handed his superior the identity card retrieved from Hugo's rucksack.

'You're a long way from home, sonny.'

'What's this then!' The younger soldier pulled out a plastic bag stuffed with grass. He held it aloft, triumphant. 'You selling drugs?'

The little dog growled.

Hugo shook his head. 'That's a research sample.'

The soldier opened the plastic bag and sniffed.

'What sort of research?'

'Grassland diversity.'

The soldier took out a strand, chewed it, then spat it out.

'Who cares about this sort of grass?'

'Wild wheat, oats and maize could be cultivated to provide food …'

'A likely story.' The soldier thrust his hand into the bag, searching for something hidden. He removed a knife roll, inspecting it before adding it to his own pack and then turned Hugo's bag upside down. Seeds spilled out onto the ground and the dog bounded forward to eat them.

'I think the Colonel might want to meet this pointy head.'

The soldiers pointed their guns at Hugo.

'Come with us.'

The dog whined but did not follow.

UBERLÂNDIA

1,700km from the gold mine, a freight train, Uberlândia, Minas Gerais State, Brazil, February

Clickety-clack, clickety-clack.

Dawn breaks as the freight train snakes through the rolling farmland of Brazil's interior.

Where am I?

I climb up the inside of the empty corn wagon and poke my head over the top. Nothing but flat farmland as far as the eye can see.

I drop back into the wagon as the wind blows black smoke into my face. The train runs on diesel, not ethanol, but at least I don't have to pay for it.

I lie back down and watch the changing colours of the sky, marvelling as if I've never concentrated on a sunrise before.

I feel like I'm seeing everything for the first time.

As the day gets hotter, the train rumbles through a town. I look up at the blocks of flats towering over the railway line, pockmarked with satellite TV dishes. The homes without air-conditioning have blinds down and windows open, the racket of daytime TV blaring out.

Why did I sell my soul to the television?

When my mother died, less than a year ago, I inherited an old portable safe, a leather-covered steel box that had belonged to my grandmother, Isabella. Among the trinkets and official documents inside, I found my son's birth certificate. And more. My baby was taken away from me, an unmarried teenager, twenty-two years ago. I was told he'd died. But the adoption certificate hidden in the strongbox revealed that he'd been sold to a Brazilian couple. I dropped everything, found a job in Brazil and set out to find him.

When I reached a dead end, I resolved to use the thing I cared about least – the family inheritance – to try and reach the one person who might care, if only he knew.

I appeared on a TV show, *The Missing*, and bared my soul to the world.

It worked.

Or did it?

A young man named Mercúrio contacted the TV station. His dates and story checked out. The moment he agreed to meet me, I borrowed one of my landlord's old motorbikes and headed south.

We were meant to spend Christmas together. Just the two of us. But after so long apart, it wasn't easy. This was no fairytale reunion, no game of happy families. We argued. He stormed out.

And that was when the kidnappers pounced. I had something Ecobrium wanted and their leader guessed I wouldn't abandon a man I believed to be my son, estranged or not. So they held Mercúrio to ransom in a boat while I raced back to England, returning with the family safe, that horrible steel and leather box constructed from secrets and lies. The maps and schedules for the gold mine were engraved on copper plates and hidden inside the walls of the box.

I kept to my side of the deal, but they reneged on theirs.

Or did they?

After what Yuko told me, I'm not sure of anything any more.

28
Ni
Nickel
58.693

Brazil produced 105,000 tonnes of nickel in 2013 with an estimated value of US$ 466 million.

Nickel is mainly used to make stainless steel. It's also used in batteries.

São Paulo, Brazil, January

The São Paulo traffic is lighter during the school summer holiday. Sunlight breaks through the smog and casts a diffuse glow over the luxury apartment in Jardins.

I get up from my desk to close the blinds.

A large painting occupies almost the whole wall behind a four-seater sofa. It's in the style of the surrealist Joan Miró, a riot of geometric shapes in primary colours – red, blue, yellow – connected by looping black lines. As my eyes go in and out of focus, the concentric circles become a hail of bullets splashing into the water.

I blink fast to stop the flashback. *Be still, busy mind.* I am making a good recovery, and nothing is going to stop me getting fit and strong again.

Lock it down. Lock it in.

The journey from the hospital in Florianópolis back to São Paulo is mostly a blur. Marina flew me back to São Jose dos Campos, returning the experimental hydrogen-powered plane to Áerex before arranging a helicopter to take me to my flat in São Paulo. I wasn't ready to face the crowds and hassle of a commercial flight or the confined space of a car in traffic.

Marina collected my phone and computer, returned my grand-mother's ring, but has arranged for most of the things I left behind at the Floripa beach house to go into storage. I don't want them. Too many memories. It was Marina who remembered about the old motorbike I borrowed to ride down the coast and Marina who sorted out its return.

What would I do without her?

I log on to the computer and stare at the website for Ecobrium. I have been working my way through their blogs. The early ones are well researched, covering deforestation, acidification of rivers, loss of natural habitats and with them a loss of native species.

The discussion accepts that this is what human beings do. They hunt. They burn. They dig. They farm. They grow and prosper by destroying the old ecosystem and creating a new one. But sustainable development requires balance, reciprocity.

The most shocking paper covers illegal mining.

Mercury can be used to capture tiny flecks of gold, too small for the naked eye, concentrating the precious metal lost from attrition in streams and rivers until you can recover whole nuggets of gold. But at what cost? The waste mercury ends up in the wrong places. The biochemical pathways are laid out in all their horror. There's a scientific rigour here that I was not expecting. Have I underestimated Ecobrium? Can this be the same organisation that kidnaps and murders?

The later blogs are more inflammatory. References are incomplete. Data is no longer shared. The nuance, the balance is gone.

What changed? I check the timeline.

Everything changed round about the time that Raimundo Elias took over. He changed the organisation from one based on science to one based on emotion, from fact to rhetoric, from the head to the heart.

One reference crops up time after time. Dr Jean Parker is regularly cited by Ecobrium to support their claims of ecological catastrophe. She's a consultant medical toxicologist in a Rio hospital and leads a ground-breaking scientific laboratory in Palmas, Tocantins, with an impressive publication record, including several papers in *Nature*.

Professor Parker is dedicated to saving life. Why would a serious, world-class scientist work with a guerrilla organisation?

Perhaps she can give me some insight.

I search for her most recent publication and try to formulate a question that is both flattering and anodyne. After adding my contact details to the email, I press send.

My phone rings. It's Carmo, a Lisbon lawyer, who dealt with my late mother's affairs and became a friend. I can't carry on ignoring her. She's helped me before; I may need her help again before long.

'Jaq, at last! Happy New Year.'

'Happy New Year, Carmo.'

'How's Brazil? It's bloody freezing here.'

Freezing to a Lisboetta probably means 12 degrees centigrade.

'Sweltering here.' I check my phone. 'Thirty-five degrees.'

The weather is one safe topic of conversation. How strangely alike are the Portuguese and British.

'Did you do Christmas *a praia?*' *Praia*, the beach, is what many Portuguese live for, and Carmo can't keep the envy out of her voice.

Oh, if only. If only things had gone as planned.

'Swimming in the sea,' I say. And almost drowning. Quick, change the subject. 'And you? How did you celebrate?'

'Just a quiet family affair.'

Carmo sounds subdued. But then she's recently lost a dear friend. Jorge Ferreira was checking out my family papers in a bank vault in Angola when he suffered a sudden, fatal heart attack.

'New year, new beginnings.' I can hear her voice grow brighter. 'I'm going to the Alentejo for a big party this weekend.'

'Great.'

'And you?'

'More beach,' I lie.

She laughs. 'Now to business.'

My heart sinks.

'I got a letter from Advogado Castanho, your late-grandmother's lawyer in Salvador.'

The ancient, fussy old man who remembered Isabella when she was my age. Claimed we looked identical.

'Or at least from his office,' Carmo continues. 'It's a bill.'

The cheek of it. 'But I was never a client. All he did was to pass over a letter from my grandmother.' A letter containing a poem and a ring. 'Is that billable?'

'No.' Carmo rustles some papers. 'This is different. A bill for a safety deposit box in the Banco Espirito Santo. Did you ask him to rent a safety deposit box for you?'

'Certainly not.'

'I thought it was a bit strange. I'll write back and tell them they've made a mistake. How's the search going?'

Not now, Carmo. Please, not now. I can't do this. I can't lie to you, but nor can I tell you the truth. Not yet.

'Entering a new phase,' I say.

'Oh, good.'

No not good. Not good at all. The good phases are over. The search phase. The contact phase. The rescue phase. I failed. I lost him. I lost everything. And now, all that's left is the killing phase.

Carmo must sense something in the pause that goes on too long.

'Jaq, what are you not telling me?'

No, Carmo. Don't ask. I can't tell you the truth. Not right now. I know it's unfair. After everything you've done for me. After all the help you've given. After all the selfless support. But I'm not ready. I can't tell you how I've messed up. And I certainly can't tell you what I plan to do next.

'Jaq, how are you? Really?'

A bead of sweat runs down between my breasts. Go back to the weather.

'Hot.' Not a word of a lie.

Carmo laughs. 'I'm so jealous.'

If only you knew.

'Have fun in the Alentejo.'

'Take care of yourself, Jaq.' The concern shines through her voice. 'Happy New Year.'

Bloody New Year.

I turn on the TV.

Rio de Janeiro, Brazil, January

The studio theatre used by Hélio TV for live broadcasts was in one of the more prosperous parts of Rio. The inhabitants of the favelas clinging to the hillside above the luxury beachfront properties of Leblon waited for an opportunity for a little redistribution of wealth.

A bodyguard stepped out of the armoured limo, buzzed the stage door of the theatre and checked the street for criminals and crazies. You could never be too careful. Once satisfied that it was all clear, he opened the passenger door. The TV presenter hurried from the limo, through the stage door towards the dressing room with his name in lights. It was testament to his fame that they only needed one word – César.

Two men were waiting for César in the corridor.

He ignored them at first, brushing past, mentally preparing for the live New Year special.

But the men stood in his way. One broad and heavily built with a livid bruise on the side of his face, the other tall and thin. César flinched at the stomp of polished black boots on the studio carpet. With their buzz cuts, clean-shaven chins, olive T-shirts tight across muscular chests and camouflage trousers they looked like soldiers from RIMPO.

César held up his hand. 'Filming. Can't see you now.'

A production assistant hovered nervously. 'I did tell these gentlemen, but they wouldn't—'

'We need to talk.'

The taller soldier wrapped his fingers around César's upper arm.

'Sorry,' César protested. 'We're about to go live …'

The broader soldier unholstered his gun. 'This can't wait.'

The production assistant gasped. 'Shall I call the police?' she whispered to César, the colour draining from her face.

'It's fine,' he said, although his voice didn't sound fine. 'Just tell the producer to fill a short break.' He turned to the thug holding his arm. 'How long will we be?'

'As long as it takes,' he growled.

'My dressing room,' César said, trying to shake free. 'This way.'

The production assistant scuttled after them as the soldiers frogmarched the TV presenter down the corridor, releasing him only so he could unlock his private room. César entered first; the soldiers followed. The broad one turned and barred the assistant's entry, slamming the door in her face.

Inside the dressing room, César collapsed onto a chair. The broad soldier remained at the door, the tall one grabbed a make-up stool and sat on it, legs wide apart.

'Where is she?'

'Who?'

'Silver.'

'How should I know?'

The broad soldier stepped forward and struck him across the face with the back of his hand. The blow brought tears to César's eyes, a mixture of pain, humiliation and terror that the blow might damage his appearance and prevent the show from continuing.

'Sorry.' César held up both hands. 'I'll tell you anything you need to know.'

'Let's start again, shall we? Where is Jaq Silver?'

'Last I heard she was surfing in Floripa, miraculously reunited with her long-lost son.'

'Her real son?'

'Well, no. I did what you asked, hired an actor to pretend to be her son. We agreed to call him Mercúrio, so everyone was clear.'

'And Mercúrio's job was to relieve her of the mine maps.'

'Exactly, and I'm sure he'll do just that.'

'Except he can't if he's dead,' growled the man at the door.

'Dead?' César looked from one soldier to the other.

'Ever heard of Raimundo Elias?' the tall one asked.

César racked his brains.

'The eco nutter? Boss of Ecobrium?'

'Ecobrium kidnapped your actor. Held him to ransom.'

César's guts felt suddenly heavy.

'I guess the actor was a little too good at his job. Looks like she fell for the story, hook line and sinker. So much so, she agreed to their demands. Anything to save Mercúrio.'

'Oh, no.'

'And what do you think the ransom was?'

'I have no idea.'

He should have been ready for the blow, but it caught him on the temple and knocked him off the chair.

'Guess.' The broad soldier loomed over him, boot raised for a kick.

'The mine deeds?' César's mouth was so dry the words were barely audible.

'Correct.'

'But Ecobrium oppose mining, why would they want a gold mine?'

'They don't.' The tall soldier said. 'They just want to stop the Colonel.'

'How did they know about her gold mine?'

The kick landed in his solar plexus. César curled up into a ball, struggling to catch his breath.

'Ecobrium knew about her inheritance because you broadcast her story to 200 million Brazilians, you beardy fucking oaf.'

Pointless to remind them that it was RIMPO's suggestion. Bullies have short memories and even shorter tempers.

'So, what happened?' César gasped.

'She gave Raimundo Elias the maps,' said the tall one.

'And then Ecobrium killed your actor,' said the broad one.

'And now we're going to kill you.'

'And then we're going to find Jaq Silver.'

'And kill her too.'

'Wait,' César screamed. 'There's something you need to know.'

São Paulo, Brazil, January

A live episode of *The Missing* is due to broadcast, so I switch TV channels to find the news.

Ecobrium is constantly hitting the headlines, but their leader is keeping a low profile. Before I knew his real name, I called him Crazy Gloves. Men who wear gloves in the heat of summer are memorable. Now I know his real name – Raimundo Elias – the man who ordered the murder of my son.

He used to appear in person at marches and demonstrations, at town-hall meetings and public lectures all over Brazil, but more recent events feature one or another of his deputies. The man I'm going to kill seems to have dropped out of the public eye. If my opportunities are limited, then my plan has to be perfect.

I turn off the TV and go back to my computer.

The painting above my desk is in the style of Picasso, a cubist representation of a seated woman. Her flat-fish face – even in profile both eyes stare at you – is bright blue and she wears a broad-brimmed orange hat. A stripy sweater-dress clings to her curves and angles. There is something solid across her knee, a long-nosed black rifle.

I need a gun.

Brazil is the second-largest producer of armaments in the western hemisphere. Anyone over 25 can apply for a licence – up to four guns for self-defence. But the gun has to stay at home, in a locked cabinet. You need a special reason to take it out with you.

Assassination might not be considered a justifiable reason in the eyes of the law.

The carry rules are different for service personnel: police and military. As an ex-air-force officer, Marina has access to a wide range of guns, and often carries. One of the many advantages of a private plane is the separate security channel, a route which can be a little more accommodating when it comes to the super-rich in their own planes.

I consider asking Marina to lend me one of her guns; but she will want to know why. And after the deed is done, she will be implicated. I need to find an untraceable weapon. I can't involve Marina in a crime.

I close down the computer and collect my gym kit. Since returning to São Paulo, I avoid the pool but spend as much time as possible in the gym. I need to get strong again.

I have a job to do.

The security guard gives me a wave as I pass. The ex-policeman has always been solicitous, especially since the break-in. Which gives me an idea.

I make a detour to greet him.

'*Bom dia, Chico.*'

'*Oi, Doutora Silver. Tudo bem?*'

I shake my head.

'I just don't feel safe here any more.'

'I can assure you that the complex is secure.'

'But after the break-in …'

I let that hang in the air and watch his reaction. This is a high-security complex and I wonder again just how someone managed to bypass all the systems and gain entrance to my flat.

'The intruder was dealt with,' Chico assures me.

'But what if he was part of a gang? What if there are others?'

'The whole security system has been upgraded.'

'I just can't sleep.' That much is true, although the demons that haunt my nights are conjured from the dark by my own regrets rather than a fear of intruders.

'I promise you, Dr Silver, you have no reason to be worried. This complex is secure now. I can guarantee that.'

'You aren't here all the time, Chico,' I say. 'I'd feel much safer if I had, you know, something to defend myself with.'

'There's no need—' he begins.

'Should I go to my landlord with these concerns?'

He bites his lip then shakes his head.

'Or could you help me to arrange something for my own protection?'

'What are you looking for?'

I tell him.

I tell him exactly what I need.

Curitibanos, Brazil, January

Graça drove straight to GG's, arriving after dark and securing the bike in her grandmother's barn at the back of the garden. She lingered for a moment beside the mango tree, gazing up into the green canopy, searching for the remnants of the tree house she'd built with her brothers when they were all still friends.

The aroma coming from the kitchen reminded her how hungry she was.

'Hi darling.' GG looked up from the stove. 'I wasn't expecting you.'

'Is it OK if I stay for a while?'

'Sure.'

GG put down the wooden spoon to hug her granddaughter.

'What's for dinner?'

'*Bacalhau com natas*.' GG pointed at the bag. 'You brought your laundry?'

'Police business.'

After dinner, Graça opened the laundry bag and inspected the metal box. The silk lining was faded, stained and torn, the leather was in tatters and there was a gap between the double-side walls where new life had taken up lodging. Where the metal was uncovered, it had started to rust. The screw holes suggested that pieces of the base were missing, but the box looked sturdy enough with its brass latches. Graça opened it. Completely empty. Whatever the soldier had been looking for had long gone.

'What's that?' GG reappeared from the kitchen.

What was it exactly? Evidence? Of what? 'I'm not sure myself.'

'It's exactly the right size for my cake stand.'

The night air filled with dramatic music. Everyone in the village tuning in to the same TV show.

'C'mon,' GG said. 'There's a new series of *The Missing* starting tonight.'

Graça returned the box to the laundry bag and pulled the drawstring tight.

Rio de Janeiro, Brazil, January

When the New Year special of *The Missing* went live, it was without César. In his place was a raven-haired beauty whom they called Gilda because her real name of Maria Beatrice was not considered sexy enough for TV.

She stood, centre stage, and opened her arms wide. 'Happy New Year, everyone!'

The lights danced and the music soared.

'Today we're going to look back on the stupendous success of *The Missing* in reuniting families after decades of absence.'

The producers had decided not to advertise the change of programme. All it had promised was a live show, it hadn't promised that César would be appearing live throughout. In truth, he wasn't in a fit state to appear. But he was in all the clips – what more could his adoring public want?

'César has chosen his very favourite episodes.'

The plan had been cobbled together in a few minutes when it became clear that the celebrity presenter wasn't feeling, or looking, his best.

'Let's start with the origin of the programme,' Gilda said. 'Our pilot episode.'

The screen behind Gilda showed a dark, dense jungle, slowly lightening to reveal the silhouette of a man's face.

'I can lead you to the bones,' he said.

His voice was disguised and came across as distorted, robotic. The music developed into slow electronic chords. The camera pulled back to show rain lashing onto a dense jungle canopy. A muddy river roared over a waterfall. A brightly coloured toucan flew into a tree, and a group of monkeys set up a chatter of alarm. The camera panned across the parked jeeps, white crosses on their roofs, and then focussed on the group of men digging into the blood-red earth. A cry went up and a woman in a white coverall, yellow boots and blue gloves hurried over and knelt down with a trowel in one hand and a brush in the other. She moved the earth away to reveal a white skull. She reverently extracted it and carried it out of the grave, laying it carefully on the ground. The camera panned up until the view was clear: thirteen partially reconstructed skeletons.

A man in a white paper suit spoke to the camera. 'We found them.'

Gilda pointed at the screen. 'In the very first episode of *The Missing*,

César persuaded the reclusive Colonel Cub to help bring closure to a group of survivors, the parents of students who disappeared forty years ago, sons and daughters who abandoned their university cities to start a people's revolution in the jungle.' She moved to one side. 'Let's see what happened.'

The camera focussed in on the screen, until the archive clip filled the frame and Gilda disappeared from view, to be replaced by César sitting on a sofa with a scientist in a lab coat opposite an elderly couple.

César spoke to the scientist.

'Can you confirm that you have analysed a sample from the human remains found in the jungle?'

'I can.'

'And can you tell us if any of them are a match?'

The doctor turned to the elderly couples.

'I'm so sorry to tell you this. 'We found a close match between your DNA and the DNA of one of the bodies.'

'Can you be sure?'

'Is there any chance ...?'

The scientist shook his head. 'It's a ten thousand to one chance that it is a coincidence.'

César put on his most sympathetic face.

'We found your daughter.'

The couple embraced.

'At last, we can lay her to rest.'

Church music played, a choir singing a lament, then the studio voice intoned.

MISSING THEN FOUND.

The camera panned back, and Gilda reappeared in front of the screen. She dabbed at her fake lashes with a tissue. 'Tragic though that first episode was, it gave such important closure to those poor folks.'

The music changed, more upbeat this time.

'But usually, César is able to bring about a happier outcome!'

'One morning, Yuko Nakamura kissed her father and left for school. When she got home, he'd vanished. Let's see what happened when she came to César for help.'

Once again César filled the screen, but this time he was sitting opposite a petite woman.

'Yuko,' César said. 'Thirty years is a long time. Why is it that you are trying to find your father now?'

'My mother is ill. She's been calling out for him.' Yuko dabbed a handkerchief at her eyes.

The studio audience sighed. Aaaahhh.

'Ladies and gentlemen, how many Brazilians have the surname Nakamura?'

A low murmur from the audience.

'There are one-and-a-half million Brazilians of Japanese descent, and Nakamura is in the top-ten surnames. There are tens of thousands of people with the name Nakamura in São Paulo alone.'

On the screen, César beamed. 'And yet we found him.'

A man appeared on the huge screen behind the presenter. The woman seated on the sofa sprang to her feet. A hand flew to her mouth, but it wasn't fast enough to muffle the cry that escaped her lips.

'Daddy?'

'Nakamura san, welcome.' César stood and bowed with exaggerated respect.

The man bowed stiffly.

'Your wife is waiting for you.'

The camera pulled back to show the man outside a hospital ward. The door opened and the camera followed him as he moved forward to be reunited with his wife.

MISSING came the voiceover, THEN FOUND, and the familiar music soared.

Gilda was back.

'And some mysteries are yet to be resolved,' she said. 'A young woman was separated from her newborn son. She was told he had died at birth. Imagine her shock to find out, over twenty years later, that he'd been adopted and brought to Brazil.'

There'd been some debate about using the clips. César had set them aside, but no one knew if he wanted to bury them or highlight them for repeat. They decided it was the latter because they were short of time.

A dark-haired woman filled the screen and spoke directly to the camera.

'My name is Jaq, and I am looking for my son.'

Curitibanos, Brazil, January

Graça leapt to her feet as a tingle of recognition turned into a buzz of excitement.

GG looked up from her knitting, startled. 'What?'

'Not what,' Graça said. 'Who!'

Facing the camera, speaking directly to the audience, the woman on TV wore a sleeveless jumpsuit with a wide gold belt and matching shoes. Her dark hair was glossy, her green eyes sparkled under the studio lights, her full lips trembled.

So that's why the CCTV footage of a woman on a motorcycle entering a multistorey car park in Floripa rang a bell in her memory. There was no doubt about it, this was the same woman.

The TV screen changed to the show title and the deep voice boomed out: *The Missing.*

'You look as if you've seen a ghost.' GG said.

Graça pointed at the screen. 'That woman on the show.'

'You into gold mines now?'

'Shhh.' Graça turned up the sound.

Afterwards, Graça found the original episode on a pirate website. She watched it right through.

What would it be like to have your baby taken away? To be told that the infant died at birth? To find out decades later that you'd been lied to?

Was the woman telling the truth? Graça's sixth sense told her so. Jaq's face shone with a fierce honesty, raw anger tempered by love. Graça switched off the TV. Would her own mother have fought for her so fiercely? Her grandmother certainly would. The brief interview had moved them both, but only GG was still crying when Graça stepped into the garden to call Zélia.

'I know who was riding the Harley.'

'Where are you? Where is it?'

'Somewhere safe.'

'You want to know where I am? Making dinner for my children before my night shift starts.'

'Busy then?'

'Just a little.'

'You want to call me back when you're not so busy?'

'I'll do just that.'

Graça was asleep when her phone rang at 2 a.m. She surfaced from vivid dreams, driving a car, speeding down a steep hill, without brakes, without even a steering wheel, completely out of control, with no way to slow or steer, towards a woman in a sleeveless jumpsuit with gold shoes.

She shook herself awake and answered. 'Yes?'

'Bit of a storm you've created.' Zélia sounded less than friendly.

'I've got a name for you,' Graça said. 'To go with the picture.'

'Picture?'

'The CCTV picture of the woman who delivered the motorcycle.'

'I'm listening.'

'Jaq.'

'As in Jaqueline?'

'Yup.'

'That's it?'

'Check for a Jaqueline flying out of Florianópolis Airport on the morning of December 19th.'

'Anything else?'

'Foreign. Definitely European, probably a Portuguese national.'

'How do you know all this?'

'She appeared on a reality TV show. *The Missing*. Episode 79 if you want to catch it.'

'I'll check it out.'

'How was dinner?'

'Chaos.'

'How's work?'

'Quiet tonight.'

Graça didn't have long to wait before the phone rang again.

'I've got an ID.' Zélia sounded excited.

'Hit me.'

'Your motorbike rider goes by the name of Dr Jaqueline Silver.'

'A medical doctor?'

'No, an engineer.'

'Portuguese?'

'Born in Angola. UK passport. Working in Brazil since July on an expert visa. I'm sending a copy of the passport through now.'

Ping.

No doubt about it. A poor picture, but there she was, the same woman who had appeared in a reality TV show in October and been captured on the airport CCTV in December.

'And there's more. This is where it gets juicy.'

'I'm intrigued.'

'I'm waiting for Interpol to call back. Looks like Dr Jaqueline Silver has a criminal record.'

São Paulo, Brazil, January

The gym in my apartment block has glass on all four walls. Three of them are backed with silver, floor-to-ceiling mirrors so you can see yourself exercising from all angles. The fourth wall has a row of tinted windows that look out over a strip of garden above a busy highway.

I prefer to watch the traffic.

After a punishing routine, I return to my flat with burning muscles and new determination.

I decide to call Bruno. My employer must be the most relaxed boss in the universe. Bruno controls my visa, my right to remain in Brazil, and yet he pays me whether I'm at work or not. I need that arrangement to continue. I'm not leaving this country until I've finished what others started.

'Jaq, Merry Christmas and a Happy New Year!' He sounds offensively cheerful.

'And to you, Bruno.'

'When are you next in the office?'

The prospect of wading through old Cuperoil safety studies, with Marco breathing leerily over my shoulder, slapping away his wandering hands, is more than I can contemplate.

I make a decision. 'I'm not coming back while Marco's there.'

Bruno sighs. 'You want to make a formal complaint.'

I cannot believe that I am the first woman Marco has harassed. I will do now what I should have done, months ago, when he showed his true colours.

'I do.'

'Leave it with me,' Bruno says.

Which leaves me free for the moment.

I'm back with only one mission.

To find Crazy Gloves.

And make him pay.

Curitibanos, Brazil, January

GG's garden was full of life, the chickens scattering as Graça entered the hen house. She'd collected five warm, speckled eggs when her phone rang.

She closed the hen hatch and moved the basket of eggs to the shade.

'Hi, Zélia,'

'Looks like your motorcycle rider took a plane to Congonhas airport in São Paulo on December 19th at 7.30 a.m.' For someone just finishing a night shift, Zélia sounded positively animated. 'She changed airports and flew to Amsterdam. The return ticket was for December 23rd, with a connecting flight to Florianópolis.'

So, if Dr Silver had returned to Floripa, why hadn't she collected her bike?

Zélia must be a mind reader. 'Bad storms over Europe meant that a lot of flights were delayed, with all connecting flights rebooked for the following day.'

Christmas Eve. 'So, she probably arrived while I was watching the bike.' And I let her slip through my fingers. Damn.

'You had a lucky escape. She's dangerous.'

'Dangerous how?'

'An explosives expert.'

'You think she caused the explosion at the airport?'

'It certainly distracted you.'

Stay with the bike. Don't touch the bike. Graça felt a pang of shame.

'That explosion blew out my car windows.'

'I'm not blaming you.' Zélia sighed. 'Though I can't speak for our boss.'

'Am I in trouble?'

'Both of us are,' Zélia said.

Graça took some reassurance from that. Zélia wouldn't let her down.

'Any idea where Silver is now?'

'News just in. Apparently she was admitted to Saint Bartholomew's private hospital in Floripa on Christmas Day.'

'Maybe she's not such an expert when it comes to explosives.'

Zélia laughed. 'Perhaps you could drop by and ask her what went wrong.'

Graça picked up her helmet.

'On my way.'

Rio de Janeiro, Brazil, January

From his hospital bed, César watched the next-day repeat of *The Missing* in dismay. Gilda had made a complete mess of his show. She'd used the very clips he'd removed from the archive to prevent them ever being broadcast again. Too late now. No one should have allowed that airhead near his programme.

But that was the least of his worries.

The emergency doctor claimed that his injuries were superficial and suggested he go home and rest. Typical idiocy of the medical profession. For a man who made his living from TV, a superficial injury was potentially fatal. Career-wise at least. César insisted on an overnight stay. In part so he could talk to the plastic surgeon first thing in the morning, but also because he felt safer here than at home.

What if the information he'd supplied to the soldiers was not enough to convince the Colonel to spare him? What if the soldiers returned to finish the job?

The Colonel was already furious, demanding that Jaq Silver be found before she did any further harm. The repeat of her episode was only going to make things worse.

If César wanted to survive, he had only one option – find Jaq Silver before the Colonel did.

Cambridge, England, January

Honey-coloured stone sparkled in the winter sunshine, the cascade of crimson ivy glowing as if on fire. Under a stone balcony with gabled windows, a wooden door opened onto a stone staircase that curved up one flight of stairs to an arched hallway, framed portraits of men in college robes lining the entrance to the meeting room.

As an alumnus of the university, and a generous benefactor to Black and minority ethnic students, Graham Dekker had access to a suite of rooms in one of the grander Cambridge colleges.

A college butler took Frank's coat and opened the heavy iron latch on the oak door. Graham was seated beside a roaring fire, a decanter of ruby liquid and two crystal glasses on a tray beside him.

'Ah, Frank!' Graham jumped to his feet and extended a hand.

It was always hard to judge his boss's age. Frank guessed he was over sixty, but his host was athletic, and his handshake was firm to the point of painful.

'Port OK for you, or do you prefer something else?' The Afrikaans drawl was the only hint that English was not Graham's first language.

Frank glanced at his watch. Two p.m. was a little early to start drinking and he needed to keep his wits about him. On the other hand it was 10 p.m. in China, and he'd barely slept since arriving. Perhaps one small glass.

'Port is fine.'

The butler withdrew and Frank took a seat beside the fire.

'Thank you for coming.' Graham poured two generous glasses and handed one to Frank.

'What's all this about?' Frank might have obeyed his boss's instruction, but that didn't mean he had to sound happy about it.

'Trouble.'

'What sort of trouble?'

'The draft report from OPCW.'

The United Nations-sponsored Organisation for the Prohibition of Chemical Weapons had launched an investigation into Frank's European division after Zagrovyl products were diverted to an illegal chemical weapons factory.

'I thought that investigation was closed.'

Frank had assisted the international authorities in bringing the Russian criminal mastermind – the Spider – to justice.

'I was completely exonerated.'

'I'm sure you had no idea what was going on at the time, Frank. But it happened on your watch.'

Frank narrowed his eyes and stared at his boss. Was this going where he feared? The responsibility argument was a tactic Frank often used with employees he wanted to get rid of. A project overruns because of scope changes imposed by others mid-construction – fire the project director. A department fails to meet its budget because it champions a promising innovation on behalf of other divisions – sack the director who ignored narrow self-interest.

But Graham couldn't have brought him here to sack him. Since being exiled to China to run the green energy division, Frank had single-handedly sorted out the rare metal supply chain. If anyone was indispensable, Frank was.

'There's a follow-up action before the final report can be issued; I'd like you to take responsibility for closing it out.'

That was more like it. Not a sacking but a potential promotion. Graham wasn't getting any younger.

'What sort of action?'

'Proof that Zagrovyl didn't benefit financially from the illegal activities of others.'

Frank nodded.

'That should be straightforward.'

'It would have been, until our US Director of Corporate Integrity got involved.'

Frank shuddered. He vaguely remembered Deborah Ives, the thin, shrew-eyed woman in a hideous frock who'd attended the global conference in Shanghai. They had been seated next to each other at the final dinner. He'd rebutted her attempts at conversation, more interested in talking golf with Graham Dekker on his right or flirting with the gorgeous Clara Sousa, head of the Brazilian Division of Zagrovyl, across the table. Was this Deborah's revenge for being ignored? Hell hath no fury like a woman scorned.

'Involved how?'

'She's hired a business transparency consultancy, an anti-corruption outfit called Pelupent.'

'Never heard of them.'

'A small outfit, based here in Cambridge.'

'What's their remit?'

'To …' Graham made air quotes round the next words, 'help us.'

Frank snorted.

'Not sure where their intelligence comes from, but they're asking a lot of pointed questions, and not limited to Zagrovyl's Russian operation.'

'Former operation. I closed it down, remember?'

'You did. But this is about the past as well as the present. And it gets worse.'

'How?'

'Corporate Integrity have helpfully asked Pelupent to widen the investigation to include all of the UK's BRIC interests.'

BRIC – Brazil, Russia, India and China, represented the fastest-growing economies in the world, vast populations leaping out of poverty with aspirations to live a more comfortable life – the very definition of the ideal consumer.

'Specifically chemical weapons?'

'Wider than that. A full review of business practices to check that the UK complies fully with the UN Convention against Corruption.'

'Of course we do. Deborah Ives must be mad.'

'I need you to work with Pelupent until this is complete. You'll relocate to England.'

'Where?'

'Wherever you like within commuting distance of Cambridge.'

Well at least that ruled Teesside out.

'And what's my role?'

'You'll keep your current job. You have a good team in China, right?'

'Right.'

'There will be a fair amount of travel. I'll let the country general managers know to give you their full support.'

Frank nodded.

'And Frank,' Graham stood up. 'I don't want any surprises.'

'Surprises?'

'Engineers aren't always the most articulate creatures, but when they get started, some of them don't know when to stop. I need someone with a bit of ... business acumen ... to ensure we manage the message. I need someone who can lead from the front.'

'Is this a promotion?'

Graham smiled. 'If you sort this out without damaging Zagrovyl's reputation, I can promise you it will lead to great things.'

'Can you be more specific?'

'Trust me, Frank.' Graham clapped him on the back.

The bastard held all the cards right now, no point in challenging him until Frank had some leverage.

Graham brought his mouth close to Frank's ear. 'I'm counting on you, Frank. Don't let me down.'

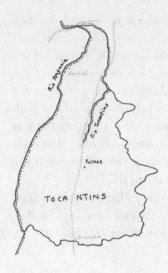

2km from the gold mine, Tocantins, Brazil, January

The Colonel's encampment lay upwind of both the mine and the miserable workers' settlement. It took an hour to reach the other side of the ridge, where a much larger river tumbled down towards the plain in a series of waterfalls and rapids. The two soldiers marched their captive up to a sandstone bluff and through a narrow defile, guarded on either side by armed sentry posts, surveillance towers with machine-gun turrets looming down from the clifftop above.

Beyond the narrow path between the cliffs was an old quarry, long abandoned except for a series of thatched conical huts that rose out of the quarry-base on stilts. The huts connected to one another with rope bridges constructed from twine, but they were isolated from the access path.

The soldiers marched Hugo to the edge and he stared down into the void. The quarry itself was about the area of a football pitch and uniformly deep. Hugo estimated a drop of ten metres to the rocky floor, more than enough to kill a man. Is this what they intended for him? Why bring him all this way just to murder him?

A light breeze gathered strength as the fierce sun dipped behind clouds. Hugo turned his face towards the wind, welcoming the cooling effect as his eyes darted to and fro, searching for a means of escape. To his left and right, armed soldiers flanked the path from the cliff. A young man, little more than a boy, scowled at him, fingers straying to the trigger of an automatic rifle. There was no way back. In front of him, a sheer drop yawned between the quarry's edge and the first of several huts on stilts.

At a shout he looked up to see a moving bridge gradually extend across the chasm, providing a pathway into the strange complex. With a whirring and creaking, it stopped about two metres from where Hugo stood.

A figure appeared at the other end.

'Who are you and what do you want?' A big man, his voice rumbled like thunder.

Before Hugo had a chance to compose an answer – along the lines of, I want these thugs to release me immediately, the older soldier spoke up.

'Dinner guest for the Colonel.'

Dinner guest? What madness was this? 'Look here …' Hugo began, until the pressure of a gun barrel in the small of his back made him think better of remonstrating.

The bridge extended the final two metres and the man with the booming voice advanced across it. A giant of a man, he wore only a pair of loose white trousers, his bare chest a magnificent work of art in itself. Hugo tried not to stare.

The giant extended a hand. 'Welcome,' he said.

Hugo winced at the powerful handshake, noting the flash of cruelty in the man's eyes. Physical beauty was deceptive, this man was dangerous.

'Follow me.'

What choice did he have?

Hugo followed the bare-chested man into the complex. It took a moment for his eyes to become accustomed to the mossy glow. The natural light shone through slits in the wall filled with a tangle of vines.

A boy, dressed in a white kaftan, descended from the top of a curved wooden staircase and bowed low.

'The boy will show you to the guest suite.'

'I'm not staying,' Hugo protested.

'You can discuss everything with the Colonel,' the man said. 'When he returns.'

1,600km from the gold mine, a freight train, Ipameri, Goiás State, Brazil, February

Chuffa-chuffa, chuffa-chuffa ... beep beep ... ding ding ... whoooo hooo.

The sun is travelling across a cloudless sky and it's getting hot inside this metal box on rails.

The steel sides of the corn wagon have no insulation. I drink the last of the rainwater before it evaporates and eat a few kernels of corn. I'll need to find fresh supplies soon.

The metal walls of the wagon are red hot, they burn my fingers as I climb up the inside and look over the lip. Nothing but fields as far as the eye can see.

I drop back, hunker down in the last patch of shade. It will be gone by noon. I don't have much time to marshal my thoughts.

When the train pulls into a siding in the middle of nowhere, I know I have come to the end of the corn line. At the hoot of another train, I climb to the lip of the wagon and watch it trundle into view. The *Siderurgia Special* is hauling a ramshackle mix of battered intermodal containers and newer hoppers towards some distant steelworks. The metals to be added to iron to temper the properties of steel – chromium and manganese, nickel and niobium – are all carried in wagons designed for bottom unloading. There's a wedge-shaped space between the ladder and bogie, a shady nook under the sloping side of the gondola.

I stand on the lip of the corn wagon and leap onto the flat roof of a shipping container, then run along the top until I reach the ladder of a hopper truck.

It's an easy jump from agriculture to industry.

41
Nb
Niobium
92.906

Brazil has over 95 per cent of the world's niobium reserves and controls most of the world's niobium production. In 2013 it produced 74,000 tonnes with an approximate value of US$ 3 billion.

Niobium is mainly used in high-grade structural steel and superalloys for jet engines and turbines.

Cambridge, England, January

An overnight frost left sparkling jewels on the college greens, and stalactites adorned weeping willow branches trailing over the dark water of the River Cam.

Cambridge might be picture-postcard pretty in the centre, but it was an urban nightmare everywhere else. Even before they'd rejected his UCAS application all those years ago, Frank had disliked the fustiness of the place. The power of the university colleges meant that any new development designed to make commerce easier always fell at the first hurdle of an ancient building. The senseless stranglehold of antiquity was perfectly mirrored in the endless traffic jams, and Frank was glad he'd hired a bicycle instead of a car.

He swung into the business park, secured the bike and removed his gloves, blowing on frozen hands. A bitter wind blew across the fens, straight from Siberia. Cambridge really was a dismal place. The only saving grace was the abundance of college chapels with lovingly maintained organs and acoustics to match. If he pretended to be considering a donation, one of the colleges would surely grant him access. Or he could just ask Graham Dekker to pull some strings.

Standing in front of the entrance to the office, Frank cracked his knuckles and spread his long hands, pressing a rubber button on the plastic housing that announced Pelupent in green letters, while imagining smooth ebony and ivory beneath his fingertips, worn wooden levers under the leather soles of his feet.

A panel lit up beside the door and a camera swivelled towards him.

'Frank Good for Nicholas McLean,' he announced.

The outside door clicked open and a man came forward to meet him.

'Mr Good, welcome.' He smiled. 'You found us OK?'

Of all the inane questions, this had to be the stupidest. But then Nick McLean looked like an idiot with his long hair and scraggly beard, ragged jumper and faded jeans stuffed into motorcycle boots with multiple buckles.

Frank nodded as he shook the pudgy hand that enclosed his.

'Ooh, cold hands. Have you cycled far?'

'From the centre.'

The serviced accommodation was a far cry from Frank's glass-walled penthouse in Shanghai. A dull little beige flat with small windows and an open-plan kitchen/dining/living area that always smelt of cabbage, despite the fact he didn't cook. But he wasn't planning on staying long, and in the meantime, it was convenient for the Pelupent office.

They called it an office, but now he was inside, he could see in a glance that it was little more than a reception area with several hot desks and a meeting room.

'Coffee? I'm afraid we're out of milk.'

'It's OK, I'm vegan.'

His host made two black coffees – there wasn't even a secretary for that – and led him to the meeting room.

'Very excited to be working with you, Mr Good. Can I call you Frank?'

Bloody cheek. 'Of course, Nicholas.'

'Oh, just Nick.'

'And your role here, Nick?'

'Founding partner,' Nick grinned. 'Wild, isn't it.'

Wild indeed. And yet Deborah Ives, Director of Corporate Integrity, had entrusted this scruffy wild man with Zagrovyl's future in the UK. What was the world coming to?

'To be honest, I wasn't expecting a senior executive from Zagrovyl to turn up, still less for him to be a vegan cyclist.'

Frank pursed his lips in satisfaction. Exactly the impression he intended.

Florianópolis, Brazil, January

Traffic roared over the suspension bridge, the longest in Brazil, joining the Island of Santa Catarina to the mainland.

Graça manoeuvred into an inside lane, signalled and accelerated down the ramp, following the signs to the hospital. She parked outside the modern building with its uninterrupted view of the bridge and bay and presented herself at reception.

'I'm here to see Dr Jaqueline Silver.'

'Let me check ....' The receptionist tapped at the computer. 'I'm sorry, we no longer have a patient of that name.'

'She left? When?'

'I'm unable to release personal information.'

'Any idea where she went?'

'I'm sorry, I'm unable to ...'

Graça flashed her police badge.

The receptionist stiffened. 'Do you have a warrant?'

'Not yet,'

'Well, like I told the other policeman ...'

'The other policeman?'

'The rude and unpleasant one who came with the soldier.' She sniffed.

'Can you describe him?'

'They all look the same to me.'

'And the soldier? Any distinguishing features?'

'One of those tattoos of a snake with a pipe.'

The description matched the soldier from the beach house. *Merda*, why had she left him to the local police? Why hadn't she shot him? Because she was a recently trained law enforcement offer, not a vigilante.

Someone else was looking for Silver.

Someone dangerous.

Someone with connections to the army and the military police.

And they were several steps ahead of her.

Rio de Janeiro, Brazil, January

If he didn't find Jaq Silver first, the Colonel's men were coming back for him. César valued his life, but he valued his good looks every bit as much, for what was life without his career, and what was his career without his good looks?

He was careful about what he ate, limited how much he drank, took regular, moderate exercise, and gave himself over to the expert hands of his barber twice a week.

Domingo worked from a small salon on the edge of Rocinha, not far from the Hélio TV studio. He kept César's beard neatly trimmed and moisturised, eyebrows thin and quizzical, hair looking natural with an even colour and always the right side of tousled. He also acted as a father confessor, confidant, invaluable source of information and occasional advice.

'*Bom dia, doutor!*'

Domingo always called him *doutor*, even though they both knew César had no university degree. It was simply a mark of respect.

'Oi, Domingo.'

'What's it to be today then?'

'The usual.'

Domingo studied his client's face in the mirror as he draped a towel across his shoulders, noting the bruises, but saying nothing.

'Great New Year special,' Domingo got out his scissors. 'One of your best.' Snip, snip. 'I like the new girl.'

The reason Domingo was still a barber working 18-hour days in a rough part of town was that although he had excellent taste in hair styles, was an expert in hair products, his abilities stopped there. Anyone who compared the finely crafted episodes that César masterminded with a cobbled-together set of clips was clearly lacking in discernment. And anyone who found Gilda impressive was badly lacking in judgement. Fortunately for them both, Domingo had no aspirations towards a career in TV production, and César occasionally found his dull, dumb, pedestrian insights of value. Domingo was a man of the people, of the *bairro*, the favela. He kept César grounded.

'I used to have a thing with Gilda,' César lied. He winked at Domingo in the mirror, and then wished he hadn't, as the muscles on that side of his face went into spasm. Fuck, it hurt.

'I bet you did!' Domingo leered back. 'Perk of the job?'

It had been once. All the beautiful people wanted to be on TV. And some of the ugly ones too. It was a competitive business, and people, men and women, would do anything to step on the ladder.

César had enjoyed himself at first, rolling from dinner to nightclub to orgy, but soon grew bored as it became clear that most of the beautiful women who threw themselves at him had no real interest in him as a person, only in what he might do for their careers. The bed of ambition was uncomfortably crowded.

Domingo lathered a razor and took hold of his client's chin. César cried out in pain.

'Trouble, *doutor?*'

César turned his head from side to side. All the foundation and powder in the world couldn't completely hide the ugly bruises left by the fists of the Colonel's men. The plastic surgeon had refused to even consider surgery until the swelling had gone down, and, in truth, as no bones had been broken, medical intervention was probably pointless.

César deflected the question. 'You don't make an omelette without breaking eggs.'

'Ain't that the truth of it.' Domingo lathered his sable brush and got to work. 'You looking for some men to help to square things up?'

'It's nothing.' César lowered his eyes. 'A little misunderstanding with our friends from RIMPO.' Domingo probably knew about it already. And if word hadn't reached the streets, he trusted his barber's discretion, that was how the barber's chair confessional worked.

'RIMPO?' Domingo sucked air through his teeth. 'Protectors

of the *garimpeiros*? The ex-soldiers who take orders from Colonel Cub? Folk from up country say that fellow is the devil himself.'

And I am stuck with him, César thought, bound in a Faustian pact of my own making. Without Colonel Cub, Hélio TV would never have agreed to make the pilot episode of *The Missing*. The runaway success of the series left him with a problem – how to extricate himself from the clutches of a lunatic?

Domingo flipped open the razor. 'Is this little misunderstanding all resolved?'

'Not quite,' César confessed. 'I have to find someone for the Colonel.'

Domingo threw back his head and roared with laughter.

'Well then, lucky that's what you do for a living.'

Except it wasn't. César was a playwright not an investigator, an actor not a counsellor. When it came to really finding a missing person, he was lost.

'It's not so easy if they don't want to be found,' he said.

'But you must know someone they know?'

Marina Querino. Stubbornly loyal. Unlikely she would rat on her new best friend.

'Not really.'

'Then use your show,' said Domingo. 'Set a trap.'

'A trap?'

'Someone may not want to be found, but sure as hell there's something they want. Find out what it is, set it up and ...' he clapped his hands together and the sound ricocheted around the room. 'Gotcha!'

César reappraised his barber as the steel blade rasped against stubble. Domingo had a way of thinking, a low cunning, that was occasionally useful. Not that César hadn't already considered such a plan, but talking it through with someone else always helped crystallise the details.

What did Jaq Silver want?

If the Colonel's men were right, she believed that Ecobrium had killed her son. In which case, she was probably looking for their leader.

He was chairing an environmental debate with a live studio audience next week. All he had to do was invite Raimundo Elias onto *Missing Nature*. Ramp up the publicity and invite Marina Querino, to be sure that Jaq got the message. When she turned up, the Colonel's men would be waiting.

São Paulo, Brazil, January

I take the pistol from its case. It's lighter than I expected, but then the last time I handled a weapon like this, I was only a child. It feels cold – of course I know that's an illusion. The second law of thermodynamics: heat moves from hotter to colder objects. The metal casing is at the same temperature as the rest of the room, about 22 degrees Centigrade. My body temperature is 37 degrees Centigrade. The high heat transfer coefficient of the metal, the ability to conduct heat away from a higher-temperature source to a lower-temperature one to achieve a balance, means that it cools my skin when I touch it.

I go through the motions, opening the barrel to check there are no bullets, spinning it, aiming and firing. It has a nice weight, well balanced in my hand, a smooth action and a satisfying click.

Was I right to avoid guns all this time? It's not that I have remained passive, not that I haven't attacked. Just that I have chosen other weapons: potassium metal and water to liberate hydrogen – boom; a smokescreen of titanium tetra-chloride – choking whiteout; cyanoacrylate to restrain a felon; polymemory for detonation. Chemical weapons. Does that make me a monster?

Perhaps the only difference is the line of sight, the honesty of intention. Choose your target, point the gun, pull the trigger. The bullet flies from the barrel and the effect is almost instantaneous. No fuse to create a delay between intention and action, only milliseconds between action and injury. No possibility to escape the full horror of an act of violence, no way to hide from the gruesome consequences. Swift, clean, targeted and, in an ideal world, less chance of harming the innocent.

But the world is far from ideal. In the messy heat of battle, collateral risk may be reduced but not eliminated.

As my brother found out, to his cost.

Lock it down. Lock it in.

I hide the gun in my luggage and set off for the airport.

I'm flying to Rio with Marina in a private plane. Different security channels and Marina has all the licences we need.

Florianópolis, Brazil, January

With the modern hospital behind her, Graça crossed the road and sat on the wall of the esplanade that curved round the bay to make a call.

'So how was the patient?' Zélia asked.

'Too late, she'd already left.' Graça said.

'Her file just came in from head office. Listen to this address.' Zélia read out an address in the exclusive Jardim district of São Paulo. 'Ring any bells?'

'Nope.'

'Guess who owns that flat?'

'Who?'

'Walter Salgado.'

'So, motorbike rider is Salty Walter's girlfriend?' Graça asked.

'Looks like it.'

'What on earth does she see in him?'

Zélia laughed. 'Other than his multi-million-pound fortune?'

'Of dubious provenance.'

'Crooks stick together,' Zélia said.

'Sounds like a trip to São Paulo coming up.'

'Graça, be careful. It looks like she's a pro. Wherever she goes, chaos follows. Dossiers as long as your arm: ongoing civil case involving multiple fatalities in England; Europol had warrants out for her arrest after a fatal explosion in Slovenia; she was even wanted for questioning by the art police after an incident in China.'

'Any convictions?'

'Not yet.'

Graça couldn't shake the conviction that it was not Silver who she should be worried about, but the people looking for her.

Rio de Janeiro, Brazil, January

The theatre is in Leblon, between the beach and the lagoon, under a pair of skyscrapers opposite a hypermarket. Posters for the show are plastered everywhere, *Os Desaparecidos do Natureza*, subtitled in English 'Missing Nature', feature a sleek black jaguar, a pink river dolphin and a cherry-throated tanager. The live debate on Brazil's environmental challenges, chaired by TV presenter César, promises to be a popular event. The Hélio TV studio has moved to a theatre large enough to accommodate the interest.

The appearance of Raimundo Elias from the eco-warrior group Ecobrium is a closely guarded secret. It is thanks to Marina that I know he is making a surprise appearance.

I've already checked the layout. The public enter from the front, up an elaborate flight of steps, or winding ramp, into a light and airy foyer with a vertical garden. The stage door is at the side, opposite the back door of a basement restaurant.

I arrive very early and take up my position, wrapped in a blanket between the industrial bins opposite the stage door.

I'm waiting for Raimundo Elias.

Plan A is to accost him before he enters the theatre. It will only work if he is alone. It's not enough to kill him. He must look me in the eyes and acknowledge what he did. There's a chance I can escape, throw the gun in the dumpster, run down the alley and get lost in the crowd, but I don't really care what happens afterwards.

Plan B is to confront him inside the theatre, to wait until he is on stage, to raise my hand to ask an innocent question, to stand up and demand an answer, to approach the stage, pull out the gun and fire at point-blank range. That way, the whole world will know what he did. And I will spend the rest of my life in prison.

After the production technicians and assistants arrive, there is a pause before the first of the 'talent' arrive. A young man with dreadlocks steps up and presses the buzzer. He's wearing a T-shirt, fluorescent baggy trousers and flip flops. The T-shirt is emblazoned with the logo 'Chemical Free Zone'. I make a mental note of the nylon beads in his hair, the aniline dyes used to colour his pantaloons and the polyurethane soles of his footwear. Don't even get me started on the fertilisers and pesticides and water-treatment chemicals and fuel needed to grow and process and transport the cotton for his clothes. A light goes on over the stage door and a camera swivels towards him. I pull back into the shadows, but I am well out of the range of the lens. He speaks into the intercom, the door clicks open, and he passes through.

A group arrives next. A woman in a tailored business suit tottering on killer heels alongside a couple of men in chinos and polo shirts. One of them is César. I burrow down into my blanket, hiding my face.

A bell rings. I check the time. The debate is due to start in ten minutes. Perhaps I missed Crazy Gloves, perhaps he came in the public entrance. I stand up and fold the blanket.

Plan A aborted.

Time for Plan B.

I spot Marina outside the foyer of the theatre. Dressed to kill in shades of green, Marina never misses an opportunity to make a visual statement. She is busy air kissing other members of the audience as I emerge from the side alley. Marina knows everyone who is anyone in Rio and all the great and the good seem to be coming to this show. It is thanks to her connections that we have tickets at all.

I feel a rush of affection for her and then a shiver of trepidation. Can I really do this? Murder a man in cold blood?

After what he did to Mercúrio?

Yes I can.

Marina is lost in conversation with someone. When I see who it is I freeze and turn away, retreating to a concrete pillar so I can observe them. Marina is talking to Beefcake. He may have grown his hair a little, covered up his tattoos with a long-sleeved, high-collared shirt, but this is not a man I will forget in a hurry. You tend to remember the people who try to kill you.

And he isn't alone. There are others like him. Once you know what you're looking for – military stance, roving eyes – the RIMPO men stand out like sore thumbs.

What are they doing here? Perhaps RIMPO are part of the debate. Perhaps the former soldiers are here to protect their Colonel, champion of the artisanal miners, the *garimpeiros*. Perhaps Colonel Cub will articulate his argument that people need livelihoods, that they cannot be sacrificed at the altar of environmental protection.

But RIMPO have never been the debating type, they are more likely to shoot first and talk later. There's no love lost between RIMPO and Ecobrium. Perhaps they are here to kill Raimundo Elias. Perhaps they'll do the job for me.

And then I see Marina smile at Beefcake. He points to his watch and Marina surveys the crowd. She takes out her phone and dials. I draw back behind the pillar.

My phone rings.

I stare at the caller ID.

Marina.

The bullet wound in my shoulder begins to throb.

And in that instant, everything becomes clear.

Marina is not my friend.

Marina has set me up.

The woman I trusted has sold me out.

The ultimate betrayal.

Cambridge, England, January

The bass roar made the whole organ loft vibrate. Frank lifted his hands from the keys, adjusted the stops and pumped his feet to sustain the glorious closing chord. Magnificent!

Graham Dekker had arranged access to his old college chapel, and Frank had taken every opportunity to explore and exploit the full power of the organ. The action was far from perfect, but the one compensation for his enforced sojourn in this freezing fenland was the opportunity to master a temperamental instrument. And master it he had. The organ scholars with their timid fiddling and footling could only be humbled by his ambition. He'd noticed them hanging around when he arrived but scurrying away before he finished. It must be hard for them to accept the superiority of an amateur.

Frank opened the college door, zipping up his jacket against the bitter wind. He unlocked his bike and pulled on gloves and his helmet.

Play was over. Time for work.

Nick was smoking outside when Frank arrived and secured his bike in the lockup.

He raised his bearded face to the sky. 'Looks like snow is on the way.'

Frank glanced up at the grey clouds. How could anyone tell? Fucking new-age hippy.

Even Frank had to admit that the project with Pelupent was progressing better than expected. Once they got down to work, things moved fast. Nick agreed to focus on Russia first, addressing the single external query from OPCW before finalising the plan to audit Zagrovyl UK's trading history with other high-risk countries.

Today they were going through the internal records and comparing them with the published figures. Nick quickly got the hang of the UK management accounts but his questions revealed that he had no idea of how a complex, multinational supply chain worked.

'The UK sold products to Slovenia. Some products were rejected but not returned to the UK. Why?'

'Because it was cheaper to send the rejected material to less-demanding customers in Russia.'

'But it never arrived in Smolensk.'

'Exactly, it was diverted en route.'

'And the UK entity made a loss?'

'Neither a profit nor a loss. Slovenia paid the UK in advance. Russia compensated Slovenia. The crooks paid the Russians.'

'Did Zagrovyl UK benefit in any way from the fact that products were diverted.'

'Absolutely not. We were the victims of a sophisticated criminal conspiracy.'

'OK, let's look at your transfer-price policy.'

Nick took regular cigarette breaks outside. Usually, he locked the screen on his computer. The outside smoking shelter wasn't visible from the meeting room, but each trip took four to seventeen minutes.

Today when Nick left the room, promising to pick up some

sandwiches, Frank noticed that he had left his account unlocked. He swivelled the laptop round and began investigating the files on the Pelupent machine.

The folders on Zagrovyl Russia contained only the information Frank, and his former financial controller Robin, had provided. The folders for Brazil, India and China were still empty.

Most of the storage was taken up with other multinational companies – a particularly fat file on the oil giant Cuperoil was password protected. And then Frank found something that stopped him in his tracks. The thumbnail of a picture not yet filed. His breathing rate doubled; his blood turned to ice as he clicked on the message from Carlos Raposa at Pelupent, Brazil. A grainy photograph emerged. The CCTV still of a woman astride a motorbike. The resolution was poor, but there was no mistaking the identity of the rider. He recognised her immediately.

What the hell was Dr Jaq Silver's connection to Pelupent?

Rio de Janeiro, Brazil, January

If I had any sense I would run for my life.

But it's not my life I care about.

If there is any chance that Raimundo Elias is in Rio, I need to know.

If he's here, I'll find him.

A café in Leblon Shopping is showing the live studio debate on a big screen normally reserved for soap operas and football. The audience is growing. Those who stop for a coffee become interested, soon joined by others. I take a seat in the middle. Anonymity in numbers.

César is a good presenter. He's not looking his best today, he has too much make-up on and his face looks a little puffy.

However much he reminds me of my ex-husband, he comes over as empathetic, insightful and intelligent. He's certainly well informed.

'So, here's the dilemma,' he summarises. 'How do we bring people out of poverty while protecting nature?'

The representative from Zagrovyl, Clara, speaks in measured, even tones. 'You talk of nature as if it is always benign and beautiful. But there are many naturally occurring diseases.'

'Yeah, nature fights back.' A young man with dreadlocks raises a fist and the studio audience cheer.

'Someone has to stop the multinationals from raping our country.'

'We have to go back to living in harmony with nature.'

'Well best of luck with that,' Clara retorts. 'Did you know that Brazil has the highest number of new cases of leprosy in the world, 30,000 each year?'

Dreadlocks struggles for something to say.

'My company, Zagrovyl, makes the medicines to combat tuberculosis and leprosy, the fibres used in anti-mosquito tents to stop the spread of dengue and malaria and the insecticides to fight river blindness and Leishmaniasis.'

I wrote a paper on that once. *Natural Danger.* It was almost as if Clara had read it. But no one is interested, they turn on her.

'You lot are causing the very problems you claim to be fighting. What about climate change?'

'We have to act now. For our children and our grandchildren.'

'We can't wait for governments to legislate, people who care have to take direct action, to take matters into their own hands.'

César holds up a hand for silence. He winces and a spasm of pain crosses his face as he stands and slowly moves to centre stage. 'And on that note, please welcome our special guest.'

The up-tempo music starts, a pounding rhythm with an accelerating beat and rising volume and the deep studio voice takes over.

From the eco-warrior group Ecobrium.

I sit up straight, every nerve in my body jangling with the music. I am only ten minutes from the theatre. I know where the 'talent' enters and leaves. I can be there before Raimundo leaves the stage, waiting for him, gun at the ready.

Please welcome ... Raimundo Elias!

The studio lights flash, swivel and go out, leaving the stage in complete darkness. A screen lights up, a rectangle on the wall behind César, and a face appears on screen: sandy haired with bushy sideburns, square jawed, cold eyed.

Crazy Gloves.

By video link.

I slump back down, grinding my teeth, as a single spotlight picks out César.

'Welcome!'

Raimundo Elias is not appearing in person. He's not in Rio. Where is he? How do I find him? How do I make him pay?

São Paulo, Brazil, January

The apartment owned by Salty Walter was in one of the most expensive parts of São Paulo. The streets of Jardins were lined with trees and the skyscrapers had helipads, air-conditioned gyms and swimming pools. They also had overzealous security.

'I'm looking for a Dr Jaqueline Silver,' Graça explained through the intercom.

'Not here,' said the guard.

'When will she be back?'

'No idea.'

'May I come in and wait?'

'Nope.'

Even her federal police badge wouldn't induce the guard to open the gate. Perhaps it was especially her federal police status that kept the gates firmly closed. What possible source of wealth allowed some to live a life of leisure in muti-million-dollar real estate while hard-working professionals struggled to cover rent in a bedsit?

Graça had come a long way, and she wasn't giving up yet.

Rio de Janeiro, Brazil, January

The coffee machine judders and hisses as espressos are dispensed, a rich aroma filling the café where I'm watching the live TV debate.

I stare at the face of the man I'm going to kill.

Crazy Gloves. Raimundo Elias.

His thin lips move; he's talking to the camera, but his words wash over me. All I can hear is the way he laughed while his men killed Mercúrio. On his orders.

Where is he?

I search for visual clues.

He's standing on a hill above a mine. The greenery has been scraped back to reveal the red earth. Deep whorls and gashes are carved into the hillside, one much deeper and wider than the others. Inside the largest excavation, men are scurrying to and fro.

The mine could be anywhere in Brazil, a vast country of 8.5 million square kilometres.

I tune in to the voice, the bass rumble making my intestines writhe.

'... 100,00 illegal mines in this state alone.'

Which state? Brazil has twenty-six, each one bigger than most European countries.

'... chopping down trees, depriving birds and animals of their natural habitat, destabilising the soil, causing floods and landslides, polluting the water ...'

So he stands up for a good cause? That doesn't make him a good man. He's nailed his colours to a popular mast. The ecology movement gives him a smokescreen to hide his true nature.

This is a man who will stop at nothing.

Unless I kill him.

One thing is clear. Crazy Gloves is not in the city of Rio de Janeiro. But RIMPO are, and they are looking for me. I must get out of this city.

I head for the airport.

São Paulo, Brazil, January

Graça sat on a wall outside the luxury complex in Jardins and watched the fast cars creep along, nose to tail, on the freeway.

No sign of Silver.

Her phone rang.

'I think we might have a hit on your gold-digger.' Zélia sounded animated.

'Where?'

'Rio de Janeiro airport. We got a call from border control. A Dr Jaq Silver tried to board a plane to São Paulo. She was detained over a visa technicality.'

'That's lucky.'

Zélia laughed. 'Luck plays no part in police work. I put out an alert the moment we identified her.'

'I'm on my way.'

Rio de Janeiro, Brazil, January

I know something is wrong when the border guard picks up the phone. I hover in front of the airport security desk, hopping from foot to foot, watching her flick through my passport.

'Is there a problem?' I ask.

She angles the microphone. 'You left Brazil on December 19th.' She points to the stamp in my page. 'When did you return?'

'December 23rd,' I say. How could I forget?

'Where's the entry stamp on your passport?' she frowns.

'Let me see if I can find something.' I hold out my hand for the passport and she hesitates for a moment before handing it back.

I scan the pages before it comes to me. Of course. I didn't come through customs or immigration. Beefcake and his merry band of soldiers were waiting for me. I got out through the Balúrdio dressing room and the retail supply corridor.

'I'm here, aren't I?' I open my arms. 'Living proof.'

She frowns. Clearly not the right tack to take.

'I'm sure border control stamped it when I arrived,' I lie, knowing full well they didn't. And since then, all my travel inside Brazil had been with Marina and her hydrogen-powered private jet.

'It was Christmas, maybe it was busy and they forgot.' I smile, hoping to engender a remnant of festive spirit. She scowls back at me. 'Or perhaps the ink faded …'

She shakes her head. 'Your visa is invalidated.'

Merda.

'Your employer will have to contact the authorities to prove you are still employed.'

Difficult, as I haven't done any work for several weeks.

'In the meantime, please come with me.'

That's not going to happen.

I turn on my heel and walk out of the airport.

I need to get back on the road. I need to find the mine where Crazy Gloves was filming.

I'm going to need some help.

That help isn't coming from Marina any more.

I pick up my phone and dial.

Cambridge, England, January

Snow had fallen while Frank was in the Pelupent office. The last of the winter sunshine was blinding, reflected from the complex crystals that clung to every surface: the roads, the pavements, the roofs and spires.

He decided to leave his bike in the lockup and walk back to the centre – bicycles were no good in snow and he wanted to reflect on what he had found. What had he found exactly? A message from the Curitiba Federal Police attaching a CCTV still of Jaqueline Silver on a motorbike. Nick hadn't yet opened the message. And now he never would. Frank took a photo of the screen and then deleted the email from Nick's inbox.

Frank took a shortcut over Clare College bridge and strode diagonally across the Backs, making firm imprints in the fresh snow.

Back in his flat, Frank poured a whisky and dialled his boss's direct number.

'Can you talk?'

'Sure, Frank. Good to hear from you.'

'Just wanted to give you a progress update.'

'Fire away,' Graham said.

'The good news is that we can close the Russia question down pretty swiftly.' Before he became a criminal, the Spider had been an accountant by profession, and a smart one at that. 'There's not a trace of any profit being made by Zagrovyl UK from the whole sorry affair.'

'Good.'

'Pelupent have found some transfer-price wrinkles that could be improved. I'll ask Robin to update the UK policies.' Not for the first time, Frank was glad that his UK financial controller had been such a stickler for the rules. 'But the UK accounts are clean.

There's nothing for the OPCW to see. We can have the final report in a couple of weeks.'

'I can hear a but coming.'

Graham Dekker was no fool.

'Do I have a budget?'

'Whatever you need.'

'I'd like to commission a separate investigation. Without involving Pelupent.'

'Connected with Russia?'

'No, this concerns … a different region.'

'I see.'

'I don't want to alarm anyone until I've … established a few facts.'

'I see.' Graham coughed. 'Why don't you keep me informed on a need-to-know basis, Frank.' Both men knew that this was not a secure line. 'No need to involve me in every detail, eh?'

'Exactly my thoughts, Graham.' Plausible deniability, that was what senior executives demanded.

'Use your company credit card for any justifiable expenses. The bills come direct to my finance team. I'll tell them not to quibble over details. You're a trusted emp …' Frank heard the word employee before Graham corrected himself, '… executive.'

'Thank you, Graham.'

Frank cut the call and turned on his laptop.

Time for a trip to Brazil to see what mischief Jaq Silver was up to.

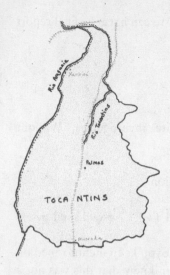

2km from the gold mine, Tocantins, Brazil, January

Whatever Hugo had been expecting, it was certainly not this. The wooden cabin occupied three-quarters of the elevated platform – a private tree house simply furnished, with a bed, a chest of drawers, a chair and desk. All the furniture was wood, hand carved with some skill, and the walls were alive with flowering plants.

A small window looked out onto the far side of the quarry and the jungle beyond. A curtain of vines led to a balcony garden with a rainwater shower and toilet closet.

Hugo had searched for an electric socket to charge his phone, but there was none. Nor was there any phone signal or internet. The room had no books.

Hugo emerged from the shower and looked around for his clothes, but they had vanished, spirited away while he washed. In their place was a clean white kaftan. He slipped it over his head and strode to the door. The handle turned, but the door remained closed.

He banged his fist against it with all his might. After a while he heard footsteps.

'Wait.'

The lock crunched and the door opened. The bare-chested giant blocked his exit.

'Why is my door locked?' Hugo protested.

'For safety.'

Whose safety, Hugo wondered. What threat could an unarmed scientist pose in this fortress? Or were there rogue elements in the complex who might attack a guest? An unwilling guest.

'When do I meet the Colonel?'

'Tomorrow.'

The man stood aside to let the boy enter with a tray of food, placing it on the desk.

'Thank you.' Hugo frowned. 'I have to leave early tomorrow.'

'Tomorrow.' The boy smiled back.

The door slammed shut, the bolt slammed home.

A crash from the balcony woke him in the middle of the night. He sat up and peered through the vines. Something hopped across the wooden planks outside. As he approached, he identified the bird as a hyacinth macaw, a large parrot with cobalt blue plumage and vibrant yellow markings around the eyes and beak. With a squawk, it backed away from him. He saw that it was in distress. One shimmering wing hung down by its side, trailing along the ground.

'Hey big fellow,' Hugo said. 'Take it easy.'

He selected some fruit from the dinner tray, a segment of *pequi* and a slice of peach, pushing them out onto the balcony before drawing back. After a while he heard the swish of dragging feathers and the tap tap of a sharp beak.

'Looks like a broken wing to me,' Hugo said from the shadows. 'Want me to take a look?'

The shriek told him all he needed to know.

In the morning, the bird was still there, huddled in the corner of the balcony. When Hugo went to wash, it panicked, flapping its good wing against the balustrade in a hopeless attempt to escape, screaming with unearthly cries.

The boy cleared away the dinner tray and laid out a light breakfast.

'My clothes?' Hugo asked. 'My shoes?'

The boy nodded and left.

Hugo sat cross-legged on the floor, just behind the curtain. Beside him lay the padding, bandage and small splint he'd extracted from his rucksack.

He took a berry from the breakfast tray and rolled it out onto the balcony.

'I won't know if that wing can be fixed unless you let me take a look,' he said, speaking softly. 'You birds have amazing bones. It could be healed in a couple of weeks. Why don't you let me try?'

When the boy brought a lunch tray, Hugo asked again for his clothes, angry this time.

The boy smiled. 'Tomorrow.'

By evening, the bird was barely moving.

'I'm leaving tomorrow,' Hugo said. 'But I can't just abandon you. That broken wing will kill you.'

Hugo stepped out onto the balcony.

'I'm sorry to have to do this, I know you're frightened, but I'm coming to get you. It's for your own good.'

Hugo bent down and wrapped a towel round the bird. It squawked and trembled, so he started singing, a nonsense song from school.

Flip, flap, flippety flop
Tra-la-la la la
Hop, skip, lickety lock
Tra-la-la la la

Inside the room, he inspected the wing, extending it away from the body.

'Well, there's good news and bad news, pal. Bad news – wing's definitely broken. Needs an X-ray and a vet. Good news – it's a simple fracture, clean break and no wound. I can do my best to pull the bones close together. Then the rest is up to you. At worst, you'll be comfortable, with a bit of luck you might even fly again.'

Hugo manipulated the broken bones together, then immobilised the wing as best he could, winding the bandage tightly, pinning both wings to the bird's breast.

He made a nest with a clean towel, and once the bird was settled, rewarded it with another berry.

When the boy came with dinner, he spotted the bird, crouching down to stroke its head, reaching into his pocket to feed it a nut.

SILVANIA

1,500km from the gold mine, a freight train, Silvania, Goiás State, Brazil, February

Clickety clack-clickety clack.

The freight train, *Siderurgia Special,* thunders across Brazil pulling three hundred wagons, each one different.

My perch under the overhang of a gondola protected me from the worst of the sun, but it is too cramped to stretch out. I'm frightened of falling asleep in case I fall onto the track.

The train must stop soon. I need to rest.

As the day turns to night, dark clouds appear and the heavens open. At first the rainwater is welcome, but soon I am wet through.

I smell the steelworks – hot metal and sulphur – before I spot the fiery-red sparks shooting from a tall chimney.

The brakes squeal and the train pulls into a giant goods yard.

I jump down to investigate.

An empty train, a brand new locomotive pulling wagons built for iron ore, pulls out of the sidings.

I select a wagon and climb on board the mine train.

26
Fe
Iron
55.854

Brazil's iron-mining industry was worth around US$ 50 billion in 2013, with 368,270,000 tonnes produced.

Iron is used to make machinery, tools, rails, ships, concrete reinforcing bars, and the load-carrying framework of buildings. Pure iron is quite soft, so it is usually alloyed with other elements (nickel, chromium, manganese, niobium etc) to make steel.

São Paulo, Brazil, January

It's disconcerting to be back in the Tecnoproject office. The textures are unchanged: concrete, glass, chrome and leather. The noises are familiar: an open-plan office buzzing with human activity. Everything appears the same, but everything has changed. I have changed.

Bruno called me to say that Marco has jumped ship rather than face a sexual harassment investigation. Good riddance.

I ignore my former colleagues and march straight to Bruno's office.

'Jaq!' he stands up, walks round his large desk to embrace me. I try not to recoil at the heat of his moist breath on my cheek, grateful that his fleshly lips don't make contact as he air kisses me, one side then the other.

'Happy New Year!'

'To you too,' I say.

He pulls back to look at me then motions to a group of chairs set round a low table.

'Coffee?' he asks.

I'm about to refuse, to save time and trouble, but I am a more decisive, less accommodating person now, and coffee is a power pause and suddenly seems like an excellent idea. 'Please.'

He gives the order to his secretary, collects a file from his desk drawer and sits down opposite me. Everything feels new and strange. It seems like an eternity since I last sat in this office.

'How was your holiday?'

He's studying me intently. What does he see exactly? I know I am leaner and paler than before. Can he see how thin my skin is? Can he sense the rage that bubbles just under the surface?

'Tiring,' I say. 'I had some family business to take care of.'

Bruno takes off his glasses and folds them carefully.

'I saw you on TV.'

I blush. Marina had advised me to tell Bruno the real reason for moving to Brazil. She suggested he might help in the search. But I didn't want my boss to think I was less than fully committed to the job that was funding my search.

I should have realised I couldn't keep anything a secret, should have anticipated the popularity of the TV show *The Missing*. After all, its reach was exactly why I had agreed to appear. I had opened up my heart to César in front of TV cameras in the hope that my message would get to the right person.

It did.

I blink back tears.

'I'm sorry. I should have told you that I had … a son in Brazil.'

I almost choke on the word had. When I came to Brazil, my son was alive. A happy young man who lived to hang out with friends and surf the ocean. And now he's dead. Because of me. But I can't tell anyone, or they'll try to stop me doing what I have to do next.

'But it doesn't stop me from working.'

Bruno nods as if he understands. He doesn't. No one does.

'Are you still searching?' he asks.

I nod. It's not quite a lie. The truth is my search has become a lot simpler, much more serious. I'm no longer searching for my son, but for the man who murdered him.

'And you're well enough to be back at work?' he asks.

'Yes,' I lie. I need the visa fixed so I can fly. I need the money to travel. I need this job.

'How's it going with Áerex?'

'All finished,' I say. I'm finished with Marina whether she likes it or not.

He raises an eyebrow.

'I'd like to focus on something different,' I say.

'I see,' he says.

He opens the file and shuffles through some papers.

'The work from Cuperoil should be coming through soon.'

The imminent Curitiba safety studies were the reason Tecnoproject employed me. The scope documents had been due to land 'next week' ever since I started here six months ago, and there is still no sign of them. Is Bruno just relentlessly optimistic? Is there a problem? What do I care, so long as he pays me.

'Good,' I say. The platitudes come easily. 'Until then, is there anything else I could do?'

'Couple of projects in bio-ethanol; energy efficiency rather than safety, but you might want to take a look.'

'Sure,' I lie. 'And anything in our mining division?'

He's seen the TV programme, so he knows about the gold mine I inherited from my grandmother.

'Let me get this clear, Dr Silver.' He shakes his head. 'You own a gold mine and want me to pay you to learn about mining?'

'It's not what you think,' I say.

And it's not. I don't want the gold. I want to find the man I'm going to kill. I can't tell Bruno that. I can't afford for him to fire me. If he does, how do I stay in Brazil?

'I'm an explosives expert. I've worked on mine safety before. I can make myself useful.'

'I have no doubt you can.' Bruno sighs. 'So where is your gold mine, exactly?'

I can't tell him that because I have no idea. Someone destroyed the original deeds held in a bank vault in Angola. Someone else – or the same organisation? – stole the copies of the deeds from a lawyer's office in Lisbon. Crazy Gloves stole the maps and schedules, engraved copper plates that were hidden inside the fabric of my grandmother's strongbox when he reneged on the ransom deal.

Where is my gold mine? It could be anywhere. But wherever it is, that's where Crazy Gloves will be found. I try distraction.

'It's very small,' I guess. 'Uneconomic.' As many mines are if you care about the true cost to the environment. 'I only mentioned it on TV to try and get my son's attention.'

This last part is true. Telling the world – or at least the world's 250 million Portuguese speakers – was the price I'd paid to interest the TV company in my story, to persuade César to run the appeal.

If I'd known the real price, I would never have agreed.

A lump forms in my throat.

'Mining is an uncivilised business,' he says. 'Rough and tough.'

'I don't care.'

'There aren't many female engineers in the field.'

'I can look after myself.'

Bruno bites his lip.

'Let me have a think.'

I hand him my passport. 'Any chance you can sort my visa out for me in the meantime?'

Bruno smiles. 'A six-month extension?'

I nod. Six months should be more than enough to find Crazy Gloves and kill him. After that I don't really care.

Bruno nods. 'I'll get my *despachante* straight on to it.'

London, England, to São Paulo, Brazil, January

Frank Good hovered outside the lingerie shop. The models who paraded up and down on the big screen were arresting, if a little intimidating. Brash, starving Amazonians with razor-sharp cheek-bones and six-pack stomachs were not really his cup of tea. He favoured something smaller, softer, rounder, less ferocious, more submissive.

Someone like Clara.

He dialled her number.

'Frank!' Her voice flowed like honey. 'Is it true? You're finally coming to Brazil?' She trilled her Rs, putting him in mind of a purring cat.

Their affair at the Zagrovyl company conference in Shanghai

had been brief and discreet. And exciting – the first time he had felt fully satisfied since Sophie had been bundled off to prison – but he hadn't given Clara another thought after they'd gone their separate ways.

'On my way,' he said.

'I'm at the beach house, but I can fly back to São Paulo, show you around.'

'No need,' Frank said. 'I have some business to take care of.'

'Maybe I can help?'

'Clara, you'd be far too much of a distraction,' he said.

Her laugh was deep, almost guttural.

'But maybe we could meet afterwards?' he offered.

He could hear her clap her little hands. 'Why don't you come and stay with me at the beach?'

He'd been working insanely hard and more than deserved some time to relax. A few days by the beach sounded exactly right. 'Perfect.'

Frank didn't stop to wonder why Clara was so keen. He knew there was more to her invitation than a desire to see him again. A shrewd business operator, she had no qualms about mixing business with pleasure: in that they were dangerously alike.

Clara headed up the Zagrovyl operation in Brazil. She'd been open in requesting his support for green energy expansion in South America, including a search for new rare-earth deposits, those tricksy little metals that went into wind turbines and solar panels, electric batteries and mobile phones. Everyone knew that it was a waste of effort. Both the Right and the Left opposed it. The Right because as long as Brazil had oil, there was no market for more expensive renewables. The Left because the environmental lobby opposed all new mining that was purely for export.

Cambridge in January meant cold and damp. A few days of sunshine and sex in the southern hemisphere was too attractive a combination to turn down.

Frank entered the lingerie shop, ignored the smiling assistant, and took in the stock at a glance. Leopard-skin bondage corsets, however appealing, were probably a risk for a second date, so he moved on to a rack of negligees. With a clear mental picture of Clara's voluptuous body, he could make a fair guess at her vital statistics and chose a low-cut confection of silk and lace: saucy and sophisticated.

Clara wasn't the only reason for his trip.

A former Zagrovyl employee, a name he had hoped never to hear again, was in Brazil. Why? What was she up to this time?

And what was her connection to Pelupent and the Zagrovyl corruption investigation?

Whatever it was that Jaqueline Silver was up to, Frank intended to find out.

The plane flew over the ring of hills that surrounded São Paulo in ever-decreasing circles. The tops of a few skyscrapers peeked out from a sea of thick, brown smog. As the plane descended into the miasma, Frank stared out of the window and began to make out the city arteries, clogged with traffic. First impressions were not encouraging.

Clara had offered to show him her city. Frank refused, and he was glad of that now. He had no interest in yet another atherosclerotic megalopolis. Once you'd seen one, you'd seen them all. Too many people with too many cars crammed into too little space.

As a first-class passenger, he embarked ahead of the crowd and passed through immigration and customs before the rabble on the jumbo jet could catch up and cause problems. He'd elected to stay overnight in an airport hotel and a representative was there to meet him and drive him the short distance to his glass and concrete haven.

The bell boy opened the door to his room and placed the suitcase on the stand. With this international luxury chain, Frank was assured of air conditioning, fast internet, reliable plumbing and a firm bed. It comforted him that the rooms were the same everywhere in the world. Same size, same layout, same quality of cotton sheet, same weight of quilt, same range of pillows, same brands of spirit in the mini-bar, same coffee maker and same room-service menu. The familiar sterility of the brand was soothing. A successful businessman like Frank had enough change to contend with in his fast-paced, wheeler-dealing job, he didn't need it in his free time.

The bell boy lingered, hovering with a passive-aggressive tip-me-to-get-rid-of-me smirk. Frank sent him away empty-handed and yawned.

Plenty of time to wash and sleep and shave. He had something important to do before meeting Clara.

São Paulo, Brazil, January

The Tecnoproject office is a safe place now that Marco has left the company: bright lights and smooth surfaces, aftershave and coffee, click-clack of computer keys and whir of printers. I spend my time on internet searches: Ecobrium, gold mining. I attend mine-safety meetings. I print the stills from César's show, the ones with Crazy Gloves in front of a working mine.

I show them to one of the geologists.

'I couldn't even begin to guess where that is,' he says. 'If anyone can help you, it's Fergus.'

'Fergus?'

'Our mining expert from Perth, Australia.'

I look around. 'Where is he?'

'Oh, he doesn't come to the office – he's a field guy.'

'How do I contact him?'

'I'll get him to call you.'

When my phone rings later that day, I reply without checking the number.

'Jaq. At last!'

My heart sinks. It's my lawyer, and friend, from Portugal.

'Carmo, hi.'

'How's things?'

'Busy.' The shorthand for, I don't want to talk to you right now. Not until I've done this thing I need to do.

'I'll keep this brief, then,' she says. 'I spoke to your grandmother's lawyers, challenged the bill, but they claim they need to talk to you. Can you give Advogado Castanho a call?'

'Sure,' I say, although I have no intention of making contact anytime soon.

'Xavier says hi.'

Xavier was my first real boyfriend, though never a lover. Portugal is a small world, Lisbon even smaller, and the Estoril-Cascais coast practically a village where everyone knows everyone else. Xavier is also a friend of Carmo's son.

'He'll be in Brazil for the kitesurfing championships.'

Just what I don't need. Distraction.

'Great!' I lie. 'Where's the competition?'

'Cumbuco, I think. Near Fortaleza.'

A long way north. Brazil is a vast country. There's no need for us to meet.

'Will you call him?' Carmo asks.

How many times has Xavier called me? To wish me a Merry Christmas? To ask how my search was going? To check if I was ever coming back? I never answered his calls. I deleted his voice-mails. I never dialled back.

A spark flared briefly between us, but never ignited. And just as well. Xavier will find someone else. Someone good.

'Jaq, you still there?'

'Yes.'

'Yes, you're still there or yes, you'll call him.'

How can I say no?

'Yes to both.'

'And you'll get in touch with Advogado Castanho in Salvador?'

'Sure.' I try to make my voice sound happy about it. It's not exactly a priority right now.

'Jaq, you don't sound yourself. What's up?'

'Lots going on. Got to fly.' Except I can't fly. Not until I get my visa sorted.

'Later then? Call me?'

'Sure.'

Carmo can tell, I know she can. She's a psychic who reads between the lines, deciphers the silences.

Best that we have no more contact for a while.

Bruno calls me into his office.

'I hear you want to talk to Fergus.'

'Please.'

'Well, I guess you could make yourself useful while we're waiting for the Cuperoil work from Curitiba. Fergus's about to start a tour of mines inland. If you can get yourself to Brasília tonight, you can join him.'

'I don't have a passport.'

Bruno produces it from his desk drawer.

'Lena will sort out travel arrangements.'

As I'm collecting my cash and tickets from Bruno's secretary, I wonder how Bruno managed to get my visa updated so quickly.

Brasília, Brazil, January

The city shimmers in the heat. A wide central axis containing the government buildings is flanked by residential areas on either side, parallel roads curving up like wings. From the air I can just make out the layout.

The flight from São Paulo to Brasília takes less than two hours, although the plane has to circle the city a few times before receiving permission to land. The capital of Brazil has grown too fast for the transport links to cope.

Inside the airport I look around for the man who is meant to meet me.

I spot a sandy-haired, wiry man with blue eyes and thin lips, wearing sturdy leather boots, shorts, a T-shirt and hat. His pale skin shows signs of an outdoor life, freckles joining into darker patches on the reddened skin of his forearms and calves. He's obviously waiting for someone.

I approach. 'Excuse me. Are you Fergus Podger?'

'I might be.' He looks me up and down. 'Who wants to know?' His smile is flirtatious rather than professional.

I hold out a hand. 'I'm with Tecnoproject too.'

A cloud passes over his eyes.

'You're Dr Silver?'

'Call me Jaq.'

'Shit,' he says, 'I thought you would be a man.'

'Sorry to disappoint. Does it matter?'

He grimaces. 'You'll soon see.'

From Brasília, we take a smaller plane that flies across Mato Grosso, almost to the border with Bolivia. My companion makes no effort at further conversation and when I find myself on the opposite end of the plane from him, I wonder if the seating arrangements are deliberate.

It's dark by the time we arrive at a small regional airport.

'You'd best spend the night there.' He nods at a sign for a hotel transfer.

'And you?'

'I'm meeting some guys.' His cold tone tells me I'm not welcome. 'Look, I don't know what Bruno told you, but it's the new wild west out here. Where we're going there are no ... facilities.'

'I'm sure I'll cope.'

'Well, stock up with whatever you need,' he says. 'We're leaving civilisation tomorrow.'

I board a rickety bus. I know I'm in the centre of town when everyone gets out, including the driver. It's an unlovely sight. Wide compacted earth streets flanked by low buildings, the brick unrendered. The hotel has a broken neon sign that fizzes and flashes, and they seem astonished to have a guest and unsure if they can accommodate me. I put down a wad of cash and they promise to try and squeeze me in. The hotel kitchen is closed, but they indicate a bar on the other side of the street that serves food. I take one look inside and decide I am not hungry. If this is civilisation, it is hard to imagine what's coming next.

In the morning things get worse.

The tenderness in my breasts and the ache in my lower back can only mean one thing.

Of all the times my period could possibly arrive early, this has to be the most inconvenient. I wash and go in search of what I need in a *mini-mercado*.

Fergus is late and looks much the worse for wear. He arrives in a Jeep driven by a wiry man with copper skin.

'Dr Silver, meet Candy.'

'Cândido,' the man corrects as we shake hands.

'Call me Jaq.'

Fergus opens the passenger door for me. 'Candy is our driver for the next three days.'

'Cândido,' I say, and the driver flashes me a smile in the mirror.

The bone-rattling, skin-bruising, teeth-grinding, muscle-aching ride in the jeep goes on for hours and hours. Either side of the crude road, the land is scorched, the original forest slashed and burned to provide grazing for cattle. My lower back aches, I feel sick, and when we stop for a 'comfort break' I have to walk for what feels like miles across the flat, ugly landscape to find the first shrub that affords some privacy, glad of the trowel I acquired in the mini-mercado to bury the blood-soaked cellulose acetate.

Fergus waits for me, tapping his fingers on the metal bonnet.

'Best if you sleep in the jeep tonight.' Fergus's Australian accent, with the upward inflexion at the end of every sentence, makes whatever he says sound questionable. 'There's nowhere suitable for your sort out here.'

'My sort?'

'Women.'

'What do men do?'

'We camp.'

'Then I'll camp.'

'You can't lock a tent.'

'Why would I need to lock it?' I guess his implication, but want him to say it out loud. Only by evaluating a threat can the risk be mitigated.

'Look, most of the guys at the mine haven't seen a woman in over a year.'

'They're men, not animals.'

'We'll, ma'am, I'm afraid some of them are both.' He opens the glove box and takes out a pistol. 'If you insist on camping, you'd better take this.'

I shake my head.

He mistakes my refusal for ignorance. 'I can teach you if you like?'

'No need.' I climb back into the jeep.

Curitibanos, Brazil, January

A cock crowed in the distance. The smell of fritters, crisp caramelised batter and sharp, sweet pineapple burst from the kitchen along with the crackling and popping of the boiling oil.

Graça dropped her bag on the kitchen floor and stretched. It had been a long and uncomfortable bus ride after yet another fruitless mission. She missed Silver in Florianópolis, in São Paulo, and then border control in Rio hadn't been able to detain her long enough for questioning.

She waited until her grandmother scooped out the last fritter and turned down the flame before shouting a greeting.

GG turned and a broad smile lit her face, arms open wide for a hug.

They sat at the kitchen table waiting for the fritters to cool. A new object took pride of place in the centre. It took Graça a moment to realise what it was.

'GG! What have you done?'

The rusty metal box from the beach house in Floripa was almost unrecognisable. GG had fixed the tattered leather and covered the box in patterned cloth, a riot of yellow sunflowers and crimson poppies. She'd also replaced the stained, torn silk with smooth wipe-clean plasticised fabric. Graça recognised the bright flowers from the curtains in the upstairs bedrooms and the checked inside from the kitchen tablecloth. GG was always clever with her hands and never threw away any spare fabric.

'All I need to do now is polish up the brass and it'll be good as new!'

Graça's phone rang.

'She's on the move again.' Zélia spoke quietly, a sure sign that

187

there were others in the offices she didn't want to share information with.

Graça knew better than to ask who. Their only communication was about Dr Jaq Silver, a woman they hoped could be persuaded to give evidence against Salty Walter. The exploration director of Cuperoil was a key player in a suspected corruption scheme.

'Where?'

'Congonhas Airport in São Paulo.'

'Where's she heading?'

'Brasília first.'

Graça sighed.

'Want me to go there?'

'No, just a transit stop, she'll be gone before you arrive. I'm sending you ticket details, but it doesn't make a whole lot of sense.'

'Why didn't border control stop her?'

'She has a new visa. That woman must have friends in high places to have had it fixed so fast.'

After eating some fritters, Graça checked her phone.

The copy of the ticket Zélia sent had two legs. São Paulo to Brasília and then seven days later Oriximiná back to São Paulo. Brasília and Oriximiná were 2,500 miles apart. How was she getting from one to the other?

Probably other flights on other airlines, stopping off other places. But where? And why?

Perhaps it didn't matter.

Oriximiná was a tiny airport in the heart of the Amazon, right on the equator. It would be much easier to spot Silver there than in crowded São Paulo. And this way, she had plenty time to prepare. Graça called Zélia. 'Any chance you can get me a flight to Oriximiná?'

Rondônia, Brazil, January

As we get closer to our destination, the flat, featureless landscape becomes more interesting. Red sandstone cliffs rear up ahead. We drive into a canyon, the cliffs growing into mountains, great saw-toothed ridges soaring into a cloudless sky.

In the front, Fergus and the driver start arguing.

Fergus turns to me. 'You still insist on camping?'

'I'll do what you do.'

'Candy here says we should make camp before the mine. He knows this area.'

Cândido turns the jeep onto a side road that winds up out of the valley, stopping on a grassy plateau.

'*Perfeito!*' I exclaim.

Cândido switches from broken English to fluent Portuguese. It has the added benefit that it annoys the hell out of Fergus.

'I'm going to fetch firewood and water,' Cândido says. 'I can show you where to wash if you like.'

'What about him?' I nod at Fergus who is pacing the area with a face like thunder.

'Mr Grumpy?' He rolls his tongue around the word *amuado*. 'Ignore him. He never washes anyway. But if we can keep him away from hard liquor for a couple of days, he becomes almost bearable.'

I prefer to reserve judgement. Grabbing my wash bag and a towel, I set off after Cândido. At the edge of the plateau, a sandy path drops down into a forest. The path levels out a little and before long I can hear water. We emerge from the trees opposite a waterfall, cascading from a notch in the high cliff, straight down into a fast mountain river, creating a deep pool.

'Is it safe to swim?'

'Safest place round here, the water is too fast for predators. No caiman, no piranhas.' He points to the stream. 'Let me get drinking water first and then I'll leave you in peace.' He smiles. 'I have a daughter about your age.'

A coded message of understanding. *You're safe with me.*

'Thanks.'

'You can find your own way back?'

'Yes.'

'Then I'll look after Grumplestiltskin.'

Lying on my back in the centre of the clear mountain pool, I stare up at the extraordinary geological formations. Right in the centre of the South American landmass, it's the most stunningly beautiful, totally unexpected vista.

What will mining do to this landscape?

São Paulo, Brazil, January

Through the tinted windows of the hotel bar, Frank watched the planes taking off and landing, crossing at unnatural angles in the sky. It looked far more precipitous, far more dangerous than it had felt, cocooned in padded comfort inside.

The stranger appeared out of nowhere, a middle-aged man dressed casually in pale chinos and a yellow polo shirt, a leather man-bag slung over his chest. He ordered a Tsingtao beer at the bar and Frank asked for the same.

'Mr Good?'

Frank nodded towards a booth by the window. He indicated a corner seat for his visitor before placing himself with his good ear closest to the private investigator.

'My name is Busco.' The PI placed his beer bottle on a mat. 'I understand you need some help.'

'I'd like you to make some discreet enquiries.'

Busco took a sip of his beer. 'Discreet is my middle name.'

Frank reached into his jacket pocket, pulled out an envelope and laid it on the table.

'I have reason to believe that an ex-employee of Zagrovyl

England is now working in Brazil. Our interests are unlikely to align, so I need to know what she's up to.' He pushed the envelope towards the PI.

Busco opened the flap and pulled out a photograph that showed an attractive woman: tall and curvy with green eyes, olive skin and dark shoulder-length hair. He glanced up at Frank.

'You want a kidnap? That way you can ask all the questions you want.'

A tempting idea. But Frank didn't fancy ending his days in a Brazilian jail. Whatever action he took, or at least anything that could be traced back to him, must be inside the letter, if not the spirit, of the law.

'No kidnap.' Frank was firm. 'Just information.'

'Anything I should know?'

'It's all there.'

Busco's lips moved as he read through the fact sheet.

Dr Jaqueline Silver. Born Luanda, Angola, to an Anglo-Portuguese mother and Russian father. Educated in Moscow, Lisbon and UK. Worked as technical manager at a Zagrovyl site in England, as an explosives expert in the Slovenian Alps and then held a series of international consulting jobs.

Busco looked up. 'There's nothing about her work in Brazil.'

Was the man stupid? 'If I knew what she was doing here, I wouldn't need you.'

'When did she arrive?'

Not just stupid. A cretin. 'I haven't the faintest idea.'

'I can find that out.'

I bloody well hope so. Frank missed his private detective in Teesside. What was his name? Sharp, Bill Sharp. A man of few words and efficient action. Until he went after Jaqueline Silver and met his death in a cold English lake.

'What is your relationship with …' Busco nodded at the photograph, 'this woman.'

What indeed? Jaqueline Silver was the sand in his shoe, the

itch at his ankle, the spasms in his spine, the pain in his neck, the monster of his nightmares. Frank reached into his pocket and found the tablets. He slipped six into his mouth and took a swig of beer.

The first time he set eyes on her, in the chrome and glass reception of Zagrovyl in Teesside, he knew she was trouble. A woman with attitude, asking inconvenient questions. Searching for a colleague he'd taken great care to 'disappear'. Things had gone downhill from there. Frank had no desire to relive those events. So how to answer the question?

'My enemy,' he said.

Busco leered and ventured a guess. 'Former lover?'

'Most certainly not.' Frank shuddered at the thought. 'This assignment is entirely work related.'

'Is she involved in industrial espionage?'

That sounded almost right. If engineers like Jaqueline Silver had their way, half the world's industry would close down tomorrow. Engineering excellence that ignored commercial reality was a form of industrial sabotage.

'I want to know who she's working for. What she's working on.' Frank leant forward. 'How she spends her time. Who she meets.'

Busco nodded. 'My office explained the fee structure?'

This PI came highly recommended, but he didn't come cheap. Still, this was a project in the best interests of Zagrovyl, so it was only fair that they stump up the money for it. Some creative accounting might be required, but they had people for that.

'Yes.'

'Payment in US dollars.'

Brazilian Real (pronounced re-yal or re-iyshe in the plural) was a basket-case of a currency, lurching from hyper-inflation to moribund stagnation. Official interest rates of 14 per cent were more like 140 per cent for the average Brazilian.

'OK.'

'In advance.'

Frank brought out a second envelope, this one stuffed with hundred-dollar bills. He removed half the notes and returned them to his inside pocket. 'The next payment when you bring me something useful.'

Busco shook his head. 'I have no way of knowing what's useful to you. I charge you the hours I spend plus the expenses I incur getting the information you asked for. That's it. This is a cost-plus contract.' He ignored the envelope. 'Unless you want a kidnapping, in which case I can do a fixed price.'

Frank was an expert negotiator, loved the cut and thrust of it, the scent of blood as the battle raged, the surge of power as victory approached. He was a tough adversary, didn't give in easily, but he was also smart enough to recognise the strength of his position. In this case, he was at a disadvantage: in a country he didn't know, among people who spoke a language he didn't understand. And not just Portuguese. He took the money from his jacket pocket, put it back into the envelope and pushed it across the table.

Busco picked up the paper package, opened the flap and riffled the notes with his fingertip.

'How do I contact you?'

Frank slid a business card across the table.

Busco tapped the number 'Your work phone?' He shook his head and pushed the card back. 'Bad idea. Take one of these.' Busco opened his leather bag and pulled out two cheap phones. Using one to ring the other, he then reversed the operation.

'You contact me using the single number in this phone, no other way, OK?'

Frank nodded.

'If it rings, you know it's me. Don't answer if you can't speak freely, but call me back when you can.'

'Understood.'

Busco stood up.

'You'll be hearing from me.'

Rondônia, Brazil, January

Cândido is right. The mining engineer is a different person in the morning. Fergus emerges in time for breakfast in better humour.

As we are packing up, I lay the stills from the TV show on the bonnet of the Jeep and ask Cândido if he recognises the mine.

'It can't be round here,' the driver says.

Fergus comes over to look.

'So, tell me Dr Silver, why are you really here?'

'I want to find this mine.' I point to the stills.

He takes off his glasses and glances at each picture in turn.

'Gold?' he asks.

All that glitters …

'Yes.'

'There are thousands of gold mines in Brazil. It could be anywhere.'

'Can you narrow it down?'

'Illegal?'

'Almost certainly.'

He picks up the picture of a cliff face to stare at it more closely. He nods. 'I can make a guess.'

'Tell me.'

He hands back the photo. 'This is personal, right?'

I lower my eyes and nod.

'But Bruno sent you here to work, right?'

I nod.

'Then we do it my way. First you help me. Then I help you.'

Heaven help me, not another Mario? *You rub my back and I'll rub yours.* I take a step back.

'Before you start looking into illegal mines, you need to understand how the legal ones operate. To understand the difference. Mining companies get a bad press in Brazil. Some criticism is fair, but you have to consider the alternative before you stop them and something else fills the vacuum.'

'Fair enough,' I say. 'But give me a general idea.'

'I'll do better than that. I'll take you there. But not until we've finished the scheduled visits.'

Fergus is in his element out here. At the first mine, he greets the owner and engineers by name, demonstrating his expertise as we tour the new developments. He allows me to translate for him, even going so far as to thank me afterwards.

The mine is just outside the protected area of a national park.

'How do you feel about all this?' I ask Cândido as we sit together in a large tent that serves as a canteen. 'Digging a mine here.'

'If there's gold, people will come.' He shrugs. 'You can no more stop the sun from rising than stop people digging. Better to licence companies who know what they are doing, who employ local people.' He indicated a group of miners. 'Who obey the law to protect the land.'

I lower my voice. 'And you think this company will do so?'

'They have headquarters in other lands. People far away worry about the jaguars and the armadillos, so they employ men like Fergus to reassure themselves.'

Jaq looks over at Fergus, locked in earnest conversation, poring over an engineering drawing spread across one of the canteen tables.

'And Fergus needs people like me.' Cândido places his knife and fork onto his plate. 'We've lost the old ways, the ways of my grandmother.'

'She grew up here?'

'I'm *Caboclo*, part Indian.' Cândido explains. 'My grandmother was from the Bororo people.'

A local tribe, at one with nature.

'How do you feel about the way things have changed?'

'My grandmother died in childbirth. My father had no education. He lived a hard life and drank himself to death. My daughter has a different future. My family need this mine to be successful.'

Trancoso, Brazil, January

If you had the right class of ticket, international air travel could be a positive pleasure. Turn off your phone, sit back and explore the entertainment options while a team of attractive galley staff waited on you hand and foot.

Domestic travel, on the other hand, regardless of class or frequent flyer privileges, was the closest thing to hell.

Frank's plane was packed with extended families heading off on summer holiday: slow pensioners blocking the aisles and noisy children kicking the back of his seat. His one-hour flight left four hours behind schedule. He arrived in the hot, crowded regional airport only to find that his hold luggage had gone astray.

Clara was there, waiting for him.

He'd been unsure about a reunion. One-night stands were usually best left at that. Attempts to reignite a spark that flared in the moment, rekindle a fire without fuel to sustain passion, were often doomed to failure. But he'd completed his other tasks with minimal effort and was free to relax.

She was looking good, better than he'd remembered. Her tight cream business suit was a guaranteed turn-on: straight skirt with side slits that made her tanned legs even longer, wide-collared jacket cinched at the waist, crimson top with a plunging neckline offering a preview of the glorious curves underneath.

He couldn't wait to get her alone.

The car passed the security barrier and swept up the hill, through dense vegetation, stopping in a clearing. Floodlights buzzed into life, and a pair of iron gates opened slowly. As they proceeded up the cobbled drive, Frank couldn't help but be impressed by the view. Not the curving coastline with its white beaches and impossible mountains, but the mansion that stood silhouetted against the dusk. The style was Art Deco, but the construction looked brand new.

Clara didn't wait for the chauffeur to open the car door, jumping out like an excited child, bounding up the steps to the grand entrance.

She turned and beckoned to Frank. 'Come on, I want to show you the pool before it gets dark.'

If the house was impressive from the outside, it was only the start. Teak floors, wide polished boards that glowed in the low light, led to a hall with a double staircase. Marble treads and gilded handrails curved around a sculpture of brass dolphins leaping up towards the crystal chandelier that dangled from the roof, three floors above.

Clara turned right, opening the door into a huge reception room with a granite-lined fireplace deep enough to roast a pig, and then out through French windows to an infinity pool above the bay.

Clara kicked off her shoes. 'Fancy a swim?'

She started unbuttoning her blouse.

Frank took a seat on a lounger. 'I think I'll just enjoy the view.'

He stared at her as she unzipped her skirt and let it fall to the ground.

'Don't be shy,' she said. 'The staff know not to disturb us.'

Frank had never been comfortable with spontaneity unless he'd planned it first. He favoured contrapuntal harmony over freeform jazz. 'I'd rather take a shower.'

She turned, giving him a chance to admire her curved backside as she plunged into the pool.

'Come on in!' she exclaimed.

Frank shook his head.

'You want to see your room?'

Why did she say your room and not our room? Not that he was complaining. In a mansion this size they could have a dozen rooms each.

'Yes, please.'

She climbed from the pool, grabbing a thick towel from a lounger and wrapping it around her body.

'Come on then.' She walked ahead of him to a modern building of low white cubes at the end of the pool.

The suite was generous. Clean modern lines with a dark tiled floor, light painted walls and a varnished wooden ceiling. The bedroom was dominated by a king-sized bed. French windows led to a private terrace with a table and chairs. Wall-to-ceiling mirrors opened onto a closet and then an en suite boasting a large shower and double sink.

A man in a crisp white uniform laid out a selection of emergency clothes – brand new shorts and short-sleeved shirts in Frank's size. More relaxed than his usual wardrobe, but they would have to do until his luggage was recovered.

'May I get you a drink, sir?'

'Gin and tonic,' Frank replied.

By the time he'd showered, his drink was waiting for him on the table, along with Clara in her soft towel.

She raised her glass, a cloudy concoction over ice, topped with an umbrella and a straw.

'Welcome to the pleasure palace.' She clinked her glass with his. 'May your deepest desires be realised here.'

When he kissed her he tasted lime and mint. And something else, something sweet and strong and intoxicating.

Later, as they lay in bed, Frank couldn't help wondering how on earth Clara could afford a house like this.

Minas Gerais, Brazil, January

After leaving the gold mine, we drive for hours before making camp. We set off again before dawn and drive all day to a small airport. We say goodbye to Cândido and fly on to a larger airport where we pick up a hire car.

I take the wheel of the jeep and follow Fergus's directions, travelling over bumpy roads.

We find separate lodgings in a pleasant little town ringed by hills. Fergus disappears for the evening, re-emerging in time for breakfast. The café is a popular spot beside a park, families stopping in on their way to deliver children to school. We sit out in the early sunshine, watching the children play in their last minutes of freedom.

A little boy refuses to leave his swing. His mother points to her watch, cajoling and encouraging. It's not until she offers him a pastry that he agrees to leave. They walk off together, hand in hand.

After breakfast, we're still early for our meeting and Fergus suggests we drive up the hillside to get a better view of the operation. The road deteriorates into a beaten earth track, and either the heat of the sun, or the hairpin bends have me sweating by the time we reach the viewpoint above the mine.

Where the gold mine was high tech and low impact, this is a cruder operation, at least on the surface. And it is very much a surface mine, the skin of the earth has been ripped up and dumped into great piles that stretch as far as the eye can see.

The land beyond the mine separates into two valleys. The main valley is broad and shallow and contains the town where we stopped for breakfast. What was once a mining camp has grown, over the years, into a prosperous town. I can make out the park next to our café, some larger buildings like the school and sports field, a church spire, the fire-brigade tower and hospital chimney. The other branch of the valley is deeper and steeper, a narrow gorge that runs straight down to the river.

'See those?' Fergus points to a series of vast, flat fields, the colours ranging from deep red to pale orange. 'Those are the lagoons.'

And I see now that they are fields of mud and water, not earth. The sun glints on the smooth surface of vast artificial lakes.

'Wastewater?'

Fergus nods. 'This mine extracts low-grade ore. It has to be concentrated before it can be sent to the smelter.'

'There's a refinery here?'

I look around for the chimneys of a furnace where the rock can be roasted until the iron melts.

Fergus shakes his head. 'Most of the iron ore goes straight to China.'

And China burns coal to melt the iron, turns it into steel to build bridges and railways, ports and factories to make and transport all the things the West wants but no longer makes itself.

'What's the price of iron ore?'

'This ore? They'll be lucky if they get US$100 per tonne.'

'And steel?'

'Good quality steel sells for ten times that, over US$1,000 per tonne.'

'So, this country tears its landscape apart, but another country extracts all the value?'

'They do some beneficiation here.' Fergus points at each of the sections in turn. 'Crushing, milling, separation and screening, all requiring vast amounts of water.'

I stare back at the lagoons.

'And what happens to all this waste?'

'You're looking at it. There are five tons of tailings for every tonne of iron concentrate produced here.'

'It stays here?'

'Stored in bigger and bigger lagoons. With higher and higher dams to contain them.'

'For how long?

'It'll take ten thousand years for the earth to recover.'

Fergus points to the earth walls that separate the lagoons. 'This company has operations all over Brazil. I'm here to persuade them to hire Tecnoproject to inspect the tailing dams.'

'Wouldn't it be better to treat the water? Re-use it?'

S&M – simplify, substitute, minimise, moderate, mitigate.

'There's a pilot plant down there.' Fergus points to a collection of tanks and columns below us. 'But this is not like the gold mine we saw. This is a high-volume low-value business. Water is plentiful in this part of the world, and it's hard to justify the cost of recycling.'

That old bollocks. Where there's a will, there's a way.

With the right technology.

How badly do rich countries need steel? For their offices and bridges, cars and aeroplanes, washing machines and fridge-freezers, wind turbines and solar panels. Is desecrating the land the price of growth? How many people know the real cost of their convenience? And if they did, wouldn't they be happy to pay a little more? How is it possible to allow a mine to operate without a technical solution for the waste? Dumping it in a 10,000-year toxic lake doesn't sound like a proper plan.

I stare at the silver towers of absorption columns glinting in the sunlight. This is what engineers are for.

Ingenuity.

Trancoso, Brazil, January

The call from Busco came a few days after their first meeting. Clara was in the shower when the burner phone rang. Frank picked it up and walked into the courtyard.

'Yes?'

His private investigator didn't bother to introduce himself – after all, he was the only one who knew this phone number.

'I intercepted a police report from Florianópolis,' Busco said. 'Shockingly poor cyber security.'

'Why are the Brazilian police interested in Jaqueline?'

'Silver was the sole survivor of a maritime accident. A scientific research boat, *Tartaruga*, vanished a few miles from Santa Catarina Island on Christmas Eve.'

'She has form with boats,' Frank growled. It rankled that she'd never paid compensation for his yacht, *Francium*.

'Silver was picked up from the water on Christmas Day.'

'Injured?' One could always hope.

Busco clicked his tongue. 'Suffering from dehydration and exposure and a minor injury but expected to make a full recovery.'

Frank ground his teeth. Silver had the luck of the devil.

'And the rest of the crew?'

'Found dead in a life raft.' Busco let out a low chuckle. 'The police interviewed her to see if she could throw any light on what happened to the boat, or to the crew.'

'And?'

'She claims there was some sort of malfunction. The boat exploded and she was thrown clear.'

A likely story. Explosions didn't just happen when Jaqueline Silver was around, she generally caused them. 'Who owned the boat?'

'This is where it gets interesting. Have you ever heard of an NGO named Ecobrium?' he asked.

Frank racked his brain. 'Rings a bell.'

'A Brazilian group committed to protecting the environment.'

'A noble aim.'

'Depends on the means employed. This lot favour radical, direct action over legal means.'

'Why are you telling me this?'

'Ecobrium owned the boat that vanished, leaving Silver adrift at sea.'

'Was she working for them?'

'Her visa says not.'

'Go on.'

'Silver was granted a fast-track visa at the Brazilian embassy in London. She flew to São Paulo in July last year. Her visa was sponsored by an engineering consultancy called Tecnoproject.'

Frank's fingers flew over the keyboard until he found the website and clicked on the automatic translation. A small engineering consultancy based in São Paulo. Fewer than a hundred employees, or associates as they were called.

'Tecnoproject carry out early design and safety studies for engineering projects. They also have a safety contract with Cuperoil, a state oil company, with a handful of engineers based in the refineries at Curitiba and Salvador.'

Frank clicked into their latest financial statement. If there was one thing he had learned from his enemy the Spider, it was the power of numbers to tell a story.

'They have a suspiciously high turnover for such a small company,' Frank remarked. If the numbers were right, each of their associates was bringing in several million dollars a year.

'They're well connected politically,' Busco said.

'What does that mean?'

'In Brazil, it means everything.'

'And what is she doing for them?'

He struggled to imagine Jaqueline Silver creating value in Brazil. Trained in the old ICI school of engineering, every detail on paper before getting on with construction, she was the sort who saw risk everywhere. He'd had his fill of her sort of time-wasting, pen-pushing engineers when he ran the Zagrovyl operation in Teesside. Forget lean, mean and fast – the cheapest way to achieve the desired business goal – Jaqueline and her sort always wanted gold-plated engineering – designs so complex they were always overpriced and late.

'She's here as a visiting expert.'

An expert in causing chaos, triggering trouble. Wherever Jaqueline Silver went, mayhem followed.

'Jaqueline is their highest-billing engineer.'

Really? Could she have changed that much? He doubted it. Yes, she worked hard, yes, she was smart, but her interest had never been in maximising profit for the companies that employed her. She seemed more concerned with the welfare of employees and safety of neighbours. All very laudable until you looked at the price tag.

'Where has she been working?'

'The hours billed are all from Cuperoil in Curitiba, but the only records of work delivered are a few days consulting with Áerex.'

So what work was Jaqueline Silver doing for a Brazilian state oil company that justified a charge of several million dollars?

'So, what's the connection with – what did you call the eco-nutters?'

'Ecobrium. Exactly what the Brazilian police want to know.'

'Is she under arrest?'

'They haven't pressed any charges, but she's attracted the attention of the military as well.'

'Attention?'

'Opprobrium.'

'Meaning?'

'Displeasure.'

'I know what the word means.' Frank made a tsk-tsk of irritation. 'What action is likely to follow.'

'I'm working on my contacts to find out.' Busco cleared his throat. 'The Brazilian military know how to deal with radicals.'

'Just keep me informed of any developments.'

'That's what you pay me for.'

'That,' Frank said. 'And more.'

When the time comes.

Or perhaps her time had already come.

If Frank left things alone, it sounded as if others would take care of Silver for him.

And where was the satisfaction in that?

Minas Gerais, Brazil, January

We drive back down the mountainside to the mine offices and are greeted by Luis, the assistant engineer who takes us on a tour.

It's only as we are walking across the broad, flat tops of the packed-earth walls that separate and contain the huge lakes of mud and wastewater that I begin to understand how these dams are constructed.

You dig a big hole in the ground to get at the rocks containing iron. You crush the solids and slurry them in water to separate out the useful minerals. The solid waste – earth and rock pulverised to sand – is used to build dikes to prevent the contaminated waste-water being released into the farmland and rivers below.

And there you have it, a tailings dam. As the mine grows, the walls become higher to contain more and more water.

'Why is that one different?' I ask. Across the narrower valley a curved concrete wall forms a secondary barrier between the mine and the river that snakes far below.

'Part of our environmental improvement plan,' Luis explains. 'To ensure no contaminated water reaches the river.'

'What about the town?'

Unlike the river, the town is not visible from the mine.

'It's a long way away.'

By road perhaps, but I had a bird's eye view from the shoulder of the mountain. Water flows downhill. And if the direct route is closed off, thanks to the new concrete dam, then it will find the next easiest path. The broader, inhabited valley has nothing but an earth bund protecting it.

'But there are people down there,' I protest.

'Which is why this mine has remote monitoring.'

As we walk across the main dike, a pyramid of earth with a flattened top, Luis points to the sensors, wires sticking out of the downstream wall every ten metres.

'What are you measuring?'

'Any movement suggesting a loss of stability,' Luis replies.

'And then what?'

'It triggers an evacuation alarm.'

'Can the people in the village hear an alarm up here?'

'There are loudspeakers with repeaters all down the valley.' He looks at his watch. 'You'll hear it shortly. We test it weekly at noon.'

I nod and smile and try to focus on something else to dampen the rising anxiety. I'm only here because Fergus has promised to help me locate the gold mine, the place where Crazy Gloves sent his TV broadcast from. I'm not the expert; Fergus is. These guys must know what they're doing. The only part of mining I understand is blowing things up.

'Do you use explosives?' I ask.

'Yes, it's a critical part of the operation.'

'Can I visit your explosives store?'

It's bang on noon when the alarm sounds. I'm walking down from the explosive store, across the corrie below the mine.

Fergus and Luis are back on the top of the dam. I stayed below to talk fuse design with Tiro, the blasting technician, a welcome distraction to get lost in a subject I understand.

Tiro is preparing to remove some bedrock. His assistant is nowhere to be seen, so I pitch in. He seems glad to have someone take an interest in what he's doing, and more than happy to have an extra pair of expert hands.

As the klaxon shrieks, I cover my ears. The noise cascades down the valley as repeaters relay the test warning. Luis was right, it would be hard to miss the alarm. I wonder if they do regular evacuation drills to see how long it takes to get everyone to safety?

Despite the palms pressed against my ears, I sense a clap of thunder. I look up at the sky but there are no rain clouds.

The next vibration comes through my feet. I scan for heavy vehicles. The mine trucks have wheels twice as tall as me and can move hundreds of tonnes with their huge shovels. But there is no sign of movement nearby. I look back to the explosives store, but all is quiet.

The test must be over by now, but the klaxons are still shrieking, making it hard to isolate or interpret the other noises. A rumbling that's building to a growl.

A note even higher than that of the klaxon cuts through.

A scream.

A whistle.

As the clamour grows from a growl to a roar, I turn to see a section of the dam folding and a wave of red-brown mud advancing towards me.

I run.

The need to move, to get away from the slurry that is about to engulf me, spurs my actions. I've done these calculations before; it's moving too fast.

The dam is ten metres high. It stores a million tonnes of silt and mud and water. The potential energy is mass multiplied by height multiplied by the acceleration due to gravity. All that potential energy will become kinetic energy. A little lost to heat and sound, but the rest converted to one half the mass times the velocity squared. Mass appears on both sides of the equation and can be ignored. Ten metres times 9.81 metres per second squared gives 98.1 m^2/s^2. Multiply both sides by two and take the square root and you get 14m/s. Multiply by 3,600 and that wave is going to move at 50km per hour. Faster than I can possibly run.

The wall of speeding, suffocating slurry is less than 500 metres away, I have about thirty seconds to escape. I can't outrun the wave, I must go sideways, find a way to get above it – my only chance.

I change direction, running diagonally towards the taller structures of the wastewater treatment plant, wasting precious seconds to find the access gate, vaulting a low fence, making a beeline for the vertical ladder on the outside of an absorption column. As

I start to climb, my hands slick with sweat, muddy feet slipping and sliding, I hear the wave approaching, booming and bellowing. I feel the filthy spray on the back of my neck, loaded with tiny projectiles that pierce and scour. Only a few seconds before the deluge will reach me. I don't dare look down as I scramble upwards, thigh muscles burning, hands jumping two rungs at a time to pull as well as push.

The noise is deafening as the wave crashes into the fence and topples it. I continue to ascend, and only when I get to the first platform do I dare look back. Through a V-shaped break in the dam, the mud is pouring through, racing down the channel, heading for the river. Was anyone else in the corrie? Is anyone hurt? I scour the stream of mud. It's lapping at my feet and rising.

'Up here!'

A man in a hard hat and boiler suit holds out a hand. I continue up the vertical ladder until I reach it and he pulls me onto the top platform.

'Are you OK?'

'A bit shaken.' I nod at the other water treatment plant workers who have congregated on the top platform. 'And you – did everyone get away?'

'Yes,' he says. 'There's a breech alarm in the control room. We evacuated immediately. We didn't think you'd make it.'

I nearly didn't.

'What about the other guy?'

'You mean Tiro, in the explosives store?'

Boiler suit gets on the radio. It crackles and then I hear the voice of the technician.

'Tiro is fine.' He takes off his hard hat and runs a hand over dark hair. 'It wasn't him I saw. There was another guy down there.'

'I was alone.'

'Someone came down from the dam, ran after you.'

We search the hillside but there is no sign of life. Whoever it was, they have disappeared.

And the danger isn't over yet.

The mountains tower over the mine. A series of deep red wounds criss-crossing the earth where the iron ore has been wrenched from the hillside. To my left is a steep gorge leading to a river valley; behind me is a broader valley at the base of which is a sleepy little town.

From high up on the pilot wastewater treatment plant, I can see the new danger.

The mud is smashing up against the concrete dam that protects the river, rebounding and moving sideways, towards the secondary dam. By closing off one route, by focussing on environmental protection of the river, they have left another route wide open. And that route leads to the town with its school and parks, hospital and houses.

The people in the town won't heed the alarm. It sounds every week at noon, they'll assume it's a test, be going about their business as normal.

'We have to evacuate the town.'

'I tried. The power's been knocked out. I can't reach them.'

'Then we have to open the overspill.'

'We need permission for that.'

'Then get permission.'

'It'll take hours.'

'We don't have hours.' I point to the red water under the earth dike. 'Look, it's not going to hold.'

I know what we have to do.

But is there enough time?

I clamber up onto the pipe bridge linking the water treatment structure to the side of the valley. A loose metal lattice supports the treated water pipe, which is pumped back up to the mine. It's about 10 inches in diameter, less than a foot wide, but I've run across ridges trickier than this.

I take a step, slip, catch myself on the pipe bridge, haul myself back up onto the pipe. My boots are too rigid, too muddy for this. I sit down and take them off, followed by my socks, and throw them back to the structure. One boot misses, bouncing of a diagonal beam and I watch it fall, tumbling over and over until it is swallowed in the seething river of mud below.

'I can't do it.'

I look back. The man in the hard hat is white faced and shaking.

'It's OK,' I say. 'Stay here.'

I glance at the sea of mud below me. As I feared, the breach is widening. It won't be long before the whole dam collapses, and the secondary barrier has no hope of withstanding the full onslaught.

'What are you going to do?'

'Radio Tiro. Tell him we need to blast an overspill.'

Barefoot, I stand up. My tightrope is a water pipe. I look up, focus on the scrub-covered slope on the far side of the valley.

'Come back.' Hard-hat puts out a hand. 'It's too risky.'

He's quite right. I'm steady on my feet, unafraid of heights, but the consequences of a slip would be fatal. If the fall doesn't kill me, I will drown in mud. Looked at in isolation this is an insane endeavour. But what is the alternative? Risk is rarely isolated, it's the balance of risk that matters.

I think of the little boy on the swing. His reluctance to abandon play to go to school. How many other children are at risk? How many adults? I might not have been able to save my own son, but I can't give up on a whole town.

I test the shoulder of the pipe with my bare soles, my feet slightly splayed, arches squarely on the top, toes curving to the edge one way, heels counterbalancing in the other direction. I don't look down but focus on my destination, a hundred metres away. I move lightly, swiftly, directly forward.

Over the abyss.

Trancoso, Brazil, January

Frank and Clara ate lunch outside in the garden, in a little pavilion with muslin curtains to keep the insects out. Afterwards, they got down to business.

Clara was dozing when the burner phone pinged. Frank slipped out of bed and wrapped a towel around his hips.

'Yes?'

'Some pictures for you. Texting a secure link.'

Frank left the bedroom and took a seat in the courtyard.

'Pictures of what?'

'Photos of the flat the target is living in.'

'And why should I care about her domestic arrangements?'

'You said she wasn't wealthy?'

'She's deep in debt.'

'Then you might wonder how she can afford to live in such luxury. Password is garden with a capital G.'

'I'll call you back.'

Frank extracted the laptop from his briefcase, typed in the link from the burner phone and went through the security. He flicked through the photos. Busco wasn't going to challenge any estate agents in the arms race of professional exaggeration, but the pictures were good enough to show that this was no ordinary apartment.

Frank called Busco back.

'New boyfriend?'

'Doesn't look like it. She's living there alone. All 150 square metres of prime São Paulo real estate for one contract engineer.' Busco clicked his tongue against his teeth. 'Did you notice the paintings on the wall?'

Frank scrolled back through the pictures. He recognised most of the artists. Miró, van Gogh, Picasso.

'What about them?'

'Originals.'

Frank whistled through his teeth. 'How much are they worth?'

'Anywhere between a million dollars for the Miró to priceless for the Picasso. And check out the garage.'

Frank glanced at a trio of gleaming motorbikes. They didn't do anything for him; he preferred four wheels.

'Collectors' editions. A 1941 Harley Davidson, a 1949 E90 AJS Porcupine and a 1952 Vincent Black Lightning. Probably worth as much as the paintings.'

'So, who owns all this?'

'Last photo.'

Frank zoomed into a photo of unopened mail. An official tax demand was addressed to *O Proprietário*, Walter Salgado.

Frank had attended a school where Latin was compulsory up to age 15. He'd loathed it at the time, but it gave him a key to understanding Portuguese. The absurd accents, hissing consonants and swallowed vowels made it impossible to communicate verbally. But when it was written down he could decipher meaning. And could see that Walter Salgado owed tax to the city of São Paulo as the owner of the apartment.

'And who is Walter Salgado?'

The splish-splash of the shower told him that Clara had given up waiting for him.

'You might find this next link quite interesting.'

Ping!

'Password car wash, all one word with a capital C.'

Frank typed the link into his laptop and went through the security again. The file contained hundreds of documents: bank statements, certified accounts, contracts.

He yawned. 'I'll need time to look at this.'

'My time is your time.'

'I'll call back.'

Frank locked his computer, walked through the bedroom with its sweaty tangled sheets to the en-suite bathroom. Through frosted glass, he could see Clara taking matters into her own hands. Now then, that would never do. A man had his pride. And his was stirring. He shrugged off his bathrobe and slid the door open.

'May I join you?'

It was almost dusk when Clara rose from the bed and started to dress.

'Don't cover up,' Frank ordered. 'I like to see you naked.' And it was true. She had a magnificent body, almost sculpted.

She laughed and cinched the belt tighter around her waist.

'Good night, Frank.'

She was leaving?

'Don't go.' He regretted the words as soon as they were out of his mouth. They sounded needy. Frank was sated and had no need of Clara right now.

'People are arriving soon.'

'People?'

'Ahead of the party.'

It was a big villa, but he hadn't envisaged having to share it.

He sat up in the bed. 'How many people will be staying here?'

'Well, there are my young cousins.'

His heart sank at the prospect of screaming children running amok and disturbing his peace. 'How young?'

'Early twenties, I believe.' She smiled. 'Carrie's a gymnast, Ruby and Jade are both dancers.' She pouted at the mirror as she refreshed her lipstick. The previous layer had rubbed off on his body, her pillow, his cock. 'I think you'll like them.'

He appraised her. 'I'm sure I will.' What exactly was she playing at?

'And then later, for the party, there is Congressman Soares and ...'

'Soares as in the minister of mines?'

She nodded 'And Crispin his geologist, Salty from Cuperoil, Grigory from the bank and ...' she raised a lovely eyebrow, and, of course, my husband.'

Minas Gerais, Brazil, January

Demolition is a skill. A different skill from construction, but a skill nonetheless.

Demolition with explosives is the most difficult of all. Placing the charges at the right points to direct the energy to the weakest areas, ensuring the structure collapses into itself instead of shattering and flying out in all directions.

The last time I did this was in Slovenia, when a melting glacier formed a new lake that hung above a skiing village. A small, controlled explosion opened a path for the water to escape in a different direction and join a mountain river. The level of the lake subsided, and the village was saved.

But I had weeks to survey, to talk to the geologists, to calibrate and measure, to set off trial explosions in similar rock.

Now I have minutes rather than months.

Tiro is waiting for me.

'What can we do?'

I point to the concrete dam.'

'I need your help,' I say. 'We need to create an overspill before the secondary barrier fails completely.'

'What about the river?'

'It's a choice between the river and the town.'

He pales. 'My wife and daughter are down there.' He shows me his mobile. 'I tried to reach them, to warn them, but there's no signal.'

Something must have knocked out the mobile mast.

'How do we open the overspill?'

'It's locked shut.'

'Who can open it?'

'It's not a local decision.'

'We don't have time to get head office's permission.'

No time for complex preparation, too much could go wrong. I

scan the cages holding the higher-energy explosives, the necklace of fuse and charges wound onto a wooden barrel.

'We'll use the charges you prepared for rock blasting.'

'Will this work?'

'We don't have time for anything else.'

Tiro and I work fast. Together we manoeuvre the rolls of charges and fuse wire to the top of the concrete damn. There's a vertical iron ladder used for inspection. I hurl myself over the wall and onto the ladder.

When I get to the overspill – a shuttered window in the dam, I call up and Tiro throws down the leading edge of the explosive necklace. I string it like Christmas lights, concentrating most of the explosive on the overspill in the centre. This is the weakest point, the easiest place to break.

Tiro shouts down

'We're out of time.'

I scurry back up to the top, in time to see the breech in the primary dam widening, the liquid mud surging towards the secondary barriers.

We race back along the concrete lip and fall panting onto the side of the rocky gorge.

'Ready?' I ask.

'You do it,' he says, covering his ears with his hands.

I take the plunger and press.

Nothing happens.

With a roar, the primary containment finally gives way. A ten-metre-high trapezium of rock spoil and mud has been undermined at the base and can no longer hold back the millions of gallons of slurry pressing against it. A tidal wave of red mud crests and surges towards us. In less than a minute it will hit the concrete dam. The concrete will hold, protecting the mountain stream that runs into the river. The full flow will bounce back and find the next path of least resistance, slamming into the earth bund with millions of tons of liquid mud, subjecting it to a force it was never designed to withstand. There is nothing between the earth barrier and the town below.

Nothing to stop this catastrophe except me.

I turn back to the plunger. My fingers fumble with the connections. In our haste something has worked loose.

I see it.

I run to it.

I fasten it, but when I let go it breaks again.

The red wave of mud is advancing. I don't have time to get back for the tools I need to make the joint secure. I'm going to have to hold it in place.

It's not the electric current that will kill me, it's a relatively low current inside an insulated copper wire. But by remaining here, either the mud will engulf me and smash me against the concrete barrier I am trying to demolish, or the detonation will be successful, the concrete dam will collapse, and I will fall into the rocky gorge and be smashed to bits.

There will be a few seconds between the detonation and collapse, and those few seconds are the only hope left to me.

'Tiro!' I shout. 'Now!'

He hesitates.

'Do it!' I scream.

He stares at me for a moment, weighing up my life against the life of his family, of all the families in the town below. Then he nods and presses the plunger.

I see the white light before I hear the blast. I drop the fuse wire and start to climb. The concrete wall shakes under my hands and feet as I move crabwise, up and sideways, away from the blast zone and above the advancing mud, scrambling faster than I have ever climbed before. My fingers reach the top of the concrete wall but as I start to pull myself up, it begins to fall away.

The concrete dam is collapsing from the middle.

I'm not going to make it.

The dam bursts open, and a jet of blood-red water fires through. The collapse of the concrete structure is gradual, a slow-motion curtsey that starts as the centre gives way and with it the keystone, the band of compression that gives it structural strength. Fatally weakened, the wall begins to fold, then rip and tear.

I'm falling.

I'm not the praying sort, but there is much I could give thanks for in my life, much I wish I could undo, make amends for. The only people who never make mistakes are the people who do nothing. I have lived life to the full. I have sought knowledge and experience and learned from unexpected masters. I have loved, oh how I have loved. Perhaps I never told those I loved just how much they meant to me.

Too late now.

A wave of thick red sludge knocks me off my feet and batters me against the collapsing dam.

My brother appears, sitting cross-legged at the base of the dam and my heart soars with joy to see him.

'Sam!' I call out to him.

He waves back.

'You're alive!' I cry.

His blue eyes darken to a shade deeper than the ocean. What happened to the mischievous sparkle, why the sorrow?

He lowers his eyelids. His eyelashes are just as long and thick as ever.

'You're dead?'

The realisation hits me. I must be dead too.

I try to figure out how to react to this. I've taken risks that others would have run from – never courted death, but never dreaded it either.

'Am I dead?'

He shakes his head and I shiver.

'No.' I answer for him. 'Dying, but not dead yet.'

I don't fear death, but I've never fancied dying. I've seen enough of it to know that the process can be swift or prolonged, painless or excruciating. Although, as an observer, it's hard to judge someone else's pain. Does a minute feel like an hour, or do days pass in an instant? I understand the biochemistry but have no idea how it feels. Is Sam here to ease my passage? My Charon ready to ferry me across the river Styx into the mouth of the underworld? My Peter at the pearly gates?

He smiles and everything is suffused in silvery light as he holds out a hand for me. My brother is not exactly as I remembered him. The last time I held him in my arms he was emaciated and wan, dirty from the dust of travel, bleeding from a bullet wound. He is older now, although not as old as I am, which is odd because he is my older brother. He looks beautiful. Gone is the awkwardness of puberty. He's lean and strong, his hair glossy, skin glowing.

I start to swim down towards him. The light from his ethereal body warms me, soothes me. He opens his arms.

Something holds me back.

'Sam,' I ask. 'Is he with you now?'

He looks puzzled for a moment. Of course, my brother died long before my son was born. How could he know?

'Your nephew,' I explain.

He shakes his head.

I'm surprised and a little annoyed, but as I don't believe in God, in a heaven or a hell, it's unfair to complain when the non-existent rules don't behave the way you would expect were there to be an afterlife.

He is beckoning to me. I crave the warmth, the strength of our bond, the joy of his unconditional love. It would be so easy to go with him.

But I'm not ready. I have a task to complete.

'D'you mind if I don't follow you just yet?'

His approval is a rainbow that lights up my heart. He, of all people, understands all about unfinished business.

I know that he will wait for me.

The silver turns to gold.

Minas Gerais, Brazil, January

I surface with a gasp.

'Jaq!'

Tiro is shouting encouragement.

I feel the swish of something in the air, a breeze against my cheek.

More than encouragement, a rope.

Tiro is throwing me a lifeline from high up on the hillside. I reach up too late. It falls away into the mud.

I haul myself onto what's left of the dam and start to climb. He hauls the rope back and throws again.

I jump into the air, catch the loop and hold on for dear life as the ground collapses beneath me and I swing out over the abyss.

I watch the concrete barrier collapse, the liquid mud roaring into the gorge, a torrent of toxic mine waste surging down towards the river.

I see a mud-covered body, with limp puppet limbs at unnatural angles. It flies over the collapsing concrete and into the gorge and I look away.

I cling on to the rope and let Tiro swing me to the hillside. I collapse on the scrubby earth, staring up at the sky, and then he is there beside me, hugging me in the most welcome embrace this year.

My limbs tremble and I am glad of Tiro's help as we struggle up the hillside.

The spill is draining away. The earth dam protecting the valley is still intact. The danger is over. Far below, the children are safe.

As the water level subsides, the valley floor is coated in red slime. The workers from the waste treatment plant come down the ladders and walk up to safety.

Luis is waiting for me at the top, ashen-faced.

'Jaq, thank the lord. I thought we'd lost you.'

'It was a close-run thing.' I look around. 'Where's Fergus?'

Luis blinks. 'I thought he was with you.'

'Did you see where he went?'

'When the breech started I had to organise the evacuation,' Luis says. 'One minute Fergus was beside me, the next he'd gone. I assumed he'd followed the others.'

Tiro shakes his head. 'He went to help Jaq.'

I bite my lip as the realisation sinks in. An unlikely hero, Fergus didn't even seem to like me much. Why didn't he stay up there out of harm's way? Why descend into danger? The poor, stupid fool.

'What happened?'

'There will have to be a full investigation.' Luis said. 'You walk under a tailing dam and next thing we know it's breeched.'

'You think I'm responsible?' I ask.

'No, of course not,' Luis says. 'It was sabotage. I think someone was trying to kill you.'

Minas Gerais, Brazil, January

If you have a plentiful supply of mercury, acid and alcohol, it's not difficult to prepare mercury fulminate. The trouble is its stability, or lack of it, which makes it ideal as a primary explosive, a detonator for the commercial explosives that are easy to come across in any working mine.

Dressed like the other miners in overalls, hard hat and boots, his face so black with dust it was impossible to make out his skin colour, a man crouched in his hiding place above the mine and watched the flood spread in the valley below.

When the first mud reached the river, the water turned blood red. That should have been Silver's blood.

He cursed her.

They were going to have to try a little harder.

Rio Araguaia

Rio Tocantins

Palmas

TOCANTINS

2km from the gold mine, Tocantins, Brazil, January

In a thatched hut on stilts above an abandoned quarry in the middle of the jungle, two men sat down to eat. Both wore loose cotton robes. One was young and strong, his shapely body plainly visible through the thin, white cotton. The musculature – sturdy calves and forearms – told of a life outdoors rather than workouts in a gym. The other man was either very old, very sick or both. He hunched forward, and ribs and elbows, hips and knees jutted through the fabric at odd angles like a bundle of sticks.

Hugo had measured time by the progress of the hyacinth macaw's wing and the new verses added to the nonsense song he sang to the parrot.

Nick, knack, nickety nock
Tra-la-la la la
Pick, pack, pickety pock
Tra-la-la la la

The bird's bones were starting to knit together when the summons finally came.

At the rasp of a key and the clunk of metal tumblers, the door opened. The bare-chested man gestured towards Hugo.

'Follow me.'

They passed over several rope bridges to the largest of the buildings before ascending a curved staircase to a vaulted room.

So this was the famous Colonel? Hugo felt simultaneously underwhelmed and hopeful.

A boy brought plates of food then withdrew.

Hugo waited for the Colonel to start eating, but his host ignored the food, sipping from a mug instead, observing his guest with piercing eyes that reflected the candle flames.

'Please eat,' the Colonel said.

The steak was so tough as to be almost inedible, but the vegetable and bean stew served on the side was passable and Hugo managed to clean the plate.

The Colonel didn't touch his food. At the clap of his hands, the boy returned with a jug and refilled his mug with steaming liquid that smelt of milk mixed with alcohol.

The Colonel took a long sip, then wiped the cream moustache from his mouth. 'Have you travelled far?'

'From Palmas.'

'Your practice is in Palmas?'

Practice? Did the Colonel think he was a medical doctor?

'I'm an academic researcher, based at the University of Manaus.'

'Ah, now Manaus is a long way away.'

'It is sir, and I'm keen to get back.'

The Colonel ignored him.

'It must be, what, 1,000 kilometres as the crow flies?'

'I have a symposium to prepare for, and some personal commitments.'

'And perhaps 4,000 kilometres by road. Maybe more?'

'I must leave first thing tomorrow.'

'Or half that by river. I'm guessing you came by river.'

The Colonel stood up.

'Well doctor, I find myself a little out of sorts today, so let's do the physical examination tomorrow.'

Physical examination? The man really was deluded.

'I'm not that sort of doctor,' Hugo protested.

'It was good of you to come all this way to see me, doctor,' said the Colonel. 'What time should we start the consultation?'

'I'm a botanist. A field researcher.'

As the Colonel stood, he stumbled, and the boy rushed to assist him.

'I'll see you tomorrow. Is 10 a.m. OK for you?'

He didn't wait for an answer, shuffling towards the exit. Before he disappeared he turned and raised a hand in farewell.

'Goodbye, doctor.' The Colonel's eyes blazed with crimson fire. 'Tomorrow, you will cure me.'

Even at night, especially at night, the jungle was alive with noise. The buzzing of insects, rustling of predators and squeals of the hunted. Hugo stood on his balcony in the darkness and listened.

What was he to do?

The blue parrot was no longer afraid of him. It sat in its nest of towels, eating whatever he gave it, occasionally venturing outside.

Soldiers had brought him to this strange quarry complex against his will and now he was expected to perform some sort of miracle cure on his host, a man who was sick in both body and mind.

Could he pretend to be a doctor? He'd had no formal medical training. Not only would it be unethical, but he doubted he could act the part convincingly. Even someone as deluded as the Colonel would quickly realise the mistake. Best to wait until morning and try to reason with his host. Surely he could make the Colonel see sense?

Hugo turned, parted the curtain of vines and returned from the balcony to his bedroom. An oil lamp flickered on the bedside table. He didn't feel in the least sleepy, so he brought it to the desk.

He opened his journal and began to write, illustrating his journey with quick pencil sketches.

After a couple of hours, the pencil was getting blunt. The soldiers had taken his field knives, so Hugo searched the desk drawers for a sharpener. There was nothing but an old-fashioned ink well – the dark blue India ink had long dried up – and a blotting pad.

He checked the chest of drawers, but it contained only clean linen sheets and towels. He grasped the metal handle of the oil lamp and took it outside, but the swarm of insects, attracted by the light, drove him back inside.

As he returned the lamp to the desk, the shadows danced, and he noticed a set of indentations on the blotting paper.

Curious now, he took the blunt pencil, rubbing it lightly over the paper, shading only the surface so that any depressions remained white. The indentations formed letters, the letters formed words.

Dearest Maria,

Someone had penned a letter, several letters, with the blotting paper underneath, and the imprint remained. It was impossible to read where sentences crossed or were written over, each letter might have had several pages, but a few fragments stood out.

... never be released.
The Colonel is quite mad.
I made the mistake of trying to reason with him, that was my downfall.
... resigned to dying here ...
So long as you are safe, nothing else matters.
Hug Luis ...
... love you ... more than life itself.
Pedro

Hugo extinguished the lamp and lay on the bed, his eyes wide open. Another man had been imprisoned here, had rested on this bed, written at the desk, had suffered in this room.

I am resigned to dying here.

Who was Pedro, and what became of him?

ANÁPOLIS

1,400km from the gold mine, a freight train, Anápolis, Goiás State, Brazil, February

Clickety-clack, clickety-clack.

I jump down from the empty ore wagon at a busy railway junction. I find fresh water and a workers' canteen with wonderfully lax security. I even sneak a bunk for the night in the railway workers' dormitory, no questions asked.

I leave early, catching the first train out, a sleek locomotive with two hundred wagons in its wake and an empty guard's van at the back with a seat and a stove – the height of luxury.

This train serves a bauxite mine, carrying aluminium ore to the port of Santos where it will be exported to Canada.

I need a plan.

I am never without a plan.

I have no phone, no money, no ID and no plan.

The best way to travel incognito is to take full advantage of the Brazilian railroad as far as it goes. There's no point in rushing if

I don't know where I'm going. This slow pace suits my mood just fine.

The sunrise behind me tells me the rough geographical direction – north-west into Brazil's vast interior.

I have enough food and water to last me several days.

Thinking time.

13
Al
Aluminium
26.981

Brazil produced 32,867,000 tonnes of aluminium in 2013, worth about one billion US$.

Aluminium is light and strong. It is used to make cars, planes, railway carriages, packaging (foil and cans), windows, doors and overhead electrical power transmission. It is almost always alloyed with other elements (zinc, manganese, copper etc).

Lisbon, Portugal, January

It took Lars two days to drive from Amsterdam to Lisbon. It would have been quicker to fly, but he didn't have anyone to leave Hettie with. Anyway, he didn't like doing jobs without her.

After the cock-up at Schiphol airport before Christmas, he was relieved to be given another opportunity to prove himself to RIMPO.

This time the mission was clear. The main target – Silver – was still at large, but there was some housekeeping to do to limit the damage she might cause. An old man in hospital who needed to be dissuaded from acting on a delayed attack of conscience and causing RIMPO more trouble.

The original plan had been to let nature take its course. An invalid, not long for this world, didn't merit scheduling valuable assets on a job in Europe with all the risks it would entail.

But old folk were unpredictable. Sleepwalking towards death's door one minute, alert and causing mayhem the next.

When news came through that the old man was about to be discharged, the priorities changed.

They sent for Lars.

Dogs were not allowed inside the hospital, but there was a garden with shade and water where recovering patients could come out to meet their canine companions. Lars sat on a bench under a magnolia tree and watched the little dramas play out. A puppy nuzzled the face of an elderly woman. A group of children played with a frisky dog while its elderly owner looked on and smiled. An elderly dog slept in the lap of a wheelchair-bound invalid. Dogs were the best medicine in the world.

'C'mon Hettie.'

Lars tied her leash to a railing and filled her drinking bowl with water from the standpipe.

She stared at him with her huge spaniel eyes.

'I won't be long.' He ruffled her ears.

Lars found a disabled toilet and donned his disguise: white coat, stethoscope, universal electronic pass. He checked the weapon. A steel case no bigger than a matchbox contained miniature darts with needle-sharp points, a tiny glass vial with a single drop of liquid and the smallest, slimmest spring activated delivery device. The instructions were simple. Point at the neck and shoot. A light squeeze of the trigger opened the glass vial to the hollow needle point and fired the first dart into the skin. A firmer squeeze sent a second dart, but if the skin was pierced, one prick was all it took.

He took a pair of latex gloves out of his pocket and snapped them on.

What was it Oskar always said?

Hospitals are dangerous places.

For the patients.

Trancoso, Brazil, January

Frank watched Clara as she greeted the first of her guests. Her white dress was cut too low, her breasts spilling out; the skirt too short, her long legs like exclamation marks in their high-heeled fuck-me shoes; the fabric clung to her body, too tight, too revealing. She was far too old to dress like that. She could do with losing some weight. In the sunlight, he could see the imperfections more clearly – the start of a wrinkle here, a little sag there. See her and hear her. Loud and brash, fawning over the visitors, he wondered what he'd ever seen in her.

Frank ignored the lawyer, the advertising executive and the property developer. His interest had been momentarily piqued by the arrival of the young 'cousins'. One young cousin for every adult man, he noticed. Was it Clara's intention to serve him a consolation prize, a gift to ease the blow of abandoning his bed for her husband's? Or perhaps the offering was for her husband, so that Clara could continue as before.

Well, she could think again.

If he was honest, sexual confidence in a woman was the biggest turn off he could imagine. A man liked to hunt, enjoy the thrill of the chase, savour the art of persuasion – resistance was exciting.

Sex was, after all, just another power game, another negotiation: advance and retreat, thrust and yield. Long before consummating the deal, you circled round the goal in ever decreasing circles, starting slowly, politely, with plenty of diversions – a drink here, a meal there, a concert or a film. You paid insincere compliments, made disingenuous promises and watched the reactions. Reactions mattered, that's how you gathered your intelligence, plotted your next move and figured out the price. Everyone had a price.

Winning was important, but there was little satisfaction if it was too easy. Sometimes your opponent tried to bluff, to walk away before the deal was made, and that's when you sprung the trap, tightened the invisible cords, until they accepted there was no other way.

And submitted.

Sometimes that's when the fun started.

Usually, it was when it stopped, and you moved on to the next challenge.

Frank called Busco on the burner phone.

'You're going to have to explain why I should be interested in Jaqueline Silver's landlord.'

'Did you look at Walter Salgado's finances?'

'Why would I bother?'

'The accounts, and there are at least three sets, are deliberately obscure.' Busco clicked his tongue. 'I believe you are something of an expert in these matters.'

Frank froze. What was Busco implying? Frank only operated legally. Yes, he might stretch definitions, search out loopholes, but who didn't employ tax experts to minimise exposure? And who didn't use specialists to engage with decision makers? From lobbying in London to advocacy in Washington, from a box at Ascot to a charity golf tournament at the Congressional Country Club. For foreign countries, a good, local consultant was essential to understand local customs, to grease the right wheels.

'Start with the background.'

'Walter Salgado is a Brazilian citizen of Angolan descent. He rose quickly through the ranks of the air force before joining Cuperoil, where he got stuck in middle management until he moved into offshore exploration. That's where he made a name for himself. He was much more successful than his predecessors at persuading government officials to grant drilling licences under preferential terms. Suddenly helpful officials were winning scholarships for their children to attend private schools, gaining access to beach houses with the use of a yacht and private jet.'

'A strange coincidence.'

'Exactly.'

'And what is Jaqueline's involvement in all this?' Much as he reviled her, he couldn't quite square this circle. She came over as priggishly self-righteous rather than corrupt.

'As far as we can tell, they've never met in person. The target arrived in Brazil in July, long after Walter left for Luanda.'

'Then why is she living in his flat? What's he getting in return?'

'We'll soon find out. Salgado will be home soon. He always spends Carnival in Brazil.'

Minas Gerais, Brazil, January

I'm sitting at the window of a guest house watching a little town go about its normal business. A post van delivers letters door to door. A bakery truck replenishes the supermarket. A school bus collects the children for summer holiday camp.

The inhabitants of this prosperous mining town have no idea how close they came to disaster. Luis asks me to hang around until the initial investigation is complete, so I extend my stay in the guest house and catch up on sleep.

I am the one who identifies Fergus's poor, battered body. His corpse is recovered from a rocky gorge where the stream changed direction before flowing into the river. The force of the torrent had broken his limbs, the mud and grit had ripped his clothes and flayed his skin, but his belt buckle and the wedding band with his partner's name engraved inside were enough for a positive identification.

I make arrangements through Bruno, who contacts the relatives in Australia and arranges for the repatriation of Fergus Podger in a closed coffin.

They find a second body soon after. Tiro weeps as he identifies his assistant Amado. They never find the missing explosives.

It doesn't take much to get Luis to agree to my version of the narrative, that the real heroes were the workforce. It was Hard-hat at the water treatment plant who'd guided me to safety and raised the alarm. It was Luis himself who had taken the decision to open an overflow and save the town. It was Tiro who'd rigged and detonated the explosives despite the immense personal danger.

They all agree it is wiser to keep me out of the story.

I am making arrangements to fly back to São Paulo when Carmo calls.

This time, I am truly, genuinely glad to hear her voice.

I don't tell her about the tailing dam disaster; it's good just to talk about the weather.

'Any news?' she asks.

I struggle to remember what she knows, how much I told her. That's the trouble with lies; they are harder to recall than the truth. Last time we spoke I was barely functioning. What did I tell her? What did she tell me? *Happy New Year.*

'How was your escape to the Alentejo?' I ask.

'Great.' She sucks air through her teeth. 'Seems like months ago, what with everything that's happened this week.'

Easier to ask questions than to answer them. 'What's happened?'

'My uncle died.'

I'll never be able to confront him now. Never have a chance to make him sorry for what he did. Incarcerating a teenage girl. Taking away her baby and her chance of ever conceiving again. Advogado Centeno was a bad man. Carrying out the instructions of a bad woman. My mother.

Who cares? They are both dead. Their hateful secrets don't matter any more. There's nothing left to uncover.

How do you phrase condolences when you don't really care?

'I'm sorry for your loss, Carmo.'

'Did you contact the lawyer?'

'The lawyer?'

'Advogado Castanho. The old guy in Salvador. About the safety deposit box.'

I had completely forgotten my promise. I have other things on my mind.

'Not yet, but I'll get round to it, I promise.'

'It might be important.'

How can it be important? Who cares what final bills my grand-mother left me?

'As soon as I can.'

'Please Jaq,' Carmo says. 'There's more here than meets the eye. I'm sure of it.'

Trancoso, Brazil, January

There was only so much sun and sand a man could take. Especially when the sex was no longer an option. He escaped from Clara and the rest of the group on the beach and set off for the house. The Brazilians insisted on using beach buggies to travel the short distance, but Frank needed the walk to clear his head.

As he entered the villa garden, strains of music caught his attention. Piano music from inside the house. The simple melody was unfamiliar to him, wrapped in a loose, free style of invention that he didn't normally care for, but something about the complex harmonic structure captured his interest.

A grand piano graced the *sala*. The rich liked to own expensive things. They bought old books by the metre to fill their bookshelves. Even unread, they gave the appearance of refinement. But the boors and fools rarely knew how to take care of musical instruments. A Steinway needed regular tuning. He couldn't bear the sound of a piano out of tune and hadn't bothered to lift the lid.

He braced himself for a tell-tale twang, a wavering, shimmering dissonance, a sour strike, but the chords were pure and clear, the harmonies bold and sweet, the intervals accurate.

He followed the sounds to the main house. The French doors were locked, the blinds drawn, so he went to the front door and rang the bell. A maid answered and let him in. He entered the *sala*, but the music had stopped. The piano lid was open but there was no one around. How strange.

He sat at the keyboard and let his fingers roam free.

Salvador, Brazil, January

The office of Castanho e Nogueira Advogados was near the container port of Salvador. With the large naval base, the lower city had the feel of a garrison town with all the familiarity and advantages that implied.

Oskar took his time, watching and waiting.

The old lawyer arrived at the main entrance at nine o'clock sharp. Gaunt and shaky on his stick-thin legs, he looked like someone who should have retired decades ago. Well, Oskar might just be able to assist with that.

There was building work going on in the office block, people coming and going, carrying sacks of dry plaster and paint tins. It wasn't difficult to slip in through the back door, bypassing reception.

The interior was much grander than the run-down exterior suggested. He ran up the curved marble staircase, past a huge stained-glass window and found the first-floor office he was looking for – it even had a name on the door.

Oskar opened it without knocking.

'Advogado Castanho?'

The old man looked up from his desk and nodded.

Oskar closed the door behind him.

'I need to talk with you.'

'And you are?'

Oskar ignored the question and advanced towards the desk.

'Excuse me, young man,' the lawyer protested. 'You can't just barge in here without an appointment.'

'I'm afraid this can't wait.'

The lawyer lifted his phone receiver, but Oskar was ahead of him, pulling the jack from the socket.

'What's all this about?'

Oskar wasn't sure whether the old man was trembling from fear or from some degenerative disease.

'You remember Colonel Cub?'

The lawyer's eyes opened wide and his mouth formed an O of surprise.

'The Colonel sent you?'

Oskar nodded.

'And how can I help the Colonel?'

'He needs some information.'

'What sort of information?'

'The current whereabouts and intentions of a Dr Jaqueline Silver.'

Oskar observed the internal struggle as it played out over the lawyer's face. He appeared to come to some sort of decision.

'The Colonel will understand that I have a duty of confidentiality to all my clients.'

Wrong decision, Oskar thought before breaking into a wide smile. This next bit was the part of the job that he liked the best.

Trancoso, Brazil, January

Frank woke to the sound of a piano playing softly. He recognised the piece instantly. Bach. Prelude in C major, BWV 846. The very piece he'd warmed up with yesterday. Radio? A recording? No. He waggled a finger as he heard the first mistake, then a pause, a reprise. The pianist wasn't note-perfect, but the mistakes were harmonious, interesting, capturing something that surely Bach himself might have approved of.

The mystery pianist again. Who was at the keys? The lawyer wouldn't fit, his enormous stomach would prevent him from drawing close enough to reach. The advertising executive had too many rings, they would clack-clack against the ivory. The property developer seemed like a smart man, but he had huge square tree stumps for fingers and would never manage those delicate trills and arpeggios. One of the cousins? Not Jade or Ruby, their fingernails were too long. Carrie perhaps, she was bendy enough, but she hadn't struck him as particularly bright, and whoever was at the piano played with sensitivity and intelligence. In any case, the house guests had all left early for a spin in Clara's yacht, a trip that Frank had no hesitation in declining.

Frank despised yachts, expensive nausea-inducing money pits. He'd given up his berth in the south of France after his own yacht sank; Jaqueline Silver had blown *The Francium* to smithereens.

Now he dressed and wandered across the garden, stopping at the French windows.

A large woman sat at the grand piano, dressed in a grey maid's uniform with a white petticoat. Her hair was in tight cornrows with a small bun at the back. She was lost in the music, utterly transported, swaying backwards and forwards as she played with great feeling, and no little technical skill.

As he entered the room, she stopped abruptly, jumping up from the piano.

'Please,' Frank said. 'Continue.'

She hung her head. 'I thought you had all gone sailing.' Her English was good, a slight American accent. 'I'm sorry.'

'You like Bach?' he asked.

'Who?'

'That piece you were playing. It's by JS Bach.'

She shrugged. 'I heard you play it.'

Heard it once and was able to play it by heart? Did he believe her? He gestured at the keyboard. 'Please continue.'

'No, no.' She shook her head. 'I should be working.'

'Your job is to look after the guests?'

'Yes.'

'And I am a guest?'

She bowed her head. 'Indeed.'

'Then I would like to play with you.'

He pulled up a second chair at the keyboard.

'I play from memory too.' Frank let his fingers wander over the keys and waited for her to remark on his prowess. 'I remember every note Bach ever wrote.' Well almost. Bach was a prolific composer, churning out over 1,000 compositions.

Frank launched into the opening of the *Well-Tempered Clavier* and was surprised to find how slowly and clumsily his fingers moved. In truth, he was badly out of practice; yesterday was the first time he'd touched a piano keyboard in a while. All his organ practice had been about slow, powerful chords and hadn't helped his dexterity.

'Sit,' he ordered.

She obeyed.

'Can you repeat what I just played?'

She played it back, note perfect. Extraordinary!

'Now follow me.'

He played a phrase; she played it back. He tried a variation; she echoed it. He nodded at her to repeat and turned it into a canon. She glanced at him for permission before launching into an extraordinary cadenza. After that, he stuck to the melody and allowed her to range freely with descant and ornamentation. He added spaces, pauses so he could focus on what she was doing. It was strangely thrilling, liberating, to watch someone let go of tempo and structure and simply experiment.

Whatever he did, she matched. Then bettered. Wherever he went, she followed. Then overtook. He lost all track of time. Frank couldn't remember being so close to the heart and mind and soul of another human being.

A bell rang, and she jumped up. 'I have to go.'

'Wait.' He put out a hand. 'What's your name?'

'Aline,' she replied.

'Well, Aline. Let's keep your piano skills a secret between us, shall we?'

'Yes sir. Thank you, sir.'

Frank liked secrets.

Secrets gave him power.

But there was something about this woman that didn't quite add up.

Curitiba, Brazil, January

The flatshare in Curitiba was a soulless place. Four bedrooms and a kitchenette in a crumbling concrete block. The lounge had been sacrificed for an extra bedroom, each of which had its own TV. Graça's flatmates were fellow police officers, a mix of trainees and undercover agents so she rarely saw them. They all worked the remotest assignments on the worst shifts. Didn't mean they couldn't wash up. Graça stared at the sink piled with dirty dishes and decided to have breakfast at the airport.

She was already tucking into a stack of hot, sweet pancakes when Zélia called.

'Trip cancelled,' she said. 'Travel agency just issued Silver a new ticket. She's flying back to São Paulo.'

'So, I don't get to go to Oriximina?'

'Why, were you looking forward to it?'

'I've never been to the Amazon.'

'You haven't missed anything, trust me.'

'Have you been?'

'Nope, and it's not on my bucket list.'

'Lungs of the planet. How could it not be interesting?'

'You're a police officer, not a bloody eco-nut.'

And since when had law enforcement and preservation of nature been on opposite sides? She'd have that argument with Zélia another time.

'So where am I going instead?'

'Come back to the office.'

'Am I in trouble?'

'No, we've just found out where Salty Walter is spending Carnival. You're back on the team.'

Minas Gerais, Brazil, January

Bruno understands my need to take a few days off. The death of a colleague and my narrow escape from a similar fate is excuse enough.

The reality is more complicated than that.

I've seen horrible deaths before. It's not that I'm hardened to human suffering, but Fergus was a fit, smart, adult man who took a stupid risk and paid the price. I didn't know him well, but I wished him no harm. I hope his end was quick.

My feelings about his death are complex. If I'm honest, the main emotion is anger.

Anger at his old-fashioned chivalry, his assumption that any woman must be a helpless damsel in distress who can't take care of herself. Anger at his stupidity for descending into the corrie below a leaking dam only to get himself killed.

Anger at Fergus's obstinacy for making me prove myself before he would reveal anything that might help me. He told me there were thousands of illegal gold mines in Brazil, but he seemed to have some idea of where it was, the one I was looking for, the one that Ecobrium tricked me out of, the one where he – Crazy Gloves – might be found.

What did Fergus know? What information did he take to his death? Why didn't he tell me?

And now it's too late.

But I'm not just angry with Fergus. I'm angry with myself. For a time on that trip, when I was rigging up explosives with Tiro, for a few glorious hours I almost forgot my mission, almost settled back into work. I forgot what I had set out to do. And others paid the price.

I arrive early for the flight. The regional airport is hot and crowded.

The definition of stupidity is doing the same thing over and over again and expecting a different result. Do I really want to return to São Paulo?

I have wasted enough time, visited enough mines for a lifetime. Did Fergus know anything or was he just stringing me along? I guess I'll never know. I am not going to find my quarry by conventional means.

My search for Crazy Gloves continues. I know his real name – Raimundo Elias. I know where he lives. Or lived, for he is no longer there, and – if his neighbours are to be believed – hasn't been seen for months.

I am not his only enemy, although I am the most determined. The police want to question him in relation to damage to logging equipment. The logging company want to find him so they can sue him. If rumour is to be believed, their investors want to find him so they can kill him.

Crazy Gloves is the scarlet pimpernel of the radical environmentalists. One minute he's in the Amazon, protesting about river pollution from gold mining. The next he's in Parana, demonstrating against corruption.

I need an in. Someone who moves in his world. Someone who can ask questions without arousing suspicion.

I walk to the window and look out over the little airport. A weather balloon floats above the runway, a flag flutters in the breeze.

Wind. Windsurfing. Kitesurfing.

It gives me an idea.

I flick back through all the messages I've ignored.

Hi,

I'll be in Brazil for the championships. Last minute sponsorship. Long story. Probably a million miles from where you are, but I could make a trip. If you want, that is. No pressure. Just thought I'd let you know. It would be great to catch up.

How are you doing?
Xav

Xavier.

I check the dates.

He's in Brazil.

For the first time this year, a smile tugs at the corner of my lips.

I call him.

'Jaq.' Xavier's voice does unexpected things to my insides. 'It's good to hear your voice.'

And it's good to hear his. Better than I'd bargained for.

'Where are you?' I ask.

'In Cumbuco until next Sunday and then a few days free. Any chance we could meet up?'

Is this a bad idea? Too much of a distraction? Or exactly what the doctor ordered?

'Sure.'

'Where are you?' he asks.

Where indeed? Lost. Fortaleza is a four-hour direct flight from here. Cumbuco a short bus ride to the north.

'I'll come to you,' I say.

'Great!' He's buzzing now. I hold the phone away from my ear as he tells me about the beach, the wind, the competition. He relays messages from Lisbon, from Carmo. After a while he must sense something because he stops mid-sentence.

'Jaq, are you OK?'

No, Xavier, I'm not OK. I'm as far from OK as I've ever been. I can't bring myself to be honest or I'll have to tell him the whole sad story. I can't do that on the phone. And for now, not even in person. Perhaps I can never tell him. Or at least not until I've done what has to be done.

'Still searching?' he asks

'Still searching,' I say.

And I am still searching. Just for a different person. No longer searching for my son, but for his killer. I'm still on a mission. Not to nurture, but to destroy.

Cumbuco, Brazil, January

The long beach is alive with colour: turquoise sea, golden sand and hundreds of triangular sails and kites and boards sporting every combination of colours in the spectrum.

I check in at the hotel, shower and head down to the beach. The noise of nylon sheet luffing and clacking in the wind drowns the roar and crash of the surf.

Xavier isn't hard to find, being interviewed by Hélio TV on the beach, surrounded by fans, beautiful young athletes who look up to him, their god of kitesurfing. And just for a minute, with his narrow hips, his wide shoulders and strong arms, his tanned skin, his black beard and body hair, he looks like a sea god. I pause for a minute to admire the view and a sudden sadness attacks me like a punch to the gut.

When Xavier sees me, his whole face lights up.

'Jaq!' he breaks away and strides towards me. 'You came.'

'Least I could do.'

He places his large hands on my shoulders when he kisses me on one cheek and then the other, his lips warm and firm and slightly abrasive.

'Where are you staying?'

'Al Mare.' He gestures to the hotel.

'Me too.'

The TV crew are waving. Pointing to their watches and then out to sea where the kites are lining up.

'Go,' I say, pushing him away. 'Go win that trophy.'

We meet again much later. I decline his invitation to a dinner hosted by Hélio TV. Just the idea of making vacuous small talk with people I don't know, don't wish to know, exhausts me. But I understand that he must go, his sponsors expect it of him. He calls me as soon as he can slip away, unnoticed.

We walk along the beach, away from the noise and lights, to a quiet spot backed by dunes.

Xavier takes my hand.

'I've been thinking about that night on Guincho beach.'

I wonder which night he means. We spent so many nights together on Guincho beach as teenagers. But I say nothing. I wait.

'The last night we spent together.'

Ah, so it was still bothering him. The night I'd taken the lead and he'd rejected my advances.

'I wish I'd behaved differently.'

The sea is lapping against the sand.

'You had other things on your mind,' he says. 'I know how that feels. You didn't need an ultimatum from me.'

He stares out to sea.

'I don't know what it is that we have between us, but I do know that – from my side at least – it's unconditional. I get that you have too much going on, that you can't make any commitments right now. It doesn't matter. I just want you to know that I'm here for you.'

'Thank you.' Xavier is a good man. Someone dependable, trust-worthy, lovable. And therefore dangerous.

'Maybe this is friendship, maybe it's love,' his eyes twinkle with the colours of the sea: sapphires and diamonds, emeralds and opals. 'Or maybe it's just plain lust.'

The small internal earthquake wrongfoots me. I tremble in the aftershock, waves spreading outward from my core.

He moves closer. I can feel the heat radiating from his body. I can smell the sea on his skin.

'I've spent every night since you left wishing I hadn't pushed

you away, dreaming of what might have happened.' He sighed.
'Should have happened.'

He extends one hand, then the other. He has big, calloused
hands. Hands that grip the control bar of his kite. Strong hands,
experienced hands, sensitive hands. Hands that could hold me fast,
steady me through this spinning maelstrom. Hands that could hold
me down. Hands that could hold me back.

No. I can't do this. Not now.

I squeeze his hand and move away.

'Let's walk back.'

His face falls. 'Sure.'

I get to my feet.

'How's Carmo?' I ask to fill the silence.

'Not great,' Xavier says. 'She lost a couple of people she was
very close to.'

'Her uncle?' My mother's lawyer.

'Yes. And a good friend in Angola. She seems to think there's a
connection.'

I stop and stare. 'A connection? I thought her uncle had been ill
for a long time.'

'Yes, but he made a full recovery. Was due to return home.
Carmo thinks his death was suspicious.'

'I see.'

'She wants you to do something for her.'

'Do what?'

'Go and find out what's in this mysterious safety deposit box.
She's convinced it may throw some light on what's going on.'

I shake my head. 'I doubt it.'

A group of young Brazilians wave at Xavier. 'Come for a drink!'
Xavier looks at me enquiringly.

'You go,' I say. 'I've been travelling all day. I'm turning in.'

'You need company?' he asks.

Oh, if only.

'I need to sleep.' I smile. 'And you need to attend to your fans.'

He looks so crestfallen; I offer an olive branch.

'Breakfast?'

'Maybe,' he says.

We kiss as friends, and I watch him head out towards the group. The women are ten years younger than me, limber and beautiful. He'll find someone to soothe his bruised ego before the night is over.

As I climb into bed, the pang of sadness takes me by surprise.

Curitiba, Brazil, January

As soon as she got the message, Graça set off for her Grandmother's house.

GG had never contacted her at work before, her generation had an almost reverential respect for authority, so it must be important.

The fifth floor of the federal police building had been buzzing with activity, there was a mountain of work to do, but family came first.

It was great to be one of the team again. Zélia had instructed the garage to finish all the repairs on Graça's car at the department's expense. In the meantime, she had the use of a motorbike. The fact that she'd swapped it with another bike also registered as a Honda 120 was known only to Zélia. Salty Walter's Harley Davidson was considerably more powerful (and many times more valuable). So long as the police continued to pay her fuel bill, Graça remained very fond of the Knucklehead.

The disciplinary case had been dropped, she'd passed her probation, her back pay had been settled and she was feeling flush.

She parked the bike in the barn, beaming with relief when GG came to the back door. Graça ran through the garden and put her arms around her grandmother.

'Steady on – don't hug me so hard I break!' GG protested.

'You said come quick. I was worried. Are you OK?'

'Never better.'

'Then what's up?'

GG put a finger to her lips. 'Come inside.'

Graça followed her into the little house.

'I found something in your metal box.'

GG placed a key on the table.

'What is it?'

Graça picked it up.

A slim, silver object in the shape of a tiny lollipop, the long shaft was notched in three dimensions and the circular head embossed with a complex pattern. A hole in the top had a slim chain and a tag. The number 196.967 was engraved on both sides.

Graça held it up to the light. Inside the circle was a triangle with letters around the three sides. *Banco Espirito Santo, Rio de Janeiro, Safe Deposit and Trust.* Inside the triangle was an engraving of a sailing ship coming into a tropical harbour.

'Where did you find this?'

'I was polishing the brass on that box you brought home, and I sort of twisted the rings and the hollow handle opened.'

'Show me.'

GG reached under the table and brought out the newly decorated box. The leather-covered handle was secured by two brass rings. GG twisted them in opposite directions and an ingeniously concealed panel sprang open. Inside the handle, a silk cushion held a key shaped hollow secured by a bespoke metal bracket: the hiding place for a very special key.

Was this what everyone had been searching for?

Cumbuco, Brazil, January

I can't sleep. The air-conditioning splutters and rattles and sends out intermittent bursts of freezing air straight at the pillow. I get up and turn it off. I go back to bed, but the room quickly becomes unbearable – hot and stuffy.

I get up, pull on shorts and a T-shirt. I'd like to go for a walk along the beach, sit and listen to the sea. If I was back on Santa Catarina Island I wouldn't hesitate; I always felt safe in that community. But I don't know this area, I have no friends here.

Except one.

Xavier is sitting in the hotel garden, alone with a book.

'Can't sleep,' I say.

'Me neither.'

'Can I join you?'

He closes the book. 'Of course.' His smile lights up the dark.

'What are you reading?'

He shows me. A slim volume of poetry.

'Do you know Fernando Pessoa?'

'Of course.'

'From school?'

'And after. Why do you ask?'

'It's a long story,' I say.

'I'm not going anywhere.' He leans back and his eyes twinkle.

Where to begin.

'I didn't ignore Carmo's request.' I start at the end. 'I know how much she's done for me.' *And at what cost.*

'I get that it's not exactly top of your list, but you can't rule out the possibility that it might be helpful to you as well.'

I'm almost ready to tell him that my son is dead, almost blurt out that nothing will help me now except finding the man who robbed me of hope. But I need Xavier to help me find Crazy Gloves. He won't help me if he knows I plan to kill the leader of Ecobrium. I can't make him knowingly complicit in a crime, can't have him go to prison for me again. I can't share this with Xavier. A problem shared is a problem doubled.

So, I try distraction.

'The first time I went to see the Salvador lawyer, I was given an envelope addressed to me as the *issue of Maria dos Anjos Sakoshansky.*'

'Issue? Ouch.'

'You get that the rift between my grandmother and mother was deep and wide.'

'They never reconciled?'

I shake my head.

'What was in the envelope?'

I don't mention the contract. It's not important.

'A verse from a poem by Pessoa.'

'Which one?'

'"The Message".'

'"Myth is the nothing that is everything",' he quotes.

'And a ring.' I take it off my third finger and hand it to him.

He holds it up to the light, between finger and thumb. 'What's the symbol?'

'I think it's the alchemical symbol for mercury,' I say. And that's when the realisation hits me.

Mercury. Mercúrio.

How could this be coincidence? Did my mother name my son Mercúrio because of this ring? Did she take him away from me, use him to thwart her own mother, to get the inheritance she craved? She might as well have put an ice pick through my heart.

'Jaq, what is it?'

I snap back to the present. I can't talk to Xavier about this.

'Nothing,' I say.

'Jaq, I'm not an idiot,' he says. 'What is it you aren't telling me?'

I lean forward to kiss him. To stop his questions. To feel his lips against mine. Suddenly desperate for human touch, the warmth of another body, hot breath on skin, to stop the conversation before it breaks down my defences and reduces me to a jelly of quivering sorrow.

At first there is no response. Have I made a mistake? Again?

Rebuffed him once too often? All his talk of love and friendship and lust, has he moved on? Has he given up on me?

And then he wraps his arms around me and moves his lips over mine and, for a while, all is well with the world and the only thing that matters is the here and now, this man with his scent of the sea and his silky black beard that tickles my neck, and the hot breath that finds my ear and whispers the things that I want to hear.

And I can't stop listening. I can't stop wanting him. Perhaps I really need him.

Just for tonight.

Cumbuco, Brazil, January

We wake before dawn and I watch him dress, pulling on jeans and a T-shirt.

The design stirs a memory, and I am brought crashing back down to earth. This is what I came for.

'What's the logo,' I ask. 'On your T-shirt?'

He turns and puffs out his chest so I can read it.

'Ecopto,' he says. 'People in Portugal are finally recognising the value of nature.'

'A Portuguese ecology movement? Something you're part of?'

'Yes.'

'Can I pick your brains?'

Xavier smiles. 'Is that why you came to see me? Not for the kitesurfing. Not even for the fabulous sex, but because I might have information.'

Once upon a time I would have blushed. But now I feel no shame in the single-minded pursuit of what I need. When did I become that person? A person who uses others. Perhaps I was born like that. Or perhaps it was when they took my son from me.

Not once, but twice. I remember something Xavier said to me on Guincho beach.

'I take no prisoners, remember?'

He sighs. 'No, you certainly don't.'

'Have you heard of a group called Ecobrium?'

'The Brazilian eco-warriors? Yes.'

'Any connection with Ecopto?'

'Loosely. Ecobrium are all about confrontation and direct action. Ecopto is all about working in harmony with stakeholders.'

'I need to find a man called Raimundo Elias.' Crazy Gloves. 'He's the head of Ecobrium.'

'I've heard of him. He keeps a low profile these days. I guess he's made a lot of enemies.'

Too right, and you're looking at his number one enemy right now.

'Is this connected to your son?'

'Yes.'

'Can you tell me more?'

I take both his hands and look into his eyes. 'One day, Xav.' And I mean it, I really mean it. 'But not yet.' I drop my gaze. 'I need to find out where he might be. Where I can bump into him and make it look like a chance meeting.'

'And you think I can help?'

'You move in the same circles.'

'Why not try a direct approach?'

'I've tried.' God knows, I've tried. 'But I'm employed to work with the very industries Ecobrium despise.' Not that I've ever done any useful work for the oil industry in all the time I've been in Brazil. Heaven knows why Tecnoproject still pays me. Far from making oil refineries safer, more efficient and cleaner, my presence on site probably caused the hydrogen explosion in Salvador when someone tried to kill me. And what about the tailing dam collapse in Minas Gerais?

'Raimundo Elias doesn't trust me. He won't willingly meet with me.' Which is true if unhelpful. The real reason Crazy Gloves will never knowingly meet with me is because of what he stole from me. Not the engraved copper maps to the gold mine – I couldn't care less about those, it's the way he extorted them from me that matters. 'He's the only one who can help me.'

'Jaq, I need you to trust me.'

'I trust you, Xav.' And it's true.

'Then tell me what's going on. Why you're so closed to me? Why all the mystery? There's something you're not telling me.'

He's right of course. And there's a good reason I can't tell him the truth. My path is set, and nothing Xavier can say or do will deflect me. I can't make him culpable, an accomplice to murder. I'm prepared to die or go to prison, but I'm not prepared to drag this fine man down with me.

Not again.

'There's a lot going on, Xav,' I say. 'Just bear with me, OK?'

'I can't begin to understand.' Xavier gets to his feet. 'If I do this for you, will you do one thing for me, for Carmo? Contact the lawyer in Salvador?'

It's a small price to pay, but still I hesitate.

'Who are you, Jaq – I'm not sure I recognise you any more?'

I am anger
I am rage
I am fury
I am vengeance
And until I make Crazy Gloves pay, I am running on empty.

Trancoso, Brazil, January

Frank stared at the pictures. The man was a similar height to Jaqueline Silver. He was bald, but otherwise covered in black hair, his beard, his chest, his arms and legs. Some of the shots showed them arm in arm, others arguing. Impossible to deny they were a couple, then. Not her usual type, she'd always gone for smooth, young, pretty boys before – the ski instructor in Slovenia, the Italian yachtsman in Crimea, the Russian dancer in China. This man looked her age or older. Clearly a sportsman with his muscled arms and a broad chest and sturdy legs. A swimmer, a surfer, and – judging by the shots on the podium – a champion.

'Who is he?'

'Xavier Fonseca – a Portuguese kitesurfer.'

'What the hell is kitesurfing?'

Busco directed him to the second folder. 'You surf with a sort of huge parachute to catch the wind.'

'What's he doing in Brazil?'

'Watersports championship.'

'And what's she doing there?'

'Whatever it is, Tecnoproject are still raking in money from Cuperoil in her name while she swans about on the beach,' Busco said. 'Xavier is leading light in the Portuguese ecology movement Ecopto.'

'What sort of group are they?'

'Pretty benign.'

'Any connection with Ecobrium?'

'They attend the same conferences, but the Brazilian outfit is much more radical, proponents of direct action.'

'Nutters, in other words.'

'Or perhaps citizens concerned about climate change.'

'Aren't we all?'

'Xavier's background is interesting though. Father was in the military. Old aristocracy. And guess who is sponsoring Xavier's trip to Brazil?'

'I have absolutely no idea.'

When Busco told him he sat up straight. What the hell were these two up to? And how could he use it to his advantage?

Cumbuco, Brazil, January

It's just a phone call. The very least I can do for Xavier, for Carmo.

'Hello, can I speak to Advogado Castanho.'

'Who is speaking?'

'Jaq Silver.'

'Please wait a moment ...'

'Dr Silver ...'

'Yes.'

'You were calling to speak to Advogado Castanho.'

'Yes.'

'May I ask what this is about.'

Impatience gets the better of me. 'No, you may not. Please put me through.'

'I'm afraid that won't be possible.'

I have a sudden premonition of what is coming next.

'I'm sorry to tell you that he recently passed away.'

'He's dead?'

'Exactly.'

A shiver runs through me.

'What happened?'

'He was a very old man ...' So was Carmo's uncle. Age is not enough to explain every death.

'A heart attack?' I venture.

'Oh.' She sounds surprised, 'How did you know?'

I ignore the question. 'A sudden heart attack at work?'

'Yes.'

'Tell me exactly what happened.'

'I'm sorry, Dr Silver, I wasn't here that day. Perhaps you'd like to speak to his assistant.'

'Yes, I would.'

'And Dr Silver, were you calling to settle your bill?'

I cut the call and book a flight.

Trancoso, Brazil, January

Frank was seated at the piano when the burner phone rang.

'Do you have access to a TV?' Busco asked.

Frank normally avoided television. He could barely tolerate the plastic music, canned laughter and applause of many BBC programmes, and British TV was positively restrained when compared to the offerings abroad. In the brief periods when he wasn't working, he preferred to read or listen to music. Baroque was his preferred style, the seventeenth his century of choice, and JS Bach his default composer. Not that he was narrow-minded. Buxtehude, Scarlatti and Couperin got a look-in when it came to the church organ, and he could tolerate some choral works by Purcell, Handel and Monteverdi. Clara did not share those interests, and the beach house had a TV in every room.

'Yes.'

'Find a programme called *Os Desaparecidos* – the English translation is *The Missing*. Go back to episode 79 – it broadcast on November 5th last year and was repeated as part of the New Year special. Tell me if the second guest is the woman you're looking for.'

Frank snorted. TV appearances didn't sound like Jaqueline Silver's normal modus operandi.

In the end he needed help to get the watch-again function to work on the TV, so he went to look for Aline.

No one told Frank that the servants' quarters were out of bounds to the guests. Clara and her friends were partying on a neighbour's yacht, overnight this time, and he'd pleaded pressure of work as an excuse not to join them.

He wandered through the lush grounds to a thick hedge with an opening where he'd seen the servants come and go. As he stepped through, the stench of an open sewer made him gag. A veritable shanty town of unrendered brick and corrugated iron lay before him. The mansion had plenty of unoccupied rooms, why were the servants not housed in better conditions?

He looked around for Aline, calling out her name. A barefoot child pointed towards a hut on the edge of the ramshackle village. He knocked and opened the door.

Salvador, Brazil, January

I stand on the balcony of my hotel room and stare down at the port at dawn. Below me, the container ship that sailed in last night is almost ready to leave. I watch the cranes lifting the last containers onto the dock. It's strangely mesmerising.

I didn't want to come back to this city, the city where Mercúrio grew up, where he was abandoned by all the adults who should have been looking after him. Last night I walked to the building where he spent his formative years. An old Jesuit mission, converted to a school and orphanage when the order was banished in 1759. It's a grand but dilapidated building looking out over the Praia de Boa Viagem – the beach of splendid journeys. This is an institution, not a home. Mercúrio wouldn't talk about his time here, but I can understand why he chose to escape into the sea, why he became a surfer.

Today I'll go and see the lawyer who has taken over my late-grandmother's affairs. I will try and find out what happened to Advogado Castanho. He was an old man, in poor health, there is no reason to think his death was connected with my inheritance. I promised Xavier I would do this one thing. And then he will set up the meeting with Crazy Gloves.

It's not a deal exactly, not an explicit you do this, and I will do that. Like so many things in life, the rules are unspoken. Give and take. Everything in life is a negotiation. If you take and take and take, after a while people stop giving. I needed Xavier to remind me of that.

Poor Carmo; it shouldn't have needed Xavier's intervention.

After all she has done for me, after all she has lost, I can close out this one last thing that's bugging her, put her legal mind at rest.

Once the sun has risen, I leave my hotel and walk to the lawyer's office: Castanho e Nogueira e Advogados Associados. I'm far too early, so I find a café in the old market and watch the world go by.

It's hot by the time I enter the air-conditioned reception.

'*Bom dia!*' The receptionist greets me as if I were a long-lost friend. 'It's Dr Silver, isn't it?'

I'm impressed by her recall.

'Advogado Nogueira has taken over your account. He'll be with you shortly.'

'I was so sorry to hear about Advogado Castanho.'

She looks away as tears fill her eyes.

'Were you here when it happened?'

She nods. 'I was his personal assistant.'

'I'm so sorry. It must have been a terrible shock.'

'It was awful,' she says.

'You found him?'

She nods.

'Can you tell me what happened?' She throws me a sideways glance. Have I pushed too far? 'Sometimes it helps to talk.'

The floodgates open.

'It was the soldier who raised the alarm.'

My hackles rise. 'The soldier?'

'Advogado Castanho didn't have any scheduled appointments, but sometimes he does pro-bono work. When I was taking a file up to the registry, I saw the soldier coming out of his room with a phone to his ear. He told me he was calling an ambulance.' She dabbed her eyes with a paper tissue. 'I rushed past him into my boss's room and there he was, Advogado Castanho, still in his chair, slumped forward onto the desk.' She let out a sob. 'His face was red, he was still warm, but he'd stopped breathing. We tried everything, but even the office defibrillator didn't revive him.'

'And the ambulance?'

'Took ages. We had to call several times. Maybe the soldier gave the wrong address.'

Or maybe the soldier was lying.

'Was there any sign of a struggle? Any injuries?'

She looked at me, eyes opening wide, before shaking her head. 'No but I keep wondering why the soldier was in his room.'

I can guess exactly why the soldier was there.

He was there to kill.

Advogado Noguiera is much younger than his recently deceased partner. Once the receptionist has stopped crying, she takes me up to his office on the top floor. The lawyer greets me stiffly.

'Dr Silver, thank you for coming in.'

'I understand from my lawyer in Lisbon that there is an unpaid bill. Can you explain?'

'Your grandmother had a safety deposit box in the head office of the Banco de Espirito Santo.'

The Bank of the Holy Spirit – if things weren't safe there, where would they be?

'She took out an insurance policy to pay for it during the lifetime of her children. That policy terminated on the death of your mother.'

So deep was the rift between mother and daughter, that whatever it was Isabella left behind, she would rather it remained hidden than risk it falling into the hands of her daughter and her communist son-in-law.

'Now you have a choice, to resume the rental, backdated to your mother's death, to ignore the demand for payment, in which case the bank will retain any property that belonged to your grandmother, or to pay the termination fee and go and empty the box yourself.'

I sigh. More family manipulation from beyond the grave.

'Any other instructions? Do I have to spend a night in a haunted house?'

The lawyer purses his lips. 'There are no such conditions attached.'

'How much is the termination fee?'

He consults his notes. 'One hundred reais.'

A pittance.

'Plus our fee,' he adds.

'And if I pay, they will send me the contents?'

He smiles and shakes his head. 'Alas no, you will have to go to the bank in person to retrieve whatever is in the box.'

I stand up. 'What's the address of the bank, I may as well get this over with.'

He hands me a card. Mr Pedro Carmargo, head of private banking in Rio de Janeiro.

I sit down again. I'm not going back to Rio any time soon. I'm ready to give up. It's only the thought of Carmo that's keeping me here.

'And the rental?'

'Ten reais a month, backdated to ...' he flicks through my file until he finds my mother's death certificate, one of three certified originals the late Advogado Castanho had demanded. 'Let's see, last year, was it?'

He reads out the date my mother died.

'Plus our fee,' he adds.

'Very well,' I say. 'Let's continue the rental until I can go in person.'

'Those are your instructions?'

'Yes.'

'Then I will draw up a document for you to sign.'

I stand up. 'Thank you.' For nothing.

'My pleasure.' He stands and extends a hand. 'Before you leave, may I see the key?'

I freeze. 'What key?'

'The key to the safety deposit box.'

I stare at him. 'How can I have a key, when I didn't even know that this safety deposit box existed until today?'

'Ah,' he sits down again and gestures for me to do the same. 'This complicates things somewhat.'

I remain standing. I want to get out of this stuffy room and away from this horrible man.

'But I am sure you can provide some further proof.'

'And how exactly do I do that?'

'Once we've established your right to the property, and we can do that for you ...'

For a fee, I think sourly.

'It's usually a three-factor verification to request a replacement key. It depends on the bank, on when the safety deposit box was rented, but ...' he pulls out a file. 'Let me see.'

He turns the letter from the Banco Espirito Santo towards me.

'Identification plus code name and number.'

'What code name and number?'

'I believe your grandmother left a letter.'

The letter contained a land purchase contract, useless without a schedule and maps, a poem, and a gold ring.

'There was no mention of a code name or number,' I say.

'Perhaps the information was hidden? Encrypted?'

'Perhaps.' Have I missed something? Do I care? I'm not warming to my late grandmother. I have no personal interest in what is in that safety deposit box. I'm only doing this for Carmo.

'In the meantime, I will write to the bank to confirm the procedure for release of a safety deposit box when the key is lost.' He stroked his chin. 'I regret that this may take some time.'

That's that then. I'm heading north, back to Cumbica, not south to Rio.

My grandmother's secrets will have to wait.

Curitibanos, Brazil, January

A fox had taken two of GG's best egg-layers in the night. Graça sent GG back to bed while she cleaned up the blood and feathers. It was unusually quiet in the garden, the clucking and crowing replaced by a broody huddle of birds facing away from the coop. Graça gave the remaining chickens some extra corn.

It took some time to find the right number, but eventually Graça was put through to the private banking section of the main branch of the Bank of the Holy Spirit.

'Yes, madam.'

'Can you remind me of the access requirements.'

'You have a key madam?'

'I do.'

'That's all you need.'

'No proof of ownership?'

'The key is the only proof required, madam. You'll need ID, of course, for the normal security checks.'

'Does the name on the ID have to match the name on the deed to the box?'

A pause. 'Are you the owner, madam?'

'I'm acting on behalf of the owner.'

'Then the fact that they have entrusted you with the key is proof enough.'

'No additional requirements?'

'No additional requirements, madam. You are welcome to call at the bank and access your vault between the hours of 9.30 and 11.30 in the morning.'

'Do I need to make an appointment?'
'There is no need, madam. We look forward to seeing you.'

Cumbuco, Brazil, January

I am indecently glad to see Xavier again. Fortunately, he is more than happy to be indecent too.

I'm lying in bed, exhausted, when he turns to me with a smile.

'I found a copy of your poem in the local bookshop.'

'My poem?'

'"The Message".'

He reaches out to the bedside table and hands me a slim volume. *Mensagem* by Fernando Pessoa.

I flick through until I find the canto my grandmother copied.

'Wait,' I say. 'Can I show you something?'

When I return from my room, I hand him the envelope. He takes it from me and removes the copied-out poem. His lips move as he reads it.

'There's something odd here,' he looks up. 'Give me the original poem.'

I hand the book back and he points to the page.

'The first couplet is genuine Pessoa,' he says.

Valeu a pena? Tudo vale a pena
Se a alma não é pequena.
Was it worth it? Everything is worthwhile
If the soul is agile.

'As is the last.'

Deus ao mar o perigo e o abysmo deu,
Mas nelle é que espelhou o céu.

God gave the sea danger and the abyss, why?
For it is a mirror to the heavens above the sky.

'But the middle couplets are fake. Unrecognisable. Nonsense.'

Confie primeiro no espírito santo
Com anel, nome e número do canto
Trust first in the holy spirit
With ring, name and verse implicit

Desmonte a caixa com gaveta falsa
A chave para o oriente, esconde na alça.
Take the box with fake drawer, dismantle
The key to the east hides in the handle.

As mapas poente, cobre entre aço e couro
Mas tenha cuidado, nem tudo que brilha é ouro
Copper between leather and steel, western maps unfold
But be careful; all that glitters is not gold.

'Wait,' I say. 'Show me.'
A light begins to dawn. I've barely glanced at the poem, recognising it as the most famous poem in the Portuguese language, one every child was forced to study at school, and thought no more of it.

But according to Xavier, the middle verses aren't original, weren't written by Pessoa. Were they inserted by my grandmother to hide a message within 'The Message'?

Dismantle the box with a fake drawer – that must be my grandmother's strongbox. What is the *key to the east hidden in the handle?* Is that the key to the safety deposit box? Where is it now?

Copper between leather and steel – that's exactly where the maps were found, engraved copper plates hidden inside the very structure of the strongbox – the *western maps.*

How did Crazy Gloves know all this? How did he know where to look? Who else saw this coded poem? Advogado Castanho, now dead. Mercúrio, now dead. I hadn't shown it to anyone else until Xavier arrived.

How could Raimundo Elias have seen it, have decoded the hidden message long before me?

I look at the poem again.

Trust first in the holy spirit – The Bank of the Holy Spirit. *With ring, name and verse* – three factor authentication – identification, code name and number.

Verse number. Canto X. The same number on the ring.

I have the ring, and the ring contains a name and a number.

I have identification and proof from the lawyer that I am the descendent of Isabella and Angie.

I could go and retrieve what is in my grandmother's safety deposit drawer.

If I cared.

But I don't.

I've carried out my part of the bargain.

Now Xavier will keep his promise, arrange a meeting with Ecobrium.

And I will kill Crazy Gloves.

Trancoso, Brazil, January

Clara lay on her stomach, her naked breasts squashed against the lounger, her shapely backside smiling at the sun, an empty cocktail glass at her side. The bottom half of her bikini, a white G-string, provided zero cover to those great orbs of flesh. What had attracted him at first now repulsed him.

She had been reading some trashy book and had bored herself to sleep. The paperback with its lurid cover fell open in her hand.

Frank put down his suitcase and took a seat in the shade.

His visit to Aline's room had been interesting, very interesting. The maid had rushed him back to the house, where she showed him how to catch up on the repeat of *The Missing* – a dreadful programme with an interesting guest.

So, Jaqueline Silver had a child. A missing child. That could be very useful information.

He called Busco.

'Yes. It's her.'

'Is the child yours?'

For fuck's sake, the man had a one-track mind. 'No.'

'Well, I guess it explains why she's in Brazil.'

'Not entirely.' Frank didn't believe in coincidences. 'Who did you say she's working for?'

'Tecnoproject. An engineering consultancy.'

'Who are their clients?'

'Mainly Cuperoil.' The giant state-owned oil and gas company. 'And a few smaller companies, like Áerex and Zagrovyl.'

Insulting to call multinational Zagrovyl a small company, but then his company's presence in Brazil was still fledgling. Frank glanced back at Clara asleep on the pool lounger. Probably because its lotus-eating senior management was more interested in cocktails than chemicals.

'I've something else for you to look into.' Frank said. 'There's a woman here who claims to be a maid. But she's hiding something. I'm sending a picture. See if you can figure out who she is and who she's really working for. Meet me in Brasilia. I have business there.'

Aline had been extremely anxious that he leave her room. Not from any sense of propriety, but because of what she tried to hide from him. It looked as if she had a veritable recording studio of quality equipment. Not the sort that musicians use, but the paraphernalia of surveillance, the tools of spies and informers.

Clara was stirring so he cut the call.

'Something's come up,' he announced and nodded at his case. 'I have to go.'

'Frank, no!' She sat up straight. 'You'll miss the party!'

That was most definitely the plan.

'I'm so sorry.' He tried to look disappointed.

'But I invited people to meet you. People who can help our business.'

He shrugged.

'Say goodbye to everyone and pass on my apologies.'

'Oh, Frank!'

She tried to kiss him on the lips, but he averted his face.

His departure was long overdue.

Cumbuco, Brazil, January

The beach curves slightly as it merges into the horizon, the palm trees shrinking with distance. Little waves in shades of turquoise and emerald lap against golden sand. The sky is azure with a few fluffy white clouds high in the sky.

If I am to spend the rest of my life in prison, I may as well savour these last moments of freedom.

Xavier emerges from the sea, casting a long shadow as he approaches.

I rub my eyes. 'Hello, Xav.' Has the competition finished already? Did he win? He always wins. 'Well done.'

He flops down onto the sand beside me.

'Hello, Jaq.' He leans over and kisses me. His lips are cool and taste salty. 'You weren't watching, were you?'

I stare out to sea. The kitesurfers are still out in force.

I pull away. 'I can't tell one kite from another.'

He roars with laughter. 'You're not much of a fangirl, Jaq.'

'I have other things on my mind.'

'Tell me something.' He picks up a handful of sand and lets it trickle through his fingers. 'Why do you want to meet Raimundo Elias?'

So I can kill him. What would Xavier do if I told him the truth?

'It's complicated,' I say.

'You think he has some connection to your son?'

Connected by kidnapping. Connected by murder. He ordered his men to tie Mercúrio up, weigh him down and throw him into the sea to drown.

'A connection, yes.' I don't meet his eyes.

'You think your son is part of Ecobrium?'

I shake my head. Mercúrio was a young man with a good heart. He loved the sea, but his passion was surfing; he left saving the planet to others.

'No.'

'I have an email address if you want to ask Raimundo Elias some questions?'

'I need to meet him face to face.'

To look him in the eyes, to ask him why. To make him suffer for what he did. And then to watch him die.

'I think I can arrange it.'

I sit up straight and stare at him.

'You found him?'

Xavier nods, water droplets sparkling in his beard.

'Maybe.'

'How soon?'

'I'm following up a chain of connections. It's ...' he waggles a hand, '... delicate.'

'I understand.' And I do. Crazy Gloves can't know it's me. 'I can wait.'

'In the meantime, now that you've decoded your grandmother's message, why don't you go and see what's in the safety deposit box, find out what it is that's caused all this trouble.'

He is loyal to Carmo, I like that about him.

I kiss him. 'After I meet Raimundo Elias.'

He smiles and shakes his head. He knows me too well.

I pretend to be offended. 'You don't trust me?'

'Jaq, you do have a habit of disappearing.'

Fair enough. In fact, doing this for him would make me feel a bit less guilty. Maybe it's a fair exchange. I'm using him to get to Crazy Gloves. But he wants something in return, so in a way, he's using me.

A smile tickles the corners of my lips.

'One last condition?'

'And what's that?'

I nuzzle his ear and whisper exactly what I want from him.

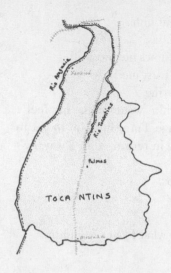

Rio Araguaia
Rio Tocantins
Palmas
TOCANTINS

2km from the gold mine, Tocantins, Brazil, January

Dawn came suddenly, the birds trumpeting a fanfare as the rosy light slanted through the curtain of vines that separated the guest room from the balcony over the quarry.

Hugo had barely slept, agonising over what he should do. Although he had no formal medical training, he'd attended some of the same biology modules as the medical students and even dated a paramedic for a while. As a field researcher, he'd completed the compulsory first aid courses. He knew how to clean an infected wound, to immobilise a broken limb, to perform CPR. He'd done enough zoology to know his way around mammalian skeletons, muscle and nerve systems, he'd successfully set the wing of a large parrot, but he knew nothing of psychiatry or neurology.

Was he being too logical, too rational? He stared at the blotting paper with the negative fragment of a letter written by a previous occupant of this room.

I made the mistake of trying to reason with him, that was my downfall.

He didn't need the skill to cure his lunatic host; he just needed to survive long enough to figure out an escape plan.

Hugo opened the first aid kit. He'd used all the bandages, padding and the smallest splint on the bird, but the usual stuff remained – antiseptic, antihistamine, plasters, tweezers, paracetamol, ibuprofen, aspirin, Imodium, sachets of rehydration salts. He also carried two syringes, one pre-loaded with morphine and another with adrenaline.

At the sound of a key in the lock, Hugo grabbed the blotting paper from the desk and slipped it under the mattress. The boy entered, bringing Hugo a freshly laundered kaftan, washed and pressed, along with a tray of fruit.

When he was alone again, Hugo fed the fruit to his avian companion and waited for the call.

A soldier came for him, leading Hugo to the Colonel's quarters, remaining silent and impassive throughout the interview.

'Good Morning, Doctor.'

'Good Morning, Colonel Cub.'

Hugo looked around. The Colonel's room was much like the guest room in layout and furnishing, significantly larger, but so muddled that it seemed cramped and claustrophobic by comparison. The floor was cluttered with mining relics – a Davey lamp, pickaxe, hammers. The walls were hung with instruments of death. Old guns and swords, memorabilia rather than weapons.

'Are you ready to cure me?'

Could he really go through with this charade? He'd always preferred to work alone. Choosing the simple honesty of field research over the highly competitive world of grant applications, laboratories vying against one another for funding, the jostling for position. Could he really pretend to be something he was not? Deceive someone else? Wasn't it better to come clean and explain he was not a doctor, could do nothing for the sick old man.

The Colonel is quite mad.

The sick old madman.

Hugo took a deep breath.

'I'll need to carry out a full examination.'

The Colonel smiled, like a child being offered a free pass in a sweet shop and began to undress.

Back in his room, Hugo sat on the bed and waited for the trembling to stop. At first the Colonel had been more than happy to talk about his ailments and Hugo had simply listened and fed back to him using Latin words. He made a show of taking a detailed history and examining every inch of the trembling, skeletal body. The laying of hands, probing and prodding every part of his host's gaunt frame, seemed to calm the man. The Colonel provided samples – sputum, urine, hair and blood – Hugo marked up the little pots and bottles and prepared slides, staring at a few drops of each of them through his portable microscope. He prescribed a change of diet, some harmless exercises and a once-a-day pill, making up a bottle from paracetamol, aspirin and ibuprofen. It would do the Colonel no harm. No good either.

When Hugo had finished his Oscar-worthy performance, he informed the Colonel that he must leave in the afternoon to take the samples to a hospital laboratory and consult with his expert colleagues.

A look of cunning spread over the Colonel's face.

'You don't like it here?'

'My first duty is to my patients.'

'And I am your patient, so you must stay with me.'

'But your samples need to go to a specialist laboratory ...' Hugo protested.

The Colonel nodded at the soldier who provided a pen and paper.

'Write the instructions, and the address.'

Hugo did as he was told.

Once the nausea had subsided, Hugo resumed his preparations for escape. He jammed the chair under the door handle. It wouldn't stop anyone from entering, just slow them down long enough to avoid any surprises.

He opened the chest of drawers and removed the sheets, using his teeth to make the first rip before tearing the linen into strips and knotting the 2m lengths together. He estimated ten metres to the floor of the jungle, but he made a double length. He needed an easy way to recover the rope after he descended, so he could use it use to climb the sheer face of the quarry. Once satisfied, he coiled the crude rope in the drawer, laid the clean towels on top and closed it again.

He replaced the chair beside his desk, took out his journal and began to write.

Not long to wait until nightfall.

The Colonel was still indisposed at dinner. Hugo took his tray out onto the balcony so he could talk to the blue parrot, now perched in the magnolia tree outside. The boy had brought yet another tough steak and the same bean stew as before. Hugo forced himself to eat it all – there was no way of knowing when he would find food again.

After the meal was cleared away, he sat in the dark and listened to the noises, inside and outside. He'd calculated the ideal time, after dinner, in darkness, before the moon rose.

Once the complex was quiet, he barricaded the door again, packed up his personal possessions and shouldered his backpack. He opened the drawer and took what he needed. Wrapping a towel around the two sturdiest balcony uprights, so his rope wouldn't rub against the wood, he fed the two ends through either side of the balcony handrail and watched them tumble towards the quarry floor with the middle secured by the wooden structure.

He took his leave of the blue parrot.

'Coming with me old friend? Let's see if we can fly.'

Hugo took a deep breath and launched himself over the side.

Tra la-la la la

He thought he heard the bird just before the knotted sheets gave way.

When Hugo regained consciousness, it was to find himself on the quarry floor struggling to breathe. The fall had winded him, but once the panic subsided, he was able to gather his senses and test out his neck, arms and legs. Nothing broken. He'd fallen onto his backpack, and his back ached, but he could move. He didn't dare to use his torch down here, too easy to spot in the darkness, so he scrabbled around until he found the rope that had fallen with him. It was worse than useless, ripped in several places. He would have to climb the sheer side of the quarry without it.

Hugo moved slowly across the quarry floor, to the point furthest away from the complex, where a fall of boulders formed a temporary hiding place. He crouched down and waited for the moon to rise.

In the moonlight, Hugo surveyed the sheer side of the quarry.

He walked round the full circumference before realising his mistake.

There was no way out.

CAMPI
NORTE

1,200km from the gold mine, a freight train, Campi Norte, Goiás State, Brazil, February

Clickety-clack, clickety-clack.

I'm not the only one train surfing. A pair of young men hitch a ride on my bauxite train. I keep my distance and jump off at the next junction, transferring to a locomotive hauling flat beds of coiled copper wire.

I lie on my back in the shadow of coiled metal and look up at the sky, following the planes criss-crossing this enormous country. Where have they come from? Where are they going? High above I spot a twin-bodied silver plane that reminds me of the Áerex hydrogen powered jet that Marina flew. I squeeze my eyes closed. I don't want to think about Marina.

As darkness falls, the train pulls into a siding and I escape into sleep.

29
Cu
Copper
63.546

Brazil produced 271,000 tonnes of copper in 2013, with a value of US$ 608 million.

Copper is used in electrical wiring, power generation, transmission and distribution, telecommunications, electronics and electrical equipment.

Brasilia, Brazil, January

They met in an airport hotel, although this time Busco had booked a private suite. At Frank's expense. Or at least at Zagrovyl's.

They sat at a circular table with a view of the runways through tinted glass. The rhythm of planes taking off and landing was hypnotically regular.

Frank dragged his eyes away from a KLM Dreamliner.

'What did you find out?'

'You were right Frank. Aline Aldo. She studied music in Belém and then did a master's degree in conducting and composition at the Julliard School of music in New York. She paid for both by temping as a sound-recording engineer. But she struggled to get a permanent job back in Brazil and my sources assure me she was recruited by the federal police earlier this year under their affirmative action plan. She was hired to work undercover in surveillance.'

'I knew it!' Frank banged the table with his fist. One musician could never fool another.

'Was she trying to entrap me?'

'I very much doubt it, Frank. No offense, but the Brazilian feds have bigger fish to fry.' He steepled his fingers. 'Who was due at the beach house party?'

Frank reeled off the list of names.

'Did you say Salty from Cuperoil?' Busco laughed. 'That explains everything. Salty is our friend Walter Salgado. This must be part of a much bigger investigation.' He frowned. 'Best you don't go back there.'

Frank snorted. As if he hadn't already worked that out for himself.

'OK,' Frank said. 'Here's what I want you to do.'

Rio de Janeiro, Brazil, January

The Banco Espirito Santo was in the old centre of Rio, a surprisingly shabby area after the glamour of Copacabana and Leblon.

The nineteenth-century building dated from the time when the Portuguese royal family declared Rio the new capital of the Lusophone empire, but it aped an older design: elaborate stone pillars and carvings in the Manueline style, decorated with ropes and knots, sea creatures and heroic sailors.

The interior had once been even grander: marble floors and jasper balustrades, crystal chandeliers and gilded carvings.

As she walked up to the reception counter, Graça sensed an air of dilapidation about the whole place. Dust on the skirting, cracks in the ceiling, missing pieces of candelabrum, scuffs on the floor.

She tapped her heels while the receptionist finished a call that – judging by the tone – had nothing to do with bank business.

'Yes?'

Graça checked her notes. 'Mr Pedro Carmargo, please.'

The receptionist raised a single eyebrow. 'You have an appointment?'

'I wish to access a safety deposit box. I was told that no appointment was needed.'

'Your name?'

'Graça Neves.'

'Just a minute.'

An immensely fat man in an ill-fitting suit arrived at the security turnstile. He walked with a limp and had the sallow skin of the chronic invalid.

'Senhora Neves?'

'Am I speaking with Pedro Carmargo?'

He shook his head. 'Senhor Carmargo is on a business trip.' He wrinkled his nose. 'A very long business trip.' He sighed. 'I am filling in during his ... extended absence.' He didn't offer his own name.

Graça produced the key. 'I would like to access a safety deposit box.'

'Please, Senhora, come this way.'

Graça walked slowly, matching her pace to his as they crossed the grand hall and skirted a sweeping staircase. The lift was tucked in behind the stairwell. Between iron pillars, a decorative grating revealed the winding gear, cables and pulleys that supported a wooden cabin. An early twentieth-century addition to a nineteenth-century building. Graça was about to suggest they took the stairs when she noticed that the bank clerk looked close to collapse just from the short walk.

For all its beauty, Rio was always an unhealthy city. Attempts by the city authorities to clean up the slums by broadening streets to facilitate waste collection and digging sewers in order to drain the stagnant pools of water where disease-carrying mosquitos bred had inevitably led to the eviction of the poorer residents. They rebuilt the slums in the hills that surrounded the city, almost out of sight, but certainly not out of mind. The health of the favelas affected the health of the city.

Now there was a new disease in Brazil, obesity. In the cities people travelled by car or public transport. A fondness for US-style fast food, burgers and nuggets and pizzas and chips, washed down with sweet sodas, finishing with cakes and pastries. Add to that an abundance of meat, rum-based alcohol and a culture of generosity, it was a recipe for disaster.

The lift arrived and a light flashed on. The clerk grunted as he scissored the iron gates apart. He gestured for Graça to enter first. The wooden cabin sank a few millimetres and Graça reached for the brass rail as the clerk joined her and made it dip and sway. Graça made a silent prayer that the cables could cope with their combined weight. She didn't want to spend her last seconds on earth plummeting into the bowels of old Rio with a sweaty stranger. The clerk turned to close the doors and pressed the button for the basement.

Somewhere high above, an electric motor whirred into action and the wooden cabin descended smoothly through the open shaft. They sank below the marble floor of the private banking reception, through the service void, stuffed with snaking cables, passed under a false roof to a busy open-plan office. Men and women in cubicles stared at green computer screens. The descent continued through a service area with water pipes and condensers, down further into the secure vault.

A security guard opened the lift door and asked for identification. Graça handed over her ID and he copied the details into a leather-bound book.

The clerk used his pass to open a barred metal gate and Graça passed through a final security check.

The clerk put his eye to a scanner. A red light clicked to green, and they entered an air lock through a thick steel door. He waited for one door to close before spinning the wheel to open the other.

Graça shivered as they stepped through into the strongroom. Inside the subterranean vault the damp air was as cold as death. The ceilings were low, and the lighting cast a sickly sheen on row after row of steel lockers, each one numbered in logical order.

'Now,' the clerk was panting from the effort of turning the wheel. 'Let me see ...'

He walked to row 196 and found box 967.

'Give me the key.'

Graça handed it over and he unlocked the drawer.

It all happened so fast that Graça took a moment to react. One minute he was standing in front of her, turning the key in the lock. There was a click and a *whoosh-whoosh*. The next minute he was sinking to the ground, clutching his neck, deflating like a balloon that had been punctured.

'Are you OK?' Graça dropped down, kneeling beside him as the clerk collapsed onto the floor. He was struggling to breathe, pulling at his shirt collar and tie. Graça helped him to loosen it. His face had turned bright red, sweat cascaded from his forehead, his mouth opening and closing like a fish out of water.

Graça looked around for an intercom or some other way to call for assistance. There was no telephone handset, no alarm or call button, just a retinal scanner beside the access to the air lock.

'Help!' she shouted.

The man on the floor was beginning to fit, spasms shaking his large body. Graça attempted to put him in the recovery position, tipping his head back to free his airways, but he fought her, snapping his teeth, straining every sinew, in a desperate attempt to breathe.

Graça jumped to her feet and ran back to the air lock door, banging against the thick steel, bringing her eye to the retinal scanner in the hope that an unauthorised attempt at access would alert security. She looked around for a way to sound the alarm. Surely there must be a panic button? She pressed the emergency button on her phone. No signal.

The clerk was fighting a losing battle. Graça returned to his side and searched his jacket as he bucked and writhed. Was he asthmatic? Did he have an inhaler? Or a nitro-glycerine spray for a heart condition? Was it an allergic reaction? Did he have an epi-pen? Was he a diabetic in need of insulin? Or sugar? How did you tell the difference? But there was no medicine or medical device in his pockets and as he began to tire, his hand reached for hers. Graça held on to him as he lost consciousness.

The moment he was still, she opened his mouth and wiped the foam away with her sleeve. There was no sign of a blockage. She inserted her fingers, but his throat was clear. Could she resuscitate him? Would CPR help? In two minutes, without oxygen, he would be brain damaged. In six minutes, he would be dead. No time to lose. She had to try.

Graça crouched over the dying man, and started chest compressions *Staying alive, staying alive*, she recited *Ah, ha, ha, ha, staying alive, staying alive.* After twelve compressions she used her fingers to open his lips, form a seal with her own and blew.

She repeated the cycle, but the effort was making her feel dizzy. Her head was buzzing and her neck was weak. She lowered her lips to his, and everything went black.

TV Studio, Rio de Janeiro, Brazil, January

In the Hélio studio, the spotlight followed César as he made his way to the sofa. He nodded at the clapping audience, making a mental note to remind the sound engineers to digitally enhance the applause and overlay with previous recordings of rapture before the show was broadcast at Carnival.

'Good evening.' He smiled so that his newly whitened teeth glinted in the studio lights. 'And welcome to *The Missing*.' He flicked a lock of hair from his eyes. 'The show that reunites some families,' he paused to stroke his neatly trimmed beard. 'And drives others apart.'

The audience laughed.

'Tonight, we have an audience with Colonel Cub.'

The relationship with RIMPO had been tricky for a while. After Silver gave them the slip in Rio, escaping the *Missing Nature* ambush he'd so carefully constructed, he'd lain low for fear that RIMPO would make good on their threat to kill him. It was only the successful recruitment of one of Silver's Portuguese friends – amazing what people would do for a bit of TV exposure – that had given him the confidence to emerge from hiding. A new meeting had been arranged between Jaq Silver and Raimundo Elias. RIMPO were ready.

It was good to be back in the studio where he belonged.

'But first, I am delighted to welcome a special guest. Please join your hands together and welcome ... Karina!'

The crowd became more animated as the guest arrived on stage. She was a stunner. Tall and slim with long flame-red hair, dressed in a short dress that showed off her long, tanned legs. César stood to embrace her, kissing one cheek and then the other. He pointed to the sofa opposite.

'Karina, welcome. Now, where are you from?'

'I'm from Palmas.'

'The capital of Tocantins, right? And what do you do there Karina?'

'I'm a nurse at the *Hospital Oswaldo Cruz*.'

The audience broke into spontaneous applause, whether from the idea of this beautiful woman dedicating her life to the sick and needy, or at the mention of Oswaldo Cruz, Brazil's great champion of public health vaccination.

'Karina, please tell the audience where you were in February last year.'

'I was on the beach.'

'And where was that beach?'

'Praia de Forte.'

'In beautiful Bahia, right?'

'Yes.'

'And Karina, were you alone on the beach?'

'No, I was with my son.'

'Your son Noah. Is this him?'

A picture of a child flashed up onto the screen behind them. The boy was aged five or six, cherub-cheeked with blond curls and blue eyes.

'Yes.'

César nodded at the box of tissues on the table, the cue to start the tears. They would cut out his prompt when they edited, and show only her lovely, tragic face.

'Tell me about Noah.'

'He was the apple of my eye.' She was dabbing her eyes and sniffling now. 'His father left before he was born, and it was just the two of us.'

There was an aaah from the crowd.

'It was hard at times, but always worth it. He was a funny, loving little tearaway.'

'A tearaway?'

'Oh, you know what little boys are like?' She shrugged at the audience and there were cries of 'Too right!' 'Don't we just.'

Good, very good, she was working the crowd.

César nodded at the studio engineer, the cue to dim the lights and change the background music from major to minor.

'How did you feel when you lost him?'

She covered her face with her hands.

'Karina, take your time.'

César poured a glass of water and handed it to her, patting her gently on the shoulder. She took a sip and wiped her eyes.'

'Can you tell us what happened that day?'

'It was our first holiday, I hadn't been able to afford the time off, but he'd begged me. Let's go to the beach for Carnival, Mama.'

'He'd never been to the beach before?'

'No, Palmas is a long way from the sea.'

'1,500 kilometres, right?'

'I don't know but it took all day and night by bus.'

'Noah's very first sight of the sea – how did he like it?'

'He was captivated by the water.'

'And on your first day there, what did you do?'

'Oh, we made sandcastles, we paddled in the shallows.'

'Did you swim?'

'No.'

'Why not Karina?'

She lowered her head.

'I can't swim.'

'You can't swim.' César repeated it for emphasis. 'And Noah? Could he swim?'

She shook her head and dabbed her eyes.

'Tell me what happened next.'

'It was getting hot. I didn't want him to get burnt on his first day. And we were hungry.'

'A morning on the beach sure makes you hungry, doesn't it, folks!'

Roars of approval.

'We ate at the café and then went upstairs to our rooms for a rest. I must have fallen asleep.'

'You fell asleep?'

'Yes, we'd been travelling all day and all night.'

'And when you woke up?'

'Noah was gone.'

MISSING came the voiceover, and the familiar music soared.

Cut!

Rio de Janeiro, Brazil, January

Beep ... Beep ... Beep ...

Graça heard machine noises, regular rhythmic wheepling, just before the smell of bleach told her she was in hospital. She opened her eyes and tried to focus on the metal frame of the bed, turning her head to examine the machines and the smooth white walls beyond. Her limbs felt heavy, but she couldn't move them and there were no restraints. She sensed movement and turned her head towards it.

'Where am I?'

A white-haired, dark-skinned woman with tortoiseshell glasses came into focus.

'I'm Doctor Rao.' She sat on a chair beside the bed. 'You are in the Blessed Martyrs Hospital in Rio de Janeiro.'

Graça blinked.

'Can you tell me your name?'

'Neves. Graça Neves.'

'Good, very good. Do you remember what happened?'

'The bank. The vault.' The memory sharpened. 'The clerk I was with, he collapsed. Is he OK?'

'I'm afraid Mr Barata didn't make it.'

Graça closed her eyes. She wasn't surprised. She'd watched him die.

'Why am I here?'

'You need to rest.'

Rest? How could she rest when she had no idea what had happened? Or what came next. She tried a different tack.

'How did I get here?'

'The security guards in the bank sounded the alarm. The bank staff found you and called an ambulance. The paramedics think you were unconscious for about an hour before they got to you.'

Unconscious? 'What's wrong with me?'

'You're making an excellent recovery.'

Graça tried to sit up. 'Can I leave?'

'Not yet.' The doctor unhooked a chart from the end of the bed. 'We need to keep you here a little longer, make sure there is no relapse.'

'Relapse from what?'

'We're still running tests.'

Graça's shoulders sagged.

'The police are outside. They need to talk to you.'

TV Studio, Rio de Janeiro, Brazil, January

At the first advert break, César cracked his knuckles and frowned at his guest. He called for the make-up team to touch up Karina's face, her crying had been pretty unconvincing so far.

And action!

'Let me recap for you. Karina is a dedicated nurse and a loving single mother. Her son, Noah, the apple of her eye, begged her to take him to the seaside. So, they saved up and made the long journey from Palmas to Bahia. After a morning of beach fun, they go back to their hotel for lunch and a siesta. And when Karina wakes up, Noah is …'

MISSING boomed the voiceover

'So, Karina.' César turned to face her. 'Tell us, how did you feel?'

'Confused. At first I thought he must be in the bathroom.'

'But he wasn't?'

'Then I thought he might be hiding. We play hide and seek sometimes. I looked under the bed, in the closet.'

'But he wasn't there?'

'No.'

'So, Karina, think back to that day. It's hot, you're still a bit sleepy. What are you thinking now?'

'Well, I'm a bit cross with him at first. I've told him before not to wander off without me. At home, he sometimes goes to see his granny or his aunty. It doesn't matter so much where we live, everyone knows us. But we're in a new place, full of strangers. I think maybe he's gone down to the café, so I go there.'

'And do you find him?'

'No.'

'And have they seen him?'

'Yes.'

'And what can they tell you?'

She gulps. 'That he headed off in the direction of the beach.'

'He's gone to the beach? On his own?'

'Yes.'

'A six-year-old boy who can't swim?'

'Yes.'

'What did you do.'

'I went to the beach.'

'You walked?' he prompted.

'I ran.'

'As if your life depended on it.' César nodded sagely. 'And when you got there?'

'It's a huge beach. And there were so many people. It was so crowded. I couldn't see him anywhere.'

'And how did you feel?'

'Complete panic.'

The screen behind them went through a photomontage. Noah as a baby, Noah at his christening, Noah on a tricycle, Noah at nursery, Noah at church. In truth, not all the pictures were of Noah. But they were good pictures.

MISSING came the voiceover, and the dramatic music.

Cut!

Rio de Janeiro, Brazil, January

The plain-clothed policeman glowered at Graça from the end of the hospital bed.

'Graça Neves?'

There was no love lost between the state-run civil police and the government-run federal police, so she didn't bother to advise him that she was in fact a fellow officer of the law.

'Yes.'

'Can you confirm that you were with Mr Rafael Barata when he died?'

'The bank employee? Yes.'

'Can you tell me what happened?'

'We were inside the strongroom when he collapsed.' Graça took a deep breath against the horror of his last minutes. Precious, precious breath.

'Before that, was he unwell?'

A morbidly obese man, his breathing was heavy as he turned the wheel to unlock the thick steel door, his movements laboured. But he talked easily and cheerfully, his skin a healthy pink, there was no warning of what was to come.

'How could I know?' Graça turned towards the doctor who sat silently at her bedside.

'Did he complain of feeling unwell?' Dr Rao asked.

'Not to me,' Graça said.

The policeman puffed out his chest, resuming control. 'Why don't we start at the beginning. From when you entered the room where he died.'

Graça tried to picture the vault. 'Mr Barata entered first, from the air lock, waited for me and then locked the door behind us.'

'Did you see anyone else in the vault?'

'No.'

'Did anyone else enter after you?'

'No.'

'Could someone have arrived before you and hidden in wait?'

Graça closed her eyes and tried to picture the dim cellar. Plastered walls, low ceilings, and row after row of safety deposit boxes, most with the profile of a letter box, a few the size of a sports locker. No place to hide.

'No.'

'Who opened your safety deposit box?'

'Mr Barata. He asked me for the key, and I gave it to him.'

'And then?'

'He unlocked the drawer, started to open it and then ...' Graça clutched her throat as the memory engulfed her. 'He seemed to recoil, cried out, clutched his neck and then he collapsed.'

'You say he clutched his neck. Do you remember where?' the doctor asked.

Graça pictured the clerk to her right, spinning suddenly, the closest hand, his left hand, crossing his chest and grabbing his neck.

'Here,' Graça pointed to her own neck. 'On the right, just below his jawline.'

The doctor scribbled something on her notepad.

'Did you hear anything?' asked the policeman.

'Not really.'

'Anything, anything at all.'

'A faint click, then a whooshing sound.'

'The click of the lock turning?'

Graça shook her head. 'The drawer was open by then, Mr Barata was sliding the box out.'

'The sliding box made the whooshing sound?'

'No, it was more like a bird's wing, something travelling through the air.'

'Any idea what might have made that noise?'

'Not really.'

'A guess?'

'Maybe an insect?'

'Did you notice any insects in the strongroom?'

'No.'

'What happened next?'

'He seemed unable to breathe. I tried to help him, loosened his tie, unbuttoned his shirt collar. Then I tried to get help.'

'And then?'

'I searched his jacket for medicine, anything that might explain his sudden attack, anything that might counteract it.'

'And?'

'There was nothing.'

'What happened after that?'

'I held his hand until he stopped struggling.'

'Struggling?' The policeman leaned forward, alert now.

'Struggling to breathe.'

'How long after collapsing?' the doctor asked.

'I'm not sure.' All sense of time became distorted in such situations. Each second elastic. A minute seemed like an hour. 'But no more than ten minutes, maybe less.' Graça held up her left wrist and put her right thumb over it. 'I felt his heart stop. That's when I started CPR.'

'How long did you attempt cardiopulmonary resuscitation?'
Staying alive, staying alive, Ah, ha, ha, ha, staying alive.
'I'm not sure. At least two cycles of compression and ventilation. The next thing I remember is waking up here.'

TV Studio, Rio de Janeiro, Brazil, January

The production assistant brought soft drinks and ammonia drops. César signalled for his hairdresser to spray mousse onto his hair and comb it through.

Action!

'Let me recap for you.' César put on his most serious expression. 'Karina and her six-year-old son are on their first ever beach holiday. While his mother is sleeping, Noah leaves the hotel room and goes to the beach. Karina runs after him, but by the time she gets there Noah is …'

MISSING. Booms the voice.

'Karina, how did you feel?'

She is crying properly now; the drops always work wonders.

'I was shouting,' she stands to demonstrate. 'Noah, Noah. My baby. Oh, my baby!'

'And crying?'

'Yes,' she wails.

'And running around.'

'In despair.'

'And then what did you hear?'

'I heard clapping.'

'You heard clapping. And what did you think?'

'I didn't know what to think.'

'Because you'd never been to the beach before, had you Karina?'

'No.'

'But our audience here know what it means.' César turned to them. 'Don't you?'

The audience started clapping, it grew to a crescendo.

César let it soar and then held up a hand, palm outwards. The clapping stopped. No conductor of any orchestra had better control.

'Then what happened?'

'A woman came up to me. She said, are you looking for someone?'

'And you said?'

'Yes, I'm looking for my baby.'

'And she said?'

'Come with me.'

'And what happened?'

'We followed the clapping.'

'Ladies and gentlemen, we have a video to show you.'

The screen behind them widens to show a typical beach in mid-summer, a jerky, hand-held camera focusses in on a woman in shorts and T-shirt, rushing over the sand, pushing through the crowds, following the sound of clapping until she reaches a little knot of people. The huddle parts to reveal a child lying on the sand, one man cradling his head, a lifeguard performing CPR on his lifeless body. The video cuts to the sound of a scream.

The audience went very quiet. They knew that each show had at least one tragedy, but they had assumed this segment was the happy ending. César enjoyed the sensation of power.

Cut!

Rio de Janeiro, Brazil, January

The worst nightmares are the ones in which you are unable to move, trapped as terrible things happen around you. Graça woke screaming.

A nurse administered a sedative.

'*Calma*,' he said. 'Just a bad dream.'

Except it wasn't a dream. It was a memory.

When Graça woke again it was light and Dr Rao was standing by the bed with an older woman.

'Good morning, Senhora Neves.'

'Graça,' she croaked.

'How are you feeling this morning?'

Graça tried to sit up, then collapsed back onto the pillows. 'Fine,' she lied.

'This is Dr Jean Parker, our chief of toxicology. She'd like to ask you a few questions.'

Graça studied the older woman as she moved closer to the hospital bed. She had the kind of face that spoke of experience. Each line and indentation earned, a woman with stories to tell.

'Why don't you tell me how you're really feeling?'

Her voice had the same gravitas as her appearance. Why dissemble?

'Exhausted. Weak. Short of breath.'

'Any pain?'

'No.'

'And Mr Barata. You told the police that it was about ten minutes between his collapse and death?'

'Yes.'

'Did the shortness of breath come first?'

'Yes.'

'And his skin colour.'

'His face was bright red.'

'Did he bleed?'

'No.'

'Was there foam in his mouth?'

'Yes.'

'Did you have any contact?'

'I tried to resuscitate him.'

'Including mouth-to-mouth?'

'Yes.'

'And that's when you collapsed?'

Graça tried to sit up, but the effort was beyond her and she sank back down. 'What's wrong with me?'

The toxicologist exchanged a glance with Dr Rao. 'May I?'

The doctor nodded.

'Graça, I have a theory. I'd like to test it by asking you to drink something I've prepared. It's not a conventional medicine. If I'm wrong, it'll do you no harm. If I'm right it might make you feel better.'

'I'll try anything.'

A nurse brought a small plastic cup with a pale green liquid.

'What is it?'

'I'll tell you afterwards.'

Graça took the little cup and knocked it back in two quick swallows. It tasted vile but she'd experienced worse. The nurse gave her a cup of water and Graça sipped until the taste had almost gone.

'What was that?'

'A cocktail made from, among other things, extracts of snake bile and puffer-fish liver.'

'Not sure it'll catch on.' Graça grimaced.

'How do you feel?'

Graça tried to sit up again. This time she was able to hold herself upright without the pillows.

'Better, I think.' She took a deep breath. 'Yes, definitely.' She frowned. 'You think I was poisoned?'

'Perhaps.'

'And your snake oil was an antidote?'

'I hope so.'

'Poisoned with what?'

'Perhaps we should wait ...'

Graça grabbed the toxicologist's hand. 'Professor Parker. I need to know.'

'I'm not sure if I should—'

'Please.' Graça squeezed the hand as hard as she could. 'I studied pharmacy before I joined the federal police force.'

'You're a police officer?'

'Curitiba branch.'

The two medics exchanged glances and then Dr Rao nodded.

'The initial lab results suggest a lipid alkaloid substance,' Professor Parker said. 'Probably one of the batrachotoxins.'

'I didn't see any tree frogs in the vault,' Graça said. 'And I certainly didn't lick any.'

'I see you know your poisons.' The toxicologist nodded. 'It's extremely unusual to find it outside of the Amazon basin.'

'Then why aren't I dead?'

'The dose maketh the poison.'

A woman who knew her Paracelcus.

'And you found batrachotoxin in my blood?'

Professor Parker shook her head. 'Undetectable in your case, but poor Mr Barata received a fatal dose.'

'Mr Barata was not a well man,' Dr Rao added. 'The paramedics assumed he'd had a heart attack. As indeed he had. The toxicology showed us the cause.'

'We were scratching our heads to figure out what was wrong with you. All the tests were inconclusive. But when Dr Rao told me that you'd tried to resuscitate the unfortunate Mr Barata mouth-to-mouth, coupled with your description of his demise, I asked them to run the full suite of toxicology tests on him as well.'

'He was poisoned?' Graça scratched her head. 'When?'

'The action is almost instantaneous. It paralyses the muscles within seconds, stops the heart within minutes.'

'But how?'

'A tiny poison dart deep in his neck.' Dr Rao pointed to a spot just below her jawline. 'Exactly where you described him clutching himself before he collapsed.'

Poisoned in the vault as he opened the safety deposit box. That click and whoosh-whoosh.

'But we were alone in a locked room. How could anyone fire a poison dart at him. And why?' Graça's fingers strayed to her neck. 'And what happened to me?'

'I admire your desire to save a man's life, but it was ill advised. You must have ingested his secreted poison while giving mouth-to-mouth. Fortunately, it was a miniscule amount, and your defences are excellent. Even so, you are very lucky it didn't do more harm.'

Each minute that passed, Graça felt her strength coming back. Breathing more easily, mind clearing, energy returning.

She swung her feet out from under the bedcovers and onto the floor. 'And now you've cured me.'

'Steady on,' Dr Rao wagged a finger. 'As your doctor, I cannot advise …'

'Has anyone inspected the vault?' Graça interrupted. 'Looked for the delivery device in the safety deposit box?'

What was inside that box that it had to be protected with a lethal weapon?

'We've only just informed the police that Mr Barata was poisoned.'

Graça stood up. 'Where are my clothes?'

'Not so fast,' said Dr Rao. 'We have to do more tests.'

Graça ignored her. 'I need to get back to the bank.'

Before someone else does.

Brasília Airport, Brazil, January

Frank was waiting in the airport transit lounge when he spotted an unpleasantly familiar figure walking down the ramp from the Fortaleza connection.

He sprang to his feet and hurried to intercept her.

'Hello Jaqueline.'

She whipped round and stared at him. Her eyes blazed with familiar fire, but there was something new in her gaze, something darker, almost haunted.

'Hello Frank.'

She spoke slowly, drawing out the words with a voice that was soft and low. Her tone was less of surprise than of resignation.

'And goodbye.'

She started to walk away.

Her reaction, or lack of it, irritated him. Surprise or curiosity, even anger or fear were all to be expected after their previous encounters. But not boredom, never that. She had dismissed him as if he was an unwelcome distraction. He followed her, lengthening his stride until they were walking side by side.

'What are you doing here?' he asked.

She increased her pace. 'I might ask you the same question.'

She might, but he saw no reason to answer her. He wasn't even sure that he had an answer. Why was he here? Certainly not for Clara, who had proved a disappointment. He'd travelled to Brazil because of Jaqueline Silver and everything she represented.

As a result he'd uncovered a web of corruption in the Brazilian arm of his own company, Zagrovyl. Perhaps he should be grateful to her. No, that was a step too far.

'Where are you going?' he insisted.

'None of your business.'

'I know what you've been up to.'

'I very much doubt that.'

'Cheating Cuperoil by invoicing them for work you didn't do.'

She stopped dead in her tracks. There was no mistaking the shock in her widening eyes. Shock that he knew? Or shock because she didn't. Could she really be so naive?

'To be honest, I was a little surprised that you would turn native so quickly. I hadn't clocked you as quite so easily corruptible.'

She pursed her lips as if she wanted to argue but was making an effort not to engage.

Now he had her full attention, it was time for the killer blow.

'But then any mother who abandons her own son can't really sink much lower.'

At last, the reaction he hoped for. A flash of anger followed by a smoke-trail of anguish. So much pain in those hazel eyes.

Their tête-à-tête was interrupted by a tannoy message. Flight 592 to Rio de Janeiro was boarding at gate 200.

Jaq turned on her heel and strode away.

Rio de Janeiro, Brazil, January

Graça arrived too late. By the time she was shown upstairs to the bank manager's office, it was the policeman with the luxuriant moustache, the one who interviewed her in hospital, who opened the door.

Sunlight streamed through the gaps in high, badly shuttered windows, revealing a desk and office chair and three large sofas around an onyx-topped table. The bank manager, a small, stocky, middle-aged man, the skin under his eyes drooping, the loose skin forming a wrinkled pouch, greeted her without enthusiasm and nodded for her to sit.

A little puff of dust rose and danced in the sunbeams. The plush fabric was slightly sticky and smelt of stale sweat.

'Senhora Neves, I'm pleased to see you have made such a swift recovery.' The policeman liked to be in charge, whatever his surroundings. 'The hospital just gave me an update.'

Her heart sank. She was half hoping that the toxicology information hadn't reached this officious man yet. But why? Maybe he could help.

'An ingenious theory, if a rather far-fetched story.'

That was why. He was an arse. Moustache for brains.

Graça turned to the bank manager, Mr Moneybags.

'I am so sorry about Mr Barata.'

For a moment he appeared perplexed, as if he'd already forgotten about his lowly employee, then realisation dawned, and he lowered his eyes.

'Terrible shame,' he muttered.

Graça turned to Moustache-for-brains.

'Have you searched the vault?'

He frowned. 'That's a police matter.'

'What about the contents of the box? What was inside?'

Moneybags coughed. 'It was empty.'

Graça could tell he was lying.

'Empty?'

He shrugged and turned his palms to face the ceiling. 'Completely empty.'

'You're telling me that someone booby trapped an empty safety deposit box. That poor Mr Barata died for nothing.'

'We don't know that the box was ... as you say ... booby trapped,' interrupted the policeman.

'Then how did Mr Barata wind up dead?'

'Perhaps you can enlighten me. After all, you were the only other person in the room.'

Graça addressed Mr Moneybags. 'Do you have security cameras?'

He puffed out his chest and drew himself up to his full, diminutive, height.

'Madam, we respect the privacy of our clients. It is absolutely imperative that they can access their private boxes, their personal belongings, without any surveillance.'

'So much so, that you left an employee to die.'

The policeman stroked his moustache.

'This theory of a spring-loaded poison dart from one of

our safety deposit boxes seems a little improbable, doesn't it?' Moneybags said.

Moustache-for-brains nodded. 'More likely that someone administered the poison in person.'

By someone, he meant Graça. Occam's razor – seek the most probable explanation first. Or the laziest explanation. Pick on the person in front of you rather than doing any investigative work.

'And why would I do that?'

The policeman leaned forward. 'That's what I'm going to discover.'

'Why would I poison myself?'

'Perhaps you didn't. You appear to have made an almost miraculous recovery.'

Thanks to Professor Parker, but there was little point in telling them about the snake and puffer-fish antidote.

Graça turned to the bank manager. 'I want to go back to the vault.'

'You no longer have a key.'

'But you do. I left it in the vault.'

He nodded. 'We retrieved a key from the lock of the safety deposit box,' he said. 'After you and Mr Barata were rushed to hospital.'

'May I have it back?'

He shook his head.

'It doesn't belong to you, does it, Senhora Neves?'

'What do you mean?'

'Just this morning we received a letter from a lawyer in Salvador, claiming that the key is lost. The rightful owner is demanding access to the safety deposit box.

'And who is that?'

'That information is confidential.'

'Let me guess.' Graça almost laughed. 'It wouldn't by any chance be a Dr Jaq Silver?'

Their faces told her all she needed to know.

Brasília Airport, Brazil, January

If Frank had been a betting man, he would have concluded three things from his meeting with Jaqueline.

The first was that she'd been used. By someone other than him this time. She was either genuinely unaware of how business worked in Brazil, something he'd twigged after one night in the arms of the voluptuous Clara, or she'd suspected something amiss but was so focused on her own agenda that she hadn't stopped to ponder.

To anyone unused to dealing with research scientists and professional engineers that might have sounded incredible. But Frank had long and wearisome experience of people with first-class degrees and PhDs who were deeply stupid when it came to the real world. They produced Gantt charts mapping every wrinkle of the future, but lost sight of the present. So focussed on their reams of data, their interminable specifications and dull standards, their nested algorithms and vast, intricate drawings, they failed to see what was right in front of their noses.

How could someone live practically rent free in a luxury flat amid a collection of original paintings that belonged in a museum, above a garage stuffed with rare motorbikes and not wonder about the owner? Had Jaqueline really asked no questions about her landlord? How could she not be curious about Walter Salgado and how he made his money? It had taken Frank less than a week to discover that Walter was the chief fixer for Cuperoil in Africa, the go-between who transferred money from business to government to ensure that the right projects were approved. At the right price. With all that money changing hands, was it surprising that a little stuck to his fingers? A tiny fraction of billions of dollars soon adds up.

How could anyone accept a salary from an engineering consultancy and not wonder why they were never given any meaningful work to do? It must have been a godsend for Tecnoproject. As a foreign consultant on a visiting visa, an expert who had to be paid outside of Brazil, they had the perfect excuse to move millions of dollars abroad.

Frank had suffered long enough in the company of engineers to recognise the inverse correlation between mathematical ability and common sense. He knew just how simple these creatures really were.

If he hadn't seen her reaction, he might have credited Jaq with a little more savvy, a modicum of emotional intelligence. But he'd seen the gears grinding behind her eyes, spotted the synapses snapping as she finally made the glaringly obvious connections.

No, had he been a betting man he'd put money on the odds that she really hadn't understood the part she'd played in this giant web of corruption.

Now she knew, she'd have to do something about it.

This was the second thing that Frank inferred. Unless Jaq had changed completely – and a leopard never loses its spots – she wouldn't be able to let this lie. Jaq would confront her employer, Tecnoproject, maybe even go head to head with the owner of the flat, Walter Salgado, or at least the go-between in the arrangement, Marina Queiros. Left to her own devices, Jaq might even investigate Zagrovyl Brazil, before Frank had time to use what he'd learned to his advantage.

The third thing that Frank resolved was that he would not let this golden opportunity slip through his fingers.

An idea was forming in his mind about how to use this to his advantage.

Rio de Janeiro, Brazil, January

From the plane window, I watch the lights of a floating oil platform heading out to sea. Out to the deep salt. Drilling deeper than man has ever gone before. The plane turns inland and banks over Guanabara Bay. The Rio lights twinkle far below.

I don't want to think about what Frank Good said to me, but I can't stop the questions swirling around in my head.

Is he right? And if so, did I know? Did I suspect? Did I even think about it?

All that mattered was finding my son.

And now all I can think about is finding his killer.

The airport bus drives past the old royal palace, a squat, subdued affair given the extravagance normally associated with the House of Braganza. The first home of King John and his entourage looks more like a barracks. Imagine if the British royal family had decamped from London, England, and moved the court and parliament to Calcutta, India, or Williamsburg, Virginia. And yet that was exactly what happened to the second-largest colonial power at the time. The Portuguese monarchy, and several thousand followers, fled from a French invasion of their homeland in 1807 and made Rio de Janeiro the new capital.

I ignore the travel advice and get the metro for the final leg of my journey. If it's good enough for ordinary Brazilians, it's good enough for me. I observe them on their way to work, all shapes and sizes, all colours and races, neither extremely rich nor extremely poor, the squeezed middle.

I emerge a few blocks away from my destination and stop for a coffee at a *pastelaria*; it's like being back in Lisbon again except that everything is bigger and brighter – from the coffee cups and pastries to the height of the ceilings and vivid colours of Art Deco stained glass.

I pay for my coffee and start walking.

I am finally meeting with Crazy Gloves. Xavier has arranged it all. Not in a gold mine, but in the safety of the Rio de Janeiro botanic gardens. All Raimundo Elias knows is that I am a wealthy foreigner with an interest in supporting Ecobrium, and that I have insisted on a face-to-face meeting. I'm to be given guest access to the private section of the orchid collection, the part that is not open to the public, and the only other guest is Crazy Gloves.

The old gunpowder factory is now a museum. It seems a fitting place to assemble my gun. The beauty of Marina's novel material – polymemory – is that I can carry all the components on an aeroplane without any risk of discovery, and all I need is an electric socket to turn soft fabric pieces into the hard grip and barrel of a handgun. I check and load before concealing the weapon in the waistband of my shorts, making sure it is covered by my loose summer blouse.

I'm ready.

And there he is. My mortal enemy. Raimundo Elias stands on the veranda of the orchid house, talking to someone leaning against a wooden pillar.

I stop dead in my tracks when I see who it is. Xavier is standing outside the orchid house. What is my lover doing here? This is one complication I don't need. He organised the meeting but didn't mention attending it. How to get him out of the firing line? He waves and I compose myself before walking towards him. I have to think fast.

Then the bullets start to fly.

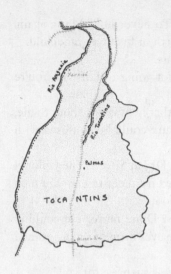

2km from the gold mine, Tocantins, Brazil, January

In the jungle complex, high above the river Tocantins, soldiers dragged a young man over the rope bridge that linked two conical huts on stilts.

'Come along sleepyhead.' The Colonel stood in the doorway of the prison hut while the soldier prodded an older man with a rifle butt. 'Today's the day.'

The Colonel put two fingers together and pointed them at Pedro.

'Bang, bang, you're dead.'

He raised the fingertips to his lips and blew away imaginary smoke.

Finally. Execution should come as a relief. Anything would be better than continued imprisonment and torture at the hands of this lunatic. Pedro struggled to his knees.

Despite himself, Pedro began to tremble. With death imminent, a wash of regret surged though him. To never hold Maria again. To leave Luis and Chica before the birth of his first grandchild.

'Please,' he whimpered. 'Don't kill me.'

'Not you, my dear little man. I'm not going to kill you. You're my honoured guest.'

Pedro almost laughed. Was it relief that he was not about to die, or the idea that incarceration and torture could be confused with hospitality?

'I'm talking about our enemy Silver, Dr Jaq Silver.' The Colonel blew on his fingertips again and grinned from ear to ear. 'My men have found her again. It'll all be over soon.'

Poor devil. Could he have said less? Done more? He couldn't even save himself, what hope had there ever been of saving others? Pedro slumped against the wall.

'And Pedro,' the Colonel said. 'I have a surprise for you.'

Pedro closed his eyes. In all his months of captivity, he'd learned that whatever the Colonel promised, it always ended in pain.

The only thing he wanted was his freedom, and he suspected that it was not the surprise his captor had in mind.

'I thought you might get lonely, so I brought you a friend, for company.'

The Colonel stood aside as they dragged the man in. He'd been beaten so badly he was barely conscious.

'This is Hugo,' the Colonel said. 'Hugo, meet Pedro. Pedro, meet Hugo. Now what do you say.'

Pedro hurried forward, as far as his shackles would allow and bowed his head. 'Pleased to meet you, Hugo.'

The man let out a cry and collapsed at his feet.

ALVORADA

1,200km from the gold mine, a freight train, Alvorada, Tocantins State, Brazil, February

The train remains in the sidings. Without motion to create a breeze, the heat is unbearable. I long for wind, for rain, even the occasional cloud to block the sun's rays. I never thought I'd miss English weather so much.

As the temperature rises, my thoughts turn to Xavier.

I've always had a soft spot for a gorgeous man. Of course, physical beauty is not enough; I would run a mile from someone who was cruel or violent, mean or stupid or whose views I despised. And some men, however gorgeous, are completely off-limits. When I was a lecturer, I couldn't get too friendly with a student; I never dated a man who worked for me – in fact I never dated anyone employed by the same company, always kept work and sex completely separate.

But a really fine man, a man with a chiselled face and gentle eyes, a generous mouth and wide, intelligent brow, a man with strong arms and a broad chest, warms my insides, and there's something about the back of a naked man that makes me melt – that geometrical perfection: an inverted triangle over two perfect squares.

I'm not that interested in bull necks or six packs or genitalia, I don't care if bodies are covered in hair or completely smooth. I don't like aftershave or deodorant – I rely on the natural scent of a man to tell if we'll be compatible in bed.

I'm rarely wrong.

And yet I was wrong about Xavier.

Not about the scent. Xavier smells of the sea. It doesn't matter how long he stands in the shower, how thoroughly he soaps himself, the moment he's dry, there's a briny green musk that makes me think of the Gods of the sea: Poseidon or Neptune.

In West Africa and South America, the sea gods are female: Olókun and Iara. Funny how the Greek and Roman sea deities were men. Big men with beards and strong upper bodies.

I was wrong about Xavier.

Not about the sex. The sex was as fine as anything I've known. I'd been so preoccupied with other things that I'd almost forgotten how good it can be. Fiery and all-encompassing and warm and sweet.

Xavier is a confident, experienced man who genuinely likes women and always tries to give just a little more than he takes: a winning combination. Not in a needy, showy – please notice how generous I'm being – or subservient, creepy – I'll be your doormat – sort of way. Taking part of his pleasure from the pleasure he gives to others. Gave to me.

Never underestimate how rare that is.

We first met when I was a teenager. A teenager in trouble. He helped me, even went to prison for me. I thought he was a friend. I wanted him as a lover. He came to me. I trusted him.

So how did I read him so wrong?

79

Au

Gold

196.967

Brazil's production of gold, 80 glittering tonnes of it, was worth about US$ 4 billion in 2013.

Gold is mainly used in investments and jewellery.

Botanic Gardens, Rio de Janeiro, Brazil, January

Oskar had always liked climbing trees. As a child he was forever disappearing up into leafy branches to avoid his father's blows. As a man he liked to work on his upper body strength in a forest rather than a gym. The botanic gardens offered many interesting arboreal opportunities, but he selected a giant sequoia with a panoramic view.

From the canopy he could see the Corcovado with the statue of Christ the Redeemer on top, his concrete arms open wide, towering above the city of Rio de Janeiro. Beneath him, the botanic gardens fanned out from a central avenue of giant palm trees. A river of clear water meandered under bridges towards the meeting point of the orchid house.

He saw Silver first. Head held high, she moved confidently across the path.

Little did she know what lay in store for her. His men were ready and waiting.

He didn't hear the throaty roar of the old motorbike until it was almost underneath him. And when he saw who was driving the Harley Davidson Knucklehead, he nearly fell out of his perch.

Federal Agent Graça Neves. What the fuck was she doing here?

Oskar steadied himself. This could only be a good thing. Two birds with one stone. And then he saw that she was not alone.

He'd expected so much more from this day, had planned to take Silver alive and take his time. Everyone had a right to enjoy their work after all. But he was a professional. In the end, the job came first and sometimes sacrifices had to be made to get it done.

Oskar put the rifle sight to his eye.

'Goodbye, Silver,' he muttered.

He pressed the trigger, felt the recoil slam into his shoulder and watched her fall.

Gunfire exploded from all angles. The police were shooting, and his men were firing back.

He took the opportunity to target Agent Neves next. He misjudged the speed and the first shot missed. She spun round and stared directly at him. He fired again – this time the bullet hit the fuel tank, millimetres away from his target. His next shot ignited the leaking fuel. The smoke and flames hid her from view. Before he could get his sights on her again, the rifle barrel leapt into the air, shot out of his hands. He made a grab for it as it fell, but it crashed through the leaves and branches to the garden below. A bullet grazed his arm, and Oskar retreated into the canopy.

Down below, mayhem had broken out, a pitched battle between RIMPO and the federal police. Oskar checked his injuries; just a flesh wound. He used his belt to reduce the bleeding. It wasn't too bad. So long as he remained here, he was safe for now. With any luck Neves was a casualty and the rest would soon forget about a lone, unarmed man in a tree.

But today he had no luck.

His men were retreating and, worse, not only was Neves still alive, but Silver wasn't dead or even injured. Like a fool, she had run towards the flaming motorbike and was attacking the blaze with a fire extinguisher from the orchid house.

Once the flames were out, Silver remained standing, defiant, surrounded by uniformed policemen.

Oskar leant forward to see what would happen next. The police were notoriously trigger happy. Perhaps they'd do his job for him, finish her off.

Neves strode up to her.

'Dr Jaq Silver, you are under arrest.'

A drop of blood fell from the tree onto the ground. Everyone looked up. Oskar drew back, but not before he saw the recognition ripple across the faces of the two women below.

His jaw dropped as he realised that Neves still had his gun.

She pointed it up at the canopy and fired.

São Paulo, Brazil, January

The runway shimmered in the fierce summer sun. From the air-conditioned comfort of the airport hotel, Frank waited for his final appointment before returning to England.

It had been an interesting trip, but he was bored with the heat, bored with the chaos, bored with the smiles of people who had so little but didn't seem to care.

At Frank's request, Busco – his PI – had contacted the federal police with a tip-off about Dr Silver. She had some questions to answer. Disclosures that would probably land her in jail. Sweet revenge. His work here was almost done.

Just one last piece of business to conclude. Some information to trade. Call it an insurance policy.

It was the PI who had drawn his attention to the link between César and Jaq's boyfriend. Frank and Busco were concluding business when a throwaway remark set Frank thinking.

'Guess who is sponsoring Xavier's trip to Brazil?' Busco asked.

'I have absolutely no idea.'

'César from Hélio TV.'

'The presenter on *The Missing*?'

'The very same.'

'So what?'

'Whatever César does, the military are never far behind.'

His guest arrived 20 minutes late but made no apology.

'Dr Good? *Boa tarde.*'

'Good afternoon.'

Frank hadn't paid much attention to César on the TV screen – he'd focussed on Jaqueline Silver – but the presenter of *The Missing* was easy to recognise; he appeared on magazine covers and advertising hoardings all over the country.

'Can I get you a drink?'

'Water, thank you.'

Frank snapped his fingers at the barman, pointed at his own glass of water and held up two fingers.

César checked his watch. 'I fly in two hours.'

'This won't take long.'

After César left, Frank checked in for his flight at the VIP desk of the hotel and waited in the bar while they sorted out his transport. It was only a five-minute walk – up in a lift, across a sky bridge and down an escalator – but the complimentary limo was part of the first-class package, and he wasn't giving anything up unless he got something in return.

Rio de Janeiro, Brazil, January

The interview room is hot and stuffy. Two plain-clothes officers are waiting for me. As the prison guard transfers my chain from her wrist to a ring in the floor, I take a few moments to look at the agent who arrested me. A plump, young woman with dark skin and intelligent eyes.

The other woman is older and takes charge.

'Remove the handcuffs,' she orders.

'My orders are—' the guard protests.

'Just do it and leave.'

The guard mutters under her breath but complies and stomps out, slamming the heavy metal door behind her.

I rub my wrists, glad to be free of the rough metal bracelets. 'Thank you.'

'My name is Agent Zélia Neto and this is Agent Graça Neves,' she says. 'We're federal police officers.'

Why are the feds involved? I don't know much about Brazilian law enforcement, but I'm pretty sure it's the state-run uniformed military police who patrol the streets and plain-clothes civil police who investigate crimes.

'And you are Dr Jaqueline Silver?'

'I am.'

'What is your relationship with Walter Salgado?'

So that's what all this is about. I almost laugh with relief. The federal police are interested in corruption. I may be planning murder, but I am not, and never have been, corrupt.

'I've never met anyone by the name of Walter Salgado.'

'That's not what I asked.'

'I have no relationship with Walter Salgado.'

She raises an eyebrow. 'But you live in his flat, drive his motorbike, spend Christmas at his beach house.'

'House-sitting while the owner is abroad. All that was arranged through a ...' the word friend is on the tip of my tongue and I have to force myself to withhold it. '... a work contact.'

'Marina Queiros?'

'That's right.' No point in denying it, they already know, and anyway, I owe Marina nothing, not after what she did to me. I'll never be able to prove it was Marina who shot at me in the sea, but I witnessed with my own eyes her attempt deliver me into the clutches of Oskar the RIMPO beefcake who tried to kill me. Marina betrayed me to RIMPO.

'So you stole his motorbike.'

'I borrowed it.' I turn to the younger officer who rode the same bike right up to the orchid house in the botanic gardens. 'Looks like you did too.'

She nods. 'Why did you leave the bike unlocked in the multi-storey car park in Florianópolis?'

I need to be careful what I tell them. I can't mention the kidnapping, my dash to fetch the ransom. After all, I still have to finish what Raimundo Elias started.

'I had to go back to England on urgent family business. I was distracted.'

A look passes between them.

Agent Neto leans forward. 'We have reason to believe that Walter Salgado is running a corrupt network. He received that motorbike, and other valuable assets, as payment for the fraudulent award of contracts.'

'A bribe?'

'Exactly. Which makes you an accessory. You benefitted from the proceeds of crime.'

I have a flashback to the lovely old Harley Davidson bursting into flames. 'I don't think anyone will be benefitting for a while.'

The flicker of a smile passes over the younger officer's lips.

'We will require a signed statement.'

I nod. 'Of course.' Given what I'm planning to do after I get out of here, this is the least of my worries.

The older officer stands. 'Graça. A word please.'

After a few minutes Agent Neves returns alone.

'Tell me Dr Silver, why are you in jail?'

Is this some kind of trick? I look at her more closely.

'You arrested me.'

'For your own safety.'

That sounds like something Xavier would say. I'm about to ask whether my lover – my former lover – tipped them off, whether he is safe, but then I think better of it. Xavier betrayed me. He's dead to me now and I'm giving nothing away until I understand my predicament.

'What were you doing in the Rio de Janeiro botanical gardens?' she asks.

'It's a beautiful place ...'

'You went to meet someone. Who?'

If she doesn't know that I was planning to meet and kill Raimundo Elias then I'm hardly going to incriminate myself.

'I'd arranged a private tour of the orchid collection.'

'You have a special interest in orchids, Dr Silver?'

I say nothing.

'Why were you carrying a gun?'

'Rio is a dangerous place.'

She stands and walks to the window, puts her hand on one of the metal bars and continues, facing away from me.

'I want to ask you about something else,' Agent Neves says. 'About a safety deposit box in the central Rio branch of Banco Espirito Santo.'

Is she talking about my grandmother's vault?

'I believe you lodged an application to recover the contents of box 196.967.'

I shrug. 'It belonged to my grandmother.'

Agent Neves turns. 'And you have the key?'

'No. I only discovered that my grandmother kept a box in the bank when I was presented with the bill.'

'Do you know what's inside it?'

'No idea.' And even less interest. Only Carmo, my lawyer in Portugal seems to think it's important.

'Have you visited the bank?'

'No.' Why is a federal police agent interested in this?

'But you took steps to protect it?'

'The only steps I took were through my lawyer.'

Agent Neves returns to the table and takes her seat.

'You have recently returned from Amazonia, correct?'

There was no point in lying. 'Yes.'

'What were you doing there?'

'I work for an engineering consultancy. I was visiting mines.'

Graça leaned in. 'And collecting poison?'

I stare at her, dumbfounded.

'The Rio police are investigating the murder of Rafael Barata, a bank clerk,' Graça says. 'He was killed by a poison dart laced with batrachotoxin. He died while trying to access your safety deposit box.'

This can't be coincidence. Does she know about the bank clerk in Angola? Carmo's friend who died while trying to access my family records in a bank vault in Luanda? There have been too many sudden heart attacks. Ferreira, Centeno, Castanho and now Barata.

I say nothing.

'I've been looking into your history,' Agent Neves continues. 'It seems that this is not the first time you have used poison. A case in China involving sweets laced with thallium.'

'I was the witness in that case, not the accused,' I say. And now Sophie is in jail.

'And yet you were imprisoned in Slovenia after a poisoning with ergotamine.'

The federal police are surprisingly well informed. Who have they been talking to?

'It wasn't poisoning.' Poor Stefan. 'And I was completely exonerated.'

'But you don't deny that there's an ongoing case against you in England. Involving nitroglycerine.'

Will I never be free of these shadows? A change made at work to improve safety that had unintended, ultimately fatal, consequences. I've been absolved in the criminal courts, and yet the families of the deceased will not give up. And who can blame them?

'A civil case. And nitroglycerine is not usually labelled a poison.'

'Indeed, it's more usually labelled an explosive.' She smiles.

'Good of you to remind me that you are also an explosives expert. Quite the arsenal you have at your disposal.'

'I'm a chemical engineer. My expertise is in safety.'

'And yet the people around you seem to wind up dead?'

I bite my lip and say nothing.

'In my experience, Dr Silver, there is no smoke without fire.'

Factually incorrect, there are plenty of decompositions that produce fumes without flame. But now doesn't seem the right time to discuss combustion.

She leans forward.

'Where were you on Christmas Eve?'

'Santa Catarina Island, Florianópolis,' I say without hesitation.

'What do you know about an explosion at the airport?'

'Hydrogen,' I say.

'Pardon?'

'There was an explosion during the refuelling of a hydrogen-powered experimental plane.'

'Were you responsible?'

'Not directly. I was several kilometres offshore, swimming in the sea.'

'Indirectly?'

'I had persuaded a ...' I stumble again over the word friend. Marina is no longer a friend. '... a pilot to fly me from Sampo in an experimental jet. I guess it was because of me she needed to refuel in a regional airport that didn't have the right infrastructure.'

'Or perhaps it was sabotage. An incident engineered to create a distraction.'

'How do you know?'

'It blew my car windows out.'

'You were there? Why?'

'I was looking for you.'

It's my turn to lean forward.

'Hang on,' I say. 'You're with the federal police. Why are you investigating an explosion in Floripa and a poisoning in Rio de Janeiro? Isn't that the job of the local police? Or is there a connection?'

'Perhaps you are the connection?' Agent Neves closes my file and sits back in her chair. 'Tell me ...' she drums the carboard with her fingers. 'What do you think is going on here?'

'I've been set up.'

'Why should I believe you?'

I run a hand through my hair. It's gritty and dirty. I think of Beefcake, his buzz cut covered in blood as he fell from a tree to his death on a gravel path in the botanic gardens.

I try a question of my own.

'The man that you killed, the soldier with the smoking cobra tattoo.'

'What about him?'

'Why did you shoot him?'

'Because he was going to ...' she looks up at me from under her lashes. She must know that he was no immediate threat. She must realise that I know it too. 'Because he is ...' she corrects herself, '... was, a wicked man. He tried to rape a young girl. He would have killed me.'

I nod. 'His name was Oskar Guerra. He tried to kill me more than once. All I can say is, my enemy's enemy is my friend.'

'You are right to trust me, but that doesn't mean I trust you.'

I like this woman. She may be with the police, but she has a spark about her, an independence that I admire. And she's my best hope right now.

'And how do I win your trust?'

'I work for the financial crimes unit within the Federal Police Bureau. We catch and convict those involved in corruption.'

I've been putting off thinking about what Frank Good said to me. About the realities of employment in Brazil.

Was I stupidly naive?

Or just in a hurry?

Look, I needed a job. A job in Brazil. A job to fund my search, to allow me to travel around, to get to know the country my son was brought up in. Tecnoproject offered the perfect solution. Did I ever stop to consider that it might have been just a little too perfect?

Yes, it was laid back, but everyone told me that business in Brazil was done in a different way. When in Rome ...

Bruno was always waiting for Cuperoil in Curitiba. I never pressed because I had other things on my mind. I was told that business development moved more slowly in Brazil, and yet my own experience with Áerex suggested the opposite. Why didn't I stop to consider? Why didn't I challenge?

Tecnoproject were happy to pay my salary, find me accommodation, arrange my travel. What seemed generous to me was a drop in the ocean to them. I never stopped to consider how it worked.

It all makes sense now.

Tecnoproject had staff embedded in Cuperoil refineries. They made proposals for work: safety studies, environmental audits, feasibility studies, front-end engineering, investment projects that never progressed but were paid for all the same.

On every real contract Tecnoproject gained, they charged many times more hours than staff worked. Some of that extra stayed in the company, paid for Bruno's fast cars. Most of it went to the fixers, the men and women who ensured that Cuperoil awarded Tecnoproject its fair share of contracts.

Fair in the sense that the consultancies carved up the opportunities. Fair in the sense that they met once a quarter and agreed which work they were interested in, negotiated who would win what, revealed their pricing and agreed not to undercut one another. Fair in the sense of everyone winning – everyone except for the shareholders and taxpayers and ordinary people of Brazil.

No wonder Tecnoproject were happy to employ me, indifferent to whether I performed any billable work or not. Because all the while they were sending millions of dollars, in my name, to the offshore accounts of political fixers, the men and women who ensure that, whichever party is in power, the system never changes.

I've been played.

How could I not have seen that there is no such thing as the perfect job?

Was I complicit? Did I fail to question? Or did I just accept with gratitude that for once in my troubled life, I could focus on what was important to me without worrying about how to pay for it?

Never look a gift horse in the mouth.

Well now the maw was open wide and I am staring at rotten teeth, diseased gums, a foetid tongue, and I'm choking on its stinking breath.

'Who tipped you off? Told you where to find me?'

'I couldn't possibly reveal the source.'

Should I tell her about Tecnoproject and the inflated bills to Cuperoil? Maybe it's small compared to Walter Salgado's schemes, but easier to prove.

'I have information that you might find useful.'

'Would you testify in court?'

I'll say anything to get out of here.

'Yes.'

'And would you help me with something else first?'

'Of course.'

Graça's phone rings and she answers it, breaking into a broad smile.

'Come on.' She stands up.

'Come on where?'

'We have work to do.

Rio de Janeiro, Brazil, January

The black-and-white mosaic had been laid out in the form of a caravel, the versatile sailing ship that brought the fifteenth-century Portuguese explorers to the shores of Brazil. Its lateen sails and high prow decorated the pavement outside the Banco Espirito Santo.

Graça opened the door to the Bank of the Holy Spirit and let her companion go ahead. Jaq approached the private banking welcome desk.

'I'm here to see Mr Pedro Camargo.'

'I'm afraid that won't be possible.' The receptionist barely glanced up. Mr Camargo is on an extended business trip.'

'Then someone in his department?'

'Mr Barata, his deputy, is sadly ...' the receptionist shook her curls, '... no longer with us.'

Graça marched forward and interrupted. 'Please inform the manager that Dr Silver is here to see him.' She smiled. 'With Graça Neves.'

The bank manager's office was at the top of a grand flight of marble stairs. His secretary came to show them the way.

'Dr Silver, welcome. How are you enjoying your time in Brazil?'

The chit-chat went on for several minutes as coffee and water were served, the rigmarole of a handbag dance, circling around rather than getting to the point. Graça could see that Jaq was well schooled in business etiquette, understood that in Brazil, it was not only rude, but counterproductive to move too fast, boundaries had to be drawn and tested.

Mr Moneybags was the first to crack.

'I have a letter from your lawyer.'

'Advogado Nogueira? Yes.'

'The key to your family safety deposit box appears to have been mislaid.'

'Indeed.'

'I'm not quite clear how that key came into the possession of,' he nodded at Graça, 'Miss Neves.'

'It's a long story.' Graça said, shooting Jaq a warning glance.

Mr Moneybags frowned. 'And then Miss Neves lost the key.'

'In your bank vault,' Graça protested.

Mr Moneybags made an expansive gesture with his hands.

'Miss Neves no longer has your key.'

'But you do.' Graça said.

Mr Moneybags held up his hand. 'Miss, I am speaking with Dr Silver.'

Jaq leaned forward. 'Then get on with it,' she hissed.

The bank manager appeared startled at the sudden change of tone.

'You have your ID?'

'Yes,' Jaq said. She slid her passport across the desk.

Mr Moneybags rang his desk buzzer and a young woman entered. She handed a file to her boss and laid a pad of paper and pen in front of Jaq.

'Can you provide the three-point verification?' Moneybags asked.

'Com anel, nome e número do canto,' Jaq muttered under her breath.

'Here's the ring.' She removed a gold band from her finger and handed it to Moneybags. 'The number is ten in Roman numerals.' She made a large X on the paper in front of her. 'And the name is …'

Graça watched Jaq form the letters Mercúrio. Where had she heard that name recently?

Jaq folded the paper and passed it across the desk.

The bank manager opened the file and nodded.

'Good, good. Well that all seems to be in order.'

'My key?'

'I'll have it delivered to your lawyer.'

'No,' Jaq shook her head. 'I require immediate access to my safety deposit box.'

'Alas,' said Mr Moneybags with a broad grin. 'That will not be possible. The vault is still closed off as a potential crime scene.'

Graça pulled out her police badge. 'Federal Agent Doutora Graça Neves demanding immediate access.'

This time they took the stairs.

Graça signed in, followed by Jaq. The security guard opened the first door of the air lock, and they stepped inside.

They were joined by a uniformed policeman who closed the first door before turning to the vault entry. He grasped the wheel. As he began to turn it, Graça had a sudden memory of Mr Barata's soft, pink hands.

The thick steel door swung open.

Inside the vault, Graça caught her breath and steadied herself against the door frame. The dimly lit, low-ceilinged cellar was closing in, her heart was beating too fast. Was there poison in the air? Affecting her breathing? Graça looked at the others.

The policeman was watching her like a hawk. Not a trace of sympathy in that cold, hard stare. But neither he nor Moneybags nor Jaq seemed to have any difficulty breathing. This was all in her head, the memory of what had happened here. Graça forced herself to take slow, shallow breaths until her hands stopped trembling and her heart rate returned to normal.

'Agent Neves, are you all right?'

Graça ignored them and stepped into the vault, pacing round the strongroom to look for hiding places. Exactly as she remembered, there was nowhere obvious. The room was about ten metres long and two metres high. Impossible to tell how deep it was, as the wall of safety deposit boxes made an impenetrable barrier. She walked to the left, then to the right and shone a pocket torch at the edges. No gap between the steel frame and the walls.

'How is the room ventilated?'

Moneybags pointed to the grilles at floor level on one wall. Graça bent down and shone a light inside, first one then another until she had inspected all four. Graça could see that the ducting was far too narrow for a person to hide in.

They walked to row 196 column 967. From the approximate position where Mr Barata had been standing, Graça made a three-hundred-and-sixty-degree survey. The ventilation grilles were too far away, the angle was all wrong for firing a dart to the neck. In any case, before Mr Barata collapsed, Graça had been standing between him and the grilles, blocking the path of any tiny missile. The poison delivery couldn't have been airborne, otherwise she would have received a similar dose. Almost undetectable in her blood, but enough to kill Mr Barata, so the delivery mechanism must have been more direct.

There was only one place the poison could have come from.

Graça pulled on a pair of latex gloves before approaching the safety deposit box.

Graça nodded at Jaq, who stepped forward and inserted the key.

'Stop,' Graça said. She motioned for everyone to move out of the way. 'Who closed the drawer?'

'I did,' volunteered Mr Moneybags.

'What's inside? Another box? A tray?'

'A tray.'

'Did you take the tray out?'

'No,' he coughed. 'The drawer was far enough open for me to see that it was empty.'

If there had been a device inside the drawer, a catapult for delivering a tiny dart, could it really have remained undetected?

'So, you inspected the inside?'

'Yes.' He coughed again. 'There was nothing.'

He was undoubtedly lying. That cough was his tell. He'd never make a poker player, which was perhaps just as well for the fortunes of the Bank of the Holy Spirit. But what was he lying about? Had he removed whatever was inside? Or had he removed a tiny spring-loaded bow that fired the dart that killed Mr Barata? Or both? The worst-case scenario was that he'd removed the contents but left the weapon. Could the action of closing the drawer have re-armed it?

Impatient with the delay, Mr Moneybags stepped forward.

'Are you going to open it?'

Graça stepped back. 'What if the same thing happens again?'

'Poison darts?' He laughed. 'You really expect us to buy that ridiculous theory?'

Graça moved aside. 'Be my guest.' *Don't say I didn't warn you.*

He turned the lock and slid the drawer open.

No click. No swoosh.

'See for yourself.'

Graça stepped forward. It really was empty. Why would someone pay for a safety deposit box that contained nothing?

If the poison-dart theory was nonsense, then how had Mr Barata died? If the theory was correct, then why had the bank manager removed the evidence?

She ran her gloved fingers along the smooth metal sides of the tray, but there was nothing. Gingerly, Graça removed the tray from inside the drawer and turned it upside down. Fabricated from a sheet of stainless steel, cut into a rectangle with shallow sides folded up and welded together, the drawer was as simple an object as you could imagine. It had no hidden compartments.

Graça propped the tray against the wall of strongboxes; it came up to her knees; she examined the drawer.

Nothing.

'Seen enough?'

'Yes.'

Graça was about to replace the tray when she saw it. A tiny tube with spring activated piston was wedged between the boxes. The fingertip gap was just wide enough for someone to prime and insert the tiny device without opening the box itself.

'Let's go.'

Moneybags brought his eye up to the retinal scanner.

Graça pulled out a clear plastic pouch, the sort that airport security insists on when sending toiletries through the scanner. She used a ballpoint pen to coax the delivery device into the pouch, then pushed the pen in with it and sealed it up.

Had there been more than one dart? *Click, whoosh-whoosh.* Graça stood with her back to the box and then paced forward, shining the torch beam onto the floor.

And there it was. A tiny shard, the size and shape of a dried clove, the sharpened flower bud of *Syzygium aromaticum*, the spice GG used to flavour her molasses cake.

Jaq had spotted it too. Did the men see? The policeman and the bank manager had their backs to the scene, lost in whispered conversation. Jaq moved to block their line of sight as Graça turned off the torch.

The men were busy opening the air lock. Graça double-bagged the evidence and slipped it into her jacket.

There was only one place to take this, straight to toxicology.

Rio de Janeiro, Brazil, January

The hospital is a hive of activity: ambulances arriving, paramedics running with trolleys, patients on stretchers being rushed to theatre.

I stand aside as a young woman is wheeled past. That was me a few weeks ago, and I might still be in a Floripa hospital if not for the medical staff who got me back on my feet. We turn away from accident and emergency and follow the signs to toxicology.

Professor Parker is expecting us.

'Graça,' she holds out both arms and they embrace.

Graça introduces me as Jaq, and we shake hands.

Professor Parker turns back to Graça. 'You're fully recovered?'

'Thanks to you.'

'Nonsense. It's a team effort in here.'

Graça nods. 'But you listened.'

'The patient generally possesses the key information required to design their cure pathway.' She smiles. 'Although few have quite as dramatic a story to tell as yours. Did you get to the bottom of your mystery?'

'Here.' Graça puts on a latex glove, removes the plastic pouch from her pocket and lays it on the lab bench. 'I found another dart.'

'I'll get it analysed straight away.' Professor Parker calls for an assistant and a young man in a white lab coat picks up the sample with a pair of steel tongs and puts it on a metal tray.

'You were lucky to catch me,' Professor Parker adds. 'I leave for Palmas this week.'

'Can I watch the testing?' Graça asks.

'Of course.'

I stand up, then hesitate at the door as Graça leaves with the technician, something tugging at the edges of my memory.

Parker. Toxicology.

And then I remember why the name is familiar. Could this be the Professor Parker cited in so many of Ecobrium's studies?

'Your research project is in Tocantins?' I ask.

'Yes.'

'Are you the Jean Parker who is looking at water pollution from mining?'

She looks surprised. 'That's right. And you are?'

'Silver,' I say. 'Dr Jaq Silver.'

She frowns for a minute as if trying to place me. I pray that my role in releasing thousands of tonnes of toxic waste into a river to save the lives of a town has not become public knowledge.

'We corresponded about Ecobrium earlier this month.'

'Of course! Now I remember.' Professor Parker smiles. 'You

asked some interesting questions about my project. I was writing a reply, but now we can talk instead.' She gestures for me to sit again.

Another time, another life, nothing would have delighted me more than to discuss scientific research with this brilliant woman. But right here, right now, there is only one mission and everything else is a distraction.

'Are you still in contact with Ecobrium?' I ask.

'The green guerrillas?' Jean Parker takes off her glasses and fixes her eyes on mine. 'Why do you ask?'

'I'm looking for one of them. The one they call the boss.'

'Raimundo Elias. You've met him?'

I nod.

'Describe him.'

'Forties, built like a bull, thinning blond hair, sideburns, angular face, deep-set eyes, protruding forehead, Porto Alegre accent.'

Jean nods. 'That sounds like Ray. And if you've already encountered him, you know to steer clear.'

'Not an option.' I shake my head. 'Unfinished business.'

'You and me both. I guess you know that Ecobrium asked me to verify some of their claims?'

'I saw your name on the early papers.'

She sighs. 'Most environmental activists do good work. They go places no one else wants to go. They talk to people that no one else cares about. They collect data to prove what is happening. Is it surprising that they get frustrated when no one wants to listen?'

'Is that how Ecobrium came about?'

Jean nods. 'A radical splinter group. Tired of legal obfuscation, political circumlocution. Committed to direct action.'

'And how did you get involved?'

'They were accused of exaggerating the problem, of using data selectively. One of their members was previously a student of mine. She knew they needed to enlist reputable scientists with an academic track record, people who would sample and analyse dispassionately.'

'And that's the way Ecobrium works?'

'At first.' Jean takes off her glasses. 'But then Raimundo Elias, Ray, took over. He'd been kicked out of his evangelical church and needed a new crusade. My student grew disenchanted and left the organisation. After that I fell out with Ecobrium.'

'Fell out, why?'

'They want my data, but I'm not giving them anything until it's peer-reviewed and published.' She frowns. 'I don't trust Ray not to misuse it. His intentions may be good, but I strongly disagree with his methods.'

Kidnap, blackmail, murder.

'You and me both.' I lean forward. 'So where would I find this Ray character?'

'It won't be easy. He keeps to the shadows these days. He's made enemies on all sides: the mining companies and the *garim-peiros*, the logging companies and the farmers, the construction firms and the labourers. There have been death threats, attempts on his life.'

And there's about to be another one, but this one will succeed.

'I need to find him.'

'Will he want to meet you?'

'No,' I say. 'Please don't mention my name.'

'I can make a few calls. My student is no longer part of the organisation, but she may still be in touch with some who are.'

'I need to speak with him face to face.'

I need to be close enough to shoot him.

By the time Graça returns with the analysis result, Professor Parker has found me the time, date and location of Raimundo Elias's next appearance, a town-hall meeting high up on a tributary of the river Tocantins.

As we stand up to leave, Professor Parker says goodbye to Graça before putting a warning hand on my shoulder.

'Dr Silver,' she says. 'Please be careful. Ray is a man who is so

consumed by self-righteous rage that he has lost sight of propor-
tionality. One day he'll go too far.'

He already has.

The tiny dart has proved positive for batrachotoxin.

Graça is excited by the incontrovertible evidence that Rafael
Barata's death was murder, that someone booby-trapped the safety
deposit box and tried to kill whoever accessed it first – in this case
the poor bank clerk. She is so focussed on filing her report that it
is easy to give her the slip.

The only thing necessary for the triumph of evil is for good men
to do nothing. Wicked men succeed when good women look away.
I am a good woman. I am a strong woman. I can be a hard woman.

I will not look the other way. I will not stand idly by. I can wield
the burning sword of justice.

I am pure, distilled vengeance.

And it feels so good.

Rio de Janeiro, Brazil, January

The barber shop on the edge of Rocinha had the best view in all of Rio, a panorama of jade mountains, golden beach and azure sea.

César turned his head from side to side, admiring his reflection in the mirror. The bruises and swelling had completely disappeared, and his new high-protein diet was paying off. Gone was the gaunt, haunted stare of a man who lived in fear.

He smiled, admiring the clean shave that made him look ten years younger.

'*Tudo bem, doutor?*'

The barber changed the towel around his shoulders.

'*Tudo bem, Domingo.*'

'How's Gilda?'

'Insatiable.' César winked at Domingo in the mirror.

In fact, he'd fired his co-presenter the moment it was safe for him to return to work. Gilda might be beautiful, but she was a liability. Airing the clip with Yuko Nakamura, after his production company had signed an agreement not to, had cost him a small fortune.

All the beautiful people wanted to be on TV. There was no shortage of willing replacements. The interview process was just part of the fun.

And now César could stop worrying about the Colonel.

RIMPO, the Colonel's paramilitary organisation, had approved the Mercúrio plan. An actor had been hired to impersonate Jaq Silver's son and relieve her of the mine deeds. Everything had been going well until the actor was kidnapped by eco-warriors. Jaq Silver gave the mine deeds to Ecobrium as ransom, but they murdered their hostage anyway. Or did they? All that mattered was that the Colonel believed it. And after the gun battle in the botanic gardens of Rio de Janeiro, Jaq Silver must be dead too.

César had fulfilled his side of the bargain, given the Colonel what he wanted, delivered Jaq Silver to the ambush. Now he was free of obligation. The Carnival special – already recorded, and what a show it was! – would be the last time the actor playing Colonel Cub appeared on *The Missing*. From now on, César was free to take whatever artistic direction he chose.

Domingo laid a hot, wet flannel over César's eyes and began to massage oil into his client's hair.

César was reliving a recent encounter on the casting couch when he noticed the silence. The barbershop banter ebbed and flowed, but it never disappeared completely. The sudden absence of noise was like a clap of thunder in reverse.

He raised a hand to remove the flannel from his eyes.

The man who stood behind him was not Domingo. This man was clean-shaven with a severe buzz cut. His sleeveless olive T-shirt stretched tight over a muscled chest. His arms were covered in tattoos.

A steel razor glinted in the bright lights. With a single swift movement, the man swept the blade across César's throat, dropped it on the ground, turned on his heel and left the TV presenter to watch himself die.

Tocantins, Brazil, January

The town has the air of a forsaken project. A fine old church at the top of a cliff is surrounded by half-finished houses. Ramshackle buildings sprawl down the hillside on either side of a deep river gorge, the two sides connected by an elaborate stone bridge. Whatever wealth paid for the eighteenth-century church and bridge has long since vanished.

The meeting in the church hall is not going well. The big blond man on stage has lost his audience. The group of subsistence farmers and *garimpeiros* were restless even before the power cut interrupted his slide presentation. Clearly rattled, he fusses for too long over batteries and generators before trying a direct appeal.

'Trust in nature, so nature can trust in you.

Invest in nature, so nature can invest in you.

Give to nature, so that nature can give back to you!'

'Get to the point,' shouts a farmer. 'What exactly are you selling?'

'All that is good comes from nature. We are stewards of the earth and responsible for its care!'

'Yeah,' shouts another. 'What's in it for us?'

'If we continue like this, we are doomed. Plants and animals are dying. The air is filling with carbon dioxide, the world is warming, glaciers are melting, sea levels are rising. We have to make sacrifices to save our planet!'

'Where are you from?' shouts another heckler.

'I was born in the south, Rio Grande.'

'Before that. Where did your family come from?'

'I'm as Brazilian as you are.'

'With your colouring – I don't think so!'

'He's German.'

'Or Dutch.'

'Your ancestry is European.' Another heckler steps forward, jabbing his finger at Crazy Gloves. 'How can you lecture us on the environment? Your lot burnt all your wood, then you burnt all your coal, then your oil. *You* filled the air with carbon dioxide. That's how you became rich. How dare you tell us to stop logging, stop ranching, stop mining, stop developing so you Europeans can breathe!'

'Get out of here!' shouts another.

'We have to do something.' Crazy Gloves ducks as missiles start flying, cans and bottles hurled at him by the furious crowd.

'Together.' He climbs down from the makeshift stage, arms open wide. 'I love this land, this flora, this fauna. I would die to protect it.'

From the back of the town hall, I watch the meeting break up in pandemonium, waiting until the last stragglers have left before approaching the podium.

Raimundo Elias, aka Crazy Gloves, is busy collecting his things – computer, projector, batteries, generator, leaflets. His neck bulges, rigid with anger. He doesn't notice me until I speak.

'Good evening.'

He looks up. 'Well, well, Jaq Silver.' He continues packing up. 'The very last person I expected to see. What brings you here?'

'You killed my son.'

He laughs and, in that moment, I hate him more than I have ever hated anyone.

'You're wrong on two counts.' He bends to retrieve a suitcase.

'Firstly,' he says, opening the lid and starting to transfer the stacks of unused leaflets, 'Mercúrio is not dead.'

I grit my teeth. I saw the shackles, the cut and bloodied clothes.

'You're lying.'

'Mercúrio is alive and well.' Crazy Gloves closes the suitcase. 'But he's not, and never was, your son.'

I unzip my bag.

'Did he agree to a DNA test?'

I pull out the gun.

'No, he didn't. And there's a reason for that.'

I flick the safety catch.

'Because he was just an actor hired by a TV show to pretend to be your son.'

Crazy Gloves would say anything to save his skin. He's lied to me from the beginning. Why would I believe anything he says now? I can't be distracted by doubt.

I raise the gun.

With a roar, a group of a dozen men burst into the hall.

'Still here?' one of them shouts. 'I thought we told you to get out!'

Crazy Gloves uses the distraction to move away from me. 'I'm leaving.'

One man swigs from a bottle of Cachaça and hands it to his neighbour. 'And never come back.'

'That I can't promise,' he says, walking towards them. He must know that I can't fire from here without collateral damage. I lower my gun. 'Someone needs to protect you from yourselves.'

It's clear that the men are too drunk and angry for rational debate.

'I think we've heard enough, boys.' The man with the bottle passes it on.

The ringleader nods to the open door. 'Let's go for a little walk.'

Two of the largest men grab Raimundo Elias's arms and drag him towards the open door.

I grab the briefcase he has left behind, lock it away in my hire car and follow the racket, keeping low and moving stealthily to avoid attracting attention. I have to go slowly to avoid tripping over tree roots or falling into holes. The roaring commotion has settled into an angry buzz. Has he escaped?

I emerge into a clearing with an elevated viewing platform, providing a spectacular view over the river chasm.

Crazy Gloves has his back to a palm tree. The men surrounding him are still angry, but they seem to have calmed a little, pointing electric torches rather than guns at him, demanding that he promise to leave and not come back. It no longer looks like a lynching, so I raise my gun.

My hand shakes; my finger slips from the trigger, my palm slick with sweat. I have to do this. An eye for an eye. A tooth for a tooth. If I don't put an end to Raimundo's reign of terror, no one will. There is no one else to avenge my son's death. Vengeance is mine and mine alone.

I take aim, but it is no longer Crazy Gloves standing in front of me.

The UNITA soldier is huge and loud, panting and swearing as he stops to catch his breath. He ignores me, a girl child cowering behind a tree; he's only interested in Sam, a boy child old enough to fight. He's going to enlist my brother, and I have to stop him. We have a gun we stole from a corpse. I know how to use it, Sam taught me, but it's too heavy so I prop it on my knee.

I take aim. I squeeze the trigger.

'No!' Sam shouts. 'Don't shoot!'

A child runs into the clearing in Tocantins, shouting for his father. I lift the muzzle just in time and the shot goes into the trees.

The men who are berating Crazy Gloves spin round to face me. Perhaps they think I am protecting him? They shout abuse. Only Raimundo understands, he knows I intend to kill him and he knows why. He turns this way and that, searching for a way out.

The insect attack comes suddenly, silently. The insects in the tree are disturbed by my gunshot, attracted by the light shining onto Raimundo Elias, the heat of his body, the carbon dioxide in his breath, the pheromones in his sweat. The bloodsuckers drop from the trees and crawl through his hair to his face. Kissing bugs, nick-named for their love of human lips, piercing the skin with a long proboscis. Crazy Gloves lunges sideways, flailing as a swarm of triatomines start feeding. Within seconds, they are in his ears, under his eyelids, up his nostrils, already congregating around his mouth, their flat abdomens swelling as they feast on his blood.

He tries to escape, lashing out at the insects that pursue him.

I watch and wait.

Astonished by the speed and ferocity of the strike, driven wild with pain as the toxins in the insect saliva, injected into his tissue, begin attacking his nerves, he careers wildly and loses his footing.

He falls backwards, tumbling over the handrail, down the side of the canyon, bouncing over rocks as he plunges towards the river far below.

The angry mob vanishes, melting into the night.

I run to the handrail, searching for him with the beam of my torch, batting away the bloodsucking insects attracted by the light. It's a straight drop down to the river from here and I can't see where he landed. I sweep the torch until I spot a rough path zig-zagging through the vegetation to my left, a steep scramble down to the river, but I can do it. I have to do it.

I vault over the rail, keeping hold of it as I move sideways beyond the vertical cliff. The path is no more than an animal track. I lose my footing and slide down, grabbing the branches of a low bush to break my fall. Thorns rip the skin of my hands, but I bite my lip and continue down, moving back towards the cliff as I near the river, dislodging stones that splash into the water until they connect with something solid instead.

I turn on the torch and my anger evaporates.

Crazy Gloves lies where he landed, a bloodied rag doll, half in, half out of the water. A cry escapes me as I take in the extent of his injuries. His spine has snapped on the jagged rocks that broke his fall. He is alive, but only just. There is little that can be done for him now.

The water thunders down the canyon, a rainbow forming in the spray as the last of the evening sun catches it and illuminates the beady eye of an alligator, just above the surface of the water, its powerful tail propelling it towards the scent of blood. I throw a rock at it, then another. It backs off a little and then skulks there, waiting.

I sit with him as he breathes his last breath.

I look around. There is no way to get his body out of the river valley. I have no boat, the river is too dangerous for swimming, broiling with hungry aquatic life, drawn by the scent of his blood.

He weighs twice as much as I do; I can't carry him back up the ravine.

When the second and third alligators slither from the sandy bank into the pool, I abandon the corpse of the man who has destroyed me and climb out of the deadly canyon, never once looking back.

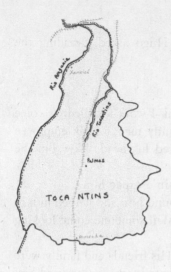

2km from the gold mine, Tocantins, Brazil, January

A gunshot rang out and a pair of bright blue birds fluttered into the sky above the old quarry.

Hugo opened his eyes.

'How are you feeling?' a voice asked.

Hugo groaned.

'Here.' A cup at his lips. The water tasted stale, but he drank greedily.

'Slowly,' said the voice, 'take it slowly or you'll be sick again.'

Christ – was it his own vomit he smelt? Hugo waited until the urge to retch had passed and then drank some more. Everything ached. The soldiers had left him in the quarry until he was too weak to fight, then they had lifted him out and beat him with fists and boots and rifle butts.

'Who are you?' Hugo asked.

'Pedro Carmargo.'

Of course. The Pedro who wrote the letter.

I am resigned to dying here in this place.

How long have you been here?' Hugo asked, dreading the answer.

'I left Rio de Janeiro in September.'

'To come here? Why?'

'The Colonel is a client of the bank I work for.' Pedro's voice caught. 'Worked for. Once I was a family man, a bank employee sent to deliver a message.' He lowered his head. 'Now I'm the captive of a madman.'

Hugo tried to sit up and a cry of pain escaped him.

'Slowly now.' Pedro put an arm around him and helped him to sit. 'Does anyone know you're here? Will someone come looking for you?'

Hugo surveyed the makeshift cell. His friends and family were used to his long absences. How long before anyone reported him missing? A week? A month? The head of his university faculty, Professor Jean Parker, had always been assiduous in the pastoral care of researchers, an unusual gift judging by the complaints of other academics, but his field work was only tangentially related to her interests.

'I work alone,' Hugo said.

Pedro began to cry.

ALVORADA

1,200km from the gold mine, a freight train, Alvorada, Tocantins State, Brazil, February

Clickety-clack, clickety-clack.

The train is on the move again. After the sweltering heat of the siding, it's good to have a breeze. I lie on my stomach beside a huge coil of metal wire and watch the track recede into the rainforest.

My mind goes back to the RIMPO ambush at the botanic gardens.

What part did Xavier play? Why was he there? His role was to arrange the meeting, not to join it. I saw him at the entrance to the orchid house before the start of the shootout. I saw him hurry Raimundo Elias to safety. They disappeared together. Did Xavier return, hiding among the bromeliads? Was he hurt? And where is he now? Do I care?

How did the soldiers from RIMPO know about the meeting? There's only one possible explanation. Xavier betrayed me.

347

If I could be so wrong about Xavier, who else have I been wrong about?

Clickety-clack, clickety-clack.

We pass over a bridge, a broad river rushes under the rail track.

I think about Crazy Gloves breathing his last in the ravine.

I abandoned his body where he fell and climbed to the top of the canyon. When I looked back down there was nothing to be seen. The alligators would finish what the kissing bugs had started.

Raimundo Elias ordered Mercúrio's murder, he deserved everything that happened to him.

Weigh him down and throw him overboard.

I set myself a task. I accomplished it. I moved on.

I didn't report his death, there were too many questions to answer.

Questions I need to face up to myself.

When someone reports Raimundo Elias missing, they will find his car and personal belongings and reach their own conclusions. Or discover his remains after the scavengers have finished. His bones, stripped clean of flesh, may be carried downriver and identified with clever forensics.

Or not.

This is a country where environmental activists disappear with alarming regularity. All it takes is for them to ask the wrong questions, challenge the powerful, threaten the business of making money.

Crazy Gloves was not a good man. He ended his days in the place he claimed to love, the ecosystem he promised to die to protect. As good as his word.

I felt no remorse at the time. It could just as easily have been me.

But now?

What if Crazy Gloves was telling the truth?

Clickety-clack, clickety-clack.

The engine lets out a blast of warning ahead of an unmanned crossing. A motorbike dashes across the rails in front of the train and roars off down a long straight road towards a distant farm. Someone was willing to risk death to avoid waiting twenty minutes for this long beast of burden to lumber past.

When I borrowed a vehicle from the garage of my landlord, I had no idea of the motorbike's value, the attention it would attract or the trouble it would cause. I barely knew my landlord's name, had never set eyes on him, had no clue how much he interested the federal police. Turns out Marina Queiros and Walter Salgado were in the air force together, back when Marina was Paulo. Marina keeps an eye on his Sao Paulo flat and Florianópolis beach house while he is away in Angola. It was Marina who suggested I could stay there, Marina who assured me I could borrow a bike. All of which makes me distrust Marina even more.

I watch the sun set over the land as it disappears behind me. Once it's dark, I drift in and out of sleep, searching for a liminal world free of reality and responsibility, trying to chase down a little thread of happiness that dangles tantalisingly just out of reach.

I sink into the arms of Morpheus, transported to a sea cove, the waves swelling underneath me, lifting me so that I can see a figure standing on the distant shore, arms wide. I let the sea carry me towards him, happiness building with every surge. But when the figure waves to me, I see that it is not Mercúrio on the beach, but Marina who is waiting there, waiting patiently for me to return.

I wake to see a twin-bodied silver plane overhead and I wonder if it's the same one.

78
Pt
Platinum
195.084

Platinum group metals are often found with gold.

Platinum is used in catalytic converters, which remove the harmful gases from automobile exhaust.

Brazil is a net importer of platinum.

Platinum world trade is currently worth about US$ 63 billion.

São Paulo, Brazil, January

The walls of the flat are closing in on me. When I close my eyes I see tidal waves of red mud, kissing bugs with blood-swollen bodies and crocodiles with bloody teeth.

My phone rings. Number withheld. I ignore it, but it rings again. I block the number – one of many, now that I've added Xavier to the list of people I will never talk to again. Friends who betray me are no longer friends.

I go to the gym. The punishing new routine is meant to help me sleep at night. It doesn't work, so I double the intensity.

I'm glistening with sweat, but I don't use the gym shower, preferring to take the private elevator to my own bathroom.

The doors ping open, and I step out.

I know immediately that I'm not alone. My sixth sense alerts me to something different. A noise? A scent? There is someone in my flat. How did they get in?

I need to alert security, but before I have a chance to turn, the doors close. I press the button, but the lift is already descending.

My heart beats in time to the footsteps from the kitchen. A figure steps into the light.

'Marina!'

Despite everything, my first reaction is one of relief. I have to remind myself that she is not to be trusted.

'Hello, Jaq,' she says. 'Why are you blocking my calls?'

Because I don't want to speak to you. And I don't want to see you. I don't need reminding of how much I miss you.

I displace the hurt with anger. 'How dare you break in to my flat!'

'It's not your flat, Jaq.'

Of course, she's right.

'I live here, and you have no right …'

'I have every right. I look after this flat for the owner.'

'You want me to move out?' I stamp a foot. 'Fine, I'll be out by morning.'

She shakes her head. 'Before Carnival is fine, as agreed from the beginning.'

'Then why are you here?'

'I have something for you.' Marina reaches into her bag and produces an envelope. 'The formal results of your analysis.'

'Analysis?'

'Your grandmother's gold ring, remember?'

It seems like another life when I gave the ring to Marina. I take the envelope, but I don't open it.

'You've done what you came to do.' I indicate the door.

She takes a step forward. 'Jaq, what is it? What happened? One minute we were going to a TV show in Rio, the next minute you're not speaking to me.'

'You tricked me.' I spit the words out with venom.

'Tricked you?'

'That event in Rio, it was a trap.'

Marina sighs. 'If that's the case, then I was hoodwinked. We were both invited by César.'

'I saw you.' I am rigid with anger. 'Talking to Oskar Guerra, the man who tried to kill me.'

'I don't know who you're talking about.'

'The soldier with the smoking cobra tattoo.'

'You mean the security guard? He said he wanted to talk to you, about protection.'

'He works for RIMPO.'

'So what?' Marina shrugs.

'The Colonel ordered him to kill me.'

'Kill you, why?'

'Because of the mine.'

Marina runs a hand through her long hair. 'Jaq, there's been a misunderstanding. Can we sit down and talk about this?'

I begin to shiver, the fierce air-conditioning making my gym sweat evaporate, freezing my skin. Is it possible that I got everything wrong? That I pushed away the people trying to help me?

If nothing else, I owe her an opportunity to defend herself.

I gesture for her to go ahead, and we move into the *sala* and sit at the table.

'Jaq, why were you so determined to find Raimundo Elias?'

'He killed Mercúrio.'

'But Mercúrio isn't dead.'

Not Marina as well. 'How dare you!' I slam my fist onto the table.

'I saw him.'

'Don't lie to me.'

'I saw him board a plane in Florianópolis on Christmas Eve.'

'You must be mistaken.'

'Yellow shortboard, right?'

'Lots of people surf. It doesn't mean you saw my son.'

'But that's the whole point, Jaq. Mercúrio is not your son.'

'Stop it!'

'Jaq – why won't you believe me? I saw Mercúrio with my own eyes. I can show you footage of him in telenovelas. *Surf Rescue Squad. Love on the Beach.* He's an actor.'

'Maybe he was an actor at one time. I never said he told me everything. But it doesn't change the fact that he was kidnapped and Raimundo Elias ordered his murder.'

I must believe that. If Crazy Gloves was innocent, if the two of them cooked up a ransom scheme to relieve me of the mine maps, then what does that make me? If what Marina is saying is true, I am – at best – a gullible fool. And at worst a murderer. I blew up the *Tartaruga* fully intending to dispatch the crew. I went after Raimundo Elias fully intending to kill him. Just because a sniper or a swarm of kissing bugs finished the job for me, I am still responsible for the deaths of three men, more if you count those I dispatched in self-defence. Could they really have been innocent? I shake my head. 'Mercúrio is dead. Ecobrium are responsible. Raimundo Elias ordered his death and the crew of the *Tartaruga* killed him.'

'It won't be the first time that César has tricked someone. Look at this.'

Marina shows me a newspaper cutting. I recognise the photograph before I see the name. The headline announces that Hélio TV has agreed an-out-of-court settlement with Yuko Nakamura.

'She was on *The Missing*.'

'So?'

'The person César introduced as her father was, in fact, an actor.'

I scan the article. 'Where does it say that?'

'It's all been hushed up as part of the settlement.'

'So, where's the proof?'

'Don't you see, it all adds up.'

'No, I don't see. And even if there was one mistake, one settlement, it doesn't mean that Mercúrio was part of a set-up.'

'I know this is hard, Jaq but why would I lie to you?'

'I have no idea.' I stand up. 'It's time for you to leave.'

After Marina has gone, I sit in silence for a while. I look at the paintings: the Picasso, the Miró, the Paula Rego. How can I not have seen it before, the things that were staring me in the face, right in front of my eyes.

I stare at the white envelope on the table. It stares back at me. After a while I open it and take out the single page. I read the analytical results of my grandmother's gold ring aloud.

All that glitters is not gold.

I sit for a while longer.

It's almost dark before I take action, and then it takes me a while to find the number.

'Hello, can I speak to Yuko Nakamura?'

'Who is speaking, please?' A female voice, I'm pretty sure it is Yuko.

'I want to talk to you about *The Missing*.'

The line goes dead.

Damn.

Cambridge, England, January

For once, Frank welcomed the cold. After the foetid heat of Brazil in high summer, the bright, clear skies of wintry England were a welcome change. A light dusting of snow sat on the well-insulated roofs and sparkled in the low, slanting sunlight.

The roads were clear, so he cycled to Pelupent.

'How was your holiday?' Nick asked.

None of your goddam business. 'How's your report coming along?'

Frank waited until late afternoon to call Graham Dekker.

'The report is finished,' he announced.

'And?'

'A clean bill of health. A simple case of theft. Zagrovyl received absolutely no profit or other benefit from materials illegally used to make chemical weapons. On the contrary, cleaning up this whole sorry mess has been an expensive business. The OPCW can rest assured there's nothing to see here.'

'Good job, Frank. I never doubted you.'

Liar.

'As soon as the board approve the report, we can formally close the Russia investigation.'

'Hmm. That won't get Corporate Integrity off my back. If anything, Deborah Ives is likely to redouble her efforts. She really doesn't like you, Frank.'

'The sentiment is wholly mutual.'

Graham sucked air through his teeth. 'Not helpful.'

'But I have something that might be. If you agree, we could feed her some information to keep her busy for a while.'

'And what's that?'

'How is Zagrovyl Brazil performing?'

'Terribly. They always overpromise and underdeliver.'

'So how would you feel about losing Clara Sousa?'

'She's always been a safe pair of hands.'

'What if I was to tell you that she invited the minister of mines to a beach party? The very minister who has the power to approve her latest project?'

Graham sighed. 'Brazil is a complicated place to do business. Nothing would surprise me.'

'And what if I told you that things went on that weekend that might give you cause for alarm.'

'What sort of things?'

'Drug abuse. Sexual favours from prostitutes posing as guests. And worse.'

'Worse?'

'A formal agreement on a schedule of backhanders from Zagrovyl to the political parties. Not just to one party, to all of them.'

'Can you prove this? Were you there?'

'No, but I know someone who was. Someone who taped the most interesting conversations for me.'

'You have tapes?'

'I do.' Or soon would have, thanks to undercover Federal Agent Aline Aldo.

'And what do you propose to do with those recordings?'

'Well, it's the sort of information that might interest Corporate Integrity,' Frank said. 'Unless you appoint me as your deputy.'

Frank smiled as he imagined Graham processing the threat. Had he overdone it? Hell – shy bairns get nowt.

'And why would I do that?'

'This is unconnected with Pelupent's investigation. The only Zagrovyl UK connection with Brazil is our sale of medicines and pesticides. Nothing to see there. The Brazil export operation reports to you in North America. If I am to sort this out for you, I need authority, so I can keep one step ahead, carry out an internal investigation.'

'And what would be the likely outcome of your investigation?'

'I'd sack those responsible for breaking company rules.'

'So Clara is to be the sacrificial lamb?'

'More of a sacrificial ewe, don't you think?'

'Frank, you are incorrigible.' Graham laughed.

'I'm counting on you, Graham,' Frank said. 'Don't let me down.'

Ituverava, São Paulo State, Brazil, February

It's easy to find the factory, I just follow the road towards the chimney towering above the fields of sugarcane, sending billowing clouds of white steam into the bright blue sky.

I roll down my window as I pull up at the gatehouse.

'*Bom dia!*'

The security guard eyes me with suspicion.

'I'm here to see Yuko Nakamura.'

'Wait,' he says.

Ten minutes later, a man in red overalls walks up to the security barrier.

'What do you want?' The name on his pocket is Castro. His moustache is larger than his face.

I get out of the car. 'I'm from Tecnoproject,' I announce brightly, handing him my card. 'I'd like to talk to Yuko Nakamura.'

Castro scowls. 'You can talk to me.'

'My name is Jaq Silver. I'm working with Tecnoproject. We offer free energy audits to selected customers.'

'Free?' Castro laughed. 'No one does anything for free. What's the catch?'

'No catch. It's government-funded.'

'Then there's the catch.'

'Tecnoproject are independent of the government, a firm of expert consulting engineers. We can pinpoint inefficiencies, tell you where you could save money. If you choose to hire us to help you improve your bottom line, then it's a win-win. But there's no obligation.' I swat at a cloud of flies buzzing in my ear. 'It's hot out here, could we talk inside?'

Castro scowled. 'Come back tomorrow when the boss is here. Three o'clock.'

'With pleasure.' I give him my warmest smile.

It has absolutely no effect.

Ituverava is 400km north of the state capital. As I stop to fill the hire car, I wonder if the fuel was made here, in the factory in front of me.

I drive straight up to the E100 pump – pure ethanol. It's the cheapest per litre, but a tankful doesn't take you as far as petrol would. The ethanol has to be two-thirds of the price of petrol to make it worthwhile, and right now it's dearer. I'm a well-paid consulting engineer and I can afford to let my conscience lighten my wallet.

Many people don't have that luxury.

After filling up and paying, I set off only to be halted at the railway tracks. Flashing lights warn of an approaching train. I sit for twenty minutes at the level crossing while a huge diesel engine pulls a mile of trucks, each one stuffed with sugar, clattering slowly past. Brazil's bounty is on its way to the port of Santos and then off to India and the USA and other sweet-toothed nations of the world.

Why drive to São Paulo tonight only to return tomorrow morning? It'll be too late for the gym tonight and too early tomorrow. Driving just to sleep is a waste of a tank and a half of fuel. Why not find somewhere to rest tonight instead? I head for the nearest town with a hotel. The bar opposite is advertising a happy hour with two-for-one cocktails.

There's no gym in the hotel, so I spend the evening in the bar.

The following day, I drive back to the factory and park in the visitors' area outside the perimeter fence. At the gatehouse I am given a pass and directed to the main office block.

The factory owner is waiting in the conference room, a young woman dressed in nude heels and a cream linen-dress suit. She is flanked by two burly men in blood-red overalls.

'Dr Silver?' she steps forward.

'Please, call me Jaq.' I thrust out my hand as she leans up to kiss my cheek. Yuko is almost a foot smaller than me, and my outstretched fingers brush her right breast. There is a moment of awkwardness as we recoil. Navigating a business etiquette designed by men, for men, we are two professional women adrift in a clash of European and Latin cultures.

She extends her hand and the tension vanishes.

'My name is Yuko Nakamura. I'm one of the owners of SucoBras.'

I pretend not to recognise her as we shake hands. She looks smaller than she did on TV, but then she was seated for most of the episode of *The Missing*. Her voice reassures me that I have come to the right place, the sweetly husky, musical timbre is as attractive as it is unique.

'This is Castro, from operations.' She gestures towards the man with the moustache.

Castro scowls. 'We already met.'

'And Lucas, my head of engineering.'

Businessmen shake hands with other men. In social situations, both men and women kiss women, right cheek then left. What are men to do with businesswomen? They take their cue from the boss and shake my hand.

We take our seats, coffee and water are served and the usual preamble starts. I have no interest in football. I do not wish to discuss my family, so I nudge the conversation towards everyone's summer holiday plans. Carnival is fast approaching, and millions of Brazilians are heading to the beach.

I've travelled the length and breadth of this country and know a fair bit about the seashore, from Ceará to Rio Grande.

I also know this foreplay can't be rushed. It is up to the host to decide when the celebration of Brazil's glorious coastline, lavish food and vibrant music has gone on for long enough. The engineer is the first to check his watch.

'I understand you're from Tecnoproject,' Lucas says.

My current employers are an engineering consultancy based in São Paulo. I took the first job I could find. In retrospect, I should have looked at the offer more closely, investigated the company finances more thoroughly, made some effort to understand why Tecnoproject were so keen to have me on their books. If something looks too good to be true, it probably is. Without a scrap of due diligence, the moment my work visa was issued, I jumped on the first available flight.

As far as SucoBras are concerned, I'm here to talk factory optimisation. The real reason for my visit will have to wait until I'm alone with Yuko. I glance over at the boss, but she is typing into her phone.

'Tecnoproject are offering free energy audits.' I launch into the official spiel, how the government wants to help the Brazilian sugar-to-ethanol industry be more competitive.

'What's the catch?'

'There's no catch.' I smile. 'It's a win-win. We identify opportunities for improvement. What you do with the report is up to you.'

'And the government pay you for this?'

In principle, it should work like that. In practice ... No, hold that thought for another day. I have enough to deal with right now.

'Exactly.'

Lucas runs a hand through his hair.

'You OK with this, Boss?'

Yuko nods.

'OK then,' Lucas gets to his feet. 'Castro will take you on a factory tour.'

Normally I jump at the chance to look round a factory. I'm fascinated by ingenuity, how humans use their big brains to adapt to their environment. My expertise is in safety, explosive safety in particular. But ever since I found my son's adoption certificate in my mother's strongbox, the need to find him pushed everything else aside, filled my thoughts and dreams.

And then my nightmares.

Yuko has information that might change things, but I need to talk to her alone.

When she looks up from her phone, something in those brown eyes makes me wonder if she's already figured out why I'm really here. Does she recognise me from TV as well? Does she understand the maze I've been lost in? Does she know what it feels like to strain every sinew and have all your efforts amount to nothing? Worse than nothing. To hurt those you only ever wished to protect.

Oh, Mercúrio. Forgive me.

Stop. Now is not the time. Lock it down. Lock it in.

Castro looks me up and down and selects a pair of overalls from a locker.

'What's your shoe size?'

I learned long ago that factories rarely carry even the commonest female size in safety footwear.

'I brought my own.' I open my backpack and extract a pair of safety boots.

I stand and address Yuko. 'Will you join us on the tour?' I ask.

She shakes her head. 'I have other work to do.'

Am I imagining a new hardness to her expression? A flicker of suspicion?

'I'll be waiting for you after the tour,' she says.

A promise or … a threat?

'Where do you want to start?' Castro asks.

I gaze out at fields of sugarcane. Any normal person would start at the beginning. But I'm pretending to do an energy survey. Hell, I might as well do an energy survey while I'm here. Energy efficiency and process optimisation were a key part of my professional training. The trick with lying is to include as much truth as possible. Maximum efficiency means starting at the point of highest-energy intensity.

I always like to start where it gets interesting.

Yuko is waiting for me after the tour. I run through my report.

'I can see some significant opportunities.' I list them: variable speed motors to adjust energy consumption in line with feed rate, improved chemical treatment to reduce scale in the evaporators, new nozzles in the steam ejectors for better vacuum, and a full survey to reduce steam leaks and root out inefficient condensate traps.

'How much?' Castro asks.

'Will it cost? Much less than you will save. I'll send you a full report.' I turn to Yuko. 'May I speak with you alone?'

She dismisses Castro with a flick of her hand.

'So, how can I help you?'

'You promise not to kick me out?'

'It depends …'

'I was looking for someone who went missing.'

At the word 'missing' Yuko stiffens.

'Are you making fun of me?' she asks.

'No, no.' I put out a hand.

'You saw me on that wretched TV show?'

'Yes, and I want to ask you …'

'I think you should leave now.'

Yuko stands up but I carry on.

'I want to ask you if César is a charlatan. Does he really find

364

missing relatives, or does he just hire people to impersonate them for the sake of drama on TV?'

Yuko stops.

'What do you think?'

'I don't know,' I whisper. 'I thought it was real, but perhaps I was tricked as well.'

'I settled out of court. I can't comment.'

'Not publicly. But surely you can tell me, woman to woman. Was that really your father?'

'My mother is dead now. What does it matter?'

'I'm sorry. My mother is dead too. And that's why it does matter. It matters very much indeed to me. It's a matter of life and death, a matter of friendship and trust. Yuko – I need to know.'

She sits down again.

'You were on the show?'

I nod.

'That man, the one who appeared on TV, he was not my father.'

I sigh. Is it relief or horror?

'But my mother accepted that he was her husband. She could barely hear or see. She wanted to believe. Whatever it was she needed to confess, she was able to do so before she died.'

'I see.'

'But I knew instantly that he was a fraud. He didn't even pretend very hard.'

'And that's why you sued Hélio?'

'Not at first. I sent a cease and desist notice that prohibited them from repeating the episode, to terminate any publicity, to avoid the lying "success stories" about me in glossy magazines. To get my privacy back.'

'I'm sorry Yuko.'

'But they showed a clip of the episode again in the New Year's Special. And once I started proceedings, it became clear that I was not the only one who'd been duped.'

'Are any of his episodes real?'

'Maybe in the beginning. Maybe the Colonel really did know the location of mass graves in Tocantins. Maybe that gave some closure for the parents of murdered students. But now it's just entertainment.'

I bow my head. The segments with the Colonel had been the only ones that I knew to be flawed. The DNA matching was nonsense. The so-called scientist had declared 'there is only a thousand to one chance of a coincidence' but in a county of 200 million, that meant the human remains could have belonged to any one of 200,000 people. If Yuko thought that was the only part of the show that might be true, then the rest must be cynical fabrication.

'I hired a private investigator, and he made a complete list of the actors involved, took their statements.'

'Mercúrio?' I whisper. But I already know the answer.

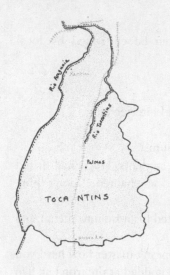

2km from the gold mine, Tocantins, Brazil, January

The correction cell in the jungle complex was one of the older huts, bare except for an iron bar supported by sturdy wooden uprights to form a frame.

The *pau de arara* - the parrots perch - was once used by Portuguese slave traders to punish disobedient slaves on colonial sugar plantations and was enthusiastically adopted by the Brazilian military.

When Hugo was dragged in, the Colonel was waiting. The shaking in his captor's limbs was even worse than usual. What disease afflicted the man?

Parkinson's? Had it affected his mind as well as his body?

'You're not really a doctor at all,' Colonel Cub hissed. 'Are you?'

'No.' It was something of a relief to tell the truth. 'I'm a botanist. A researcher.'

'Why are you here?'

'I was collecting samples from the riverbank,' Hugo said.

'What sort of samples?'

'Varieties of edible grasses that can be cultivated by local people.'

'Who sent you?'

'No one sent me.'

'So you're a communist?' the Colonel interjected.

'I'm sorry?'

'You're a filthy, dirty, stinking communist.'

'I'm not, as it happens.' Like many students, Hugo had flirted with radical politics before becoming disenchanted. 'I don't think my politics have anything to do with...'

The Colonel held up a hand. He lifted his nose into the air and made an exaggerated show of sniffing.

'I can smell communists, you see. Doesn't matter how hard you protest; I can always tell.' The Colonel nodded at the iron bar. 'Do you know what that is?' he asked.

Hugo shook his head.

'I hear you like parrots.' The Colonel flapped his elbows and made a squawking noise. 'So, you're going to love the parrot's perch.' He turned to the bare-chested man beside him. 'Is he ready for the interrogation?'

The huge man nodded.

'No!' Hugo protested.

Arms seized him and turned him on his side, wrenching his arms and legs back, tying each ankle to its corresponding wrist. A metal pole was threaded through the unnatural circle then placed between two uprights. Hugo was left hanging upside down from his knees, his spine twisted backwards, every joint in his body on fire with pain.

And then the interrogation began.

500km from the gold mine, a freight train, Tocantins State, Brazil, February

Clickety-clack, clickety-clack.

How long have I been riding freight trains? Ten days? Eleven? Twelve? I escaped death in the sugar factory by stowing away on a corn train, swapping to a soy train, then iron ore, then bauxite powder. I've lost track of time.

The limbo land has given me time to think, time to put together all the pieces of the puzzle.

But there's a piece left. The piece that I've been refusing to look at. The piece that connects everything else.

My grandmother's mine.

After Marina left the flat in São Paulo, I opened the envelope and read the analysis report, discovered the composition of my grandmother's gold ring. I stared at the results for a long time.

At last, I know what I have to do.

But can I do it alone?

I look up as the train pulls into a station.
  PALMAS
  Why is that name familiar?
  Who do I know in Palmas, Tocantins?

46

Pd

Palladium

106.42

Palladium is rarer and more expensive than silver or gold.

Palladium is invaluable in hydrogen-storage technology.

Brazil imports more palladium than it exports.

The world trade in palladium is currently worth about US$ 25 billion.

Palmas, Tocantins, Brazil, February

The toxicology lab is inside a university building in the centre of Tocantins. I march past security, up the stairs and straight to the office of Professor Parker.

The toxicologist from the hospital in Rio de Janeiro looks up from her desk as I knock and enter, breaking into a wide smile.

'Dr Silver!' she exclaims.

'Jaq,' I insist, and we kiss, one cheek then the other.

'What brings you to this wilderness, Jaq?'

'I came to find you.'

'And now you have!'

'I can't tell you how glad I am to see you, Professor Parker.'

'It's Jean, please.' She looks at me more closely. 'I was just heading for lunch. Care to join me?'

We walk side by side to the staff canteen. My mouth waters at the aromas as we stand in the queue.

'Did you go to the Ecobrium meeting?' Jean asks.

What to say? People may have seen me there. Can I lie? No, there have been too many lies.

'I did.'

'Did you see Ray?'

'Yes.'

'And?'

'He didn't get a very friendly reception. I left before things got nasty.'

Nasty with alligators. Time to change the subject.

We reach the food counter and I pile a plate high. Jean leads the way to a table in a quiet corner.

'How are you, Jaq?' Jean waits until I have finished wolfing down the food. Even after a night in a hotel, with a limitless buffet, I am permanently hungry.

I meet her eyes. 'Physically, I'm fine.'

Jean looks into my soul.

'Which suggests that other things are not?'

There is no cure for my grief. A grief compounded by a growing sense of guilt. I can't undo what's been done, but I can prevent further harm.

'How long have you been running a lab here?' I ask.

'I set it up years ago. One of my first serious research projects.'

'Batrachotoxin?'

'Something much more dangerous.'

'More dangerous than a poison frog?'

'Mercury poisoning. It's endemic in these parts.'

The beat starts in my throat, a little pulse of excitement. 'From illegal gold mining?'

'Exactly.'

'And you're here to treat the victims?'

'Alas,' Jean shakes her head. 'The neurological damage is usually irreversible. The best you can hope for is to stop further damage, but to do that you have to find the source.'

The mine.

'And how do you do that?'

'I have a group of researchers sampling the soil and the crops and the animals who graze them, the rivers and the fish that are caught.'

'And what do you do with the information?'

'We build up heat maps. Warn people where they shouldn't fish or farm. Alert the authorities to the likely source.'

'You mean you could pinpoint an illegal gold mine?'

'That's exactly what we've been doing.'

'And the authorities close them down?'

Jean takes a long sip of water. 'How much do you know about politics in Brazil?'

I hold up a hand and make a zero with thumb and index finger. I know nothing and care even less.

'The health of the poor is not high on the agenda where money is to be made.'

'That's true the world over.'

'And it's not just the rich and powerful exploiting the poor and helpless, although there's plenty of that. Gold fever takes over, the dream of riches, the promise of escape.'

Jean runs her fingers around the rim of the glass.

'People round here have so little opportunity, so little hope. Working in a gold mine is entering a dangerous lottery. Everyone knows someone who knows someone who made it big. One nugget of gold, and their life changes overnight.'

'But not always for the better.'

'Easy for us to say. We're used to a roof over our heads that doesn't leak, drinking water that doesn't make us ill, food that doesn't poison us, services to take our waste away, vaccinations against preventable diseases, access to good seed and fertiliser, teachers and books, doctors and medicine, tools and telecommunications.'

Jean puts her elbows on the table and leans closer.

'Who are we to say money doesn't make you happy? A real lack of money, below subsistence, makes people very unhappy indeed. It robs them of hope and then it kills them, slowly.'

'But risking mercury poisoning? Isn't that even worse?'

'People aren't good at assessing risk. The poisoning comes slowly, it takes years and years. Everyone thinks they're different, they can handle it, that they won't suffer as badly as the shaking, dribbling fool whose place they took. They pop worthless pills in an attempt to protect themselves, improve the ventilation, the washing, moving the problem elsewhere.'

Jean sighs and takes another sip of her drink.

'At least the illegal miners become ill from choice, however absurd that sounds. It's the innocents downstream that suffer the most. The people who have no option. The miners are exposed to mercury vapour. It's not nearly as dangerous as the organic mercury that their waste creates in the rivers and soil.'

'Your heat map? Can I see one?'

'Sure.'

We stack our dirty plates and glasses on a trolley and return to Jean's office, where she links her computer to a large TV screen and flicks through slides tracking the concentration of mercury found in samples of grass, cassava, banana, fish, meat, followed up by targeted investigation of soil and water. Above a background level, the sample points are marked with a colour, progressing from light green through yellow to orange and deepening shades of red.

I point to where several deep-red dots intersect.

'And the mine is here?'

'That's an old mine from the 1980s. Since it closed, we've been monitoring the soil remediation and water treatment. There's much worse than that. Here.'

She flicks to another map.

Something catches my eye. The sinuous bends of a river. The pattern is exactly like the etching on one of the engraved copper plates that Crazy Gloves stole from me. And I stole back.

'Where is that?'

'North of here. A colleague of mine is helping me on this one.'

Surely this is it? I'm finding it hard to breathe normally.

'What are those?' I point to a symbol that appears several times on the map.'

'Waterfalls.'

'And the contamination is upriver?'

'Yes, although Hugo wasn't able to confirm the source last time we spoke. It's wild up there, bandit land, crawling with ex-soldiers who've gone rogue.' She pulled out her phone. 'Let me check if he's in the lab today.'

I wait in the office, staring at the map, while Professor Parker is called away.

She returns, shaking her head. 'The analysts say they haven't heard from Hugo in a while. But he did send some samples.' She shook her head. 'This is odd, very odd. The samples were human. With the highest level of mercury we've ever seen.'

'Taken from your researcher.'

'Definitely not.' She shook her head. 'They came with a rather odd message.

'Can I see it?'

She shows me the paper.

Urgent run
Please carry out the following tests
-6 then 082 and 863
-48 with 192 or 942

'Do those numbers make any sense?'

'No.'

Jaq stared at the paper, then broke into a smile.

'What if you take out the words. You can make a pair of negative numbers with six digits after the decimal point.'

'I don't understand.'

'Latitude and Longitude.'

'Aha!'

Jean enters the numbers and a new location appears on her map.

'Right where the mine should be!'

I stand up.

It's time to go and take a look.

The gold mine, Tocantins, Brazil, February

There are certain sorts of material that are soft and malleable one minute, hard and rigid the next. Like the composite in *Transform*'s revolutionary material, Cub's pubescent brain had received extraordinary stimulation at the most impressionable age. In the case of *polymemory*, an electric current promoted crosslinking of carbon nanotubes, stiffening the pliable material until it was rock hard; in Cub's case, witnessing the torture and execution of a number of neighbours had turned him from a rather weak, cowardly boy into an implacably violent man. But unlike *polymemory*, there was no route back, no reverse warming to softness, no mechanism in his grey matter to unsnap the synapses. In fact, the subsequent burial, exhumation and burning of the bodies of those same villagers, and the students they sought to protect, strengthened rather than weakened the new structures in his brain.

While strength with elasticity can be a powerful combination, there is a certain kind of stiffness that is only strong under pressure. During war, for example, and the Araguaia Guerrilla War was one of the worst, the ability to follow orders without question was an undoubted advantage. But in peacetime, his unquestioning brutality, inflexible certainty and rigid intensity led to a dangerous brittleness that bordered on insanity.

The early exposure to mercury vapours didn't help.

Mercury is an amazing substance, the only metal that is liquid at room temperature. It forms an amalgam with gold, seeking it out, collecting it from the pores and interstices of dull grey ore, extracting tiny flecks from the wash water channelled over it. The mercury can be removed by heating – in a puff of smoke the mercury evaporates leaving pure gold behind.

Unfortunately, mercury is a serious neurotoxin, one of the worst. If you inhale the vapours from a gold furnace, or worse, ingest it from fish caught in contaminated water, it will cause long-term, irreversible effects.

Why was everyone so interested in this gold mine?

Colonel Cub because the gold mine bankrolled RIMPO. Professor Parker because the mercury used for extracting the gold was poisoning the villagers downstream. Ecobrium because they wanted to protect the flora and fauna, even the alligators and triatomine kissing bugs.

And her grandmother Isabella, why did she want to stop the *garimpeiros*? Was it because their crude methods failed to extract the true value of the deposit? The analysis of the ring indicated that the reserve contained metals that didn't form an amalgam with mercury, metals that had to be extracted by more sophisticated means than those the *garimpeiros* employed. The ore was rich in platinum and palladium, metals used in the green revolution, in catalytic converters and power storage.

Metals even more valuable than gold.

The precious metal mine, Tocantins, Brazil, February

At the top of the ridge, the grassy slope falls away before rising again. Between sunlit hilltops a dark circular depression is now visible, a fault line in black and white amid the technicolour vegetation of rubber trees, açaí palms, bitter cassava shrubs and swaying grass.

I approach the lip of the crater and hold my breath. There is movement below me, little pale grey larvae are being transported by black insects, moving in orderly lines, following well-defined trails, carrying something up from the bowels of the earth.

It takes me a full minute to comprehend the scale of what I am seeing. This is the mine everyone has been looking for. The movement far below is human, not insect, the absence of colour is because everyone and everything is covered in mud.

On one face, the rock has been hacked away into giant cubes, each ledge about six meters square and six metres above the next one. These colossal steps are connected by crude ladders, lashed together with wood and twine. Opposite the stone face is a cliff of smoothed earth. A single ladder, perhaps two hundred meters long, runs from the floor of the mine to the first flat section. There are several of these enormously long ladders side by side, and at first it looks as if each of them has been covered with a giant knitted scarf. Except this human scarf is moving. Each wide pale sack, carried across broad shoulders, is separated from the next by a long black back, plain then purl, repeated over and over again, hundreds of times. A ribbon of men hauling rock from the depths of the earth using the power of their own muscles.

The low buzz resolves into identifiable noises, the slap of feet on mud, the groan of effort, a sharp cry of pain, the rasp of stiff hessian sacks rubbing against bare shoulders, the creak of wooden supports bending under the weight of so many men.

And they are all men, these mud hogs, and mostly black men. Bare-chested with only shorts or a crude loincloth for modesty, some wear shoes, most are barefoot, some wear hats, most use a rectangle of old sacking to cover their heads and shoulders. The bags of rock are tied with rope, looping around the forehead of each man. He bends forward, using his back to support the weight, one hand gripping the rope to stop it moving, prevent it sawing into his flesh, the other hand gripping the ladder, his head inches from the rump of the man above, his legs and feet hidden by the head and shoulders of the man below. If one man slips, or a bag of rock falls, hundreds of men will topple, all those below him, all climbing the same rickety ladders with no space between them, forced upwards by the pressure of the impatient queue below.

There are soldiers too. White men with guns. Their fatigues might once have been khaki; now they are coated with the same grey mud as the miners, from the tips of their boots to the peaks of their caps.

If Fergus was to be believed, the soldiers in illegal mines are not here to force the men to work, but to provide security, to protect them from one another. These miners, *garimpeiros*, have come here of their own free will. They dreamed of riches that would free them from their lives of subsistence farming, a nugget of gold that would catapult them from the daily grind of poverty in the harsh interior of Brazil to the high life in one of the coastal cities.

Perhaps even to Miami or LA.

As I draw closer, I can see how strong the workers have to be: broad chests, muscular arms and powerful thighs. Few have escaped injury. From scratches and bruises, black eyes and split lips to terrible suppurating lesions, their bodies are marked by the hellish labour and close proximity to other desperate men with gold in their souls. What happens to those who rupture ligaments or suffer broken limbs? There can be no place for them here.

But it isn't the backbreaking, manual labour that shocks me; the most horrific part of this operation is outside the mine itself. The extraction of the gold with mercury makes me feel physically sick.

On a broad, flat stretch, just above the artisanal gold mine in this remote part of Brazil, the sacks of mud and earth and rock are emptied and inspected. Any nugget of shining precious metal not already pocketed by the miners down below is picked out by hand. Fergus, the mining expert, told me that in an illegal mine, if gold was found in a section, each worker from that section was entitled to pick one of the sacks they brought out. A rich find is a passport out of hell.

The rock is crushed to dust and washed with water. The heavier particles separate by gravity, are collected and loaded into a mixer. Mercury is added to bind the gold.

A silvery river of liquid metal collects at the base of the mixer and runs down into a pan on a crude, open furnace. The mercury evaporates, leaving behind a layer of solid gold, and the deadliest of foul air.

The spent rock from the mixer is dumped on the ground in great heaps of spoil. The residual mercury leaches into the soil, joined by the mercury evaporated from the furnaces as it condenses with the next rainstorm. The mercury reacts with organics, and methylmercury, the most toxic form of all, is washed into the streams, rivers and lakes below to be ingested by fish and eaten by pregnant women who give birth to infants with damaged brains and twisted limbs.

Children born before the pollution start to suddenly lose their spark. They stop learning, unable to process the rudimentary schooling the state offers in these remote places, forget the things they have already learned, become listless, forgetful.

Adults begin to stumble as they walk, shake with uncontrollable tremors, find it increasingly difficult to swallow.

No wonder Crazy Gloves wanted to stop this criminal enterprise.

The Colonel is hard to miss. He stands at the top of the ridge in full military uniform surrounded by his soldiers. Uniformly white, male, muscled, with buzz cuts and tattoos, RIMPO could really use a diversity policy.

As I approach, I see that the Colonel holds the leashes of two thin animals in one hand. The captives are not greyhounds or monkeys, but men. Two poor wretches on all fours, completely naked bar a metal collar around each neck, connected to chains that join a leather leash.

The men are painfully thin, ribs and hips jutting from skin marked by torture: cuts from whipping and bruises from beatings, burns from fire and the midday sun. The older man is in bad shape, he keeps toppling to the ground, only to be kicked upright. To call Colonel Cub mad as a hatter would be an insult to hatters.

'Dr Silver, I presume?' he waves at me. '*Enfim!*' he cries. 'I was wondering when you might show up.'

I keep walking.

'Meet my pets. This is Pedro,' He kicks the older man, who lets out a low sob of pain. 'And this one is Hugo.' The younger man grits his teeth and remains silent as a boot hits his flank.

At a nod from the Colonel, a soldier takes the leash and urges the two wretched men forward. They move slowly past me, on all fours. Hugo looks up and I am taken aback by the intensity of his deep green eyes. I reach out a hand and touch his shoulder.

'Help is coming,' I whisper.

The soldier yanks the chain, and the men are gone.

'You look like her, y'know,' the Colonel says.

I stand up straight and face him. 'Like who?'

'I saw the resemblance immediately. Silver, ha! You can't hide behind an anglicised version of your name. You are a Ribeiro da Silva through and through.'

He stinks of rum, and something else, something sour and rank.

'Isabella, lovely Isabella. I met her, y'know. I was only a boy, but I knew quality when I saw it. Only quality would wear a beautiful dress to visit a mine in the jungle.' He giggles. 'That was forty years ago. What relation was she to you?'

'Isabella Ribeiro da Silva was my grandmother,' I say. 'Although I never met her.'

'An impressive woman. Strong and wise. The writing was on the wall for Angola, so she planned to do what the Portuguese aristocracy have done from time immemorial when things get chewy – move to Brazil.'

He laughs, a long, manic screech.

'Things were different in those days. She didn't just buy the land; she bought a veto on the mining rights. Very unusual.' He scowls. 'How can it be fair that a foreign family has rights over land they have never lived in? How can a piece of paper make that just?'

He clears his throat and spits onto the ground.

'It didn't help them. They left it too late to leave Angola and...' He makes a slurping noise as he draws a finger across his throat. 'The communists got them.'

What had really happened to Isabella and Robert? There were few records from that brutal period of Angola's history. The newly independent country became a battleground for the cold war, with Cuba and Russia pitted against South Africa and the USA.

'We know all about communists here. We've been fighting them for decades. Not that they put up much of a fight.'

He unclips a flask from his belt and removes the screw cap with a shaking hand.

'The Brazilian communists wanted to form a peasants army. Ha, what a joke! A peasant might fight to protect his own land, maybe even that of his family, but take him five kilometres from his village and he is lost. What does he care about Marxism–Leninism? How does he know if Stalin or Mao or Hoxha got it wrong? Suddenly all these useless children arrive from the cities, full of grand ideas of revolution but without a clue how to survive in the here and now, how to handle a hoe or milk a cow. Instead of liberating the peasants, those urban guerrillas exploited them, leeches who ate and drank at the expense of those who worked from dawn to dusk.'

He takes another long sip from his flask and then wipes his mouth with the back of his hand.

'Oh, they talk a good talk, with their beards and sandals and man-of-the-people rigmarole, but what most citizens want is peace and stability.' He puts the flask to his lips again and, finding it empty, throws it on the ground. 'They don't want committees and congresses; all people crave is a strong leader.' He puffs out his chest. 'Someone to tell them what to do. Someone to reward the good ones and punish the bad.'

A soldier retrieves the flask and narrowly avoids a kick from the Colonel's boot.

'My *garimpeiros* have worked this land for decades. I can't let anyone jeopardise my operation.'

He signals to his soldiers, who raise their weapons, pointing them at me.

'Which is why I'm going to have to kill you.'

I pull the cord and the Transform jet pack propels me into the air, high above the Colonel's men. Right on cue Marina and Graça arrive on trail bikes, followed by a swarm of federal police on

ATVs. The whir of helicopter blades echoes back and forth across the sandstone cliffs as the white parachutes of the air force float down from platinum skies.

When my train pulled into Palmas, someone was waiting for me.

Yuko had raised the alarm after finding my car and bag abandoned in the visitor's car park and human remains in her filters. Everyone had assumed the worst. Everyone except Marina. She'd figured out my escape route and inspected trains from the air until she spotted me, then faithfully followed my slow progress into the heart of Brazil. It was Marina who took me to a hotel in Palmas, let me wash and eat, bought me new clothes for my meeting with Professor Jean Parker. It was Marina who contacted Graça and together they brokered the support of the air force and federal police.

'*A cobra vai fumar!*' Colonel Cub screams, the battle cry of the smoking cobras.

The battle doesn't last long. The *garimpeiros* scamper back down their long ladders, retreating to the base of the mine, more worried about protecting their patch than helping the Colonel. His soldiers take a second look at the fit, well-armed, highly trained men advancing towards them and make a calculated bet. The rag-tag band of poorly trained RIMPO men melt into the hills, leaving the Colonel alone.

I cut the nitrogen propulsion on my jet pack and drop back down to face him.

He moves with surprising speed, grabbing me around the throat, and pressing a gun to my temple. It feels like being trapped by a skeleton. His ribs press against my back and I sense the tremors that shake his bones. His breath is foul, but he has the strength of a lunatic.

'Let her go!' Marina advances.

'Come any closer and I'll kill her.'

Graça opens her palms. 'We can talk about this.'

'The time for talking is over.'

'What do you want, Colonel?'

'I want what's mine. All the gold.'

'Let Dr Silver go. Then we can talk.'

I assess my options. My captor is so unstable, mentally and physically, the slightest move might set his gun off. I remain still. Trying to reason with a drunken, mercury-damaged psychopath is unlikely to yield results.

A bright blue macaw flies overhead, making an almost human cry.

Tra-la-la la la.

After the bird call comes the rattle of clanking chains. The Colonel turns his head. The dog men, Pedro and Hugo, launch themselves onto their torturer with animal cries, snarling and biting as they wrap the chain that connects them around his neck. The Colonel fires and Marina falls to the ground.

I scream and rush to her side, falling to the ground beside my friend as blood gushes from her body, staining the earth red.

'Marina! No!'

TV Studio, Rio de Janeiro, Brazil, February

The music stopped, and a photograph with a black border filled the screen, followed by the dates of César Correia's birth and death.

The camera pulled back from the screen and the studio lights came up to reveal an empty stage. A spotlight shone on César's vacant chair and the theme music from *The Missing* began to play at half the tempo, an octave lower and in a minor key.

Gilda entered the stage, wearing a long black sheath dress that emphasised her fabulous curves, a white lace handkerchief in her black-gloved hand.

'Ladies and gentlemen!' she announced. 'We are not here to mourn César's passing but to celebrate his life.' She dabbed her eyes, careful not to smudge the thick mascara. 'It's what he would have wanted.'

'Tonight, we are going to show the final episode of the programme he completed just before his untimely death.'

She spread her arms wide.

'All hail César!'

The screen behind her lit up.

'Let me recap for you.' On the screen, César was addressing his audience. 'Karina and her six-year-old son are on their first ever beach holiday. While his mother is sleeping, Noah leaves the hotel room and goes to the beach. Karina runs after him, but by the time she gets there Noah has been pulled lifeless from the sea.'

César sat and put an arm around Karina.

'Karina, was that your scream on the recording?'

'Yes.'

'What did you think?'

'I thought my baby had drowned and that it was all my fault.'

'What did you do?'

'I pushed them out of the way; I fell to the ground. I pulled him up and I hugged him as hard as I could.'

'And what happened?'

'He came back to me.'

The video resumed. The woman is on the ground holding the child, and suddenly his little arms are around her neck, hugging her as if he will never let go.

MISSING THEN FOUND!

The dramatic music changes to happy music and the audience goes wild.

'How did you feel?'

'I was so happy.'

'Can you point to the man who rescued Noah from the sea?'

Karina pointed to the man on the sand who had been cradling the child's head while the lifeguard attempted to resuscitate him.'

'And what did you say to the man who rescued Noah?'

'I said thank you, thank you.'

'And what did he say?'

A deep voice boomed over the stage. 'I said, can I buy you dinner?'

The audience cheered in delight.

César beamed. 'Ladies and gentlemen, please put your hands together for Lucas, the man who saved Noah.'

The applause was rapturous as Lucas strolled onto the stage. César rose to greet him; they hugged and slapped each other's backs. A handsome man in middle age, he embraced Karina and sat beside her on the sofa as César returned to the host seat.

'Welcome Lucas. So, what were you doing at Praia de Forte?'

'I work at the Turtle Sanctuary.'

A video started playing, this time a professional film about the work of the nature reserve, protecting the endangered sea turtles that lay their eggs on the beach.

'So, Lucas, can you tell us what happened?'

'I was repairing the fence near the beach when I saw a little boy on his own. It's a fine place at low tide, but at high tide, the waves can come right up to the wall.'

'Did he look lost?'

'No, he looked very happy, running up and down. I assumed his parents were with the crowd of people in the water or on the beach.'

'Then what happened?'

'It all happened quickly. He tripped and fell, just as a big wave came in. Next thing I know he's being dragged out to sea.'

'What did you do?'

'I tore open the fence and jumped in after him.'

'Did you hesitate?'

'Not for one second!'

The audience clapped and cheered.

'I couldn't see him at first.'

'He'd gone under the water?'

'It gets deep suddenly, and the sand was making it difficult to see.'

'What did you do?'

'I dived down. Once, twice. I stopped to feel the current, followed the undertow and dived again. The third time, I found him.'

'He was swimming?'

'No. I thought it was too late. I started yelling for help. When I got him onto the sand I checked, but he wasn't breathing, so I started mouth-to-mouth.'

'Did he respond?'

'No. A lifeguard arrived and took over.'

'And still nothing?'

'No response.'

'But nothing beats a mother's love?'

Lucas took Karina's hand and they smiled into each other's eyes.

'Nothing at all.'

The audience went wild.

César let the cheers and whistles of approval sing for a while and then held up a hand.

'So, Karina, now, do you understand the clapping?'

'Yes,' she smiled. 'When a child is lost on the beach, people clap so that they can be reunited.'

César addressed the studio audience. 'OK folks, shall we give it a go?'

The clapping moved through the crowd, the spotlight following the relay of noise until it stopped and focussed on a little boy with blue eyes and sandy hair sitting on the knee of a production assistant at the back.

'Ladies and gentlemen, please welcome NOAH!'

The production assistant held his hand until he reached the

stage. Lucas bent down and lifted him onto the sofa and his mother put her arms around him.

'Noah, can you tell us what happened the day you were lost.'

'I wanted to see the sea.'

Tutting from the crowd.

'But you know you shouldn't go off on your own?'

He bit his lip. 'I was naughty.'

Aaahs from the crowd.

'I won't do it again.'

'Why not?'

'Because now I have a daddy.'

Lucas reached out and took Karina's hand.

César mimed surprise. 'Is this true?'

Lucas nodded. 'When I saw that beautiful woman running over the sand, her face so full of love for her son, I realised what was missing from my life. Since my wife died, I've barely been able to see friends, let alone make new ones.'

'It was love at first sight?'

'For me, yes.'

'And for you, Karina?'

She blushed. 'I wanted to thank him. I agreed to meet him for dinner.'

'And then?'

'We saw each other every day until the end of the holiday.'

'When you went back to Palmas.' César turned back to Lucas. 'And how did you feel when Karina went home.'

'I missed her, and Noah.'

'So, what did you do?'

'I flew to Palmas. I met her family.'

'And then?'

'I asked Karina to marry me.'

'And what did she say?'

Karina flashed a ring. 'I said yes.'

'And you're all going to live in Palmas?'

The crowd roared with laughter as if this was the finest of jokes.

'No, we're all moving to Praia de Forte.'

Little Noah piped up. 'And my new daddy is going to teach me to swim!'

Palmas, Tocantins, Brazil, February

As the theme music for the memorial edition of *The Missing* fades, I click the remote to turn the television off.

'You have to hand it to César,' Marina says. 'He knew how to put on a good show.'

The bastard.

I lay a hand on the hospital bed.

'How are you doing, Marina?'

'Good,' she nods. 'Really good. I can leave as soon as they take the stitches out.'

'You didn't half bleed,' I say. 'I thought you were a goner.'

'You saved my life,' she says.

'No, you saved mine.'

'Can you make sense of it all now?' Marina asks.

'I'm beginning to.'

'Then can you help make sense of it for me?'

'I can try.'

80
Hg
Mercury
200.592

Brazil is a net importer of mercury.

Mercury is liquid at room temperature and forms alloys, called amalgams, with other metals such as gold, silver and tin. The ease with which it amalgamates with gold made it useful in recovering gold from its ores. Mercury amalgams were also used in dental fillings.

Cacimba do Padre Beach, Fernando de Noronha, Brazil, March

The swell is building nicely now, a soul-stirring point break with a sweet, sandy landing, the ridge so long that several riders can catch the same wave and remain safely apart. But that's not my intention.

I watch the rider approach on a familiar yellow shortboard and pick my moment to join him. It isn't easy to catch the break at the midpoint, far from the optimal take-off zone. I ride a backwash warble, a pyramid of dark water moving sideways, hunting for a last second on-ramp, a portal onto the face of the wave. For once, my timing is perfect. I pop up right in front of him, making him swerve. He curses and regains his balance before setting off in pursuit.

The lip of the wave curls over, and I enter a turquoise tunnel, the sunlight causing the barrel to shimmer and glow. I zigzag up and down the wall of water, one dazzling turn after another, relishing the exhilarating rise and fall, allowing him to catch me on a more direct line down the wave.

As he draws close, I turn and smile. The expression on his face is priceless.

We race out into sunlight, one last figure of eight to escape the wave before it shuts down, and glide to a stop in the flats.

'Hello Jaq.'

'Hello.'

'How did you find me?'

I nod back to the beach where Marina stands gazing out to sea. I'm keeping her under close observation since the shooting.

It was Graça who supervised the field surgeon, made sure the stitches were made neatly under Marina's hairline. Pedro and Hugo, dehydrated, starved and exhausted by their final act of defiance, needed urgent medical attention, and all three were flown together to a hospital in Palmas.

It was too late for the Colonel, his neck broken by the frenzied assault from his two captives. An assault that saved my life.

As Marina recuperated, we completed the missing pieces of the puzzle, bringing us to Fernando de Noronha, an island off the north coast of Brazil.

'Marina recognised you from a TV soap.'

'I've had so little TV work; I'm amazed she spotted me.'

'So, it's true. You're an actor.'

He hangs his head. 'I'm sorry.'

I paddle towards the lagoon, and he follows.

'Did you even grow up in Salvador?'

'No.'

'Were you ever sent to an orphanage?'

'No.'

'Is your name Mercúrio?'

'No, it's Mateo.'

'César concocted that whole story and paid you to approach me?'

'Yes.'

'Why?'

A small set breaks closer to shore and our boards bob in the surf. We wait until another surfer paddles past.

'To earn your trust and find the box with the maps of the gold mine.'

'Wouldn't it have been easier just to ask me?'

'Everyone assumed you had an agenda. That you'd want the mine for yourself.'

We're in shallow water now. I jump off my board and turn to face him.

'And you. What did you think?'

'By the time I was sure that you weren't part of a conspiracy, that you were genuinely unaware of the power you had to stop the Colonel, I was in too deep.'

'Who thought up the kidnap drama?'

'Ecobrium. I knew that the Colonel would kill me if I didn't deliver. Ray promised me a way out.'

Crazy Gloves tricked us all.

The man who pretended to be my son rolls off his board, into the water. 'I'm sorry I lied to you, Jaq.' He swims up beside me and takes my hand. 'If I didn't already have one, I'd quite like you as my mum.'

I pull my hand away.

'At least you're safe,' I say.

'There's something you should know.' He bites his lip. 'After Hélio TV hired me to play Mercúrio ...'

He makes it sound like a part in a play or a film.

'... someone contacted them with a very credible story. César tried to put them off, destroyed the records.'

And now César is dead, taking his secrets to the grave.

'Why would he tell you?'

'A warning. To be careful. That someone else might turn up, looking for you.'

I stare at him.

'And did they?'

'No.'

I turn away.

'Jaq, somewhere out there, your son is alive and searching for you.'

I turn my board round and pull myself on. Lying flat on my stomach, I begin to scull away.

'I hope you find him, your real son,' he calls after me.

A new set is lining up sweetly, an emerald-green wall shimmering against the cyan-blue sky as I paddle out to sea.

Notes

Sugarcane

Saccharum officinarum is one of the most efficient photosynthesisers on the planet. The plant uses the sun's energy to convert carbon dioxide in the air and nutrient-rich water from the soil into sugar. The state of São Paulo in Brazil provides the perfect subtropical climate – plenty of sun and rain – and lots of land.

The factories have to be close to the fields, as natural enzyme action begins to degrade the sugar the moment the cane is cut.

Pre-harvest burning reduces pests and plant disease, makes the woody stalks easier to cut by hand and improves the quality of the juice, but the traditional practice causes air pollution and contributes to global warming.

The producers crush the cane to extract the juice – *garapa* – which is then filtered, treated with sulphur dioxide and slaked lime, and concentrated to crystallise the sugar, which is then steam-cleaned, air dried and packed.

The residue, a thick molasses, goes to the fermenters to make ethanol. The molasses is sterilised and fed to the fermenters, along with yeast, and four to twelve hours later we have weak ethanol, which is distilled to 96 per cent.

The solid waste, *bagasse,* is burnt to raise steam to generate power to run the factory and export to the grid. The best factories are self-sufficient in energy and produce both sugar and ethanol, varying the split depending on the market prices.

Since the 1970s, all cars in Brazil must be designed to run on an ethanol/petrol mix. Flex cars can run on any concentration up to 100 per cent. The Brazilian government varies the amount of ethanol in the national fuel blend depending on the harvest

– lower harvest, higher price, lower percentage of ethanol in the blend.

Brazil is the world's largest producer of ethanol from sugarcane.

Caipirinha

The cocktail, Caipirinha, represents sugarcane – *saccharum officinarum* – in all its forms. The rum is made from cane juice, *garapa*, fermented to produce ethanol. The waste solids, *bagasse*, are burnt to provide the heat and power: steam to distil the alcohol to Cachaça strength and electrical energy to power the freezer and make ice.

Lava Jato – Exposing Corruption

Operation Car Wash started with an investigation into money laundering and illegal currency trading from the office of a small petrol station in Curitiba. The code name is ironic; the only thing the petrol station lacked was a car wash. As the police operation grew, it uncovered widespread institutional corruption in Brazil that had been going on for decades and benefitted all political parties. A cartel of engineering and construction companies conspired with the state oil company, Petrobras, to overcharge for work, channelling money to politicians in return for lucrative contracts for members of the cartel.

Criminal investigation into money laundering and political corruption, led by the Curitiba branch of the federal police, resulted in the impeachment of the president, Dilma Rouseff (arguably the least corrupt president in Brazil's history) and the incarceration of Lula da Silva, her predecessor, preventing him from contesting the 2018 elections, which brought Jair Bolsonaro to power.

Lula was released from prison and the conviction annulled in time for him to contest – and win – the 2022 election.

Major Curió

Sebastião Curió Rodrigues de Moura (born 1934) led a clandestine operation on behalf of the Brazilian military dictatorship (1964–1985) to stamp out the Araguaia guerrilla movement, kidnapping, torturing and murdering suspected communists. One of the founders of the city of Curionópolis, he was town mayor before being found guilty of corruption and fraud.

Wallace Souza

Wallace Souza (1958–2010), a disgraced policeman and Amazonia politician, presented a controversial news programme – *Canal Livre* – which broadcast live footage of crimes being committed in Manaus, Brazil. In 2009 he was accused of arranging murders to boost ratings for his programme. Souza died before he could be tried, but his son Rafael was sentenced to nine years for homicide.

Flavio Souza and Eike Batista

In February 2015, Judge Flavio Souza ordered seizure of the assets of the richest man in Brazil and arranged, even before trial, to auction them off. The judge was then photographed driving a white Porsche Cayenne seized from the man he was prosecuting. He claimed to have taken it home because he didn't want it damaged by rain and sun in the impound lot. After investigation, it transpired he had taken another of the cars home and placed Eike's piano in a neighbour's apartment. Further investigation revealed he'd stolen US$300,000, seized in an unrelated drug trafficking case. He was sentenced to eight years in jail.

The Federal Police

The Brazilian police is separated into multiple state-run forces. The military police focus on crime prevention with uniformed, armed officers on the streets. The civil police are responsible for the investigation of crimes. The federal police have country-wide jurisdiction and look after border control and white-collar crime. Federal Police Agents (Agentes de Polícia Federal) must have a bachelor's degree and pass highly competitive admission tests. No previous police experience is required but it is one of the most sought-after government jobs.

Batrachotoxin

Batrachotoxin is a natural poison found on the back of tree frogs. It was traditionally used to tip the arrows of hunters in Brazil.

Fundão Dam, Mariana

On 5 November 2015, the Fundão Dam collapsed at an iron mine in Mariana, Brazil, killing 19 people. The wave of sludge levelled the town centre of Bento Rodrigues and turned the Rio Doce (Sweet River) toxic blood-red, killing entire fish populations. Two weeks and 620km later, the tailings reached the coast and fanned out into the ocean.

Brumadinho Dam Disaster

On 25 January 2019, a tailings dam at the Córrego do Feijão iron mine, near Brumadinho in Minas Gerais, Brazil, failed catastrophically. The sludge swept through the mine offices and canteen during lunchtime and 270 people were killed.

Train Surfing

The Malha Paulista freight railway carries almost 3 million tonnes of sugar each year. The FRS carries 5 million tonnes of soy and 4 million tonnes of corn. Both connect with the MRA, which carries 121 billion tonnes of iron ore every year. It is theoretically possible to join the Ferrovia Norte-Sul railway and travel by freight train from the port of Santos on the coast to Palmas in the geographical centre of Brazil.

I haven't done it myself, but here's a link to the map I pored over instead:

https://apicatalog.mziq.com/filemanager/v2/d/003f6029-d45a-44ac-9c9e-869fe5df83fc/cf6a5fc6-1616-28f1-1809-6b8f5218b398?origin=2

Sebastião Salgado

Sebastião Salgado, a Brazilian photographer, documented the working conditions of ordinary men and women in his series *Trabalho*. I first saw his photographs at an exhibition in Lisbon in the early 1990s. A huge black-and-white print covered one wall of the gallery. It looked like a mosaic, tessellated geometric shapes. Only when you looked closely could you see the movement, thousands of miners hauling canvas sacks up vertical ladders: a living hell.

Portugal and Great Britain

Portugal and England have the oldest unbroken alliance in Europe. From the Treaty of Windsor in 1386 to support for Portugal joining the EU in 1986, Portugal and Britain generally choose the same side. The sister of Henry IV, Philippa of Lancaster, married King John I of Portugal. Catherine of Braganza married Charles II. While the Spaniards and Italians are clearly and exuberantly Latin, Portugal is unreservedly Celtic.

Mad Hatters

The illness, first described as mad-hatter syndrome, was common among those who worked with mercury for a living. The phrase 'mad as a hatter' comes from the use of mercury in hat-making from the eighteenth century onwards. The best sorts of top hats were made from beaver fur. The individual hairs on the beaver pelt have serrated edges; they connect to one another, crosslinking to form a mat, and it is easy to turn beaver fur into a lustrous felt.

As beaver fur became more expensive, the animals hunted almost to extinction, hat makers looked to cheaper, more plentiful options like rabbit skin. By brushing the rabbit fur with a mercury-nitrate solution, the smooth hair roughened. The process was called carroting because it turned the fur bright orange. The roughened hairs were shaved from the pelt and formed into a felt. The mercury-saturated felt was then boiled in acid, steamed and ironed into shape. The mercury evaporated and some was inhaled by the hat makers in poorly ventilated workshops.

The symptoms of mercury poisoning, or erethism, include slurred speech, tremors, stumbling and delusions. Despite all the evidence for one of the earliest industrial occupational diseases, mercury was only banned in the twentieth century. Cynics might note that mercury nitrate was needed to make detonators for bombs used to fight the Second World War.

Global Spot Prices 17 Nov 2022

Metal	US$/kg
Palladium	$ 89,380
Gold	$ 48,102
Platinum	$ 28,052
Silver	$ 693
Niobium	$ 45
Mercury	$ 6
Iron	$ 0.06

Brazilian Metal Exports 2013

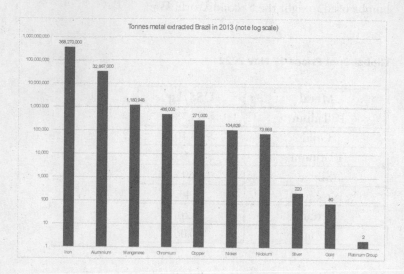

Tonnes metal extracted Brazil in 2013 (note log scale)

Sumário Mineral Brasília Volume 34 2014 ISSN 0101-2053

Note: Platinum group includes platinum, palladium, rhodium, ruthenium, iridium, and osmium.

Books

***Brazillionaires: The Godfathers of Modern Brazil* – by Alex Cuadros**

This is the single book I'd recommend to anyone interested in contemporary Brazil. It opens with the fatal collision of a sports car and a bicycle and proceeds to explore the taxonomy of inequality. Focussing on the ultra-rich – the Brazillionaires – Cuadros never ignores the experience of ordinary folk struggling to survive. Metal shutters descend over bulletproof glass, blocking out a fine view of Ipanema beach; the shower-sized maid's room in the same apartment is windowless by design.

***This Is the Place to Be* – Lara Pawson**

I have worked or travelled in most of the countries I write about, but I haven't yet been to Angola, so I'm grateful to Lara for taking me there. In beautiful, short fragments she paints a vivid picture. In another book: *In the Name of the People,* her in-depth retrospective analysis of the 27 May 1977 revolution inside the ruling MPLA is as fascinating as it is depressing. Power corrupts and absolute power corrupts absolutely.

***The Mechanism: A Crime Network So Deep it Brought Down a Nation* – Vladimir Netto, translated by Robin Patterson**

***Nemesis: One Man and the Battle for Rio* – Misha Glenny**

Wai-Wai: Through the Forests North of the Amazon – Nicholas Guppy

Barbarian Days: A Surfing Life – William Finnegan

Conundrum – Jan Morris

Acknowledgements

Thanks:

To Jean Parker who won the RNLA charity auction at Bay Tales in 2022 to have a character named after her. The real Jean Parker retired after 41 years teaching at St Anselm's College, Birkenhead. I hope the fictional Professor Parker has done justice to her great inner spirit.

To Gordon McVie and all the wonderful book bloggers – too many to name here – thank you for your passion, generosity and commitment. Where there is dark, you bring light by sharing all that's good about books.

To all the fabulous book festivals – Edinburgh International Book Festival, Harrogate, Crimefest, Bay Tales, Bloody Scotland and Newcastle Noir, to name but a few.

To all the libraries and bookshops who spread the joy, with a special mention for Stockton Libraries, Newcastle and Gateshead Libraries, Drake the Bookshop in Stockton, Forum in Whitley Bay and Waterstones Durham.

To my Angolan-born friends who told me their stories. Rosario, who learned to handle a Kalashnikov in a camp in Angola and introduced me to São Paulo. José Leite Pinto, who became separated from his parents and travelled the length of Angola at the height of the civil war in search of his family.

Rui Centeno, who described growing up on a farm on the fertile high plains of Angola in such memorable detail.

To my Beta readers – where would I be without you? – Marjory Flynn, Barry Hatton, Andrew Erskine (senior), Lorraine Wilson, Ivan Vince, Mark Dufty, Emma Christie and Judith O'Reilly.

To the Northern Crime Syndicate – Chris McGeorge, Rob Parker, Adam Peacock, Robert Scragg and Trevor Wood, with an extra special mention for founder Judith O'Reilly whose wise advice came at a critical time.

To my agent Juliet Mushens and all the team at Mushens Entertainment, to my editor Jenny Parrott, copy-editor Francine Brody, head of production Paul Nash and all the team at Oneworld, there would be no book without you.

To my family for putting up with the far-away look in my eyes.

And to anyone who made it this far – thank you for reading!

Fiona Erskine is a professional engineer based in Teesside, although her work has taken her around the world. As a female engineer, she has often been the lone representative of her gender in board meetings, cargo ships and night-time factories, and her fiction offers a fascinating insight into this traditionally male world. She is the author of The *Chemical Detective, The Chemical Reaction* and *The Chemical Cocktail. The Chemical Detective* was short-listed for the Specsavers Debut Crime Novel Award. Her second thriller in the Jaq Silver series, *The Chemical Reaction*, was short-listed for the Staunch Prize.